Day
Dreamer

ALSO BY SUSIE TATE

Gold Digger

Outlier
coming August 2025

Day Dreamer

SUSIE TATE

Arndell

Arndell

DAYDREAMER
Copyright © 2024 by Sett Publishing,
excluding new exclusive content to this edition.
This edition has been published by Arndell,
an imprint of Keeperton, in 2025.
1527 New Hampshire Ave. NW
Washington, D.C. 20036

10 9 8 7 6 5 4 3 2 1

ISBN: 978-1-923232-14-3 (Paperback)

Excerpt from Gold Digger Copyright © 2024 by Sett Publishing

Library of Congress Control Number: 2025932914

Printed in the United States of America

Edited by Joanna Edwards
Formatted by Kirby Jones
Cover design by Arndell
Cover image by Vitalii Arkhypenko, Unsplash

Sydney | Washington D.C. | London
www.keeperton.com/arndell

For all the Daydreamers.
I stand with you, my friends.

CONTENT WARNING

The novel contains descriptions of workplace harassment and assault. Please read at your own discretion.

CHAPTER 1

General crapness

Lucy

"Lucy, are you listening to me?" Felix snapped, and I flinched in the chair. The honest answer to that was no. I had instead been focusing on the way his beautiful, thick, dark hair brushed the collar of his shirt.

I started to nod, but when my focus moved to his stern expression, I shook my head instead. Felix sighed, throwing his hands up in the air in that expressive Italian way the Moretti family seemed to have retained, even though they'd been in the UK for two generations now.

"This is *exactly* what I'm talking about. This constant daydreaming is completely unacceptable. Will's complained about you *again*."

Bloody Will. That slimy bastard could take a running jump. I bit my lip, and my gaze dropped down to my lap. Looking at Felix for too long was like staring at the sun — he was just that blindingly handsome. Deeply tanned skin, brown eyes so dark they were almost black, strong jawline with close-cropped, perfectly styled stubble, broad shoulders, tall enough to dwarf my hobbit-like stature, with the lines of his designer suit exactly tailored to his muscular frame. He was the most attractive human I had ever met in real life. Even as a child, he'd had this Italian loose-limbed grace which we pasty English folk of a more awkward persuasion could only marvel at.

I cleared my throat so that actual words could make it past the lump that had formed.

"I don't *mean* to daydream," I said in a small voice. "It's just that my mind tends to wander, and I sort of… lose time."

As an abject coward, I was loath to tell him the truth – that this job was just so *boring*. I was well aware that as executive assistants went, I was the worst this company had probably ever seen, but meetings and deadlines and emails and prescribed tasks were honestly *not* my bag. It didn't help that my direct boss, Will – or Mr Brent as he preferred me to address him – was an unrelenting prick.

Everything about this office felt like a cage. Even the décor screamed prison cell. Yes, okay so Felix and the bigwigs had floor-to-ceiling views of London, but the rest of the office floor, beyond their heavy oak doors, had barely any natural light. The plant I brought in for my desk had withered in a matter of days. Everything was grey and white. Even my colourful pens and notebook were frowned upon so much that I had to hide them in my bag most days.

But worse than the aesthetics of this place was the atmosphere. The partners were feared and revered like gods. Emphasis was put on a certain kind of cut-throat dynamism that was completely foreign to me.

Only now was the reality sinking in, that coming to London had been a big, fat mistake. I should have stayed at home. At least in Little Buckingham, I wouldn't be berated on a daily basis about my general crapness.

I looked up as Felix moved around the desk to stand directly in front of me, crossing his arms over his broad chest and leaning back against the solid wood of his desk. His suit jacket strained under the bulk of his arm muscles, and my mouth went dry at his proximity.

This crush I had on Felix was totally inappropriate. He'd be *completely* horrified if he knew about the fevered dreams I had involving him and his desk. I felt a mortifying heat rise to my cheeks just thinking about it.

"I made a promise to your mum, Lucy," he said in a serious tone. "I don't want to let her down, but you're making the situation impossible. People line up for this job. We've basically handed it to you on a silver platter, and you're squandering the opportunity."

I had to lean back in the chair and tilt my head to look directly at him. It made me feel even smaller than I usually did around him. Guilt swelled at the thought of letting down my mum, and for the people who would have taken this job in a heartbeat – who no doubt would have made the absolute most of it. I imagined them lining up outside the building looking like they just stepped out of *GQ* magazine: severe expressions, trendy glasses, glamorous pencil-skirt-wearing women, Clark Kent lookalike men, briefcases ready to smash me out of the way.

"I–I'll try harder," I said, my voice coming out just above a whisper as I twisted my hands in my lap, pulling the sleeves of my jumper down to cover my fingers and pushing my thumbs through the holes that had formed there from frequent use. Felix's gaze flicked down to my hands and his eyes narrowed.

"And *this* is another problem," he snapped. "These ancient woolly jumpers you wear have *actual* holes in them. Have you not noticed how the rest of the office dresses, Lucy? You can't just keep chugging along in all your scruffy little outfits. This is a serious business I'm running here. I'm not saying you have to power dress, but you could at least ditch the moth-eaten clothes and the Uggs that have seen better days – those days being back in the nineties when people *wore* Uggs."

I bit my lip as I looked down at my feet. They were practically toe to toe with Felix's, and the contrast couldn't be starker. His shiny Italian leather next to my scuffed, faded, fluffy boots. As

I thought about how the rest of the office were turned out I winced. None of the women wore anything lower than four-inch heels.

"And you can't keep carrying stationery around in your hair either," he said, and then, to my shock, leaned over me, his hand coming up around the back of my head to touch my hair (dear God, the man *touched my hair*) and plucking out the four-colour pen I had shoved into my messy bun.

I swallowed, still recovering from the giant rush of adrenaline in response to the contact.

He frowned and cocked his head to the side before plucking out another four pens (two gold Sharpies, a biro and a fountain pen) from deeper in my mass of hair. He placed all my pens down on the desk before turning back to me. My heart felt like it was beating outside my chest.

"Do you see any other women in the office carrying sundry items in their up-dos?"

I thought about all the sleek blondes and glossy brunettes that littered the office, and tried to imagine any of them shoving pens into their perfectly coiffed tresses. I shrugged and forced myself to make eye contact with Felix again. But having all the intensity of his dark gaze directed at me was mega intimidating, so I chickened out and focused on his shoulder instead.

"I... er, well, sometimes I just kind of need a pen," I muttered to his suit jacket. "And I'm really not that great at keeping hold of them, so my hair is the logical place."

"You need *five* pens in your hair at all times?" he asked in a dry tone.

I shrugged again but didn't really know how to respond. To be honest, yes, I did need five pens in my hair. If I had a plot idea or a character development strategy, I had to write it down immediately. Years of painful attempts at recall after the fact had taught me it was better to always have access to pens and my notebook. But there was no way I was telling Felix that little piece of information.

Just then there was a knock behind me. Both Felix and I looked over as the office door swung open, and Tabitha, Felix's executive assistant, stepped into the room.

"So sorry to interrupt, Mr Moretti," she said, not sounding sorry at all. The gust of air from the door caused me to shiver in my seat. That was the other thing about this bloody office – it was *freezing*. Tabitha threw me a brief, dismissive look before focusing back on the boss. "But I've got a message from Mr York wanting to rearrange tomorrow's meeting. Apparently, his wife's got an appointment for an antenatal scan."

I swivelled away from her critical gaze to focus back on Felix. His expression flickered with annoyance before he hid it. The man was such a workaholic that he probably couldn't get his head around the idea of anyone needing to attend anything outside the office that couldn't be "outsourced". He likely thought that unless you were incubating the baby yourself, your presence in the ultrasound room was completely surplus to requirement.

Well, I'd spied on Harry York with his wife Verity when they came to the office last week, so I wasn't surprised that the man put his wife and future child above business. They were very sweet together – he guided her through the office space with his hand at the small of her back as if negotiating a minefield and not a few desks; then held her hand whilst they waited for Felix outside his office.

"Fine, whatever," Felix said, his voice laced with annoyance. "Thanks, Tabitha. Could you set it up for next week, or am I full then?"

"You're always fully booked, but I'll make it work," she said, efficient as ever. "I'll get on and sort it now." She turned on her perfect, red-soled, four-inch heels and swept out of the door, leaving a trail of expensive perfume in her wake.

The gap between women like Tabitha and me had never seemed so wide. Her pristine white silk shirt was paired with a tight pencil skirt that stopped just above the knee. The entire outfit was almost freakily wrinkle-free. Even if I spent hours ironing a shirt like that, I knew it still wouldn't be fit to wear. But then, ironing had never really been my forte. Not a hell of a lot of practical things were, to be honest.

My shoulders dropped and I sighed. This was completely pointless. I was, and always would be, a lost cause. This whole job business had been a good idea in theory, but it was becoming very clear that coming to work for Felix was not the stepping stone to broadening my horizons that I thought it might be. It might even be making things worse.

My vision of moving to London and having gal pals to bowl about with was *very* naïve. I hadn't met one person that wasn't super intimidating. Instead of popping out for drinks and meeting in cafés as I had envisaged, I went home to my empty flat every night, ordered a lonely takeaway and sank back into my fantasy world – the same fantasy world that I'd spent the last ten years constructing back in Little Buckingham. Nothing had changed. Coming here was pointless. I really should have stayed back home. At least there I had Mum, Emily and Mike.

Painful shyness and a touch of weirdness were my problems. I was confident in the fictional world I had created, but in the real world... not so much. That's why I'd never left Little Buckingham before, never moved out of my family home, never had a boyfriend – the list went on.

But the hope that getting a job in the big smoke would boost my confidence was slowly dying. As was the hope of making some new friends outside of my village bubble. The very idea of making friends with a woman like Tabitha was completely laughable. When she wasn't displaying open contempt for me, she was largely ignoring me.

Then there was the other secret hope I didn't admit to anyone – the hope that Felix might finally notice me as something other than his best friend's slightly odd little sister.

Well, that was the most far-fetched idea of the lot.

CHAPTER 2

That sounds... fun

Lucy

"Maybe I should just quit," I said, crossing my arms over my chest so I could tuck my hands into my sides to keep them warm and suppressing another shiver. The futility of carrying on in this environment was becoming painstakingly clear now. I was better off stagnating in Little Buckingham; at least I had some mates there.

I was staring at Felix's tie now. How did you even manage to get a tie to appear so perfect? Everything about this man was immaculate. I was feeling more like a scruffy little nobody by the minute.

"You can't just quit!" Felix's affronted tone shocked me into meeting his eyes again. He had pushed away from the desk to fully loom over me. Felix was very good at looming. His expression now was furious. "What kind of attitude is that?"

I frowned up at him. "I thought that's what you were hinting at? Listen, we're on the same page about my crapness. I've got past form for being crap at stuff. Honestly, I'm surprised you haven't fired me sooner."

"I'm not firing you, Luce," he shot back, a panicked look on his face now. "Don't tell your mum that I'm firing you. That is *not* what's happening."

My mum had been Felix's nanny for his entire childhood. We grew up in the same village. Well, sort of the same village: my family had lived in a small cottage right next to the pub in the heart of Little Buckingham; Felix's lived in a vast manor house with acres of land on the outskirts of the village. And whilst my brother Mike and I went to the village school, Felix had been sent off to a posh boarding prep school miles away.

But it was my mum who looked after him when he was home. He spent a lot of time in our tiny cottage, and he absolutely loved my mum and my brother. Mike and Felix were both six years older than me, and although their lives had now gone in different directions (my brother was a carpenter, Felix a business tycoon), they still considered themselves best friends, together with the other third of their trio, Ollie, whose family lived in the neighbouring estate to Felix's.

I was always fascinated by the beautiful, loud, expressive, glamorous boy who would fill our little cottage with his magnetic energy. I followed him, Mike and Ollie around the village like a puppy back then until my brother would tell me to bugger off.

But Felix would argue my case for me. He always let me tag along. I must have been really annoying, but he never got frustrated with me. There's no denying I was a rare one with my endless stories and quirkiness, but Felix always humoured me. He was always kind.

When my guinea pig died, I insisted on a formal funeral – a directive that my brother completely ignored, but fifteen-year-old Felix turned up in a fitted, designer black suit, looking grave and appropriately sombre. He even gave a brief eulogy for Coco, something along the lines of how he'd always remember the way Coco pooped in Mike's shoes, that he had a very soft head for stroking, and that he'd only ever bitten Felix's finger once (which he'd probably deserved as he'd been putting him in Mike's shoe at the time so that he would poop in there again).

"God, don't encourage her, mate," Mike had grumbled. "She's mad as a box of frogs."

"Don't listen to him, Shakespeare," Felix had said as he ruffled my hair. "The last thing you want to be is normal."

I sighed. It was clear that grown-up Felix didn't have the same appreciation of my quirks as he'd had back then. But to be honest, he was quite different now to the boy I'd known. I couldn't see the Felix of today being happy listening to my crazy stories for hours on end and calling me Shakespeare. This Felix had sharp edges; he was hardened. He only did Very Important Things with Very Important People. He only dated supermodels or famous actresses. He was ruthless in business, cut-throat even. Everyone in the office was scared of him, he never smiled – I hadn't once spotted his dimple the entire month I'd been working here. This Felix didn't want some oddly dressed blast from the past haunting his office and dragging down the tone.

But, despite the fact that he was now a billionaire, ran his own multinational property development empire and was one of the top two hundred richest people in the country, he *still* didn't want to disappoint his nanny. So he was stuck with me.

"Er... right, well, what *is* happening then?" I asked in confusion. The last half hour had definitely seemed like he was working up to firing me, and with good reason. "I won't tell Mum that you fired me, if that's what you're worried about."

"I'm not firing you," he said again through gritted teeth.

I shrugged. "If you say so."

"Lucy, for someone who *needs* this job, you seem very at peace with losing it."

I sighed. "Felix, I'm crap at this. There's no getting around it. And I don't fit in here at all." I bit my lip before I carried on with the next bit, willing my eyes to stop stinging. I would not cry in front of this man. "It's not working out. Coming to London might have been a mistake."

Felix crossed his arms over his chest and stared down at me. I attempted to keep my cool despite the intensity of his gaze. God, he was beautiful.

"You just need more confidence. For a start, you'll feel better if you're wearing the appropriate stuff. Hold on."

He swivelled round and pressed the intercom like we were in a bad movie about an arrogant CEO. It should have been cheesy, but the gorgeous bastard made it work.

"Tabitha, would you mind coming in here, please?" he asked.

"Of course, sir," said Tabitha in that super-efficient, intimidating tone I was used to from her. A few click-clacks of her heels and she was back in the office. She looked between me and Felix again, probably wondering why I wasn't already collecting up my stuff and vacating the building.

"Lucy needs some help," Felix said, and I blinked in confusion. "She needs office-appropriate clothes. A whole re-vamp. And I'm not sure that, left to her own devices, she can manage that much of a transformation."

Tabitha fixed me with a piercing stare, her eyes raking from my messy bun to my Uggs and back again. She was an expert in disguising her emotions. The only way I knew that she was angry was the twitch in the corner of her left eye.

I felt my face flood with heat. I'd always had a terrible blushing habit. I couldn't experience the least bit of embarrassment without turning tomato red, and I wasn't sure if I'd ever been so embarrassed in my life. I was a twenty-seven-year-old woman who clearly could not be trusted to dress myself. When Tabitha didn't reply, Felix cleared his throat.

"You can take the company credit card. No spending limit."

"Fine," she said, turning her attention from me to Felix and smiling as if it was no problem whatsoever to take a socially backward and fashion-challenged loser out for a shopping trip. "When would you like us to go?"

"You can both go now," he said, waving his hand through the air.

"But it's the meeting with Anderson Corp – don't you need me there?"

"Don't worry, I can handle Nick Anderson. And John can fill in for you."

"Right." Her smile was fixed now and looked like it might actually be hurting her face. Her eye twitch was going crazy. The woman was furious.

*

"Er, this is... a lot," I said. My voice was muffled by the pile of clothes that Tabitha had just dumped into my arms and which came up above my mouth. "I don't think I've ever tried on this many clothes before in my life."

"Clearly," she snapped, gesturing towards me and my general attire, her lip curling just slightly. "Could we hurry this along, please? *You* may not care about your job, but *I* was integral to the Anderson deal, and I don't appreciate being chucked out of the office to baby you through a bloody shopping trip so that fucking prick John can take all the credit."

"Oh no," I said as my stomach dropped. "I'm so sorry. That's really shit of Felix. I–I can manage on my own. You might catch the meeting if you hurry back now."

She narrowed her eyes at what was visible of me behind the pile of clothes. "Are you *really* this dense?"

I swallowed. My throat felt thick, and I had a terrible feeling I was going to cry. Tabitha hated me now, and I couldn't blame her. She was the only person I'd had much contact with since joining the office (apart from Will, but he didn't count), and it was clear she was not going to be open to a friendship. I blinked rapidly, hoping to push back the tears.

Tabitha sighed again. Her expression had softened, just a tad.

"Look, if I go back now, I'll arrive at the meeting late. That's worse than not showing up at all." She moved to me, laid one hand on each of my shoulders and turned me around towards the changing room then gave me a little shove forward. "But I would very much like not to miss the rest of the working day, so if you could hurry it up, that would be great."

"Yes, sure, of course," I said, rushing forward, glad that I was now facing away from her, and it didn't matter that a tear had made it down my cheek.

What followed was an exhausting hour of ruthless efficiency. I'd been poked and prodded and forced into all manner of outfits. When I almost fell arse-over-tit in the heels Tabitha picked out for me, she conceded that I might need to go down by an inch or two.

"But you can't go *too* low," she warned me. "You're short."

I blinked at her – okay, five foot two is not exactly supermodel height, but I wasn't a total pee-wee.

"And any lower than three inches would look out of place."

She was right there. But weren't women supposed to be liberated now? Why were we still forced into these contraptions, making walking an exercise in balance and stamina?

When it was time to pay, Tabitha brought out the company credit card, but in an unusual display of assertiveness, I made her put it away, insisting on paying for everything myself and then wincing at the cost. But there was no way I was letting Felix absorb the financial burden of replacing my crappy wardrobe. Even if I hadn't wanted said crappy wardrobe replaced in the first place.

On the ride back to the office in Felix's town car, I swallowed down my nerves and attempted to break the stony silence.

"So, um… do you like working at Moretti Harding?" I forced myself to ask in a small voice. Tabitha spun around from staring out of the window and levelled me with a condescending glare.

"Like it?" she asked in an incredulous tone.

I cleared my throat and bit my lip. That had been the most innocuous question I could think of, but it was still being met by open contempt.

"You don't *like* a job like mine," Tabitha said slowly as if she was explaining how the world worked to a backward five-year-old. "You work your arse off, claw your way through the shit, put up with all manner of crap to drag yourself up the corporate ladder."

"Oh, er… right. That sounds… fun."

Her eyebrows were in her hairline. "Fun? Are you insane? Of course it's not fun. I work with no natural daylight; the entire office staff is poised on the edge of a panic attack the whole time. I have to fight constantly against the horrific boys' club culture. Fun does not enter into it."

"Maybe you could suggest some changes? Brighten up the space a bit? Doesn't the company have a whole interior design team? Maybe there's a way of bringing in some light from—"

"Lucy," Tabitha said in a dry tone, cutting me off. "Stick to staring off into space and squeaking like a little mouse when someone asks you a basic question, okay? You know nothing whatsoever about business."

"Okay," I whispered, feeling small and stupid again. Forgetting that my old jumper was now stowed away in one of the many shopping bags, I tried to pull the sleeves down to cover my hands and push my thumbs through the small holes, but encountered the cuffs of the silk shirt I was wearing instead and had to sit on my hands for the rest of the car journey to keep them warm.

I shivered. This clothing experiment was all well and good, but if I died of hypothermia it would all be a big waste of time. I envisaged Felix looming over my dead body, berating me for my inefficiency and lack of ambition as I slowly turned blue. My snort of suppressed laughter was met by a glacial look from Tabitha, so I shrank further back into my seat to avoid angering her further.

Not for the first time I wished I'd never agreed to this plan. But Mum had been absolutely insistent that I work for Felix.

"Such a lovely boy," she'd told me.

Hetty Mayweather might be the last human being in England to call Felix a lovely boy. As one of the most ruthless

13

and intimidating men in London, he was anything but *lovely* or a *boy*.

"He'll look after you in London," Mum had assured me.

Yeah, right. If you could call looking after someone criticizing them for their many shortcomings daily and forcing them into a load of uncomfortable, cold clothes, then Mum was right.

CHAPTER 3

Think of it as armour

Felix

"Right, that's sorted then. The clothes are an improvement," I said briskly. "Much more professional."

Lucy gave me a weak smile and shrugged her shoulders. "I guess."

I cleared my throat and rubbed the back of my neck. Calling Lucy in here had been a mistake. Agreeing for Lucy to come to work at the office at all had been a bigger mistake. But when Hetty had asked me, I really hadn't known how to get out of it.

I mean, I *liked* Lucy. Granted, I hadn't seen her in years until she came here last month, but I'd always had a soft spot for the quirky kid who used to tell the most bizarrely addictive stories. She'd been a cute, shy little girl with freckles on her nose and muddy knees. Mike, Ollie and I let her trail after us in the holidays, those big blue eyes watching as we played football, battled in video games and hung out in the treehouse (the Mayweathers' house may have been small, but they had the *best* treehouse).

It was clear that Hetty worried about her even back then.

"She's a dreamer, that's the problem," the ever practical and sensible Hetty would say. "Head in the clouds when she needs her feet on the ground. God knows how she'll survive in the wide world."

Lucy's father, Henry, didn't share Hetty's opinion though. He'd doted on her, called her *his little dreamer*, and, if anything, wanted that instinct to be protected rather than corrected. But after he died when Lucy was eight, Hetty stopped trying to pull her into the real world, and Lucy seemed to want to avoid it even more.

That year, Mike and I were tasked with taking her trick or treating in the village. Half an hour after she'd gone up to her bedroom to grab her witch's hat, Hetty sent me up to see what was going on. Lucy was sitting on her window sill, staring out into the night, knees up to her chest, her arms around her legs, head resting on her knees.

"Luce?" No answer. I moved to sit on the opposite side of the window seat. She was perfectly still, her big eyes just staring out of the window. It was like I wasn't even in the room. "Hey, Shakespeare. Time for sweets."

It was only when I put my hand on her small shoulder and gave her a little shake that she seemed to come back to the room, flinching where she sat, her eyes flying to me and her mouth falling open.

"Hi," she said, smiling her gap-toothed grin. "Whatcha doin'?"

"Lucy, we're going to go trick or treating, remember? You went to get your hat?"

Her eyes went wide, and she bit her lip. "Oh! Oh dear, I must've gone doolally again."

"Doolally?"

"It's what Mummy and Da… I mean Mummy says I do when I forget and go to my thinking place." A lump formed in my throat as Lucy corrected herself. Accepting that Henry wasn't there was still hard for her; if I was honest, it was hard for me too.

"Is this your thinking place?"

She shook her head, her bunches flying from side to side and becoming even more lopsided. "No, silly. My thinking place is in my brain."

I smiled. "What were you thinking about?"

And that was when little Lucy would become animated. Anytime you asked her what she was thinking about when she was daydreaming, she'd launch into one of her stories.

"So, there's this king, he's half human, half fairy and—"

"Half fairy?" I said. "Isn't that a bit girly for a king?"

Lucy shook her head again; one of her bunches gave up the fight and came out completely. "Fairies are *not* girly. They're stronger than humans, they have magic, they're way faster and they are more vicious. They can rip your throat out before you even know they've moved."

That was the thing with Lucy's stories. They weren't what you would imagine a standard eight-year-old girl would come up with. There was too much blood and guts, and too few princesses and ponies. But they were always completely riveting. After twenty minutes of hearing about this bloodthirsty king, Mike's head popped round the door.

"What the bloody hell is going on?" he said. We were both still sitting on the window seat opposite each other, and Lucy had just got to the part in the story where the king's brother had tried to kill the mother of his unborn child. "Come on, all the sweets will be gone."

Lucy told me dozens of stories over the years. In fact, there were a few times when I was an angry teenager, furious at my dad for being the piece of shit that he was, when Lucy's stories seemed like the only distraction that really soothed me. So, of course, I had a soft spot for her. But having full-grown Lucy in the office was definitely a mistake.

The moment she walked in here a month ago with the same freckles on her nose and the same big blue eyes blinking up at me, I'd felt winded. It didn't matter how huge and tattered her woolly jumper was, how her hair was in an inexplicable mess on the top of her head with pens sticking out of it, how she didn't wear a scrap of make-up. She was absolutely beautiful. Not in the way I usually appreciated beauty. Not like my ex had been beautiful – long legs, perfectly put together, sophisticated, chic. No, Lucy's beauty was of the natural, cute but captivating variety. It wasn't my cup of tea, or at least it shouldn't have been, but the moment I saw her again, it felt like coming home. Being around her made me *feel* more than I had in a long time, and this bone-deep longing to touch her was worsening by the day.

What made things even more painful was her crush. She probably wasn't aware of how obvious she was, but Lucy stared at me *a lot,* and it was hell on my self-control. All I wanted to do was pull her into my office, kiss those freckles on her nose, strip her monstrosity of a jumper off, lay her on my desk and then give her what I could sense she wanted from me. For hours.

And weirder than even my dirty fantasies about Lucy were the post-coital ones. Because after I'd taken her very thoroughly, and when her guard was down, I imagined asking her what she was thinking about and having her tell me one of her stories again. No sex fantasy with any other woman had been quite so bizarre.

But I *had* to snap out of it. This was Hetty's and Henry's daughter, Mike's sister. Without Hetty and Henry, I wouldn't be half as well-adjusted. They raised me. Without the Mayweathers' house as my sanctuary, my childhood would have been bleak. I couldn't let Hetty down, and I'd promised I'd help Lucy. I mean, Hetty had been so desperate that she'd even told me I didn't have to pay Lucy. How on earth she expected Lucy to live in London without being paid was beyond me, and I certainly wasn't going to have her work for me for free. Clearly, Hetty was still supporting her daughter, which must be putting a huge financial strain on her.

I hadn't been back home in over five years after that final straw with my father – when he crossed the line so completely there was no coming back from it. I was justified in staying away from him. But I felt the guilt of not checking in with the Mayweathers. I'd been so focused on trying to outdo my father in business that I'd let everything else fall by the wayside. Even my own mother had only seen me a handful of times and then only in London on neutral ground. I loved Mum, but nothing would get me back to Little Buckingham.

So no, I wasn't going to give in to the desire to simply take Lucy home and keep her all to myself in my house so she could daydream to her heart's content out of my window seat. I was going to help transform her into someone her mother didn't have to worry about. I was going to toughen her up. Because the world isn't kind to dreamers like Lucy. There's no room for daydreaming in this reality. It's harsh and cruel, and the sooner Lucy woke up to that, the better.

"You'll feel more confident now you're in professional clothes," I told her. "Think of it as armour."

"Hmm," she hummed under her breath, turning to look out of the window and rubbing her hands up and down her arms. "That's a bit depressing, isn't it? Needing to wear armour for work. Is it really that much of a battle?"

I frowned. "Of *course* you need armour in the corporate world, Luce. We're not in Little Buckingham now. It's dog-eat-dog here."

Her mouth turned down, and her shoulders slumped. "Oh, right. Dog-eat-dog. Okay." It didn't sound okay at all. It sounded the opposite of okay, but what did she expect? This was London. If she didn't change, she'd be chewed up and spat out in an instant. I'd learned that the hard way – people took advantage if you showed any sign of weakness, and that included not dressing the part.

Anyway, there was no denying she looked beautiful. These new clothes were a huge improvement. She should have been happy. *I* should have been happy. I was sorting the brief Hetty had handed me after all. I was transforming her daughter. She *completely* looked the part now. But as I surveyed the new Lucy – fitted suit, high heels – I felt an awful ache in my chest and a profound sense of loss. I shook my head to clear it. I was losing my mind.

"So, now you just have to buck up your ideas a bit," I said. "No more daydreaming. Right?"

She bit her lip but gave a slow nod.

I sighed.

"Lucy, honestly, you can't stare into space when you're a personal assistant. There's a shit-ton to get done every day." It was time to stop playing Mr Nice Guy. Lucy needed to really knuckle down if she wanted to succeed. "You can't carry on being unrelentingly crap. It's not fair to anyone. You've got your armour now. You can go out there, fit right in and get on with the bloody job."

She nodded slowly, looking unconvinced. There was a knock on my door, and I frowned, not finished with Lucy's motivational talk.

"Yes," I snapped.

Will walked in, doing a double take when he spotted Lucy. Then, to my deep annoyance, he looked her up and down, and a slow smile spread across his face.

"Christ, what have you done to her, Moretti? Who knew this was what mousy little Lucy was hiding under those god-awful jumpers." He'd stepped closer to Lucy now and touched the lapel of her suit jacket, feeling the material between his fingers. Lucy startled and flinched away from him. His grin widened, and I narrowed my eyes.

"Leave it out, Brent," I snapped.

His smile dropped, and he shoved his hands into his pockets.

"So, is this new Office Lucy actually going to deign to answer the fucking phone?" Will said, his eyebrows going up.

My instinct was to go over there and punch the smug prick in the face, but I shoved that down. I was letting my feelings for Lucy get in the way of reason. Could I honestly be angry with Will for wanting a real, functioning assistant? He was handling one of our most high-profile land deals at the moment, and I'd saddled him with a real dud.

"Lucy's totally on it now," I said. "Aren't you, Luce?" Silence. When I looked over at her, she was looking out of the floor-to-ceiling window of my office, fiddling with the button on her sleeve. I sighed and rubbed my hand over my face.

"Lucy!" My voice cracked across the room, and she jumped; her gaze flew to me. I spoke slowly, trying to tamp the anger in my tone down. She really was impossible.

"You're ready to do better, *aren't you*?"

Lucy flashed a nervous look at Will and then gave a quick nod. Her hands came up to rub her arms again as she took another faltering step away from him.

"Sure," she said, sounding anything but. "Er... best assistant ever. From now on. Brownies' Honour." She actually held her hand up in a Brownie salute, and I sighed as Will snorted back a laugh.

CHAPTER 4

The very worst assistant

Lucy

I clenched my jaw to keep my teeth from chattering. The office temperature had been just about bearable in my thick jumpers, but in my current silk shirt, fitted suit and four-inch-heels combo, it was freezing. Plus, my ankle was throbbing from when I'd savagely twisted it earlier on the way into the lift. Unfortunately, I'd arrived there just as Will the Slimeball was getting in – he'd spotted me coming through the large double doors this morning and insisted on holding the lift for me, even though there were two others I could have gone in. I'd tried to wave him away with a smile, telling him I'd catch another, but he just ignored me, keeping his foot shoved against the automatic doors to keep them open.

Will was just plain mean and gave me the creeps. He had even less patience than Felix with my daydreaming. I was mostly relegated to office gopher-slash-tea-maker, which, to be honest, was probably for the best.

When I'd been making the tea for him and his clients last week, after he'd instructed me not to "fuck it up like you always do" right in front of them, I'd overheard him telling the others that I was "total shit as an assistant but pretty fuckable for someone who dresses like a tramp". This was met with a ripple of contemptible boys' club laughter, which made my flesh crawl. I'd had to slink back in there, completely mortified with a tomato-red face, and serve those dickheads their tea. I cursed my blushing habit again as I moved around the room; some of them did look deeply uncomfortable when they glanced at me – it must have been pretty obvious that I'd overheard them. Will, however, did not seem in the least bit uncomfortable with the situation.

The bastard seemed to revel in my discomfort in general. He'd even cornered me by the kettle two days ago on the pretence of reaching for his *favourite* mug in a cupboard above my head. The process of reaching for it seemed to involve a fair bit of side-boob contact. When I scuttled away, he actually laughed.

"You're a skittish little thing, aren't you?" he'd said in that self-satisfied smug tone. "Don't worry, my taste doesn't extend to scruffy country bumpkins."

Well, that may have been the case, but it didn't seem to stop him from grabbing me this morning as I fell into the lift after going over on my ankle, and then hauling me up against him as he dragged me inside. I did not want to feel my boss's junk against my stomach at eight in the morning. The whole thing made my flesh crawl. When I scuttled away, he laughed.

"Just making sure you stay upright," he said through his smug smile. "First time in heels? Must say I like the new look. Always suspected those jumpers were hiding a passable body."

I was ashamed of myself. I should have been able to tell him to fuck off. But in reality, I *was* a country bumpkin. Navigating an urban predator like Will, who was soon to be a junior partner in the firm, was beyond my capabilities.

So I just ran out of the lift as soon as the doors opened like a frightened rabbit, twisting my ankle *again*.

The day had deteriorated since then. I'd been thinking about a really annoying plot hole in my latest book (how was Astrida, the Queen of Light, going to get from the Black Kingdom to the Fae underlayer and still retain her powers?) when fingers snapping in front of my face brought me back to the present.

"Do you think she's had a stroke?"

I blinked, and my heart sank as I looked up at the CFO of Moretti Harding. How she made it to the top with the level of misogyny around here was a mystery, but Victoria Harding was properly terrifying. Completely emotionless. I don't think I'd ever seen the woman crack a smile. She rarely actually condescended to speak to anyone. Usually, everything was communicated via her assistant Lottie.

Now, Lottie *did* smile. To be honest, she seemed to be the friendliest face in the office and the only one who didn't seem to fit the corporate vibe completely. Pretty with caramel, curly hair and an easy smile. Don't get me wrong, she wore the same power suits and heels, but her multiple ear piercings, the small tattoo behind her ear and the neon trainers I saw her change out of when she arrived at the office yesterday told a different story.

But then Lottie could get away with anything because of how powerful Victoria was. I didn't have that luxury.

Weirdly, I actually knew Victoria from childhood. My brother's friend Ollie was her half-brother. But I'd only seen her a few times when I was growing up, seeing as she was the product of Ollie's dad's affair and so lived with her biological mother. This was quite the scandal as Ollie's dad was the Duke of Buckingham at the time (he'd since died and Ollie had inherited the title).

Mum said that aristocrats had affairs all the time, so it wasn't really that shocking.

One of the few times I'd met Victoria had been at our small cottage when I was seven and she was nine, although she didn't speak to me. Mum told me that Victoria didn't actually speak to anyone back then – selective mutism or something. She certainly wasn't mute now, though.

My ankle twinged with pain again as I shifted in my seat to look up at Victoria and Lottie. Victoria was looking at me with a curious expression, her head tipped to the side like I was a bug in a microscope. The way she'd asked if I was having a stroke in that emotionless manner summed her up perfectly. As did her outfit – a winter-white trouser suit with high heels, blonde hair scraped back into a perfect bun, make-up on point.

Where Lottie was pretty with a girl-next-door vibe, Victoria was intimidatingly beautiful in an untouchable way.

"Shit," I muttered. "I mean… sorry, I'm fine. I must have just drifted off for a minute."

"You are Lucy Mayweather," she told me, and I nodded slowly. I'd been in the office for a month, but it was as though this was the first time Victoria had actually seen me.

"Your mother was Felix's nanny."

I nodded again. This conversation didn't seem to need much input from me anyway.

"She is a kind lady."

I blinked in surprise and then felt my face soften. "Yes, she is."

"Do you have a condition?" Was what Victoria blurted out next.

"Er…" I blinked at her. "Well, I—"

"Vicky," Lottie said, flashing me a smile and then looking up at her boss. "Remember we talked about being blunt and being rude?" Victoria nodded, her attention still on me. "Well, this is one of those times where you've edged into rude. You can't really ask people if they have a *condition* like that."

Victoria frowned. "But if she has epilepsy, then her inattention at her desk could be explained by an absence seizure."

"I don't have epilepsy," I rushed in to say.

"Then why were you staring into space, not aware of your environment?"

"Vicky, give it a rest," Lottie muttered.

"It's okay," I said, my face heating. "Sorry, I was daydreaming."

"Daydreaming?" Victoria said in a confused voice as if she was only just hearing about this phenomenon for the first time and found the entire concept too bizarre to be real. "Well, that's a shame. Epilepsy absence seizures have potential treatments. I don't think the same can be said for daydreaming."

I pressed my lips together to hold back a laugh. Meanwhile, Lottie was rolling her eyes.

"Don't worry," I reassured Victoria. "I don't need treatment."

In fact, daydreaming was pretty much essential to my real career, but I wasn't going to tell these women that. I shivered again, still feeling the cold and Victoria's sharp eyes took that in as well.

"You're cold," she stated.

I bit my lip and slowly nodded.

"It's eighteen point five degrees in here," she went on to tell me, and I blinked. Point five... was this woman for real? "That is *not* a low ambient temperature."

I looked left and right for some sort of out from this weird conversation, but the office space around me was deserted. Where was Slimy Will when I needed him?

"Why are you cold?" Victoria pushed.

I shrugged. "I have cold intolerance. It's been a problem since I was small. Everyone else will be in t-shirts and I'll have to wear two jumpers. I think my own personal thermostat is a bit screwy."

"Let me see your hands," she commanded.

"Honestly, Vicky," Lottie said in a hushed voice. "Leave the poor girl alone. We're going to be late for the meeting."

"They'll start without us. William has clearly gone ahead. He should be capable of introducing the scheme."

Lottie sighed and mouthed, "I'm sorry," as Victoria turned back to me.

"Now, show me your hands."

I lifted my hands up onto the desk. The tips of three of my fingers had gone white.

"You have Raynaud's," she said; again, not a question, but I nodded anyway.

The Raynaud's had developed in my mid-twenties in addition to the cold intolerance.

"Fascinating."

Wow, calling someone's painful medical condition fascinating was cold.

"Vicky, come on now," Lottie said in a gentle voice, and I wondered why she had to be gentle with such a seemingly spiky woman. "We do need to get to that meeting. Will might be capable sometimes, but he's also perfectly capable of pissing everyone off too."

Then Lottie reached over and put her hand over Victoria's wrist. This gesture seemed to be some sort of trigger to pull Victoria away from her focus on me.

"True," Victoria acknowledged. "Goodbye," she said to me, making a sharp turn on her heel and walking briskly down the corridor towards the conference room.

"Sorry," Lottie said to me through a wide smile. "She can be a bit much. I better catch her up before she goes in there. Who knows what she'll say otherwise? See you later." And off she went at a jog after her boss.

I stared after her, thinking that Lottie was probably more my type of person, but I was simply too shy to approach her, and besides, she was always with Victoria. I tried to imagine myself finding her later and asking if she wanted to go out for a drink or something, but just couldn't see it happening.

I jumped as the phone next to me rang. Like an idiot, it was only after five rings that I thought to pick it up.

Seriously, I was the very worst assistant in the history of the world.

CHAPTER 5

Hop-a-long

Lucy

"Why weren't you at your desk?" Will snapped over the phone.

"I was."

"Then why did it take you so long to pick up? Honestly, I'm not sure how many neurons are actually firing inside your tiny mind most days. We need tea. You can manage that, right?"

"Yes, I can manage that," I muttered miserably.

Fifteen minutes later I'd set up the tea trolley with the help of the lovely catering lady whose job it actually was to deliver the tea; Will just wanted me to do it as some sort of power trip. He was *such* a dick.

I hobbled into the meeting room and then froze at the entrance. At one head of the long conference table was Felix, looking absolutely delicious as always. The rest of the table was filled with various executives and partners, including Will and Victoria, but I did a double take when I spotted Ollie, the duke, sitting next to his half-sister and looking just as intimidating as he always did. Fortunately, Ollie barely glanced in my direction – nobody ever really noticed the tea lady after all.

But even more shocking was the man sitting at the other end of the long table: Harry York. I stared at him like a deer trapped in the headlights, praying that he didn't realise who I was.

I'd only met him very briefly about a year ago, at my agent Madeline's insistence. Harry ran an investment company, but he and his wife were massive epic fantasy readers. He'd contacted Madeline and offered to provide financial backing if she could broker a deal with a production company to do a series based on my books. Part of the reason was so I would consider meeting his wife who was also a fan. It was going to be an anniversary gift to her.

Unfortunately, at that stage of my life I'd barely left Little Buckingham, and by the time I'd made it into London, I was totally overwhelmed. I was supposed to be meeting Harry and Madeline at a crowded restaurant. It was really fancy, and I felt completely out of place. Luckily, Maddie was there before Harry. Once I made it over to her, I didn't even sit down at the table. I just burst out with, "Sorry, I can't do this," and basically ran out of there.

But on my way out I collided with Harry (I recognised him from my extensive Googling). He didn't know who I was of course, so he just reached out to steady me with his hands on my upper arms, said sorry even though it very much was not his fault, smiled down at me then walked away towards Madeline once I was safely on my feet.

I felt awful afterwards, but I did make sure to send him signed books for him and his wife in time for their anniversary. Madeline was exasperated, but she knew me pretty well by then and was used to my reclusive ways. She said she'd just told Harry that I was "a bit of a rare one" and that I didn't leave my hidey-hole very often (which was a fair comment).

That incident had been one of the triggers for me moving to London. I knew I needed to stop being such a wussbag and get out there. Nowadays, if you didn't show your face at book signings everyone could just assume you were some sort of AI robot, which wasn't a good look.

Plus, I did actually *want* to meet my fans. To connect with them in the real world. The letters and emails I got from them were wonderful and meant a huge amount to me. The least I could do was woman up for them and come out of hiding.

I hadn't even really meant for my identity to be a secret. LP Mayweather was my actual name. But I was never comfortable with having author photos taken and nobody had ever made the connection to me, so it was really just an open secret. If people asked, I would have told them – but nobody ever asked.

I was fairly confident that Harry York wouldn't remember me from that brief encounter in the restaurant – especially not after my recent transformation, and in this environment. When he and his wife came into the office last week, I'd made sure to keep myself hidden in the background; now I was front and centre, pushing a squeaky tea trolley.

Felix glanced at me and then scowled. He seemed to be having trouble getting used to the transformation that he himself had asked for. God knows why. I was now a carbon copy of every other woman in the office. I gave him a brief smile. He opened his mouth to speak, shut it again, and then shook his head to clear it.

"Right, well, as I was saying," he said in that sharp, commanding tone that I found so sexy. Missing dimple aside, there were some aspects of Business Felix that really buttered my muffin. I could have listened to his bossy voice all day. "The Hyde Park Project is now set in stone. To suggest that it's not a sound investment is deeply insulting. And to block us from using Blue Sky Designs is unbelievable."

"Bullshit," Harry York said, and I nearly dropped the teacup I was holding. Crikey, people thought I was unprofessional wearing a jumper to work? This guy said the s-word in meetings! "You haven't even managed to broker the land deal fully yet. How do we even know that planning will go through? I'm not letting the Buckingham Estate throw good money after bad. And as far as my wife's architecture firm goes – I'm not willing to have them involved in such an unstable project."

I watched in fascination as Felix's hand on the table clenched into a fist. It was the only sign that Harry was getting to him. His face remained perfectly calm.

"She was absolutely fine with it when she came into the office last month," he gritted out. "What's changed?"

"Now now, chaps," Ollie spoke up. "No need for tantrums."

He was the only one smiling, and his comment was met by stony glares from both Harry and Felix. I decided I'd better actually serve the bloody tea rather than stare at Felix like a deranged stalker, so I picked up a teacup and started limping to the table.

"I will not be drawn into a—" Felix broke off just as I'd reached Victoria with her tea. I was hoping I'd got it right. There was an actual colour chart for Victoria's tea preference, citing the exact shade she wanted it at different times of the day. The woman was certainly strange. Unfortunately, I was pretty sure the tea I'd presented to her now was more the five-o'clock lighter shade than a ten-in-the-morning shade.

"Lucy," Felix snapped, and I jerked in surprise at the use of my name. Half the tea spilt onto the saucer as I was putting it down. "Why are you limping?"

My eyes went wide as I looked across at him. He was staring at me expectantly, totally ignoring the fact that there were at least ten other people listening to this exchange and that he was interrupting what seemed to be an extremely tense meeting.

I cleared my throat, glancing around at the curious faces and then back at Felix.

"I twisted my ankle. But, er... it's fine. I guess I just need a bit more practice in heels." I let out a small, nervous laugh, which he cut off.

"You need to go to the emergency department," he said in that commanding tone. Now, whilst I'm not saying the commanding tone didn't do it for me, *actually* being issued commands (and ridiculous ones at that) was slightly irritating, however sexy the command-issuer was.

"It's fine. I'm fine. Wouldn't want to waste NHS time and all that." I gave another little laugh in an attempt to lighten the atmosphere, which fell very flat.

"Felix, let Hop-a-long serve the tea," said Will in an amused tone, edged with irritation. "She's been limping all morning. She's fine."

Felix's gaze flew to Will, his expression so cold I almost shivered. Will shrank back in his chair, his smile wavering.

"Lucy," Felix said. "Take a seat at the table. We'll talk about your ankle after the meeting. Will, get the fuck up and serve the fucking tea yourself."

I opened my mouth to try and say again that I was fine, but Felix's eyes flashed back to me again.

"Sit." His command snapped through the space, and without any conscious thought, I sat straight down in the chair just behind me. Felix stared at me for a second more, something working behind those gorgeous dark eyes, his mouth pulling up at one side in what might have been the ghost of a self-satisfied smirk before he masked it. He turned his attention back to Will. "I wasn't fucking around, Brent. Stand up and serve the tea. Now."

Will's face flushed and he shot me a murderous look before pushing back from his chair and storming over to the tea trolley. I twisted my hands in my lap as heat hit my cheeks.

"Lucy Mayweather!" My head shot up at Ollie's deep voice. He was grinning at me from across the table. "What the fuck are you doing here, love? Last time I spoke to Mike he told me you never left the village."

"Er..." I glanced around at all the faces staring at our exchange and I flushed with embarrassment. Christ, these entitled public school boys just said and did whatever the heck they wanted, didn't they? "Hi." I gave Ollie a small wave, and he grinned across at me. But then, proving my earlier point, he got up from his seat and strode around to my side of the table. When he reached me, he pulled me up from my chair, gave me a hug and then pulled back to stare at me.

"Jesus, you look so grown up. Not a woolly jumper in sight."

"For fuck's sake, Ollie," snapped Felix. "Let her go so she can sit down. She shouldn't be on that ankle."

Ollie rolled his eyes but did release me so I could sit back down on the chair. "He always this bossy?" he muttered in my ear once I was seated and I bit my lip. With another grin, Ollie gave me a quick kiss on the cheek before striding back to his own seat again.

"Sit the fuck down," snapped Felix, sounding absolutely furious. He was glaring across the space at Ollie, his hands on the table as if about to push up to standing, a muscle ticking in his tightly clenched jaw.

"I guess the answer to that is yes," said Ollie to me with another grin. When he took his seat, he looked between a still-furious Felix and me and raised an eyebrow.

But when I glanced around the table, I realised that Ollie's surprising display of affection was the least of my worries. Harry York was staring at me, a small frown marring his forehead.

CHAPTER 6

"Lucy Mayweather?"

Lucy

Why did Ollie have to use my full name? After a long moment staring at me, Harry blinked and shook his head as if to clear it. I breathed a sigh of relief. Maybe I'd got away with it? After all, Mayweather is a fairly common name, and he only glanced at me for a second in that restaurant over a year ago.

"If the reunion is over, can we get back to the actual numbers on the project and how they don't add up? I'm sure we don't want to waste His Grace's time," Harry said.

Felix rolled his eyes. "His Grace," he muttered. "Christ, you're *such* a kiss-arse."

Felix and Harry continued to volley increasingly aggressive insults until, to my surprise, it was Victoria who interrupted the deadlock.

"Enough!" she said, that one word cracking through the room, silencing the meeting. "Neither of you are using logical reasoning skills here. Felix, I know Ollie's your friend."

"He's *your* brother," Felix snapped. "Where's his sense of family loyalty?"

"Half-brother," Victoria corrected automatically.

"Careful, Felix," Ollie put in, his smile dropping.

Victoria just rolled her eyes. "The financials on the Hyde

Park development are solid. I will prepare a presentation and I'll deal with your concerns. Let me assure you, Mr York, I have no interest in putting any Buckingham Estate money at risk, despite what you may have heard about my parentage."

"Vics," Ollie said softly. "Nobody would think that, darling."

Victoria gave a jerky nod, a flare of some unidentifiable emotion breaking her cool exterior for a moment before she masked it.

"Lady Harding, I didn't mean to imply that—"

"I am not Lady Harding. The title does not transfer to illegitimate children," Victoria said, cutting Harry off. Silence fell over the boardroom. "I'll prepare the figures by next week when we should have heard more from the planning application. This meeting is no longer productive. Lottie, arrange another meeting *excluding* Felix. As far as Blue Sky Designs goes, I am already negotiating directly with Verity York. Good day."

With that, Victoria pushed back her chair and simply left the room without a backward glance. The woman was a total badass. Ollie muttered his excuses and stalked out of the room after her.

"Right," muttered Harry York. "Well, I—"

"Jolly good," the guy next to Harry said briskly (I assumed he was Harry's business partner, Toby). "As usual, Ms Harding cuts through the bullshit."

Everyone started packing up their stuff. I started to push up to stand, but Felix's sharp "Lucy," from across the table, caused me to sit back down. "Stay a moment, please. You as well, Brent."

Will shot me another poisonous look, then sat back in his chair and crossed his arms.

"Lucy, is it?" Harry asked me as he approached my side of the table.

"Er, yeah. Hi," I said in a small voice. He tilted his head to the side as he stared down at me.

"Lucy *Mayweather*?"

I swallowed past the lump in my throat, suddenly regretting my decision not to go with a proper pen name. The leap from LP Mayweather to Lucy Mayweather wasn't a big one.

"Yes," I whispered. Recognition flashed in Harry's eyes, and my heart sank. He opened his mouth to speak again, but with my wide eyes fixed on his, I gave a very slight shake of my head. He frowned, his gaze flicked around the room and his eyebrows went up, but he did snap his mouth shut.

"What the fuck?" Felix snapped as he strode around the table to me. "Leave my employees alone, York."

Harry gave me one last searching look before focusing on Felix.

"Alright, Moretti. Keep your knickers on." Harry winked at me before picking up his bag and moving to the double doors. "I'll be seeing you," he said, his eyes on me just before the door closed after him.

"What was that about?" Felix asked, crossing his arms over his impressive chest.

I just shrugged. "No idea," I squeaked, and he frowned down at me. I'd never been a great liar. Finally, he looked from me to Will, uncrossed his arms to put his hands on his hips.

"Right, want to tell me what you're playing at, Brent?" he asked.

"I don't know what you mean."

"If Lucy is limping, you don't just ignore it. You bloody well tell her to get it checked out. At the very least, you don't have her walking around the office at your beck and call. You certainly don't call her *Hop-a-long*."

Will rolled his eyes. "She's a full-grown adult, Felix. She can sort herself out. I'm not here to babysit her. I've babied her through the last month as it is. Anyway, she knows it's all just bants, don't you, darling?" He winked at me, and I think I might have vomited just a little in my mouth.

"Watch it, Brent," Felix said in a low, dangerous voice. "Do you understand me? Now, Lucy won't be available for the rest of the day. She needs to go for an X-ray."

"Whatever," Will said under his breath as he got up to leave. "No loss to me. About as useful as a chocolate teapot."

As the double doors closed after Will, Felix turned his attention back to me, and I wanted to sink through the floor with embarrassment.

"Felix, I am *not* going to the emergency department."

Felix narrowed his eyes.

"Are you going to shout at me again?" I meant my voice to come out stronger than it did, but I tried to square my shoulders and brace for criticism. But Felix just looked up at the ceiling and rubbed his temples. I felt bad for the man. He had enough stress going on without me adding to it every day.

To be honest, I couldn't understand anyone wanting to live life at the pace he did. It looked exhausting to me. I needed *way* more downtime than everyone else here seemed to require. The relentless peopling Felix did would break me. I fiddled with the sleeves of my shirt, wishing again it was the warm wool of my holey jumper that I could pull over my fingers.

"Lucy, I've never shouted at you," his voice was softer now, but I could still detect the irritation. All I seemed to do was annoy Felix these days. He used to be much more tolerant of me when we were kids. I turned to stare out of the window again and heard Felix's exasperated sigh. "And you *are* going to A&E, right? Lucy? Are you listening?"

I forced myself to look at him, and it was my turn to narrow my eyes. "Yes, I'm listening. No, I'm not going to A&E."

"You're a lot more stubborn than I remember."

I shrugged.

"Well, fine. If you want to be an idiot, be my guest. You'd better get back out there and answer the bloody phone then."

He was clearly irritated. I got the impression that he considered all his interactions with me a massive waste of time.

His loyalty to my mum must be a real millstone around his neck.

"You've got the proper clothes now. You can start getting on with the job properly."

I forced a smile. "Right, yes. Er… are you sure you don't want to just fire me? It'd probably be easier."

"Lucy," Felix snapped. "This defeatist attitude is bullshit, you know? You owe it to your mum to really give this opportunity a chance."

A huge wave of guilt assailed me then. Felix had really gone out on a limb for me, and I was fucking it all up. Not to mention all those poor, much more competent people who should be doing this job instead. I promised Mum I'd give this a go. I had to stop being a big wimp and get on with it. Creeps like Will were everywhere in the real world. So were offices full of unfriendly people. If I wanted to live in the real world, I needed to start toughening up.

"Okay," I said. "I'm on it. I promise."

The trouble is that being *on it* had never really been my natural state. More often than not, I was unaware of what *it* actually was.

CHAPTER 7

Good girl

Lucy

I sat bolt-upright on the sofa when the banging started, then blinked across at the hallway and my front door beyond it.

"What on earth?" I muttered as I tried to disentangle myself from my duvet cocoon. This place was a bit on the draughty side, to be honest. Period properties were fine if you didn't mind a cold wind blowing through your living room.

I flinched as another series of loud bangs sounded again, and then finally managed to untangle myself.

"Bollocks," I cursed as I skidded on the polished hallway on the way to the door, falling on my arse again. I couldn't even blame the heels this time.

When I finally made it to the door, I paused and then went up on tiptoes to peer through the peephole. Upon seeing Felix's handsome but frustrated face on the other side, I stumbled back and fell on my arse for the third time that day. Once down, I decided it was safer to stay there. Maybe if he thought I was out, he might go away. There was no way I was letting him see me dressed like this. Not only was I in the most deeply unsexy and embarrassing pyjamas known to man, but I had a massive fluffy dressing gown over the top, which Emily had reliably informed me made me look like her Aunt Becs (not a flattering comparison, believe me). On my feet were my enormous fluffy pink and purple slippers, my hands were in fingerless gloves, and I had a bobble hat on my head.

"Lucy, I can hear you in there," Felix said. "Open the door."

I winced. He was clearly running out of patience. Great, if he didn't think I was a useless weirdo before, he was definitely going to think it now.

With no other choice, I clambered to my feet and resigned myself to my fate. When I got through the many locks and finally pulled open the door, my breath left me in a whoosh. There he was in all his glorious intensity. His stubble was end-of-the-day thick, his tie was loose and his hair was more ruffled than normal.

My mouth went completely dry when his dark eyes locked with mine, and then I felt heat rise in my cheeks as he did a full body scan from the bobble on my hat to the fluff on my slippers. His lips twitched once, and that dimple made a very brief appearance before he blanked his expression.

Then he just walked right in, closed the door behind himself and bizarrely started inspecting the locks.

"Er, what are you—"

"Good girl," he interrupted in a low voice, and my head started to spin. I challenge any heterosexual woman to be unaffected by Felix Moretti calling them a good girl.

"W–what?" I whispered, hoping he'd say it again.

"Good girl for not opening the door right away. Good girl for checking the peephole and good girl for having so many locks on your front door."

That was four good girls in under a minute. I was going to pass out. Then Felix's head tilted to the side as he scanned me again.

"Is your heating on the blink?"

"What?" I whispered again, as clearly this was the only word I was capable of saying from now on.

"Your heating," he said slowly. "It feels warm in here, but you seem to be dressed for some sort of weird polar expedition."

I pulled my hat off and threw it onto the side table in a sudden movement. It landed on one of my many houseplants. Felix watched its progress, and then his gorgeous eyes came back to me. I cleared my throat, hoping I was now able to form words.

"It's draughty," I said, just above a whisper, and honestly, I was proud of myself for getting that much information out. Felix Moretti in my flat was not something my brain was able to cope with.

Technically, I should have been prepared. The amount of times I'd fantasised about having him here was insane. But Imaginary Felix was nothing compared to the real thing – well, apart from the fact that Imaginary Felix would have ripped my clothes off by now and started doing bad, bad things to me. Then again, Imaginary Lucy would not be looking like Emily's Aunt Becs. Imaginary Lucy was in a silky sleep-shorts set with lace trim and her imaginary cleavage on show so...

"Lucy," Felix snapped, and I blinked. Whoops, zoned out again. "Did you hear anything I just said?"

I pulled my lips in between my teeth and widened my eyes. He shook his head in exasperation and stalked past me into the living room. I made a sound no human should make – sort of a cross between an "eep" and a "squee" as I hustled after him. My living room was an absolute state. He stopped by my sofa, looking down at the duvet nest and the many, many books that were littered around it. When he looked back at me his dimple had returned.

"Still read five books at a time then?" he asked. I gave another deeply embarrassing "eep" in reply as my vocal cords had now entirely given up the ghost. He picked up *The Hobbit* from the top of the nest. "Still keep a Tolkien going while you read the others?"

I shrugged one shoulder in response. It was something I'd done since I was small. I'd read all the Tolkien books early, but then I could never really let them go. So I just re-read them whilst I read other books, sort of like literary palate cleansers. It did mean lugging a lot of weight around in my school bag and made me even more of a target for bullies, but it was just the way I wanted to do things.

Felix felt the well-worn cover of *The Hobbit* for a moment and then carefully placed it back on the duvet. A warm feeling spread out from my chest at the amount of care he took over that book. He knew how much it meant to me. He remembered that much at least.

"Right," he said, all business now as his dimple disappeared and he crossed his arms over his chest. "I'm here to take you to the emergency department. No arguments."

I blinked up at him, anger piercing through the daydream I was starting to have about Felix on top of my duvet nest.

"No," I said, my voice much stronger than before.

"Lucy, I spoke to your mum and—"

"You spoke to my mother?" If anything was going to throw cold water over my Felix sex daydreams, it was chat about my mum.

"Yes, of course," Felix said slowly. "She entrusted you to my care and—"

"Oh my God," I said, anger helping me to fully regain control of my vocal cords. "I am not a child! Felix, I'm twenty-seven years old. I don't have to be *entrusted* to anyone."

He huffed. "Lucy, I would believe you if you weren't still limping and not getting anything checked out. Instead you're freezing to death in this flat that... wait a minute." Felix pulled at his shirt collar and shrugged off his suit jacket. "You said there was a cold draught? It's bloody boiling in here."

I scowled at him. "Felix, I feel the cold. Now, did you just come here to lecture me about my post-injury care?"

He rolled up his sleeves and frowned at the extra heater I had blasting the room. "How are you still cold?"

I huffed. Seriously if he was going to come here and boss me about in a deeply non-sexual way, then he could just bugger off so I could go back to fantasising about Imaginary Felix who banged *me* instead of banging on about going to the hospital and my cold intolerance.

"It's very, er, orange in here," he said slowly, taking in the rest of the room. It was my turn to cross my arms over my chest.

"Not all of us like unrelenting grey and white, Felix."

"Clearly," he muttered, moving across the room and fingering the leaves of one of my many plants. I enjoyed colour, plants and lots of books in my environment. Organised clutter was how I liked to term it. *A bloody mess* was more my brother's description. Felix cleared his throat. "Right, well if you won't let me take you, then I at least need to look at your ankle."

I made another deeply embarrassing "eep" sound.

Felix rolled his eyes. "Lucy, look it's my fault that you twisted your ankle in the first place, by making you wear those shoes. I feel responsible and I need to know that nothing's broken."

Then he moved to me, put his hands on my shoulders and pushed me down onto the sofa. It was dangerously close to what Imaginary Felix would do in this situation, and I had another head rush at the feel of his large hands even though it was through three fairly thick layers. Another "eep" escaped when he sat next to me on the sofa, right on the duvet nest, and picked up both my fluff-covered feet from the floor into his lap.

"I just want to say at this point," I said in a hoarse voice, "that I do not think this is necessary, and—" My lips clamped together in shock as Felix pulled off the fluffy slipper on my injured leg.

"Jesus Christ, how many socks do you have on?" he muttered as he pulled off the thick sock underneath, then the medium-thickness thermal sock under that. When he finally made it to my actual foot he pushed up the leg of my flannel pyjamas and froze. I watched him stare intently at my foot and ankle for a long moment before he swallowed and his jaw clenched tight.

43

"Your feet are really small," he said, and it was his voice that was hoarse this time.

I blinked at him, unsure how to respond to that comment. Was it a compliment? He sounded like he was actually in pain and he still hadn't moved.

"I…" he trailed off and swallowed again. "Lucy, I'm going to touch your ankle now, okay?"

He tore his gaze away from his intense inspection of my lower leg to look up at my face. All I was capable of was a short nod. Then his hands were on me and it felt like my heart might just stop in my chest. One of his large, warm, dry hands enclosed my ankle, pressing on both sides whilst the other tilted my foot from side to side.

"Does it hurt?" he asked, his voice now so hoarse and low he was almost growling.

"N–n–no," I managed to stutter out. To be honest, I doubted that in that very moment, I was able to feel any pain. I would have probably told him a gunshot wound was fine right then. At my voice, his gaze snapped back up to mine, and our eyes locked. He searched my face for a long moment, his jaw ticking as his hand on my ankle slid up just an inch under my pyjama leg. I sucked in a sharp breath, willing him to go on, feeling like I'd die if he didn't, but then he blinked rapidly, breaking the connection.

"Shit," he muttered under his breath before he sprang up from the sofa like it was on fire. I was still frozen in my duvet nest, the head rush from having his hands on me making my thoughts fuzzy around the edges. He tore his hand through his hair and took two rapid steps back from me. "Right, right." He cleared his throat before shoving his hands into his pockets. "Okay, so that's good. No need to take you to the emergency department. I'll… er, I'll see you at work."

He stalked out of my living room and down the hallway, slamming my front door behind him before I even had time to blink. I sat there frozen for a full minute before a series of sharp

44

knocks sounded from my door again. I managed to make it to the door on wobbly legs just as Felix said, "Lock up, Lucy," through the wood. I nodded even though he couldn't see me, and after I'd pushed the last deadbolt in place, I swore I heard "Good girl" again before I heard his footsteps retreat down the steps away from the door.

CHAPTER 8

"She's unhappy."

Felix

"I'm trying, Mum. Really I am." Lucy's voice stopped me in my tracks on my way out of the office. What was she doing here this late? It was after seven. The rest of the desks were long deserted. I'd had to stay to try and sort a planning application that was up the spout. But there was no reason for *her* to be here. "But you don't understand how very crap I am at this job. I got a whole spreadsheet of stuff wrong today so now I have to stay to sort it out, except I don't bloody understand Excel at all. So I'm about as likely to sort it as the Buckingham Rovers are of winning the league."

I smiled at the mention of the most crap football team of all time. Mike, Ollie and I had spent many summers playing for their youth squad. After terms of amazing sporting equipment and top-class sports teachers at school, coming home and playing for the Buckingham Rovers, where the footballs were barely kept inflated and Barry the coach with his twenty-a-day habit wheezed his way through the most bizarre football advice ever given, was quite the contrast. I had the piss taken out of me for being a posh wanker, the tackles were rarely legal… but it was bloody good fun.

I kept walking towards the sound of Lucy's voice but paused just around the corner from her desk when she sighed, and I heard a small hitch in her breath as she did it. She sounded a little hoarse when she spoke again, and for some reason, that made my chest tighten.

"My boss is really mean," she said, just above a whisper. "And I don't blame him because honestly, I'm *so* crap, but... Mum, nobody likes me here. I haven't made a single friend. And I'm cold." Another pause. "No, no, I have to wear this *fancy* stuff now. No jumpers. It's like a bloody fridge in here."

My eyebrows went up at that. A fridge? I kept the office at a comfortable temperature. It wasn't exactly Baltic.

"I know, I'm wearing it now, Mum. But I can't very well trot around the office in a puffa jacket that goes to my ankles and essentially looks like I'm wearing a sleeping bag all day. That's not professional... Mum, I don't think you understand what kind of business Felix's running here. It's not a jolly, cosy little office. And he's not the same. I'm never going to fit into this world. Coming here was a mistake. I think I need to come back home."

Bloody hell. I was failing Hetty. I'd never been very good at accepting failure. I'd just have to turn this around. I owed it to Hetty to sort Lucy out. When I strode around the corner, Lucy jumped in her chair, and her eyes went wide. She looked utterly ridiculous in a huge puffa coat that was zipped up to her chin, a pair of fingerless gloves that had seen better days on her hands, and a fluffy wool hat pulled down over her ears.

"Er... Mum, I—"

Before she could make up any excuses for her mother, I snatched the phone out of her hand.

"Hetty?"

"Oh! Felix, dear. Lucy didn't say you were there."

"I think I surprised her. I was just leaving and heard her on the phone to you."

"How much did you hear?"

"Enough."

"She's unhappy."

47

"I know."

Hetty sighed, and I felt the weight of her disappointment all the way from Little Buckingham. "Maybe it was too much to ask of you. I think that—"

"Lucy's coming to a party with me tonight," I declared, watching Lucy as her eyes went even wider than before.

"Oh!" Hetty sounded delighted. "A party. That sounds wonderful. Just what Lucy needs. A nice party."

"She'll meet people there. Network. It'll do her the power of good."

"Er… Felix, love," Hetty's tone was slightly more hesitant now. "I'm not sure you really understand. Networking is not… well, I don't think…"

"It's *exactly* what she needs," I said. "Getting out there and amongst it. She'll have a great time."

"Right, okay," Hetty sounded a little happier now. "A *great time* is good. She needs *that*. I knew you'd be able to sort things out for her. You always were such a good boy."

I felt Hetty's praise wash over me just like I was ten years old again. It reinforced my determination to see this plan through.

"You can rely on me," I said.

"Wonderful, dear. Off you kids go then. Have a lovely time! And Felix, don't forget your mum's birthday next month. You know she'll be disappointed if you're not there again."

"Hmm," I muttered, non-committedly. My mother's birthday dinners were tortuous and there was no way in hell I would ever be in the same room as my father. The last five years I'd convinced Mum to come and visit me in London for a fancy meal out. That way, I didn't have to see *him*.

Hetty sighed.

"She does care about you, love," she said softly, and I cleared my throat. "I know your father—"

"Great to speak to you, Hetty. I'll be in touch." There was a pause, and when Hetty spoke again her voice was soft.

"Okay, love. You kids have a nice time now."

At thirty-three and CEO of a major financial company, it was a long while since I'd been called a kid.

I held Lucy's phone out to her, and it took a few seconds before she managed to reach for it with her glove-clad hand. Her face, which had drained of colour when she first caught sight of me, was now glowing red.

"Wow," she muttered, slipping her phone into her puffa's pocket. "*That* was mortifying."

"Why are you sitting in all those clothes?"

Lucy's face glowed even brighter, which I wouldn't have thought possible. "I feel the cold. I told you that."

I frowned, realising that this wasn't a new phenomenon. Memories flashed through my mind: Lucy wrapped in various blankets in the warm Mayweather house despite how cosy the cottage was; Lucy permanently plastered against the boiling Aga like a kitten; Lucy wearing the most ridiculous winter coats even on relatively warm days.

"You're cold here?"

She shrugged. "It was okay when I could wear my jumpers and stuff, but silk shirts, skirts and thin tights are freezing."

I felt an arrow of guilt at that. Lucy had been freezing her arse off in the office for a whole week at *my* instruction. She still had a slight limp as well, and that was from wearing the heels *I* had insisted on. I came around the desk to look at her feet now. They were stuffed into her massive fluffy, pink and purple slippers, her heels abandoned on the floor next to her.

"Er... thanks for putting Mum off the scent there with the party thing. It'll get her off my back for a while if she thinks I'm getting out there."

"I wouldn't lie to Hetty," I said, crossing my arms over my chest as I stared down at Lucy. "You *are* going to come to a party with me."

Lucy's eyes went wide, and her mouth dropped open. "Tonight?"

"Yes." I shrugged. "Why not?"

49

She bit her lip and looked to the side. When she did turn her gaze back to me, it was infuriatingly my tie that she directed it at.

"I'm not that great at parties."

"You'll be fine," I said briskly. "And this will help you get into the swing of things in the corporate world. A certain amount of socialising is expected in this business."

Lucy grimaced. "Oh, is this a businessy party? I defo don't think that'll be my bag, Felix. And I'm right in the middle of *The Mandalorian*." I gave her a blank look. "You know – Mando, Baby Yoda?"

I tamped down my irritation. Any other woman, especially one working in my industry, would absolutely leap at the chance to accompany me to an industry party. But Lucy was instead talking about random *Star Wars* spin-offs and preferring to spend her time watching a small green alien puppet.

"You're coming," I said in a firm voice. "It'll do you the power of good, and I promised your mum."

"You always were bossy," she muttered, standing up and shuffling across to put on her massive scarf. When she was done, only her eyes and the freckles over the bridge of her nose were visible under all her layers. She looked both totally ridiculous and heart-stoppingly pretty. She started shuffling off towards the lift with her fluffy slippers still on her feet. I pinched the bridge of my nose and looked down at the ground.

"Luce, you can't go out in those."

She looked back at me, and I pointed to her feet.

"Oh, right," she said, her voice distracted. "You wouldn't believe the number of times I've been to the shops or pub back home in these bad boys. Totally slips my mind."

I could just see Lucy traipsing around in those ridiculous slippers back in Little Buckingham. Nobody would have batted an eyelid. I wondered for the hundredth time what on earth this girl was doing in London and how the hell I was going to help her even vaguely fit in.

"Don't suppose it'd be a good look for your posh party, though," she said. I couldn't see her mouth, but I could see her eyes crinkling above her scarf as she smiled. Shuffling back to the desk, she toed off her slippers and put on the heels from earlier, wincing as she bore weight on them. I sighed.

"Just put your Uggs on," I said.

"Oh great," she replied, pulling off the heels and reaching for the furry Ugg boots I knew she kept under her desk.

Well, at least she most likely didn't have that god-awful jumper on underneath the puffa. Maybe this wouldn't be a complete disaster.

CHAPTER 9

Not really a party person

Lucy

This was a complete disaster.

I looked like a right numpty in my jumper and Uggs. But Felix had said it was a *house party*. What he failed to mention was that it was in one of the poshest houses in London, complete with a shiny marble entrance hall and multiple servers circulating with champagne and canapés.

A house party back in Little Buckingham consisted of a six-pack of beer, maybe some cider if we were feeling fancy and a large bag of Wotsits. Sometimes Trina, who worked behind the counter at the Post Office, would wear the occasional mini-skirt, but that was as smart as it got. Every woman here was immaculate. They were all in heels and looked like they had collectively stepped off a shoot for *Vogue*. The men had all clearly come straight from work in their tailored suits. There wasn't a pair of jeans or a bottle of beer to be seen.

With all these people and the fancy environment, I felt like I was drowning. It took all my willpower not to bolt back out of the front door. I tried to stop the rising panic with the techniques Mum had taught me: look for three things you can see, two things you can smell and one thing you can feel.

Okay, well, three things I could see – Felix looking

absolutely gorgeous as always, Will smirking at me from across the room and now a glamorous, tall woman sweeping up to Felix and kissing him on the cheek. *Okay*, none of that was exactly helping with my impending panic attack.

"Felix, darling!" the woman cooed. "Where have you been hiding, you naughty man."

As I stood next to him, feeling like a spare part, I tried to move on to two things I could smell. Well, the only thing I could smell was this woman's overpowering, expensive perfume – so no help there either.

"Felix, mate." A suited man approached him from our other side. "How's it going? Heard about the Hyde Park development. Bit ballsy thinking you'll get the planning?" As various glamorous people engulfed Felix, I was pushed further and further out of the increasingly large circle forming around him. Okay, something I could feel – I fiddled with the sleeves of my jumper, realising this one had particularly large holes in it and feeling super awkward.

"How do you like Felix's house?" I startled at the voice right next to me and turned to see Tabitha standing there, holding a glass of champagne, staring down her nose at me.

"Er… is this Felix's?" I asked stupidly, willing my heart rate to slow down and the nausea to recede. At least Tabitha was a familiar face.

But Felix hadn't told me that it was *his* house party. Wow, his house was massive. Wasn't it a bit weird to live somewhere this huge if it was just you? Somehow that wasn't how I viewed Felix. He'd always preferred Mum's cottage to his parents' mega-mansion. I'd just assumed he would want to live somewhere more cozy. This was anything but.

Tabitha's eyebrows went up. "Yes," she said slowly. "I thought you were family friends or something? Bit weird that you don't even know where he lives."

"I think family friends is stretching it a bit," I mumbled, feeling more and more out of place. "Felix just owed my mum a favour." I scuffed my foot on the floor and bit my lip. Truthfully, it was a little hurtful that I hadn't even seen his house so far when I'd been in London for a month.

Tabitha snorted. "Your *mum* got you the job? That must have been one whopping favour he owed her."

I forced a small laugh. "Mum was Felix's nanny."

A waiter came past and offered me a tall glass of champagne. There weren't any pints of cider, so I took it with a muttered thanks, suppressing a grimace – fizzy wine was gross.

"Oh, so she was *staff*. Not exactly a favour she did him then, more a term of her employment."

Wow. Tabitha was a bitch. I tried to give people the benefit of the doubt, but there was simply no getting away from this fact. I looked left and right, trying to see an out as I felt my pulse beating in my ears. Felix was still engulfed in people. Someone bumped into me from behind, and I flew forward a step. Unfortunately, it caused the contents of my glass to fly out over Tabitha's shirt.

"Oh shit," I said in a horrified whisper. "Tabitha, I'm so sorry." I started trying to dry up the champagne with the sleeves of my jumper, but Tabitha shooed me back, her face red with fury.

"You are such an unrelenting idiot," she muttered, holding her soaking shirt away from her skin.

"Ah, Tabitha," Vanessa, who worked in the publicity department of Moretti Harding, came up and kissed Tabitha on the cheek followed by David, a sort of colleague I'd exchanged the odd greeting with over tea in the break room. "How are you, darling? Christ, what's happened here?"

I started to edge away, but Tabitha stopped me in my tracks.

"Lucy happened," Tabitha snapped. "Did you guys know that she's Felix's nanny's daughter? Apparently her tenuous connection to Felix gives her the right to work at one of the top companies in the country and throw champagne over unsuspecting, connectionless employees."

"Tabitha," David's voice held a note of warning. His brows were lowered, and he looked supremely uncomfortable with her tirade. "Hey, Lucy," he nodded awkwardly towards me. "I come in peace, and this shirt is new, so…"

I smiled at him. "Don't worry, I'm unarmed." I said, waving my now empty champagne glass (at least I didn't have to drink the stuff anymore).

"Oh hi, Luce," Vanessa said, giving me a friendly smile. "Thanks again for helping out this week."

I'd taken a panicked phone call from Vanessa a couple of weeks ago about the publicity campaign for a new Moretti Harding housing development just outside London. She'd wanted me to pass a message onto Will, but I realised that with my experience with advertising, I could actually help her myself. So that's how I ended up sorting some of the ad copy for the campaigns they were running.

Tabitha's eyebrows were in her hairline. "Lucy helped you? Seriously?"

"Er… yes, of course. Lucy's really creative."

Tabitha rolled her eyes then gave me a fake smile. "Maybe you might like to put the same effort in at your actual job, Lucy?"

"Oh wow, look at the vultures descending on Felix," Vanessa said in an obvious attempt to change the subject. "I don't think he'll be coming up for air for a while."

They all started talking businessy, financy, property stuff and, as was my way if faced with a situation I couldn't deal with, I zoned out.

"What do you think, Lucy?" Tabitha's voice snapped me back into the room, and I blinked.

"Er… what?"

"What do you think about Dyson?"

"Oh…" Why was she asking me about hoovers? God, how long had I been daydreaming? "Well, Mum's got a handheld one. She uses it for the car mainly. Swears by it."

David's shoulders started shaking, Vanessa was valiantly holding back a smile, but Tabitha didn't bother. She openly laughed at me. "That's interesting info, Lucy," she said through her amusement. I felt my cheeks start to heat. "But I was actually referring to the crash of their stock last week and how it should influence the market."

"Oh, right. Sorry, bit of a dunce when it comes to all this finance stuff really."

"Yes," Tabitha agreed. "Which begs the question: why are you working in a job that you have no interest, no aptitude and no talent for?"

"Tabitha, that's enough," David snapped, the amusement now leaving his expression.

"It's a fair question," Tabitha said. She looked furious. But it wasn't like I could explain that I just wanted to potter up to London, see if I could make some new friends, come out of my shell a bit and gain a bit of confidence so that I wasn't stuck as a recluse in Little Buckingham for the rest of my life, never getting to meet any of my readers.

University hadn't really been an option for me after school. Mum didn't have the money to afford the fees, and I wouldn't have managed working as well as doing a degree. Also, at that stage, I just didn't want to leave home – my friends were all staying in the village, and I'd never been particularly outgoing. I wasn't ready for independence at eighteen.

In fact, it was becoming increasingly obvious that I wasn't ready for it at twenty-seven. Perhaps I should have set my sights much closer to Little Buckingham. Looking back, I don't know why I decided on the nuclear option of London. But Mum had been so keen when I brought it up. And when she'd suggested asking Felix for a job, I'm ashamed to say I jumped at the chance. Maybe, I thought, now that I was older, I might stand a *small* chance with him. Maybe he wouldn't just see me as a quirky kid anymore. Looking around the room at all the glamorous women I felt really stupid. I was living in cloud cuckoo land if I thought Felix would ever look twice at me.

"Yes, well," I said in a small voice, avoiding eye contact with the others. "I can see how that's annoying. Erm... sorry, guys. I'd better be going. I've, um... got a thing. So..."

As I shuffled away from the group, I heard Vanessa call my name, but fortunately it was easy enough to slip unnoticed through the crowd. Now, if I could just find the bloody exit, that would be great. I was starving as well. The only thing that had been offered to me here was tiny little food on trays, but it was all fish eggs and fancy scallops – not a sausage roll or a Wotsit in sight.

I started to scan the crowd, looking for Felix so I could say goodbye, but then slammed into a large body and nearly fell backwards.

"Look who's come out to play," Will said. I took a quick step back from him, but my retreat was hampered by the crowds around us. "Still rocking hobo chic, I see, Mayweather?" As he leaned in then to speak into my ear his hand came up to grab my arm, and his voice became a harsh whisper. "Where are those tight little skirts from earlier, huh? Back to hiding the goods away, are we?"

I yanked my arm down, dislodging his grip. His face darkened at my rejection, settling into a familiar scowl.

I felt a shiver of fear go up my spine.

"Got to admit it's a bit galling that an incompetent, scruffy little upstart managed to get me in the shit. Couldn't just serve the tea without making a bloody scene, could you? Had to make me look bad." He grabbed my arm again, squeezing tightly through my jumper. "What's your hold over Felix anyway?"

I was backing away from him now and trying to shake my arm free, but his grip was too tight.

"What are you doing?" At the sound of Victoria's commanding tone, Will dropped my arm and retreated as if I was radioactive. We turned to see her and Lottie right next to us.

Victoria was wearing a beautiful jumper dress with a slight gold shimmer and high-heeled boots, and Lottie was in one of the formal business dresses that she seemed to cycle regularly (her wardrobe didn't seem to be nearly as extensive as everyone else in the office). Both of them were scowling at Will.

"Don't know what you mean," he said, shoving his hands in his pockets and clearing his throat. "Luce and I were having a chat."

"We saw you grab her, twice," Victoria said, her voice still didn't betray any emotion. It was like she was describing the weather, not reporting on a man grabbing a woman without her consent.

"Don't be ridiculous," Will scoffed. "Luce and I were just bantering."

"Take your banter," Lottie said, her voice tight with anger. "And sod off. Right?"

Will gave Lottie a filthy look, muttered "jumped-up sidekick", then stalked off, pushing his way roughly through the crowd.

"You okay?" Lottie asked. I turned from watching Will's retreat to Lottie's concerned face and gave her a shaky smile.

"It's fine. Will's just a bit pissed off. He thinks I showed him up at the meeting."

"Lottie put it in my diary for tomorrow. I need to go to the board to have Will fired."

"No!" I said, feeling a bit panicky. "Honestly, it's fine. I don't want to get Will fired." The last thing I needed was for this all to be escalated, causing more problems for Felix. "He's a bit of a dick, but to be fair, I am a *really* crap assistant."

"It is not acceptable to grab someone like that," Victoria informed me. "If that happened to me…" she shuddered, which was the first bit of human reaction I'd ever seen from her. "Well, it wouldn't be good. I don't respond well to unwelcome physical contact."

"Honestly, it's fine," I said. "Please don't say anything. He's not worth the trouble."

Victoria cocked her head to the side, considering me. "This is your decision to make, isn't it?" She turned to Lottie. "This is one of those times when it's *not my choice*."

"Yes, hun," Lottie said. "It is one of those times, I'm afraid."

Victoria looked frustrated but resigned. "That is highly annoying."

I smiled at her. "I'm sorry."

She nodded. "I find it difficult to accept people making illogical choices."

"Vicky can have a bit of a tricky time accepting other people's autonomy," Lottie put in with a smile. "But I have to say on this one, I agree with her. So if he ever does anything like that again, you come to us, okay?'

"Okay."

"So, you enjoying the party?" Lottie asked.

I shrugged. "Not really a party person," I explained. "At least not parties like this."

"I couldn't agree more," Victoria put in. "Sheer torture. Lottie, how much longer do we have to stay."

Lottie laughed. "Come on. You've spoken to all the peeps on your list. We can go now. Lucy, need a lift?"

"No, you guys go on. I came with Felix, so I'd better let him know before I leave," I said, scanning the packed room for him.

Lottie and Victoria said goodbye, Lottie with a brief hug and Victoria a small head jerk, and I started pushing through the people towards where I thought I'd last seen Felix. Trouble was, I couldn't find him no matter which way I turned. Being shorter than most other people was not ideal when trying to pick someone out of the crowd, and the lack of heels really exacerbated the problem.

Eventually, I found myself on the other side of the room at the entrance to a small corridor. I heard Will's obnoxious laugh from somewhere nearby, and on instinct scurried away down the deserted corridor, pushing open the first door I came to.

When I shut the heavy wood firmly behind me, all thoughts of the party, the people, Felix, Will, Victoria and Lottie left my brain as I took in the huge room. It was in the same minimalist style as the rest of the house, which I wasn't a huge fan of – minimalism always freaked me out slightly. I mean, where's all your stuff? I was way more of a cosy knick-knack type of girl. But this room had an advantage over the rest. A beautiful desk stood in the centre, with Felix's laptop resting on top of a large proper ink blotting pad. And the stationery. Oh my God, the stationery: beautiful fountain pens, pencils of all grades, different coloured gel pens, all organised in a leather container.

I took a deep breath in. Felix's expensive cologne lingered in the air. This room was clearly well-used.

After I swiped a blanket from the window seat, I sat in his large leather office chair and held back a moan at how comfortable it was. Leaning back, I let the silence and the smell of Felix wash over me, and my mind started to drift. The thread of a story sparked in my imagination, and my eyes flew open. I knew from bitter experience that if I didn't sketch the outline then and there, it could easily dissipate in my brain like smoke.

I moved Felix's laptop out of the way and selected a beautiful pen which was the perfect weight in my hand and was definitely coming home with me. Then I looked down at the first sheet of the blotting-pad, and I started to write. My outlines were like spider diagrams. They looked a bit crazy to the outside eye, but it was the only way I could organise my thoughts. I'd soon filled the first page and moved on to the one underneath. I was on a roll.

CHAPTER 10

"You ate my toast"

Felix

"What the bloody hell are you doing?" I barked, and Lucy jumped in her seat. She was wrapped in a huge blanket which was bunched up around her ears. Only her hand was visible from the folds, holding a pen poised over a large piece of paper on my desk. Around the desk were loads of other sheets, full of complicated diagrams and small, tightly packed writing. Lucy dropped the pen and spent a good while and some considerable effort fighting her way free of the blanket.

"Oh, hi," she said breathlessly as she scrambled to gather all the sheets together. I walked over to the desk and reached down to one of them that had slipped onto the floor, but before I could read it she'd snatched it out of my hand.

"What's all this?"

She bit her lip. "Oh, just something I'm working on." She rolled all the bits of paper together and then clutched them tightly to her chest. Clearly, she did not want me reading them. Working? What possible work could she be doing on blotting paper in my office?

"Lucy, why are you hiding in my office?"

"Oh, er... I just popped in here for a bit. I was about to come and find you to say bye. Got a bit... distracted."

I crossed my arms over my chest and raised my eyebrows. "It's two in the morning. I last saw you at *eight*. What have you been doing for the last *six hours*?"

Her eyes went wide. "Ooh. Wow, that's a record, even for me."

"What do you mean?"

She made an eek face, and I tried not to let myself consider how unbearably cute that was. I was annoyed with Lucy. I'd been looking for her all evening. I'd tried ringing her phone, which I now saw was lying on the armchair across the room.

When I found her coat, scarf and hat still in the hallway, I knew she wouldn't have gone out in the cold without them. The last of the guests left an hour ago, and I'd torn the house apart trying to find her. Now she was telling me that she got distracted? Who does that?

"Well, I tend to zone out a bit sometimes. I can lose time."

"I told your mum that I'd take you to a party to meet some people," I said with what I thought was a fair amount of patience. "You have to actually make an effort, Luce. I can't do *all* the heavy lifting for you."

Lucy started fiddling with the sleeves of her jumper. It was a nervous habit that I recognised from childhood, and was the reason that so many of her jumpers had frayed cuffs. "Your mates are all a bit intimidating, Felix. I'm not so good with parties like this. You said it was a house party. I assumed you meant sharing a takeaway with a few peeps."

"Lucy, this is a party where you make connections. Where you network, it's an opportunity."

"Oh, right," she said. "Networking." She made networking sound akin to being tortured on a rack. "Yeah, I'm not sure that that's my thing to be honest."

"God, you're impossible."

"Listen," Lucy snapped, angry colour flooding her cheeks now. "I never said I wanted to *network*. You try turning up somewhere looking like a right numpty compared to everyone else, absolutely starving, only to be offered tiny, weird food and fizzy wine, which I *hate*; then be cut adrift and expected to just cope. I'm starving and pissed off. Your parties suck. *You* suck, Felix Moretti."

I blinked. Tiny, weird food? The canapés were from one of the best Michelin-starred restaurants in London. And fizzy wine? That champagne was three hundred pounds a bottle. Her stomach chose that opportunity to grumble, highlighting how inadequate my tiny, weird food had been, and I clenched my jaw in annoyance.

"Fine," I snapped. "Come with me."

*

The sight of Lucy plastered up against my Aga with a slice of Marmite toast in her hand gave me a sweeping sense of déjà vu. How many times had I seen her in the exact same pose, holding the exact same snack back in Hetty's kitchen in Little Buckingham?

After the stomach grumble and the tiny food remark, I'd marched Lucy through the house to the kitchen, given her a bottle of cider I had in the fridge and made her Marmite toast – her favourite. Maybe this party was an unmitigated disaster, but I was not going to be accused of starving her to death.

"I knew you'd like Marmite eventually," she said through another bite.

I rolled my eyes. "You lot wore me down."

Eating Marmite was almost a religion in the Mayweather family, and I had been berated daily about my failure to accept it as the superior spread.

Truth was, I never got into Marmite until after I left the village behind me. At uni I'd seen it on the shelf of the supermarket one day, and my chest had tightened with acute homesickness for that cosy kitchen. I'd shoved the jar in my basket on autopilot and then eaten toast with it on back in my student digs, fully expecting to hate it. But Marmite was one of the few things in my life that I'd really been wrong about. If you get the Marmite-to-bread ratio correct, there's no better nirvana of taste combination.

Any pro-Marmite Brit will tell you that they themselves have to do the spreading or risk an imperfect balance: too thick and you're in a salty nightmare; too thin and there's not enough to satisfy.

I took Marmite *very* seriously now.

"Hey, what's happened to your fingers?" I was just noticing that Lucy was eating the toast with her left hand while her right hand was pressed up against the Aga. Two of her fingers were completely white from the knuckles down.

"Oh," she said, waving the offending hand in the air for a moment before pressing it back against the Aga. "Yeah, my hands like the cold even less than me. Raynaud's. I've always been cold intolerant, but I developed Raynaud's a few years ago. Your home office is a bit brass monkeys, and I had to have my right hand out to write. It just takes a bit of time to rewarm, then the colour will come back."

"Jesus," I muttered, covering the distance between us in a couple of strides whilst I focused on her poor delicate hand. I'd had a good amount of champagne that evening, not to mention a couple of shots with a client that I didn't feel I could turn down, and I was just that little bit buzzed, just slightly disinhibited. So I didn't think as I reached for her freezing hand and held it between my own, engulfing it in my warmth.

Lucy's eyes widened as she took in a shocked breath.

"You weren't kidding when you said you feel the cold."

The toast she was holding tipped to the side as her grip on it loosened.

I grabbed it from her before it could drop to the floor, took a bite and then put it down on the Aga. Colour rose in her cheeks. This close, I could see every freckle across the bridge of her nose, could see the flecks of green in her blue eyes as her pupils dilated.

"You ate my toast," she whispered, and my gaze dropped to her mouth. She bit her lip again, those perfect white teeth digging into her naturally pink bottom lip. That small freckle next to the corner of her mouth became more prominent.

"You weren't eating it," I muttered, moving in so close now that I could smell her delicate floral shampoo. A lock of her dark hair had fallen out of her ponytail. I reached up and tucked it behind her ear, grazing the side of her cheek with my fingers. She blinked and inhaled a short, sharp breath. When I looked back up at her eyes, I realised our faces were only a few inches apart. She was so beautiful. I felt my gut tighten with need so acute that I could feel my control slipping. The tequila was still pumping through my system. All I could focus on was how much I wanted her.

"Felix, I—"

Her uncertain voice was like a splash of cold water. God, what was the matter with me? This was Lucy – Hetty's daughter, Mike's sister. Hetty and Mike trusted me.

I forced myself to take a step back, dropping Lucy's hand. She blinked up at me in confusion, the flush of desire still staining her cheeks, her pupils still huge. She looked so young standing there in my kitchen in the exact same pose as when we were kids. Mike would kick my arse if he knew what I almost just did to his sister. Taking advantage of an employee was lower than low, and it was not my style. Taking advantage of a Mayweather was completely unacceptable.

But there was a small voice in the back of my head asking me why. Why couldn't I have Lucy? I was rich enough, and I'd worked hard enough to have what I wanted, surely?

However, the most prevalent voice (the one that sounded suspiciously like my father's) questioned whether I deserved Lucy. What could I really offer her? It certainly wasn't a meaningful relationship – not with my track record and inability to trust anyone. And did I want to risk my relationship with my best friend and my surrogate mum?

"Right," I said briskly, crossing my arms over my chest and pulling away from Lucy altogether. "Better get you home. I'll call my car for you."

I watched as Lucy's shoulders slumped just a little. Better a small disappointment now than the heartbreaking kind later.

At least, that's what I told myself.

CHAPTER 11

Go away, Felix

Lucy

"What is this shit, Mayweather?" Will snapped, and I wished I had the backbone required to slap him. The man had a very slappable face.

"Er... it's coffee."

"It tastes like a baboon's arse. What have you put in there?"

"You asked for soy milk," I said through my now-chattering teeth. Will was really putting the effort in now to torment me. His current favourite was to send me on the most ridiculous errands. He almost seemed to get off on it. Hence this Costa run in the pouring rain for his over-complicated drink order. I was soaked to the skin and totally dishevelled as it was half a mile away and the traffic was gridlocked, so I'd had to jog there. And now he was in his office with two other executives he seemed hell-bent on humiliating me in front of.

He laughed. "Do I look like a fucking woke, hippy, soy-drinking dickhead to you?"

I hesitated, wanting to say exactly what I thought he looked like but not having the ladyballs. My hesitation was enough to infuriate him though. His eyes narrowed as he stared at me.

"Go back and *get it right*." Each word was said slowly and

67

carefully as if he was addressing someone who was intellectually challenged.

"But it's quite a—"

"Gentlemen," Will cut me off, looking at the other two suits in his office who were shifting uncomfortably in their seats (one of them was David, who I had previously thought wasn't a total wanker) clearly not at peace with how much of a knob Will was being, but also not ballsy enough to stick up for me. "Your orders?"

They both demurred, but Will pressed it so much that eventually they gave in, and as I was a big wussbag and terrified of Will, I resigned myself to going back to the cursed Costa through the now torrential rain.

On my way back, the coffees were shaking so violently as I shivered that it took all my effort and concentration to keep them upright. So I didn't notice the sleek, low-slung sports car pull up beside me. Not until the beeping of horns from the cars behind it was blocking started.

"Lucy!" Felix shouted, and I almost flipped the tray of coffee. His window was down now, and he was scowling at me from the driver's seat. "What the fuck are you doing?"

"What does it look like?" I called back. "This is my job. I'm *assisting*. You said you wanted me to do it better. This is me doing better."

"I didn't say go out in a howling gale and get hypothermia."

"Go away, Felix," I said and turned to carry on walking. I was cold, pissed off and I'd had it with this man. I really thought he was going to kiss me last week at his house. My disappointment was so acute that I was having a hard time being rational.

To know that this fierce, almost painful attraction was still one-sided after having had that small glimmer of hope was unbearable. And I was sure that for a moment, just for a second, he'd felt it too. But then I'd been bundled into my coat and shoved into one of his cars that he seemed to have on twenty-four-hour call like I was radioactive. I was crushed. And I was not up to dealing with him yet.

At the office, I'd managed to avoid him, especially as I was spending more time with Vanessa to help with the ad campaigns in lieu of Will actually doing his job. But after the first day, I realised he was avoiding me as well, which was even more galling. Probably worried that silly little Lucy would get the wrong idea.

"Get in the car."

"Bugger off." The beeping had escalated now. Felix was causing a massive backlog of traffic – which in London was quite possibly a hanging offence.

"You can't tell me to bugger off." He sounded so ridiculously affronted that I almost laughed, although I doubted that would have been possible given how hard my teeth were chattering.

"Felix Moretti, I've known you since you had your first snog with Melanie Green behind the outdoor bogs at The Badger's Sett. I can tell you to bugger off if I want to." That had broken my little eight-year-old heart back then, and I was still letting him do it to me now.

"Right, fine," he bit out, bringing his car to a complete stop and putting the hazards on. People in the cars behind him were swearing now and gesturing out of their windows.

I stopped in my tracks and my mouth dropped open as he rounded his car, totally ignoring the chaos he was causing, and closed the distance between us in just a few long strides. Before I could react, he grabbed the tray of coffees out of my hand, chucked them in the bin next to us, turned back to me, put a shoulder to my stomach and lifted me over it.

"What the hell are you doing?" I screeched.

The honking behind us had fallen silent. They were probably just as shocked as me. I heard the car door open, and I was lowered, then dumped into the deep bucket seat. Felix, still in the torrential rain, which had already soaked his hair, leaned down to unzip my soaking puffa, pulled it off me somehow, then took off his own coat and threw it over me. Still not finished, he pulled the seatbelt across me and his coat and plugged it in like I was a child. When he moved back to slam the door shut, his shirt was soaked and clung to his muscular torso like a second skin.

He flipped off the cars behind us and rounded his bonnet to fling himself into the driver seat. Continuing to ignore the horns, he yanked up the thermostat on his car and I was blasted by warm air. Finally, cool as a cucumber, he casually drove away.

There was water dripping from his hair down the line of his jaw and into his stubble. I tried to drag my eyes away from his arms and chest, revealed by the wet shirt in all their glorious detail, but it was a losing battle. He was almost too perfect to be real.

"When do you get the time to work out?"

Yes. Yes, that is what came out of my mouth. If my blatant staring wasn't enough, I actually asked the man how he cultivated his perfect muscles. Felix's eyebrows shot up, and his severe frown was replaced by a small smirk. I felt my face flood with heat, but even with my embarrassment, I was thrilled to see the dimple on his right cheek finally make an appearance.

"Er... any chance we could forget I just said that?" My voice was muffled as I'd buried my face in my hands in mortification.

"I have a home gym," Felix told me. "And I get up at five every day."

"Every day?" I squeaked out, managing to lower my hands to look at him. "Even on weekends?"

"Even on weekends."

"Bloody hell, you must be exhausted."

"It's called discipline, Lucy."

I scowled out of the window. There was that superior tone again. I was so tired of being talked down to. There were different types of discipline. Okay, so mine was of the more haphazard variety, but that didn't mean I never achieved

70

anything. And, to add insult to injury, I just could not stop shaking. Felix glanced at me as we pulled up to another traffic light and frowned again.

"Why were you walking to get coffee in a heavy downpour?"

"I told you," I said through chattering teeth. "I was being a good assistant. Mr Brent wanted coffee for his meeting."

"He can get it at the office."

"He didn't want shitty instant coffee."

"But—"

"Felix, you've got a fancy coffee machine in *your* fancy office. The rest of us have to survive on instant."

Yet another example of the ridiculous hierarchical system at work. The partners hogged all the coffee, most of the space and even all the natural daylight. It was the least open environment I'd ever set foot in. The sad state of the withering mini tree I'd brought in during my first week, back when I didn't realise the office was where dreams and plants came to die, was a good representation of the general vibe there.

When we made it back to the office car park, I shoved Felix's coat at him and jumped out of the car at double speed, booking it to the lift and hoping that he wouldn't be able to keep up. This hope was in vain, seeing as his legs were much longer than mine, and *he* didn't have to wear ridiculous death-trap shoes.

When we were standing in the lift, I started shivering again, and he put his coat over my shoulders. The combination of his hand brushing my neck as he did that and the clean, masculine scent coming off his suit jacket was enough to make my cheeks feel like they were on fire despite how freezing I was. When I glanced at Felix, his jaw was clenched tightly as he stared ahead, his fists bunched by his side. He looked almost angry. Well, I didn't ask him to stop and force me into his bloody car. What a high-handed prick.

As soon as the lift doors opened he strode away without a word, and I followed, feeling like a total weirdo. The office fell silent as we emerged into the common space. We were both still soaked and dripping water onto the carpet. I thought Felix would duck into his office, happy to be away from me, but then he took off in the opposite direction. By the time I realised where he was heading, it was too late.

"What the fuck do you think you're playing at, Brent?" Felix had thrown open the door to Will's office and was glowering at Will and the two other executives from the doorway.

Will cleared his throat. "Er... problem, Felix?"

"Yes there's a fucking problem, you twat," Felix snapped.

Oh dear, I knew very well how things would go for me if Felix had a go at Will. The be-a-total-shit-to-Lucy campaign would ramp up significantly. I rushed forward to try to stop him but unfortunately tripped over those stupid heels when I was a foot away. I would have face-planted into Will's office had Felix's strong arm not shot out to catch me around my waist and haul me back up to my feet. My hands had automatically gone to his arm to steady myself, and I could feel the hard muscles under my fingers through the still-damp shirt.

His jaw clenched again, and he looked almost in pain before he abruptly let go of me once I was stable, stepping back like I had a contagious disease.

I heard Will mutter, "Fucking liability," under his breath.

If someone could die of embarrassment, I would have expired on the spot. There were some chuckles from the other two men in the room before Felix shot them a furious look that I was surprised didn't incinerate them in their seats. David at least had the decency to look ashamed of himself.

"Don't send Lucy out to get coffees in a fucking rainstorm."

"Look, I'm sorry, Felix," Will said, his voice full of frustration. "I didn't realise it was raining." Felix's eyebrows went up. Rain was currently beating against Will's windows. Will huffed. "And exactly what else do you expect I ask her to do? She doesn't even answer the phone properly half the time."

"Felix, please," I begged, tugging on his sleeve to get his attention. "Just let it go."

He glanced at me. His eyes flashed as he tracked a raindrop splash from my eyelashes onto my cheek, and he huffed out a sigh.

"No more errands in the bloody rain," he said, turning back to Will and pointing at him. "And you two better watch yourselves as well." Geoffrey's small smirk dropped, and he sank back in his chair. David shot me an apologetic look. Felix spun on his heel, ushered me out in front of him and slammed the door to Will's office behind us. Then he turned to me.

"Don't let him push you around."

I frowned at him. "Don't fight my battles for me." I crossed my arms over my chest and glared up at him. "You'll only make it worse. Anyway, you yourself told me that I should be a better assistant. That does actually mean doing what the man says, you realise?"

His hand went to the back of his neck, and his head dropped back to look up at the ceiling. There was so much pec, biceps and forearm muscle action under the wet shirt involved in that manoeuvre that I felt my mouth go completely dry.

"You come to me if he gives you any more grief. Right?" He was looking at me again now as he crossed his arms over his chest. My eyes slid to the side. I was not going to go to Felix if I had another problem with Will. Why he thought I would was a total mystery. Nobody complained in this soulless place, and he was the very last person I'd run to if there was a problem. He already thought I was totally useless and spineless.

"Sure," I muttered, and, to my shock, his hand came up, and his fingers gently grasped my jaw to lift my face towards his. He was close now. I could smell a heady combination of rainwater and Felix, and I could make out the golden flecks in his dark brown eyes. My breath caught in my throat, and then I stopped breathing altogether.

"You come to me, understand?" His voice was low and commanding. I told myself that I hated him bossing me around like a child, but there was something about that voice that went right through me, causing my stomach to hollow out with such fierce need that I couldn't help swaying towards him just slightly. At my movement, a muscle ticked in his jaw and his pupils dilated. When I licked my lips, his gaze moved to my mouth. Two flags of colour appeared high on his cheeks.

"Felix," I whispered. He blinked once, and the spell was broken. His hand fell away before he stepped back. I noticed his hands clenching into fists again at his sides again before he lifted one to point at me.

"Don't go out in the rain again," he said, his voice now hoarse. All I could do was nod as he turned to leave like the hounds of hell were chasing him. Once he was out of sight, I slumped against the wall, trying to control my breathing. The buzzer on the intercom from Will's office made me jump.

"Lucy, if it's not too much trouble, could you actually *make* us some fucking coffee? Or am I going to get shat on by the boss for asking you to do even that?"

I rolled my eyes and pushed away from the wall. Yeah, there was no way in hell I was tattling to Felix about any of this. It only made things worse.

CHAPTER 12

Pathetic heroine in a romance novel

Lucy

"Emily, I can't speak for long," I said into the phone with difficulty as my teeth were still chattering.

"You sound freezing," Emily snapped. "Does that shit, Felix, know about your cold intolerance? If the tight git has got his office at Baltic temperatures, I'm telling your brother. It sounds like a hellhole there anyway."

I rolled my eyes at her drama. I had not described Felix's company as a "hellhole". I might have mentioned the lack of natural light and comfy furniture, along with the fact that everyone seemed to be a corporate robot apart from me. Emily didn't understand why I didn't tell them where to stuff their job.

"It's not worth it just to ogle your childhood crush all day long, Luce," she said, and I hastily put down the mug I was holding to take her off speaker.

"Ems," I hissed. "I am actually in the office *now*, you know. Can we not talk about my pathetic crush on the completely unobtainable, out-of-my-league human ever, ever again? I'm not working here because of that."

"Right," Emily drew out the word, and I gritted my still-chattering teeth.

"I wish that twelve-year-old me had known better than to tell twelve-year-old you my deepest, darkest secrets."

Emily snorted. "Twenty-seven-year-old you *still* tells me everything, so there was never much chance of that."

"I don't tell you everything," I snapped, immediately wishing I could take back the lie.

"You dirty bitch," Emily cried, sounding way too excited and way, way too loud. I glanced around the empty kitchen space nervously. "Are you getting yourself some and not telling me?"

I sighed and then heard a commotion on the other end of the line. It sounded like furniture falling followed by some kids shouting.

"Marcus put the baby down!" Emily screamed so loud I had to take the phone away from my ear or risk permanent hearing damage. "Oh bloody hell, Luce. I'll have to call you back. But I'm so fucking excited that I could – no, I did not say the f-word Marcus, I'm talking to your Auntie Lucy about ducks... yeah, there's *loads* of ducks in London. Oh shit! Don't you dare—"

The line went dead, and I breathed a sigh of relief. Saved by Emily's feral child. I shivered again, and a wave of homesickness swept over me. Emily's kids were a lot, but I loved them to pieces. I could just imagine the chaos at Emily's house right now. If I was at home, I'd go over there to help out, then if we were lucky Emily's mum would babysit and we'd all go to the pub as it was Friday night. Maybe play some darts. Definitely drink some warmish cider – The Badger's Sett had never quite figured out how to chill drinks appropriately.

"Miss Mayweather?" I startled, dropping the mug again at Frank's voice. Frank was Felix's driver, a nice chap in his sixties who'd driven me a couple of times before.

"Oh, hi, Frank," I said, clearing my throat as I flicked on the kettle to start to make shitty coffee for Will and his minions.

"Mr Moretti wants you to go home now, miss," Frank said. "He said you need to get changed and warm up."

I gritted my teeth to stop them chattering and gave Frank a smile. "That's okay, Frank. I'm fine."

Frank sighed. "He was quite specific, love," he said. "I'm to take you straight home."

I was still shivering, so making coffee was proving trickier than normal, and I was no expert at the best of times – yet another thing I regularly fucked up as the worst assistant ever.

"Well, I've just got to—"

"*I've* been sent to do that," Tabitha snapped, grabbing the kettle away from me. "Apparently you're too fragile after being out in the rain. Kind of like a really pathetic heroine in a romance novel." Tabitha looked me up and down, and her lip curled. "I'll be assisting Mr Brent for the rest of the day. You can go and swoon elsewhere."

Great, yet another black mark against me with Tabitha. Clearly, Felix had once again pulled her out of something important to have to come and sort me out. My eyes started stinging. I really wasn't that great at the whole people being mean to me thing. It had never been my jam, even as a child. But back in Little Buckingham, I'd been allowed to live in my dream world. If anyone even looked at me wrong, Mike or Emily would be on them like a ton of bricks. If this was the real world, then the real world sucked. Big time.

"Tabby," Frank said in a warning tone, and I was surprised that he was so familiar with her. She rolled her eyes.

"Whatever," she snapped. "Just bugger off, yeah?"

"Right, okay," I managed to croak out, on the verge of tears but managing to swallow them down just about. I let Frank lead me out of the office and down to Felix's town car, which was absolutely boiling inside with the heating blasting.

"Jesus, Frank," I said as I slipped into the passenger seat, loving the warm air around me. "Do you always leave your heating running?"

Frank turned to me and raised his eyebrows. "Mr Moretti was very specific about what temperature the car should be at in order for me to drive you home," he explained. "Above twenty-five degrees, closer to thirty if possible."

I blinked and looked out of the window as Frank negotiated his way out of the car park. Molly-coddled was the word that came to mind. Well, I didn't want Felix to molly-coddle me. I wanted him to do X-rated, dirty things to me – not view me as a careless child that he had to look after. "Bloody bossy," I muttered under my breath.

"He cares about you," Frank returned, and I snorted. Felix cared about what my mother thought, not me. "You don't believe me? I've never driven any other employee home ever before. I've certainly never been instructed about the car environment before. Even with his—" Frank broke off and shifted uncomfortably in his seat.

"With his what?"

Frank cleared his throat. "Nothing," he said in a strangled voice.

"With his what, Frank? Tell me, or I'm getting out at the next set of traffic lights."

"With his *lady friends*," he muttered, looking acutely embarrassed. "Even when I've driven them home, he's never given me a ten-minute lecture on how to do it."

The mention of Felix's lady friends made my chest feel tight. Of course, I'd seen him in magazines. I knew he'd dated all sorts of women, some of them famous in their own right, all of them glamorous in the extreme. I sank down into my chair, feeling very small and more than a little stupid.

As if Felix would be interested in me. The reactions I thought I'd seen were probably just acute embarrassment that the kid with a crush on him was now haunting his working life as an adult.

CHAPTER 13

"Why wouldn't I buy my own clothes?"

Lucy

"What the—?" I jumped in my seat as everything went dark, then blinked when my head popped out of a jumper. Felix was towering over me with a grumpy expression as he pulled one arm then another through the sleeves of the massive jumper he'd just dumped over my head. I must have zoned out again as I hadn't heard his approach. The jumper smelt of him – clean, masculine with a hint of his expensive aftershave, and the warmth from it enveloped me immediately.

I was in my new uniform, as I thought of it: thin tights, silk shirt, small, tailored jacket and matching skirt. And I was bloody freezing. I'd contemplated sitting in my puffa again but, however fashion backwards I might be, I did have insight into how weird that would make me look. Plus Will had called me a "deranged hobo" when I wore it yesterday, so I'd thought better of it.

Felix's jumper wouldn't be much better, to be honest. As I stood, the damn thing reached nearly to my knees, and I had to bunch the sleeves up to a ridiculous degree to even find my hands.

"Why are you going around shoving jumpers on unsuspecting women?"

"You were shivering," Felix said in an accusatory tone, as if my shivering in his office was a personal insult to him. "You do know it's twenty-three degrees in here now? I asked them to yank up the thermostat. Pete from accounting is about to pass out with heatstroke. I've had to come up with another solution. It's not raining today, so even if Will did send you out, which he better not have done, I can't understand how you've got this cold."

I bit my lip. "Oh dear. Don't boil everyone alive, Felix. Honestly, I'd be fine if I was in my old stuff. It's just these fancy outfits are so flimsy."

Felix huffed and crossed his arms over his chest. "Why didn't you say anything when I asked you to change your clothes? Your mum would kill me if I let you freeze to death in my office."

I narrowed my eyes at Felix and put my hands on my hips (unfortunately, the effect was slightly ruined by the bloody sleeves falling down over my hands again and dangling almost to my knees). "Felix, I'm twenty-seven years old, not a child that you're looking after for my mother."

Felix totally ignored me as he looked over his shoulder at Tabitha who was at her desk a few feet away.

"Tabitha, the stuff you got for Lucy. It's not warm enough. She needs to get some—"

"Woah, woah, woah!" I said, jumping forward to block Felix's view of an increasingly angry Tabitha. I stepped closer to him and tried to lower my voice so that Tabitha wouldn't hear me. "I can sort the clothing sitch, Felix. You're making me look like a right numpty."

His eyebrows went up, and he gave me a doubtful look. "Lucy, no offence, but I'm not sure that—"

"I'll sort it," another voice clipped from the doorway.

I peered around Felix to see Victoria behind him with Lottie in her wake. Felix turned to them and put his hands on his hips.

"Vicky, I—"

"I heard you two from my office," Victoria said. "And I already know about Lucy's inability to regulate her temperature. I've done some research."

Felix's hand went up to the back of his neck. "Vicky, we've got one of our most important investors coming in the afternoon. You don't have time to go out and—"

"Go out?" Victoria asked, her perfect nose wrinkling in disgust. "To shop in *public*? Are you insane? We can order it all. Can't we, Lottie?"

Lottie was smiling at me as she walked forward to draw up next to Victoria. "Sure we can. And if anyone has to go out in public, *heaven forbid*, I think *I* can handle it. Come on, Luce." Lottie dropped Victoria's arm, moved to me and started pushing me in the direction of Vicky's office. I glanced back at Felix. He still had his hands on his hips, but his head was tilted to the side as if struggling to work out the dynamic between Victoria and me. Granted, we didn't exactly have a lot in common. I was as confused as him.

I almost gasped when we made it into Victoria's office.

"Crikey, I thought Felix had a big one."

"That's what she said," Lottie said without missing a beat, surprising a startled laugh from me.

Victoria frowned for a moment before her expression cleared. "Oh yes, I remember. You taught me this one last week: if someone comments on the size of something, or says that it won't fit – anything of that nature – then you can follow up with the 'that's what she said' line. And it's funny because people think you're referring to a man's pe—"

"Okay!" Lottie cut her off. "Thanks, hun. But I think Lucy gets it."

"Hmm," Victoria hummed. "So what were you referring to, Lucy, if not Felix's penis?"

Lottie snorted a laugh.

"His office," I replied quickly, feeling my cheeks heat. "His big *office*. Yours smashes his though."

"I like space," Victoria said, then shook her head. "No, it's more than that. I *have* to have space. And light. I can't breathe without them."

"Well, you're alright here then." Her office had so much square footage that you could have hosted the entire clientele of The Badger's Sett and still have had room for more. Two of the walls were completely glass from floor to ceiling. The desk in the centre was huge and L-shaped with two computer stations on either side.

"Right," Victoria said briskly, pulling out her office chair and sitting down at her computer. "Lottie, bring up the tabs I saved. This shouldn't take long."

*

Wow. Vicky, as I was now to call her, was a genius. A very weird, asocial genius, but a genius nonetheless. I was warm, and I didn't look like a crazy Polar explorer. In fact, I even looked… nice. I was wearing a roll-neck, fitted, thick cashmere dress, fleece-lined tights, and fur-lined boots with only a small heel. Underneath the dress I had on very thin, fine merino wool, lace-trimmed, crazy-comfortable thermals. I didn't own much smart clothing, but I was definitely a convert. It was like magic. I'd given Vicky an unwelcome hug after changing into the new clothes, such was my excitement. It didn't go down well. But as I blinked at myself in the full-length mirror, I was glad I'd done it.

And Vicky wasn't content to stop there. She told Lottie to sort *the works* for me. It soon became clear that this involved hair and make-up at an upmarket salon. My hair was down and in soft waves around my face. My make-up was perfect. Having pretty much given up on make-up a while ago, this was a huge shock. I didn't think it was something I'd be able to reproduce. I felt like someone else. Someone glamorous. Someone who *belonged* in London.

Vicky and Lottie had been to their Very Important Meetings during my transformation. They'd sent me off to the salon after telling Will that I'd be unavailable for the rest of the day. This information had been met with unveiled hostility from Will. Why he was cross that I wouldn't be on hand was anyone's guess. I'd already done his work for him with the publicity department, something that he was now getting all the credit for. And for the PA stuff Tabitha was far more capable. Having me around was only ever a hindrance. I suspected that he just didn't like not having me there to torment. He had probably cooked up some further humiliation for me today and was not pleased to have his plans thwarted. But Vicky was his superior. There was no arguing with her really.

"Yowsers!" Lottie shouted when she found me back at my desk later that day. "Transformation complete, I'd say. Right, you can't let this go to waste. Come out with us."

"You're not going to a party with tiny food, are you?" I asked. "It's just that didn't really turn out to be my thing."

Lottie laughed. "No tiny food in sight, I promise. Just an office outing to the pub. Doesn't happen too often and Vics doesn't normally go but she's agreed tonight."

"For practice," put in Vicky and I tilted my head to the side in confusion as I looked at her.

"Practice?"

"Practice for interacting appropriately with other human beings."

"And for fun, right, hun?" Lottie said, giving Vicky a gentle look.

Vicky blinked. "There is nothing fun about this scenario."

"Wow," I said, smiling at Vicky. "We're as bad as each other."

"I seriously doubt that," Vicky said with conviction.

Lottie cleared her throat, bringing my attention back to her. "Hey, listen, you didn't take the company credit card earlier. Felix's made it clear that you weren't to spend *your* money on the clothes and stuff."

I frowned at her. "Why wouldn't I buy my own clothes?"

Lottie glanced down at what I was wearing, then tilted her head to the side. "Well, I guess because it's kind of a requirement of the company to wear this stuff and, well, no offence, but I know what it costs. That's crazy money."

I shrugged. "Felix's done enough for me. I'm not sponging off the company for clothes."

I didn't explain that the last person who needed financial funding was me. There was no way I would take that money.

What Lottie, Vicky and Felix didn't know was that I had decided that I wouldn't be working for Moretti Harding for much longer. The guilt at being paid to consistently fuck up was too much for me.

Okay, so I had offset some of those fuck ups with the work I'd been doing with the publicity team, I knew that, but it didn't justify staying. I was going to finish the month here and then stop this charade altogether. It was just a case of plucking up the courage to go to HR.

Seeing as when I previously tried to quit Felix's head almost exploded, I was keeping it to myself for the moment. What I needed to do was to stop pining after Felix and start doing what I came to London to do – get out of my shell, meet people, maybe even find a man who was interested in me for God's sake. Otherwise, what was the bloody point of leaving Little Buckingham at all?

CHAPTER 14

"Where are your freckles?"

Felix

"Woah? Is that… is that *Lucy*?"

I spun around to follow the direction of David's gaze, and there she was.

"Looks like Piers is trying his arm," David grumbled. "Sneaky bastard always gets in there before the rest of us. He's got some sort of totty radar or something."

Piers was indeed boxing Lucy in at the bar, the overbearing dickhead. I felt my blood pressure climb when he leaned right into her and said something close to her ear which caused her to giggle, some colour flooding her cheeks. The bar was heaving and as a result, boiling inside. All the other women I could see were wearing minimal clothing but not Lucy. Lucy was in a jumper dress – cream wool from her neck to just above her knees with sleeves that fell to cover her hands. Compared to the skimpy dresses on display in the bar it shouldn't have been that sexy or eye-catching. But the wool skimmed close to her figure, showing off her curves in a way that was even more effective.

She was talking to Piers now, a bright smile lighting up her features. Her nose scrunched at his reply. I wasn't close enough to see her freckles, but I was infuriated that Piers was. In fact, this whole situation was totally unacceptable. What on earth was Lucy doing out and about by herself? Where was shy Lucy who hid in my home office last week instead of mingling at a party? Why was that stupid sod Piers getting to see her freckles close up and not me?

Ignoring my colleagues, who were also now all watching Lucy, the shady bastards, I slammed my drink down on the table and pushed up from my seat. All I was really focused on at that stage was my anger. I probably should have taken a moment to ask myself if I had the right to be angry. Unfortunately, as with a lot of my dealings with this woman, rationality seemed to have deserted me. Plus I'd downed at least four shots already to celebrate closing on a piece of land just outside London.

"Piers," I snapped as I pushed myself into a space next to them at the bar. "What the fuck do you think you're doing?"

Piers jerked in surprise at my words and turned his head to face me. My annoyance ratcheted up a notch when he didn't drop his hand that was resting on the bar next to Lucy.

"Er…" he frowned at me. Piers and I had always got on pretty well. He was about my age and a hedge fund manager. We'd been out on the town fishing in the same waters for many years. He'd shagged a fair few of my exes and me his; it never caused an issue before. "Well, I'm talking to Lucy. Interesting girl."

I narrowed my eyes at him. "I bet."

"Yes," Piers said slowly. "Yes, she is. She was explaining to me about how she works. It's fascinating really."

My eyebrows went up. "Fascinating? Lucy's work?"

Piers was looking at me like I was a little mad. "Yes, of course."

What on earth had Lucy told Piers about the job she was doing, fairly incompetently, now? I didn't think she was the type to stretch the truth.

"Well, you can continue to be *fascinated* from a safe distance, you oversexed prick."

86

"Felix!" Lucy said, clearly annoyed, but I wasn't going to be deterred. She'd thank me when I explained to her what an absolute dog this guy was.

Piers straightened from the bar, widening the distance between himself and Lucy so he could turn fully to me, but at the same time keeping his hand firmly in place next to her. I felt a burning sensation in my gut that I refused to term as jealousy. No, I was simply protecting Lucy from unwanted advances. Hetty would kill me otherwise.

"It's not like you were staking a claim, Moretti," Piers said as he looked between me and Lucy. "If *I* came to the pub with Lucy she wouldn't be out of my sight. Seems like you took your eye off the ball, mate."

"It's not about staking any claims, you Neanderthal," I said in a haughty tone. "I'm looking out for her is all. She's like family, like a little sister."

Piers's eyebrows went up and then I saw the bastard suppress a small smirk. "Big brother, *right*," he said, drawing out the last word and losing his battle with his damn smirk. "Okay, *bro*." He lifted his hand away from the bar and held them both up in surrender. I felt that band around my chest loosen as he finally stepped away from Lucy. "Fascinating chat, babe," he said to Lucy before turning back to me, that smirk still in place. "Good luck, *big bro*. Few sharks circling tonight worse than me, I'd say."

He melted into the crowd, and I took his place next to Lucy at the bar just as I could see another one of these cocky city boys approaching. I crowded Lucy and gave the city boy a glare which sent him in the other direction. A small fist landed on my shoulder, and I looked back down at an infuriated Lucy. Her eyes were flashing with annoyance, and the colour in her cheeks was heightened. It was the first time I think I'd ever seen Lucy with make-up on. My mind blanked, and I said the first thing that came into it.

"Where are your freckles?" I mean, she looked beautiful, but *my* Lucy had freckles. I decided I wanted them back.

She blinked up at me like I was insane. Maybe I was.

"My freckles? Why are you asking about my freckles?"

"Your freckles are gone."

"You were the one who wanted me to fit in at your office. To smarten up. Make-up is part of that."

"I didn't mean for you to cover up your freckles," I said in a grumpy tone.

"Have you gone mad? And what the hell was that for with Piers?" she snapped.

I gave her what I thought was a patient look and went for a patient tone to go with it. This might not have been the best policy as it only seemed to infuriate her further.

"Piers wants to sleep with you, Lucy. Guys like him are only after one thing."

Lucy was so annoyed then that she actually growled. It was cute. I decided not to point that out to her – she looked murderous enough already.

"Felix," she said in a low voice, vibrating with fury. "You're *unbearable*, you know that? I can do what I like. I don't need *another* big brother throwing his weight around."

"I can't have you taken advantage of. What would your mother say?"

"Oh my God!" she semi-shouted. "My mother would be the first to tell me to get on and have some fun. 'Play the field' is how she put it. 'Have a few rides.' And, my personal favourite, 'Get out there and get a proper seeing to – do you the power of good'. My *mother* would have expected me to go home with Piers in a heartbeat. Why on earth do you think she encouraged me to leave Little Buckingham? Do you know how many single men there are back home, Felix?" I shook my head dumbly, still having trouble getting over the shock of Hetty telling her precious daughter to *get proper seen to*. "Zero. There are exactly zero. Emily married Pete, the last relatively attractive single man in the area. You remember Pete? Nice chap, but not

88

exactly George Clooney. The vicar's single, but he's old enough to be my grandad, so that's out."

I blinked. "Is that why you came to London? To meet men?"

She sighed. "Not just men. I've never lived away from home before. Never even went away to uni. I wanted to get out there in the big smoke. And well, I needed to get used to... people and such. Why did you *think* I came here?"

"For the career opportunities."

Lucy looked up at the ceiling as if she was seeking patience with me, which was totally the wrong way around. "What exactly did Mum say to you when she asked you for this job?"

"Well..." I rubbed the back of my neck. "She said you needed to get out of Little Buckingham."

"Did she mention furthering my career? You think I want to work in property development or finance?"

"What was I supposed to think, Lucy?"

She sighed and looked down at her feet for a moment. "You really don't know *anything* about me at all, do you?" she muttered in a dejected tone.

How much was I supposed to know about Lucy? I'd barely seen her for the last few years. I mean, I avoided going home like the plague, and the few times I'd met up with Mike it had been in London and had involved beers and shit-talking each other. Information about his little sister was not top of our agenda.

"Listen, Lucy Mayweather," I said in my most commanding voice. "You will not be having *any* rides with anyone, and that includes bloody *Piers*."

"Have you considered that maybe I can make my own decisions, you high-handed prick? Maybe I might want to have some fun after being cooped up in Little Buckingham for nearly three decades. Maybe Piers should be careful around me – huh?"

I frowned, then took Lucy by the hand to lead her away from the bar and out into a large alcove near the exit, away from anyone who might be watching us. She took a step back but I followed her, leaning in with my arm on the wall above her head, and registering the sharp intake of breath she took at our proximity. She was still bristling with anger, but I could feel her attraction to me through the waves of fury. Colour crept up from her neck to her cheeks, and her chest rose and fell with her fast breathing.

"Do you *want* to sleep with Piers?" I asked, my voice low, my face so close to hers that our lips were almost touching.

"I–I maybe I do," she stuttered out, her voice hoarse now. Anger coursed through me, and I felt my jaw clench. "B–b–but that would be my choice. You're not the boss of me."

"Aren't I?" I replied, my voice dropping even lower now.

"N–no, n–n–not here. Not outside work. You can't tell me what to do." She was breathless now, and her pupils were so dilated that only a thin rim of blue was evident around them. She shivered as my mouth moved to the shell of her ear.

"See I think I *am* the boss of you. I think that's what you *need*." At this point, I had definitely lost my handle on self-control. It was the smell of her shampoo, those goddamn freckles trying to show through the make-up, the rapid rise and fall of her chest, plus the alcohol coursing through my system, lowering my inhibitions.

"I think you've come here to drive me out of my mind so that I'll remind you of that. Remind you who your boss really is." My mouth moved from her ear to her neck, and I grazed her soft skin below her ear with my lips. Her pulse was flickering frantically in her neck as she let out a small sound from the back of her throat. I could feel the anger morph into confused excitement as my mouth moved to her delicate jawline, and another small shiver went through her. When I reached the corner of her mouth, I spoke again, this time against her lips. "You're not going to be doing anything with dickheads like Piers. Isn't that right, baby?"

"W–what," she whispered, our lips now a hair's breadth apart.

"Be a good girl and say, yes Felix," I said against her lips.

"Yes, Felix," she breathed. I smiled slowly then my mouth covered hers. She jerked slightly in shock, separating our connection and stared up at me for a moment with wide eyes. God, what was I doing? This was completely out of order. I was out of my drunken mind.

"Christ, sorry Lu—"

It was her turn to cut me off this time. Both her hands came up to frame my face then into my hair as she pulled me back down to her level. Her soft mouth sealed over mine, and she let out a small moan, which flipped the switch on any control my lust-addled mind had been exerting over my body.

My arms closed around her, one wrapping around her back with my hand splaying between her shoulder blades so I could pull her body into mine, the other low on her waist to do the same. Everything about her was small and soft and unbearably delicate, but also raw and intoxicating. It was a lethal combination. I could taste the sweet cocktail that prick Piers had probably bought her mixed with unique Lucy.

"Woah! Now I get it." Will's shouting broke through into my fuzzy brain, and I managed to pull back from the kiss. Lucy had clearly been so swept up in the moment that she hadn't even heard Will, despite his obnoxious shouting. Her eyes were still closed, and she leaned forward to follow my retreat. I almost smiled, but then I remembered bloody Will was standing right next to us. His finger was up now, pointing between us. "Family friend, *my arse*. Why didn't you just say you were fucking her, man?"

Lucy's eyes had blinked open, and I felt her body go rigid. When I glanced at her shocked face, I saw the colour drain out of it.

"Fuck off, Brent," I snapped, grabbing Lucy's hand and pulling her away from the alcove, pausing only to nab her coat off the bar stool beside her. As usual, Lucy tripped, and I caught her just before she went down, hauled her up against me and then pushed our way through the crowd and out of the bar.

91

When we got to the exit, I let her go, but only to shake out her coat and bundle her into it. She still seemed too dazed to fully function. I texted Frank, and then I pulled Lucy outside onto the pavement. She only had to shiver once, and I was done for. I put my arms around her and pulled her into me so that her face was in my chest, and she was practically inside my coat as well as her own. Her small hands were pressed against me, and she looked up at me as I kept her in the circle of my arms.

"Er... what's happening, Felix?" she whispered.

"You kissed me, that's what's happening."

She blinked once, opened her mouth to speak, shut it again, then shook her head as if to clear it.

"Are you angry with me for kissing you?" she asked, her voice both tentative and confused. I couldn't really blame her, but I did smile despite still feeling fucking furious with Will.

"No, love. I'm not angry with you. Brent can go fuck himself, but you've done nothing wrong."

She shivered at the endearment, and I didn't think it had anything to do with the cold. Warm satisfaction flooded through me, and I pulled her small body closer to mine. After kissing Lucy and holding her in my arms, all my stupid reasons for not doing this sooner were rapidly melting away. So what if Hetty and Mike thought I was taking advantage? I'd prove to them otherwise. So what if it was inappropriate behaviour with a subordinate? I'd sort it out with HR myself. So what if I had a talent for fucking up relationships? I'd just have to do better with Lucy. Frank pulled up then, and I grabbed Lucy's hand.

"Come on," I muttered, pulling her to the car and then opening the door for her, indicating she should get in first.

"Hi, Frank," Lucy said, giving him a small wave. "How are the grandkids?"

Frank smiled at her. "Lucy, this is a surprise." He glanced at me, a hint of disapproval in his expression, before turning back to Lucy.

"Ha! For me too," muttered Lucy.

"I'll take you home first, then," said Frank.

"Oh," Lucy said as we pulled away from the curb. She sounded disappointed. I was still holding her hand, and she gave it a squeeze before she moved to whisper in my ear. "Isn't your home closer?"

"Yes."

Her face had that adorably confused expression again as she looked up at me and I just couldn't help it. Despite the waves of disapproval coming off Frank, I kissed her. It was brief, hard and claiming. When I pulled back, her face was flushed as she blinked up at me. She paused for a moment and then squared her jaw, a look of determination replacing the confused expression from before.

"I think I want to come home with you," she whispered. Then, seeming to lose her nerve, she bit her lip, and her eyes slid to the side. I used the opportunity to kiss her cheek and then moved to whisper in her ear.

"You should probably be the one to tell Frank that. He clearly thinks I'm kidnapping you as it is."

"Right," she whispered back, then louder. "Er... Frank, actually we're going to Felix's so... um, just go there. Er... please?"

"It's no bother to take you back to your place, love," Frank said in a firm tone, and I smiled but controlled the urge to roll my eyes. What Frank didn't do was alter his direction. I remembered how far Lucy's house was from the office and wondered how she got to work every day. Did she take the tube at night and walk back after dark? My smile dropped as I imagined her walking home from the tube in the dark at night, freezing and totally vulnerable. How had I not taken an interest in this before? What if she'd been attacked? I tightened my arm around her as a few different scenarios flew through my mind.

"Well, that's kind, but I just really want to go to Felix's place," Lucy was trying to make her tone as firm as possible, but it wasn't quite having the effect I was sure she was going for.

"I'm sure you're best off getting home," said Frank. As much as the old bastard was annoying me, I also had to suppress a laugh. Clearly, he did not approve of Lucy being with me. I couldn't say I blamed him. Frank had driven me home with a fair amount of women over the years and rarely twice.

I knew I had some sort of deep-seated commitment issues, but I had a very good reason for that, and for the last few years all the women I dated, even if only briefly, knew the score. Some of the models and actresses were just happy with the extra publicity anyway, so there was often a symbiosis to the relationship – not particularly romantic, but I wasn't disappointing anyone. I always made it clear where I stood on commitment, usually before I'd even kissed them and definitely before they agreed to come home with me to make sure there were no expectations on either side.

Funnily enough, the thought of having *that* conversation with Lucy made me feel vaguely ill. With her, I realised, I had all *sorts* of expectations, not least that no other man touched her ever again. Quite the demand for someone I'd only kissed twice. Frank still hadn't changed direction, the stubborn sod.

"Frank, we're going back to mine," I put in, raising my voice just slightly. I caught his eye in the rear-view mirror, and he frowned at me. I raised one eyebrow, daring him to contradict a direct order. He made a low, disapproving noise in the back of his throat.

"Right, well, if you're *sure*, Lucy," he said finally. Lucy relaxed against me, her nose buried into my side, and my chest swelled as she inhaled.

"Totally," she said in a soft voice.

CHAPTER 15

Davey Turnbull

Lucy

"You are so handsome," I breathed as I looked up at Felix. We'd made it in from the car but not far beyond the front door. I hadn't even taken my coat off before I turned to him, wrapped my arms around him, looked up at his gorgeous face and blurted that out. Not exactly as smooth as I'm sure Felix was used to, but I was a couple of cocktails down and I'd spent the last twenty minutes breathing him in on the car ride. There was only so much a girl could take. And he *was* handsome. So handsome it was almost unreal.

I wasn't sure what was driving him to take me home tonight, to kiss me, but I wasn't going to question it. If this was the only time I ever had with Felix, I was going to make the most of it, and that included telling him how handsome he was. He smiled down at me, his long-lost dimple making an appearance for the second time that evening, reached up and tucked a lock of my hair behind my ear, searching my face in that intense way that made my stomach flip over.

"You are so fucking gorgeous it's almost painful," he murmured before he kissed the corner of my mouth again. Another tummy flip and a wave of desire so strong I thought I probably would have sunk to the ground had I not been secure in the circle of Felix's arms. I'd never had a compliment involving the f-word before – it had a certain extra kick.

"You're really good at this," I said, and he chuckled against my neck.

"Come on," he muttered through a smile, taking my hand and leading me to the stairs. He paused at the bottom step. "Do you want a drink?" I shook my head vigorously, and he smiled again as if I was funny. "Toast and Marmite?" Another head shake. "Tea?" His tone was teasing now, and I narrowed my eyes.

"Felix, take me upstairs," I said, trying to make my voice as firm as possible, but it just made his smile widen.

"Bossy little thing, aren't you," he said in a low voice before he brushed his lips against mine again, causing a whole body shiver and another head rush, making me feel almost lightheaded. This time, I did stumble slightly. Felix's eyes narrowed at that, and his smile dropped. "How much have you had to drink, Lucy?"

I shrugged. In truth, I was pretty buzzed. Being a cider drinker, I think I may have underestimated how strong those cocktails were. That was probably why I hadn't been a bundle of nerves in the crowded bar. Definitely why I opened up to Piers about my writing. But there was no way I was going to let that ruin my chance with Felix. This might be the only opportunity I had with him. If he thought I was shitfaced, I knew he wouldn't go any further with me. And we were going further, goddamn it. I'd been dreaming of this since middle school. Nothing was getting in my way.

"Hardly anything," I said, trying to look as sober as possible. He narrowed his eyes and pulled away slightly.

"Maybe we should pause things tonight, love," he said.

"No!" I semi-shouted, and his eyebrows went up in surprise. "There will be no *pausing of things*. Look, I'll prove how sober I am." I pulled away from him to walk up the corridor in a straight line, heel to toe. Unfortunately, seeing as I *was* a wee bit shitfaced and wearing stupid heeled boots, I listed to the side, and Felix had to catch me before I fell on my arse. He laughed as he pulled me against him again and gave me another brief kiss.

"We don't have to do anything now," he said softly as he looked down at my frustrated face. "There's no rush to—"

"I swear I'm sober. You try doing that in these stupid boots."

"Lucy, I—"

"Felix Moretti, if you don't take me to your bedroom right now and do bad, bad things to me, I will... well, I don't know what I'll do, but it'll piss me right off. I haven't been fantasising about you for the vast majority of my life only to have you put the kibosh on it just because you think I'm a bit squiffy. That's not going to fly, boss or no."

His body was shaking with laughter now, and it only served to piss me off more. When he'd finished laughing, he looked down at my scowling face.

"You've wanted me for that long?" he asked, his tone low and intense. In the back of my mind, I realised that sober-not-lust-crazed Lucy would be mortified to be revealing that much to Felix. But tipsy-Felix-addled Lucy was very much in charge at the moment, and *she* was going to be sorted out tonight in Felix's bed. I leaned into him and stared deep into his eyes.

"Felix, I promise I know what I'm doing. Please."

The amusement died in Felix's expression as he searched my face. "Christ," he groaned. "I'm going straight to hell."

Then he kissed me. Not briefly this time. This time, it was deep, long and demanding. My knees went weak, but his strong arms were around me holding me up as my tongue slid into his mouth and my hands found their way under his shirt to feel his warm skin and the muscles underneath. I swear Felix's body temperature ran a few degrees higher than the average human. He was such a perfect counterbalance to me. I always felt cold, but with Felix, I was so warm I felt like I was burning up.

"Take me to bed," I muttered against his lips, and he groaned again before pulling away, taking my hand and dragging me towards the stairs.

When I stumbled on the third step, I thought he was going to go all noble again and suggest putting the brakes on. But instead, he bent down and swept me up with one arm under my knees and the other around my shoulders. He then proceeded to jog up the stairs, taking them two at a time, with me held up against his chest as if he didn't even register my weight at all.

We made it to the top landing, and Felix, clearly still not feeling me capable of independent ambulation, turned and strode down the corridor, before kicking open one of the doors and taking me into what must be his bedroom. I only had a moment to take in the deep grey of the walls against the stark white of the bedding on his huge bed before I was deposited on the soft duvet. I came up on my elbows to watch Felix shrug his coat off onto the floor, loosen his tie, undo the top button of his shirt, then do that incredibly sexy man-manoeuvre I'd only ever seen in films when the man grabs their shirt from the back between their shoulder blades and whips it off in one.

"Oh my God," I breathed as I took in his torso. Tanned skin, defined muscles, broad shoulders. He smiled at me then, wide and glamorous, his white teeth standing out against his dark skin and thick stubble, his dimple making me catch my breath. All the blood seemed to leave my brain and sweep down south.

He was just that beautiful.

He climbed over to me then, and I sank back onto the bed as my elbows gave out. His still-smiling face hovered above mine, the muscles of his arms bulging with tension as he held himself above me. Then he lowered himself down, his delicious weight pressing me further into the bed, an intense warmth flooding from his body to mine.

"Breathe, baby," he whispered roughly in my ear, and I let out a puff of air that I hadn't even realised I'd been holding, then pulled a sharp breath in. He rocked against me, and I made a sound I'd never imagined myself capable of – a desperate sort of small moan from deep within my chest.

That seemed to trigger a loss of some of his control. He groaned again, and his mouth sealed over mine with another demanding kiss. One of my hands went into his thick hair to hold him to me, and the other went up around his back, feeling the muscles move under the scorching skin again as he continued to rock into me.

"You have way too many clothes on," he muttered against my lips as he started to wrestle with my coat, throwing it onto the floor, then moving onto my jumper dress, which he pulled over my head to follow the coat.

"What the fuck?" he said as my next layer of merino wool dress was revealed. When that layer went, he started laughing when he encountered my full-length lace-trimmed thermals.

"Are you even in there?" he asked, and I giggled. But I stopped when he tore off the thermal layer, and I was left in my underwear. Suddenly I wasn't feeling so buzzed from the cocktails anymore. My shyness and insecurity started poking through the Felix lust haze, and I bit my lip, scared to look up at him.

"Lucy," Felix breathed, his voice rough with desire, and I plucked up the courage to raise my gaze to his. Rejection, after I'd pined for him for so long, would have killed me, but that was not what I saw in his face. His jaw was clenched tight, a fierce expression on his face as his eyes swept the length of my body.

"Fucking hell," he breathed, then he moved. Before I knew it, he'd unhooked my bra, thrown it to the floor and slid his hand behind my back to pull my body flush with his, my softness against his hard chest, and he was kissing me again.

"You are incredible," he said against my mouth, that rough quality back in his voice. I was beyond forming words now. Now that his hot skin was directly against mine, his hardness moving against me. He kissed down my throat to my chest until his mouth closed over one of my nipples.

I arched off the bed and made another desperate noise in the back of my throat.

His hand traced down my stomach until he was right there, skimming inside my knickers and pressing his thumb at my centre whilst his fingers glided into me. He started a slow steady rhythm with his hand, exerting just the right amount of pressure as I squirmed beneath him.

Eventually, I lost all control and was literally riding his hand, completely disinhibited. Then the sharp tug of his mouth at my other nipple tipped me over the edge. He bit me lightly as I flew apart with a near scream, stars exploding behind my eyes.

It was so intense that I actually felt like I'd left my body. When I came back to myself and blinked up at Felix's focused expression, another wave of desire swept through me.

"Jesus Christ," he said in a rough, almost strained voice. He had a wild look in his eyes, and his whole body was strung tight as if holding himself back. I could feel the tense muscles under my hands on his back as I slid them up to his hair.

"Blimey," I breathed. "You're really bloody good at that."

That broke through Felix's intensity. His body started shaking before he collapsed onto me and laughed into my throat. "Thanks for the performance review," he said against my skin through his laughter, and I smiled.

The weight of him and his movement was starting to build up the tension in me again, and I started moving against him, a small moan escaping as I kissed his ear. Then some sort of sex kitten Lucy emerged, and I took his ear between my teeth before licking it with my tongue and whispering, "I need you, Felix."

His laughter merged into a groan. And when he pulled back to look at me, that intensity was back in his expression. Before I knew it, my knickers were on the floor along with the rest of his clothes, and he was reaching into his side table for a condom, which he sorted in record time. Then his cock was right there, pressing forward. I inhaled sharply and tensed for a moment at his size. A muscle was clenched in his jaw, and his body was trembling with the tension of holding back.

"Lucy," he said in a rough voice. "Baby, are you a virgin?"

"What? Oh no... well, I mean not *really*."

He swallowed; it looked like it was costing him every bit of self-control. His body was trembling over mine. "What do you mean by *not really*?"

"Er... well, I've had sex before with Davey Turnbull, you know the farmer's lad up in Lower Winton?"

Felix closed his eyes slowly and let out a huff of breath, which sounded like a half-laugh, half-groan, almost like he was in some extreme pain but finding it amusing.

"It's just that Davey was—"

"Please, Luce, when I'm nearly inside you in my bed, please can we not talk about 'Davey the farmer's lad'?"

"Well, see, Davey wasn't quite as... er, blessed in that area."

"Davey had a small cock."

"Not really, it's just you seem to have a... well... a... rather large... er..."

More of his weight settled on me as he slid further in. I grunted as I adjusted to his size.

"Enough said, baby," he said into my ear in a rough whisper, slowly pushing forward. I moaned as I stretched around him. I was so full it was almost uncomfortable, but I craved more, pushing my hips up to take more of him. "Christ," he ground out. "Keep still, love. I can't—"

"Please, Felix," I breathed. "Fuck me."

That snapped his control, and I gasped as he thrust forward, now fully seated inside me, so deep it was verging on discomfort but in a delicious way. He paused a moment to search my face, his eyes wild. "Are you okay?"

"I–I think so? I mean you're really big. Maybe too big? But in a good way. Like, I feel so *very* full and... well like I want you to move. Maybe?"

He made a sound which was half-laugh, half-groan before he did just that, slowly at first then building pace until his thrusts were shaking me on the bed as I climbed back up to the peak. Then he was kissing me and hooking one of my legs over his arm to get the exact angle I didn't even know I needed.

His movements were wild as I broke again, convulsing around him with pleasure so intense it felt like I might black out with the force of it. Then I got to watch as Felix's rhythm became more forceful, uncontrolled and uneven before everything in his incredible body strung tight. He let out a hoarse cry then after a long moment he collapsed on top of me, letting me take all his weight for a few seconds before he managed to roll to the side. He pulled me along with him so that I was sprawled over his chest, my leg up on his thigh, and my face tucked into his neck. Then he tugged the duvet over both of us before his arms came up around me to hold me to him tightly.

We were breathing heavily, the intensity still in the air but now mixed with acute relief. Then Felix started laughing again.

"Hey," I snapped, slapping his chest in indignation. "What's so funny?"

He looked down at my frowning face and kissed me through his laughter. But he didn't stop laughing, the bastard. Was sex with me that comical? I started to pull away, but his arms tightened around me to keep me in place and against his warmth.

"I think that's a first for me. A performance review after I made you come was one thing, but the discussion of a past lover, including his full name and who he worked for in the village I grew up in when I was practically inside you, was... unusual."

"You asked me!"

"You could just have said, 'No, Felix, I'm not a virgin'. You didn't have to give me the full name, profession and dick size of your last partner."

"My only partner," I muttered grumpily into his chest. He kissed the top of my head and started stroking my back.

"Not anymore," he said in a very satisfied tone.

"Well, I'm sorry if sex with me is weird. I'm not fully up on the etiquette."

Felix laughed again, then pushed me onto my back, settling his weight on top of me again, both his hands coming up to my face to push my hair gently back behind my ears.

"Sex with you is absolutely incredible, Lucy," he said through a smile. "Even if I have Davey Turnbull's name burned into my brain for eternity, I wouldn't change a thing."

Then he kissed me again, deep and long and so thoroughly I forgot to be cross. In fact, as he hardened against me again, I forgot everything apart from his warmth and the pure need flooding through me.

CHAPTER 16

You remember that, do you?"

Lucy

"Tell me a story, Shakespeare," Felix muttered into my neck.

It was the early hours of the morning, after round three. The second time had been slower, with a pulsing intensity that brought tears to my eyes it was so beautiful. In fact, one tear did fall after I finally came. I had hoped that Felix wouldn't notice, but the man seemed to be aware of everything when it came to me. He looked up just at the right time and brushed the tear away with his lips as it tracked into my hair, then kissed me deeply, still connected to me, and I didn't think I'd ever been so happy. We'd passed out after that.

The third time had been this morning in the shower – Felix's suggestion after he rolled us both off the bed. I was sceptical about the logistics of shower sex, but Felix disabused me of that notion pretty quickly as he lifted me with ease under the warm spray, held me up against the side of the shower and showed me how easy it was with sufficient strength and motivation.

Now we'd collapsed back in bed again. Felix had pulled off our towels and his head was lying on my chest, his large arm slung over my tummy as I stroked his hair. It was Saturday, and

I knew he usually worked Saturday morning, but he'd shown no sign of going to the office yet and I didn't want to break the bubble of bliss we were currently in.

"What?" I said softly.

"A story," he repeated. "You know, like you did when we were kids."

I took a short breath in and let it out slowly. My throat felt tight, and I had to clear it before I could get any words out. "You remember that, do you?" I said, trying to make my voice light, but it was an effort with the amount I was feeling.

"Of course I do. I loved your stories."

I swallowed and blinked rapidly to push back stupid tears. I knew that Felix had no idea about my writing, and I knew that was partly my fault for not just bloody telling him. But it still stung that he'd never asked Mikey about me, never wondered about it. What did he think I'd been doing for the last nine years? Did he think I just sponged off Mum back in Little Buckingham? No wonder he felt he had to give me a job.

What made it worse was how much of a sad case I felt given how avidly I had followed Felix's every move. I'd grilled Mike after every time he met up with Felix in London, wanting to know all the details of Felix's career – whether he was happy, whether he had met someone?

Granted, I had an advantage in following Felix's progress. When he wasn't featured in financial papers, he was often splashed across the tabloids and magazines out and about with various extremely glamorous, often famous women. It would be a little harder to find out what I was up to in Little Buckingham I was sure. But not impossible. Mikey or Mum would have told him if he'd bothered to ask.

So my pride was just a bit hurt. That was why I couldn't bring myself to tell him that my stories weren't just childish inventions anymore. They were a career. But then I owed some of that career to Felix, didn't I? The boy who was always prepared to listen to anything my weird brain had dreamed up. The boy who never found my ramblings boring, who encouraged me to keep going. *Tell me another story, Shakespeare.* Felix had no idea how many times I'd conjured his voice over the years to help motivate my writing.

But this man who'd inspired me, who'd given me the courage to go for it – he didn't even know what I'd achieved. One of the tears made it out, trickling down into my hair. I wiped it away before Felix could notice and cleared my throat.

"Okay, so there's a fae King called Taurus," I started when I was sure my voice wouldn't betray any of the emotion I was feeling. "He's the leader of the Western Territory and the only one of the fae ever to claim back the city of Mendes from the Shadowlands. But he's become obsessed with the prophecy of The Girl. The one to lead the fae out of darkness. The one whose light will flow into every corner of all the territories."

I talked for nearly an hour, recounting the plot line to my first book. Had Felix wanted, he could have heard this story years ago. There was an audiobook version after all, with better narrators than little old me.

"Why have you stopped?" Felix said in a grumpy voice, giving me a squeeze. I smiled as I ran my hands through his hair and kissed his forehead.

"You need to feed me," I told him, not able to tell him that I simply couldn't go on recounting this story. It felt weirdly like lying, which I guess I *was* kind of doing by omission. But in my defence, Felix hadn't actually asked me directly at any point about anything specific. I used to talk about being an author as a child. Did he just assume I'd given up on my dreams?

I pushed the annoyance and resentment down. I didn't want to waste this time with Felix. Who knew how much longer I had with him? I wasn't under any illusion that I'd be enough to hold Felix's interest. If he didn't stay with all those other glamourzons there was little hope for me. But I was absolutely resolved to savour every fantastic moment with him now. I wasn't missing a thing – not his warmth, not his smile, not his sense of humour, not his gentle teasing, not his incredible, unnaturally warm body. It was all mine... for now.

My stomach chose that moment to let out a low grumble. Felix pushed up and flipped fully on top of me, caging me in with his arms, his hands planted in the pillow on either side of my head. He leaned down to kiss me once and smiled his glamorous, white smile, complete with dimple, making my breath catch in my throat at just how handsome he was.

His stubble was thicker this morning, his hair deliciously tousled from where I'd had my hands through it, his tanned skin a stark contrast to my lily-white complexion. He looked good enough to eat. He groaned and let out a low laugh.

"Don't look at me like that, baby," he muttered. "Or we'll never leave this bed, and you need to eat."

He kissed me again and rested his forehead on mine for a moment before jumping out of bed and pulling on a pair of jeans from the back of a chair.

I shuffled out from under the duvet, feeling exposed now that we weren't actively shagging or lying naked together under the sheets. I became a little frantic as I searched for my underwear, breathing a huge sigh of relief when I managed to find my knickers and nearly fell over in my haste to pull them on.

Felix stopped me as I was about to go back to grab the next item of clothing I could see. I no longer cared about the order; I'd wear my bra over my jumper dress if I could just get them on in a matter of seconds. He took my hand in his as I reached for my thermals and pulled me back upright and against him, encircling me again with his warmth.

"Hey," he said softly into the top of my head. "You okay, love?"

I buried my face into his chest and swallowed my embarrassment. "Y–yes, I just..." I let out a small laugh. "I just feel a bit weird now. I mean the other women you've been with... I..."

"What about them?"

"Felix, I've seen the pictures. I'm not exactly in the same league. You can't really blame me for being a little self-conscious."

Felix pulled away slightly so that he could look at me. When I kept my gaze firmly on his chest, he used both his hands on either side of my jaw to lift my face to his.

"Lucy, you are the most beautiful woman I have ever seen in my life," he said. My eyes went wide, and my mouth dropped open.

"Y–you can't mean that. I—"

"Listen, I should be the insecure one," he told me, a small smile tugging at the corners of his mouth. "Davey Turnbull's a hard act to follow. At least I'm not recounting my previous dates' full names."

I narrowed my eyes at him. "I know full well that you are not in the least intimidated by a farmer's lad from Lower Winton."

He shrugged. "You're the one who brought him up just as we were about to—"

I slapped his chest but did smile. "Don't say it!"

He kissed me again and then held me against him, my body melting into his. Then he shuffled me over to his chest of drawers, pulled out a shirt and slipped it over my head. It came down to my knees, and I had to roll the sleeves up a few times to find my hands.

"Forget about clothes for a moment," he said. "I want you to potter around the house in just my shirt." He went back to the drawers and pulled out a pair of thick socks. "Wear these, and I'll crank the heat right up to thirty degrees. I have underfloor heating."

"I'll look ridiculous," I mumbled.

"Trust me, you'll look gorgeous."

"Fine," I snapped, taking the socks and pulling them on. "But only if you keep your shirt *off.*"

He laughed again. "You've got a deal."

CHAPTER 17

I've created a monster

Lucy

So that's how we ended up in Felix's ridiculously large kitchen, scrambling eggs, me in just his shirt and him in just his jeans.

"Do you want me to make Mum's eggs?" I asked.

"Fuck, yes," Felix said. "I bloody love your Mum's eggs."

His contribution to the scrambling process was to stand behind me at the kitchen counter, caging me in with his arms either side of me, his heat at my back, alternating between stroking my hair back from my neck and kissing me below my ear. I dropped the spoon twice until I abandoned the eggs and started kissing him again. This led to him lifting me up on the counter next to said eggs, lying me back against the granite with the cold at my back contrasting with the immense heat from his skin at my front. Just like in the shower I was doubtful about the logistics, but when I voiced this to Felix, he made it clear that was not a concern.

"I'll make it work, I swear," he said against my mouth, then proceeded to kiss down my neck to my chest, undoing the buttons of his shirt as he went, then further to my breasts, down my stomach. I gasped when he dispatched my knickers in one fluid motion, and then his mouth was right *there*.

So yes, he was right, the counter was indeed the perfect height. In fact, this should probably be our routine at breakfast from now on I decided as I came so hard I would have fallen off the granite without Felix holding me up.

"Wow," I gasped as he moved up over me, his body covering mine again, and his arms came up to lift me off the counter against him.

He smiled and then groaned as he slid deep. Our heavy breathing filled the kitchen as he effortlessly held me up away from the hard countertop. I'd have been content to just hold on for the ride and watch Felix lose control, but he wasn't having any of that. As his thrusts became deeper and more out of control, he slid his hand around between us, his thumb pressing just where I needed it, and we fell over the edge together.

When I recovered enough to speak and he'd settled me back down on my feet, I quickly pulled the shirt sides together and started buttoning the front. Felix had said I was beautiful but there was no point giving him full frontal views in the unforgiving morning light of the kitchen for longer than I had to. I didn't want to push my luck. I could feel my face heat as I pulled on my knickers, realising that I'd left his socks on throughout all of that. I was beginning to get that insecure feeling again in the pit of my stomach. Would Felix ask me to leave after breakfast? When I straightened, he seemed to read my mind again and reached for both my hands, tugging me forward and dipping down to kiss me.

"Okay?" he said softly, dropping one of my hands so that one of his could come up to tuck my hair that had fallen in front of my eye behind my ear. "Was that too much? I was a bit rough and—"

"No," I cried, my eyes going wide. The last thing I needed was for Felix to think I was some delicate flower. What if the opportunity for dirty kitchen counter sex cropped up again, and he didn't take it because he was afraid it would be *too much*?

I wasn't missing out on any of the kitchen counter sex, thank you very much!

"It's just that's the second time you've gone all skittish after, though, love," Felix said gently. "I want you to tell me honestly if there's anything you're uncomfortable with. It's really important."

I felt my face heat as I looked to the side.

"Lucy," Felix called, his hand sliding to my jaw to gently turn my head to look at him. "Baby, please. You can tell me."

"Ugh," I huffed out. "You're getting the wrong end of the stick. I'm only uncomfortable after because... well, during *stuff* I'm in the moment so I forget to be embarrassed. But then afterwards, I kind of come back to myself and realise that..."

"Realise what?"

I sighed. "Firstly, I've hardly ever been naked in front of anyone before. I'm not sure I even took my top off with Davey." Felix growled in warning at the mention of Davey's name and I rolled my eyes. "Look, I've never even stepped inside a gym. I like my mum's carrot cake. And I was voted pastiest villager at the church fete. I'm not overly keen for you to get an eyeful and be put off."

"Lucy, look at me," he commanded in his Boss Voice. I blinked up at him as I bit my lip. "I am completely obsessed with your body exactly the way it is. There will be no gyms in your future – clearly, you need any excess energy to keep yourself warm. But you really have to tell me if anything we did was—"

"No, no!" I repeated. "That was amazing. I've never done any of that stuff before, but trust me, I'm on board. I want to officially declare my full enjoyment and formally request further kitchen exploits." Felix's shoulders started shaking.

"Formally request?" he said through a laugh. "Do you want to submit it in writing?"

I felt myself blush again and bit my lip. Maybe I'd revealed a bit too much.

"I—er, well, that's if there are further opportunities. I—er, don't want to presume that you want to..." I trailed off and closed my eyes in frustration. Why was it that my words could flow so effortlessly when I was writing, but I became a tongue-tied imbecile so often in real life, especially around Felix?

He gathered me close and kissed my lips again, this time soft and unbearably sweet.

"You better believe that there'll be 'further kitchen exploits', gorgeous," he said against my mouth. "Formal request or no." I relaxed into him, feeling some of my nervous energy drain away. At least it seemed that Felix wasn't thinking that this was just a one-off.

"Now," he said in a playful tone. "Make me my eggs, woman." He pushed me towards the Aga and lightly smacked my bottom as I went. Even that small action made me want to turn around and rip his jeans off again. I was turning into a full sex maniac!

We ate the eggs at his kitchen island. Felix ate his with one hand, the other resting on my thigh under his shirt. He closed his eyes with the first bite and hummed his approval, an action that also turned me on an unreasonable amount. "Oh my God. This is just like Hetty's. I haven't had eggs this good in over a decade."

"Mum's good at eggs."

"Your mum's the best at most things," Felix muttered, turning back to his eggs with a pensive expression, his hand now moving to rub the back of his neck, leaving my thigh cold in its absence. "I owe your mum a lot, Luce."

"I know you love Mum, Felix," I said softly. He was frowning now and had stopped eating altogether. "Listen, I'm not going to go all bunny-boiler on you if you want to er... well, *when* you don't want to carry on..." I was stumped. What did I say? Carry on shagging like rabbits? It wasn't like we were dating. We hadn't even gone on a single date. The party at Felix's house didn't count – there were hundreds of people there, and I only saw him briefly before he left me to my own devices to embarrass myself and then hide. "Er… carry on sleeping together? Being fuck buddies?"

"Lucy," Felix snapped, putting his fork down to glare at me. "We are not fuck buddies!"

"Okay, chill," I tried to reassure him. "I mean, I'm not that up on the terminology. But we're not exactly dating, more… doing the horizontal stuff. Oh well, actually, some of it wasn't altogether horizontal, was it? Impressive, by the way – demonstrated lots of upper body strength."

Felix groaned and buried his face in his hands with his elbows on the granite in front of him. "Your mother is going to kill me."

"Look, don't get so stressed out. Let's go back to before the eggs. Back when you were shagging me on the kitchen counter and smacking my arse."

"No," Felix said with determination. "We're not doing any more of that." My heart sank, and I tried to swallow down my disappointment along with the eggs that were now sticking in my throat. "Not until I take you out on a proper date. We've done this all the wrong way around. Christ, your brother! Mike's going to have my guts for garters."

"A date?" I spun on my stool to look at Felix. My eyebrows went up in surprise. "We're going to go on a proper date? Like we're dating?" I tried, I really did, but I did not think I was successful in keeping the excitement out of my voice. The whole bouncing on my chair may rather have given me away as well.

Felix turned his frowning face to my excited one. "Lucy, of course we'll date. Did you think we'd just be *fuck buddies* as you put it? What the hell?"

I slid off my stool and walked into the space between Felix's legs. He immediately enclosed his warm arms around me as I pressed my hands against his chest and looked up at his handsome face.

"I'm just happy to be with you," I said softly through a smile. "I don't care how it's labelled. Every hour with you is more than I could have ever hoped for."

"Oh God, Lucy," he groaned. "You're killing me."

He leaned down and kissed me softly first, then, as seemed to be the way with us, the kiss went deeper, his hands smoothed up the back of his shirt, warm on my skin. My hands went up to the back of his neck and into his hair. A small moan escaped the back of my throat before he wrenched away.

"Bloody hell," he breathed into my hair at the top of my head as he pulled me into his chest. "Right, no more fuck buddy stuff until we have a *proper date*."

"For the record. I think that's a stupid rule." My voice was muffled by his chest, but I knew that he heard me because he started laughing softly.

"Finish your eggs," he said, setting me away from him and lifting me back onto my own stool, turning it firmly towards the plate and away from him.

"We better be going on a date in the next hour," I said in a grumpy voice at my eggs. As much as I wanted to go out with Felix, I wasn't that keen to wait for more fuck buddy stuff. That seemed grossly unfair just because *he* was worried about my mum and brother.

"I'll take you out tonight," he said. "How's that, FB?"

I rolled my eyes. "Only if you'll promise to put out."

He laughed again and kissed the side of my head. But then his phone buzzed, and he picked it up with a frown.

"Shit," he muttered. "I forgot, I'm meeting Ollie and Vicky tonight. Trying to smooth everything over after that shitshow of a meeting with York."

"Oh."

"Come with us. We can eat before, then we'll meet them."

I bit my lip. "Nowhere fancy is it? I'm not so comfortable in those places. Takes bloody ages to get served and they don't have any proper cider."

"I'm meeting them in a pub in Soho. Don't worry, you'll get your cider." He was still smiling. "You can even wear your Uggs."

I squinted at him. "This counts as an official date, right? You're not going to be withholding any more sex?"

He rolled his eyes. "Bloody hell, I've created a monster."

CHAPTER 18

Parking is sexy?

Felix

Lucy was running out of the house as I pulled up outside her flat in Putney, and her eyes were smiling. I couldn't see her mouth due to her huge scarf. She wore a bobble hat pulled down low over her ears with her hair poofing out from under it and that long puffa coat that made her look like she was walking around in a sleeping bag. And yes, her Uggs were on her feet.

"I told you to wait, and I'd come to your door," I said as she skipped to me. A one-woman homing missile, only stopping when she collided with me, her gloved hands landing on my chest and her excited face smiling up at me. Her nose was pink under her freckles, her eyes bright, and I felt my chest squeeze with the unexpected force of my feelings. She was just that adorable. It was almost scary. My arms closed around her, and I pulled down her scarf to get to her mouth for a brief, hard kiss.

"I missed you," she breathed when I pulled back slightly, and I started chuckling.

"You only saw me six hours ago," I teased, and she gave me a grumpy look.

"Didn't you miss me? Not at all?"

"Nope," I said, slinging my arm around her and leading her

over to the car. "I had work to do. I didn't think about you for a second," I lied.

She harumphed as I opened the door for her and crowded her into the passenger seat. I'd decided to take the car myself tonight, determined to stay sober and keep at least some of my self-control around Lucy. I smiled when I got into the driver's seat and glanced at her. Her arms were crossed across her chest, and she was still frowning. After cranking the heat right up on the console, I leaned over Lucy and grabbed her seatbelt to pull it across her body, clicking it into place but not moving back; instead, my hand slid up her jaw, turning her face to mine and I kissed the corner of her mouth softly.

"Do you want to hear that I couldn't get anything done today? That I've probably fucked up a multi-million-pound deal because all I could think about were these freckles." I kissed her nose then my voice dropped lower as I started kissing down her neck. "That I couldn't get the taste of you out of my mouth, couldn't get those breathy little sounds you make when you come out of my head? That my hands have been itchy all day to feel your soft skin? That I've been hard as nails wanting to bend you over my desk and fuck you till you scream."

"Er... w—well, yes," she stuttered out as I gave her small earlobe a light graze with my teeth, and she shuddered in her seat. It took all my self-control, but I pulled back and gave her thigh a couple of pats and a brief squeeze through her coat. There was a short pause before she cleared her throat.

"For the record, I'm pro dirty talk," she said, and I chuckled. "I might have to work up to it myself, but I give you leave to continue along the same dirty talk lines." A short pause again, then, "And I'm *very* pro the desk thing. Just so you know."

I groaned, rock hard again. When I spoke, my voice was just a little strangled. "Right. Feedback received and noted. Now that we've established that, let's go."

"Well, we don't have to go *now,* do we?" Lucy said, glancing up at the house she'd just come out of and then back at me. Her cheeks were pink, and she was biting her lip. "I mean, we could…"

"Lucy," I said in a firm tone. "I'm taking you on a bloody date. Stop trying to take advantage of me." I smirked as she sucked in a furious breath.

"I am not taking advantage, Felix Moretti!"

"I can't blame you really," I said in a resigned tone. "Not when you're confronted with all this." I swept my hand up and down my body to emphasise my point before checking the mirrors to pull away from the curb. Lucy giggled.

"You always were an arrogant sod," she muttered as we drove down the leafy street.

I gave her a quick smirk. "You love it. Listen, FB. We'll have plenty of time for horizontal fun. There's a ton of other stuff we haven't tried."

"There is?" She sounded excited now, and I held back another groan, resisting the urge to perform a dangerous U-turn and take her back to her place. I swallowed and gripped the steering wheel harder.

"Lucy, we are going out on a proper date." It was a promise to myself as much as to her.

"Alright," she said in that same grumpy tone, sitting back in her seat and crossing her arms again.

"How have you managed to afford this flat anyway, Luce?"

"Er… well I got a really good deal." She cleared her throat, seeming nervous, which I didn't quite understand. "So, what's the plan?" Her voice was high-pitched now, but I allowed the abrupt change of subject.

"The food at the pub's pretty good. None of those tiny little canapés or the fizzy wine you hate so much." I gave her a side-eye, and she rolled her eyes. "So I thought we'd get there early and eat. The others won't arrive till nine-ish. Vics never eats out really anyway."

"Oh right. How did it get so awkward with Ollie? You two were always good mates. You could cut the tension in that meeting with a knife."

I sighed. "No, I'm still mates with Ollie, but he's been pissed off since I made Vicky a partner. He's weirdly protective of her. Vicky's... well, she's unique."

Lucy laughed. "Yes, I'd noticed that."

"Do you remember her from when we were kids? She was about the same age as you but she wasn't around very much. Only occasionally in the summer holidays."

"She came to the cottage a couple of times but she never spoke to me. I thought it was because she was snobbish but Mum said she was a bit... different."

"Vicky didn't speak for years when she was a child. Selective mutism. Things weren't easy for her. Staying with the Hardings in the holidays must have been... difficult with her being her dad's love child."

There was a pause before Lucy spoke again.

"Felix, is Vicky Autistic?"

"I mean, I think so," I admitted. "But it's not something the Hardings ever discuss and she's never brought it up. To be honest I'm not sure it's ever been handled the right way. She was bullied very badly at school. That's one of the reasons Ollie's so protective of her I think."

"So why is there friction about her working with you?"

"Ollie's an arrogant sod. He thinks Vics would be better off working for the Buckingham Estate, but she had other plans. And okay, there were some teething problems to start with. Vicky is very... truthful and... direct. It can put people's backs up. But since she hired Lottie to be her personal assistant that hasn't been a problem anymore. Lottie is sort of like her own personal empath – helps Vics read the room, stops her going off on one or insulting people. It works well. Only problem is that Ollie hates Lottie."

"What? How could anyone hate Lottie?"

I chuckled. "That's a long story. Not sure we've got time for me to spill all the tea on that one."

"So you think Ollie's using York to spite you? Because you stole his sister and you're employing his enemy?"

I raised my eyebrows. "Jesus, Luce. You've still got a flare for the drama. Much as I hate to admit it, I think Vicky's probably right – York manages the relevant investments for the Hyde Park project and he does have legitimate concerns. He was just a bit a of prick about them."

I parallel parked outside the restaurant and when I was in the space, with my arm around the back of Lucy's seat to look out the back window, she reached up to kiss me.

"That is so sexy," she breathed against my mouth, and I started laughing.

"What? Parking is sexy?"

"Yes!" she said, her hands going into my hair to pull me down for another kiss. "It's all that manly sling-the-arm-over-the-passenger-seat-to-look-out-the-back-spin-the-wheel-one-handed sexiness."

I growled into her mouth and wished I'd agreed to just come into her house instead of going out. Lucy was so open, so honest about her feelings for me and the strength of her attraction. It was like nothing I'd ever experienced before, and I found myself wanting to take her and hide her from the rest of the world, from people that I knew would crush all that trusting honesty.

"You're easy to please," I said before kissing her again, one of my hands cupping the back of her neck under her scarf and the other going around her side to pull her to me. I could barely feel Lucy under the bulk of her coat. "How many layers do you have on exactly?" I asked as I pulled back. We couldn't stay necking like teenagers in the car all evening.

"Eleventy billion," she said with a smile as I pushed open my car door.

"Stay," I told her as I levered out of the car and then slammed the door before going round to her side to pull her door open for her.

"Yikes, this *is* a proper date," she said as I helped her out of the car. I tucked her into my side once we were on the pavement and led her over to the restaurant. "It'd better not be fancy. You promised I could wear my Uggs."

As we moved to the pub in front of us I felt her body relax against mine. The King's Head certainly could not be described as fancy.

She smiled at me as we sat down at the table I'd reserved next to the fire, and then the unwrapping began. First the coat, then the sleeveless puffa underneath, the scarf, the hat, the gloves until she was left in a denim skirt with thick tights which were the same blue as her very fluffy, high-necked jumper.

"Aren't your legs cold?"

She shook her head and smiled. "Fleece-lined," she said, lifting her jumper and peeling down the top of her tights to show me the fluffy lining within. It shouldn't have been sexy. I'd always considered myself much more of a tiny underwear and stockings kind of man, but Lucy's thermals were weirdly a massive turn-on.

I took a seat at the table before I embarrassed myself in public. Despite all the layers, when I looked at Lucy's hands on the table I could see a couple of her fingers were white. So, I moved from opposite her to sit by her side and took both her hands in mine to warm them.

"I need to get you heated gloves," I muttered as I tried to get as much warmth into her fingers as possible.

Lucy was looking down at our joined hands. When she looked back up at me, she had that dreamy, blissful expression on her face again, like she couldn't really believe she was here with me, like *she* was the lucky one.

I felt an arrow of guilt at that. There was the niggling worry that her long-term crush on me was clouding her judgement. That I was taking advantage of her. But I pushed it aside, not willing to let anything stand between us.

CHAPTER 19

Your Grace

Felix

In true Little Buckingham fashion, Lucy ordered a steak and ale pie and a pint of cider. I got the scampi because I knew that was also her favourite. I'd eaten enough times with the Mayweathers in the past to know what they all liked.

"How's Mike?" I asked when our food arrived, and Lucy's face lit up. She'd always adored her brother. We talked about life back home – Mike's carpentry business (he made bespoke, high-end rustic pieces that sold for massive amounts), her mum, her old mates in Little Buckingham (I remembered Emily – she was a feisty kid and the opposite of Lucy, but they'd always been thick as thieves).

But, when we got onto the subject of *my* family, despite the warm fire, the cider and the comfort food, I clammed up. I didn't want to bring the evening down by talking about them and all the reasons I hadn't gone back to Little Buckingham for years.

My father was a very successful corporate lawyer for one of my competitors. The only thing he really understood was money. I had hated him even before his serious betrayal five years ago, but since then I avoided him at all costs. So, I made damn sure that I built up my company into an empire which made his financial situation look like child's play. I can still hear my dad's sneering voice to me as a ten-year-old child:

"You'll never make anything of yourself. No backbone. You have to be ruthless in this world, or you'll get trampled over."

Well, I'd proved him wrong. It was well known how ruthless I was. The amount of business my own father's company had lost to mine was proof of that. But then, sitting here opposite Lucy, my dad's voice faded, and another took its place:

"Aren't we lucky?"

Henry Mayweather would say that sentence nearly every week. Even just on an ordinary Tuesday afternoon with his family and me squashed round the kitchen table, sharing a packet of ginger biscuits. And he meant it too. The Mayweathers didn't have any money really. Henry was a gardener for my parents and for the Buckingham Estate; Hetty was my nanny. Neither job paid particularly well, but success and happiness for Henry wasn't about that. It was about a tiny kitchen full of laughter and the people in it whom he loved.

I blinked at the sudden jolt of grief I felt for Henry Mayweather. Lucy tilted her head to the side as she looked over at me, but luckily, before she could probe any further, Ollie chose that moment to arrive.

"Well, this is cosy," Ollie said from the side of our table, and Lucy jumped in surprise, dropping the scampi she'd been about to steal from my plate.

"Bucks," I said, standing to do a man hug, back slap. Ollie's official title was the Duke of Buckingham, but for as long as I could remember, I'd called him Bucks – everyone at school had. "Right." I moved back and then around to Lucy who'd stood from the table and was looking between us with wide eyes. "Don't paw her like the last time, you bastard."

Ollie laughed and did pull Lucy into a brief hug, making me grind my teeth, but he didn't push his luck as far as before.

"Hey, freckles," Ollie said in a smooth tone, and I rolled my eyes. He'd always had a crazily powerful effect on women. In addition to the whole duke thing, there was the fact that even I could admit he was objectively good-looking, and he had this innate charm that seemed to impress the opposite sex. He was well aware of it too, the cheeky sod. I wasn't having him use his knicker-melting abilities on Lucy.

Lucy blinked up at him after he released her and then did something that made amusement chase away my jealousy. Holding the sides of her denim skirt and sinking so low that I thought, given her clumsiness, she would topple over, she performed some sort of weird curtsy. Ollie's shoulders started shaking, and I had to hold back my own burst of laughter.

"Your Honour," she said reverently, which was when I lost the battle with my amusement as I steadied her and pulled her into my side to laugh into her hair.

"Baby, you don't have to curtsy to him."

Lucy abruptly straightened, her face bright red as she scowled at me.

"You could have told me that before," she whispered furiously. "Ollie's a duke now, for God's sake. What am I *supposed* to do?" Ollie moved forward, having suppressed his own laughter but still with humour dancing in his eyes. He placed his hand on Lucy's arm to get her attention, and I stiffened.

"It's actually *Your Grace*," he told her, and her mouth dropped open before he let out another laugh. "Joking! Please call me Ollie still."

Lucy managed a small smile for him. "Right, okay, Ollie. If you're sure I won't get locked up in the Tower of London for insubordination." Her expression softened. "I'm sorry about your dad, by the way." Ollie only inherited the title after his dad died of a heart attack five years ago. His eyes warmed as he looked down at her.

"Thanks," he said softly, reaching up to give her arm a small squeeze. "But no more curtseying or Your Graces. I'm only thirty-fifth in line to the throne, you know. I'm not sure anyone cares what you call me. And even my cousins don't expect curtsying."

"Right, your cousins. *Right*," Lucy breathed, a fair amount of awe in her tone. We all knew who Ollie's cousins were. The whole world knew that. He still had his bloody hand on her arm. I moved her back with me so that he was forced to break contact. Ollie tucked his hands back into his pockets and tilted his head to the side, looking at us with curiosity. I didn't blame him. I'd never been a very territorial guy in the past.

"Hello," Vicky's voice cut through the tension, and we all turned to her. She looked between the three of us, and her eyebrows went up. "Lucy. You're here."

"Er, hi," Lucy replied with a small wave.

"Felix has his arm around you," Vicky put in, and I cleared my throat. This seemed to be Vicky's talent – uncomfortable observations. "Are you sleeping together?"

"Vicky," Lottie made it over to us then, slightly out of breath. "Remember, we talked about questions that are okay."

Vicky turned to Lottie. "But you want to know this too, correct? As far as we knew Felix was *not* sleeping with Lucy. But he's here, and he has an arm around her. Why can't I be direct?"

"Lucy's embarrassed, hun," Lottie said softly, touching Vicky's wrist briefly. Vicky looked at me.

"Oh," she said.

"You ask whatever questions you want to, Vics," Ollie said in an irritated tone. He'd stepped next to Vicky and she looked up at him. When they made eye contact, he hesitated until Vicky gave a small, almost imperceptible nod, then he hugged her. It was brief, but it was more affection than I'd seen Vicky accept in the past from anyone else. When he moved back, he gave Lottie a filthy look. "Don't tell her what to do, Forest."

Ollie's hatred of Lottie was getting old now. The problem was that originally Lottie had worked for Ollie, not as his personal assistant... as his cleaner. And back then, he certainly hadn't hated her, not by a long shot. I never got to the bottom of it, but one minute Ollie had been complaining about having a crush on his cleaner, then next he'd fired her, hated her guts. He was furious when Vicky, who'd met Lottie when she was working for Ollie, hired her after he fired her.

In my opinion, Ollie could be a stubborn bastard and would never have considered that maybe he'd got this one wrong. He certainly wasn't going to stop me having Lottie as part of my company. She worked brilliantly with Vics, and her ability to read the room was almost supernatural and great in difficult negotiations. Ollie was just jealous.

He told me he had good reason not to trust her, but she'd been a permanent fixture in Vicky's life for months. She was her personal assistant in name, but in reality her role was much more involved. Everywhere Vicky went, Lottie wasn't far behind.

Ollie insisted that Vicky was vulnerable and that Lottie was on the make. Apparently, he had evidence to that effect, but Vicky wouldn't hear a word against Lottie. Ollie was used to getting what he wanted, so he found the whole situation very frustrating. His solution was to be an unrelenting prick to Lottie, hoping to make her go away. But Lottie wasn't so easy to break. She took a grey rock approach with him: not reacting to any of his insults or barbs, pretending they didn't affect her.

It was only if you observed her very carefully that you could see the small flinches, often just a slight tightening around her eyes or a brief despondent look when he was in full prick mode. I'd told him on a few occasions to lay off, but he just maintained that she was a scheming user.

True to form, Lottie acted as if Ollie hadn't spoken, turning to me and Lucy instead.

"I knew that jumper would suit you," Lottie said as she hugged Lucy. "You look like a fierce, wool-wearing badass."

Lucy laughed. "I'm not sure how many badasses wear fleece-lined tights."

"So, am I allowed to ask if Lucy is your girlfriend?" Vicky asked. She was staring at me now. I heard Lottie sigh and saw Lucy stiffen as she released Lottie from the hug. Immediately, I grabbed Lucy's hand and pulled her to my side.

"Yes, Vicky," I said with conviction. "Lucy is my girlfriend."

"I am?" Lucy squeaked, and I frowned down at her.

"Of course you are." Then it was like the others didn't even exist for her anymore. She looked up at me with a soft look. A slow smile spread across her face, her eyes shining with happiness.

"Awesome," she breathed. No artifice, no game playing, no hiding how absolutely into me she was. I couldn't help it, I had to kiss her. Lucy tensed in my arms when Ollie cleared his throat, bringing her back to reality.

"Does Mike know about this?" Ollie asked, a hint of accusation in his tone. We all knew the rule: no messing about with little sisters. My throat felt tight as I imagined Mike's face when I told him.

"Not yet," I said. "But he will, alright? I'll sort it."

Ollie whistled. "He's going to *lose his shit*. Please, let me have a front-row seat to that nightmare."

"Mike's not my keeper," Lucy put in. "And *I'll* tell him. He's *my* brother."

"I'll come to your funeral, mate," Ollie said to me, and Lucy growled in frustration.

"Well then," Vicky cut in. "At least we've established what's going on." Lucy tore her gaze from mine to look at Vicky. "I'm sorry, Lucy," Vicky explained. "But I'm much better with social interactions if all the dynamics are made super clear at the start."

"Vicky's not good with grey areas. It's just that..." Lottie broke off midsentence when Ollie made an annoyed noise at the back of his throat. She slid him a nervous look, then forced a smile. "Shall we sit?"

"I can't sit here," Vicky snapped, glancing at the table.

"I know, hun," Lottie muttered. "We'll sit in a booth, all right?"

Vicky nodded and her shoulders relaxed. In all my time knowing Vicky, I'd never eaten with her. She always arrived after a meal. I'd asked Ollie about it and he said that it was just "one of her things". Personally I thought it went deeper than that, but that family had always been secretive around Vicky's difficulties, so playing down her quirks around food was not unexpected.

Once we were settled in the booth, and despite the frosty atmosphere between Lottie and Ollie, surprisingly the conversation flowed. I'd assumed that adult Lucy would be even more shy than the Lucy I'd known as a child, but it was clear that in the right environment she was anything but shy. In fact, in a small group in this relaxed pub atmosphere, she was very animated. I'd forgotten how naturally curious she was. How many questions she'd ask. How she'd really *listen* to your answers, as if what you were telling her was fascinating. She was a daydreamer at work, but it was clear that when it came to other people her concentration could be laser-focused.

We didn't even get onto the Hyde Park development until two hours had gone by. By then we'd already talked extensively about horses, something Ollie and Vicky shared a passion for, boarding school, what it was like to be a duke. It was actually Lottie who held herself back from the conversation the most, not Lucy.

Lottie, I'd noticed, was very adept at deflecting personal questions. I had no idea where she was from, or who her family were. But somehow Lucy managed to get out of her the fact that she had actually worked for Ollie before Vicky. I was surprised as normally neither of them *ever* mentioned that connection.

"Oh, wow," Lucy said. "I had no idea you worked for the Buckingham Estate before. Did you ever go to Little Buckingham?"

"I only worked at the London house," Lottie said in a small voice as she shifted on her chair, clearly uncomfortable.

"Less said about that the better," muttered Ollie into his beer and Lottie's face reddened as she shrank further into her seat. "And now you're a personal assistant to one of the leading financial brokers in London. Cleaner to executive. Perfectly logical transition."

"Lottie's very good at what she does, Ollie," Vicky said, frowning at her half-brother. Often Vicky didn't seem to notice Ollie's digs at Lottie, as they were too subtle for her literal brain to catch, but this one didn't seem to go over her head.

"*Right*," Ollie drew out the word. That was when Lottie stood up from the booth.

"I think I'd better leave," she muttered, avoiding eye contact with Ollie and turning to Vicky. "I'll see you tomorrow."

"But—" Vicky started, and Lottie leaned down towards her. "Ollie's here, hun," she said softly. "You'll be good with him. You know that." Vicky looked panicked for a moment, then glanced at Ollie, who was frowning at them both.

"Of course, I'll sort you out, Vics," he said. "Let the girl go home."

Just *the girl*, not Lottie. I kicked him under the table, but he just shrugged at me. Lottie said a brief goodbye and made her escape.

"Okay, arsehole. Now that you've successfully acted like a prick, not for the first time. How about we talk about the Hyde Park development?"

Ollie was watching Lottie's retreating back with a frown on his face. "What the fuck kind of coat does she think she's wearing for this weather?" he muttered, completely ignoring me. I looked over my shoulder to see Lottie shrugging on an, admittedly thin, denim jacket. When I looked back at Ollie he was still frowning.

"Er, why the hell do you give a fuck?" I asked in surprise. "Given how much you dislike her, I'd have thought you'd be glad of the chance for her to freeze to death."

Ollie barely acknowledged me. Instead, without a word of explanation, he shoved his chair back and strode after Lottie.

We all watched as he blocked her way to the exit, causing her to run into him and nearly fall. His hands shot out to steady her before she could land on her arse but once she was upright he released her as if she'd burned him. They exchanged a few words then she dodged around him out of the double doors and we lost sight of them both when he stormed after her.

"What is his problem?" Lucy muttered.

"My half-brother is totally illogical when it comes to Lottie," Vicky told us. "I've given up trying to reason with him."

After a couple of minutes Ollie was back, looking windswept and pissed off.

"Vics, make sure she wears a proper bloody coat," he said as he took his place back at the table. "She must be able to afford one on the salary you're paying her."

Vicky shrugged. "I don't police what other people wear. That would be weird. You're being weird. Stop being horrid to Lottie. I *need* her."

Ollie sighed. "You don't *need* her, Vics. I just—"

"Anyway, Felix's right," she said, cutting him off. "We need to talk about Hyde Park and there's another opportunity that's just come up from the Framlingham Estate."

Ollie sighed and rubbed his hand down his face. He glanced at Lucy. "Luce, we can trust you, right? This is all confidential stuff, not to go any further."

Lucy sat up straight in her chair, and I could feel her discomfort coming off her in waves. She put her hands on the table and went to stand. "Oh, don't worry, guys," she said, flustered, which pissed me off. I wanted relaxed, chatty Lucy back. "I'd better get going anyway. If you need to talk super-secret, businessy stuff, I'll just be in the way."

"You're not going anywhere," I said in a firm tone, my hand on her leg pushing her to sit down. "I trust Lucy completely. And she's not exactly corporate spy material."

Ollie gave me a look, and I frowned at him. He knew what had gone on five years ago. I hadn't really trusted anybody since then. That I was willing to trust Lucy now was a huge step – Ollie understood that.

Lucy let out a shocked laugh. "Corporate spy!" She laughed again. "Sorry, Ollie, but the idea of me even understanding enough of what you might talk about to use it as a corporate spy is funny. But seriously, I can just grab an Uber and—"

"No, it's fine," Ollie said with a smile at Lucy. "I'm sorry, but I just wanted you to know that this is really sensitive stuff. Don't go. Felix'll be grumpy if you take off and we won't get anywhere. I'll try to keep it brief so you're not too bored."

"Okay," Lucy agreed. "If I can have another cider. Ooh and a chocolate pudding."

So, Lucy drank her cider and ate her pudding whilst the three of us hashed out the details of Ollie's investment in Hyde Park, then laid out the Framlingham Estate plan. I kept my hand on Lucy's thigh, rubbing small circles on her tights. About ten minutes after she finished her pudding, I felt her lean a little more heavily into my side, her body relaxing. When I looked down at her, she was fast asleep. I leaned back onto the wall in the corner of the booth and put my arm around her so that she could snuggle into my chest more comfortably and held her to me. I couldn't really blame her for being tired. I hadn't let her sleep much last night. Ollie looked between us and raised an eyebrow.

"She's not that into finance and property development then?" he observed.

I laughed quietly. "Good for her. Finance is bloody boring, and we're all boring bastards."

"What *is* she into?" asked Vicky.

I blinked at her, opened my mouth to reply and then snapped it shut when I realised I had no idea, not anymore.

CHAPTER 20

Dog-eat-dog

Lucy

"Where have you been?" Felix demanded in a low, furious voice as he took me by the elbow and led me into his office, shutting the door behind us. "Will's been looking for you. There's been nobody answering his phone for the last hour. Clients have been calling, Luce. You can't just swan off any time you want in the day just because we're together now."

I flinched as if he slapped me and took a step back. He dropped my elbow and then crossed his arms over his chest as he watched me. We were alone in his office, and the atmosphere was thick with his anger.

This Felix wasn't *my* Felix. This Felix was Ruthless Business Bastard Felix. It wasn't the Felix who made me laugh, who fussed over my temperature regulation, who cuddled me in bed and watched *The Lord of the Rings* with me. And it certainly wasn't the Felix I'd known twenty years ago – the one who had found me and looked after me after we lost Dad. That was *my* Felix. If I was honest, Ruthless Business Bastard Felix reminded me a little of his father, which I knew *my* Felix would hate more than anything.

"I thought Will was managing his phone for a bit," I said. "And I was with Vanessa because—"

"There's *no* reason for you to be with Vanessa," he snapped, his hand slashed between us through the air. "You are *not* Vanessa's assistant. Listen, I know you don't like Will that much. Believe me, I'm not his biggest fan either. But at least he gets on with the job in hand, and he deserves an assistant who's at least present."

My throat started burning, and I felt a stinging at the back of my eyes, but I managed to push back the tears – I wouldn't give Felix the satisfaction. He hadn't even asked what I was doing with Vanessa. Just like he didn't ask about my stories. He probably just assumed all the maps and spider diagrams I created and the words I typed on my laptop were just a hobby. To him I was just a directionless waste of space.

And to think I'd actually started feeling guilty about keeping so much from him. I'd promised myself that if he asked me a direct question, I would explain everything. But sadly, the questions never came. We'd been together for two weeks now, and I'd spent nearly every night at his place.

I sighed and crossed my arms as well. I should really tell Felix where to go. If I had any self-respect I would call him out on being such a prick. Unfortunately, when it came to Felix, my self-respect was sadly lacking. He just made me so happy. I felt like I'd die if I couldn't be with him. In fact, even the distance between us now, standing separated by a few feet was making my stomach hurt. This was why I hadn't quit my job yet. Even before we were together, I had thought that any time I spent with him in any capacity was a bonus.

And now my dreams had come true and we were together, I had no idea how long it would be until he got bored of me. I was going to make the most of my remaining time in London with him. He was like a drug. But this was unhealthy. Being around him at work was not a good idea. I needed to confirm my notice period with HR today. No more slimy Will. No more stuck-up finance people.

I'd still see Lottie and Vicky of course. Over the last couple of weeks we'd regularly been going for lunch and coffee. They'd sort of adopted me. Vicky was so salty and literal that she ended up being hilarious most of the time. And Lottie was one of the most positive people I'd ever met (just as long as the Duke of Fuckingham, as she called him, wasn't around – Ollie was about the only person I'd ever seen effectively dampen her mood).

It was easier for us to meet up in the daytime as Lottie had custody of her eight-year-old sister, Hayley – a carbon copy of Lottie, with caramel curls and big brown eyes. So the few times we met up in the evening we'd either hung out at her flat (although it was tiny and her neighbourhood was a little scary) or mine or Vicky's, so that Hayley could be there too. So no bars or horrid business parties.

Like me, Hayley wasn't big on crowds. Before Lottie took custody of her, Hayley had been through some traumatic stuff with her alcoholic mum which had left her selectively mute – she only spoke to Lottie. But she was a cute kid and could get her point across without words, most of the time anyway. She seemed to have an affinity with Vicky which made sense given Vicky hadn't spoken either for many years as a child. It made me wonder about Vicky. I was aware of Hayley's trauma that led to her mutism, but what had been Vicky's? But any even vague reference to her childhood or biological family was always shut down quickly by Vicky so I never got to the bottom of it. Hanging out with them was fun, and they weren't into fizzy wine or weird small food either.

Finally I had friends in London. Mum was so proud. I hadn't told her or Mike about Felix yet. At first, it was because I knew Mum would get ridiculously excited, and I didn't want to then disappoint her when it came to nothing. Also, the last thing I wanted was to affect Felix's relationship with my mum or Mike – I knew they meant such a lot to him.

But now, I was keeping quiet about our relationship at Felix's insistence. He was adamant that we shouldn't tell my family, and looked a little pale if I even mentioned it to be honest.

When I'd casually brought up the possibility of a trip back to Little Buckingham, he'd reacted with a firm, "No fucking way". I knew he hated going back there for some reason, which he wasn't willing to share with me. But my family was in Little Buckingham, and I missed them. I wanted to share my news about Felix with them; I wanted us all to sit around Mum's kitchen table together.

It was almost as though he was ashamed of me. Or maybe he was worried that telling Mum and Mikey would make things too official? But then he didn't seem too bothered about making everything official elsewhere – he'd informed HR at work straight away. So the office was aware, but he still remained strictly formal with me here. There had been a fair bit of eye-rolling and muttering behind my back, especially from Will, but I was willing to suck it up if it meant being with Felix.

"Right, okay, I'll get back to my desk," I said in a small voice. Felix sighed and rubbed his hands down his face.

"I'm sorry," he said. "I don't mean to snap at you, but there was a really important client that couldn't get through because you weren't there. I might be able to salvage the deal if I work on it with Will, but it's a bit of a shitshow."

There was no point telling Felix that Will *told* me to go down to the publicity department as he knew I could do that part of his job way better than he was able to, considering that he didn't have a creative bone in his body to help with the ad copy. That it was Will being rubbish that meant the call was missed. That, in addition to him being rubbish, he kept touching my hair, brushing my shoulder, and caging me in. Unless I had something concrete to complain about, I would just look weird and like I was trying to make excuses for being a crap employee. I *was* a crap employee, I freely admitted that. That's why I was *going* to quit once I grew some ladyballs.

But despite my crapness, I did think I'd managed to help Vanessa out over the last few weeks, so at least my contribution here wasn't *all* negative. But that wasn't enough to make me stay. Plus my agent had rung this morning – I had a lot of shit going on over the next month. I needed to keep up with my deadlines. In fact, I had to meet her this afternoon which was going to look even worse.

"I'm sorry," I said, just wanting to get this over with and be back to smiling Felix who would have taken me into his arms by now in other circumstances. His expression softened.

"Just try a little harder, Luce. Be a bit more on the ball. I can't have people thinking I'm letting you off the hook because you're my girlfriend. Or that I'm letting myself get distracted. I've already taken too much time off recently."

I resisted the urge to roll my eyes. Time off? Felix was home late every night and still worked on weekends. And I could hear the resentment in his tone. Clearly he wasn't happy with this particular distraction. It hurt my feelings but, like a lot of things recently, I swallowed it down and didn't rock the boat.

Just like his birthday last week when I made the mistake of making a lopsided cake and bringing it into the office. I *may* have been just a bit too overexcited to give it to him and I *may* have barged into his office, interrupting a delicate meeting with potential investors. His face had been like thunder. He'd made me promise *never* to come into his office without express permission from then on.

I wasn't making that mistake again. So, instead of arguing with him now I just nodded and turned to leave. He caught my hand, pulling me towards him until I was only inches away from his heat. I looked up at him and his expression softened.

"I'm only trying to help you, Luce. For your own good. It's dog-eat-dog out there. You've got to sharpen up."

I tilted my head to the side, feeling an ache in my chest for this man who had such a cynical worldview. Who hated the fact something had distracted him from his work. He sounded like his father again. He'd be horrified at the thought, but it was true. I gave him a smile and laid my hand on his chest, leaning into him as he took a deep breath in.

"It doesn't have to be that way, Felix," I said softly. "Not everything has to be dog-eat-dog stressful. We don't have to be tough all the time."

It wasn't the first time I'd tried to gently address Felix's ultra-stressed-out lifestyle. I personally didn't think it was healthy, but it was clear he was not open to any suggestion that there might be an alternative way. He was surprised about how depressing I found the office, about how I didn't think the atmosphere of fear here was productive.

"There's not even natural light for the rest of the lower mortals, Felix," I'd told him yesterday whilst drawing small circles on his chest in bed. "Couldn't you try to brighten the place up a bit? Maybe chuck in a few beanbags and a nice communal, bright space?"

He'd just sighed and told me that I "didn't know the first thing about running a successful financial institution", that "his employees thrived on fear" and "didn't need any poxy beanbags to get the job done".

I mean he was right: I'd never run a company like his, but I knew human beings, and they *did not* run well on fear. And I knew that the best ideas I ever had came along when I was "doolally" as Mum would say. There was value in daydreaming sometimes.

Felix shook his head and closed his eyes briefly before focusing back on me.

"What am I going to do with you?" he muttered before his gaze dropped to my mouth. Then he kissed me, softly first until my mouth opened under his. He groaned, pushing me back against his door, one of his arms slipping under my thighs to lift me up against him as my legs wrapped around his back, his other hand spreading across my back to hold my body to his. He froze as he was kissing down my neck. It took me a few moments to realise that someone was buzzing the intercom.

"Shit," he snapped, letting me drop down to the floor so suddenly I was lucky I didn't end up in a crumpled heap, and then stepped back rapidly.

I shivered in the sudden absence of his heat as I pulled my skirt back down over my fleece-lined tights.

"Look, just get back to work, Lucy," he clipped, smoothing down his tie and tucking his shirt back into his trousers. "I can't afford all this distraction the whole time. And do your bloody job."

He was frowning as he answered the intercom, clearly even more angry with himself than with me. Felix had never been very good at accepting that he was human. Kissing in the middle of the workday, being distracted by me – he viewed that as weakness, and it had been instilled in Felix long ago that you never showed weakness.

I could remember one of the only times I'd been in the same room as Felix's dad, and how terrifying the man was, his face red as he screamed at Felix for being *spineless* and *weak*. The worst thing had been how Felix had just taken it. No crying, very little outward reaction to his father's awful, shouted words. A shiver went up my spine at the memory.

I slipped out of the office so that Felix couldn't see any tears forming in my eyes. I'd talk to him later, I decided. I'd tell him then that there was something off about Will, that Will made me uncomfortable, that I was quitting the job. I'd explain about my work with Vanessa. And I'd drop the bomb that I never really *needed* the job in the first place. Now that would be a fairly embarrassing conversation as it would eventually lead to why on earth I would take a job I didn't need. I'd have to admit that it wasn't just to get out of Little Buckingham and help me overcome my reclusive tendencies.

Because really, buried deep in the back of my mind, I knew it was so I could be near Felix. I mean it had worked out great now, hadn't it? Surely he wouldn't be that angry?

"Were you fucking him in there?" Will's voice brought me up short as I walked away from Felix's office. His large body was blocking the corridor and he looked absolutely furious. "Is that how you always weasel out of him firing you?"

"Get out of my way, Mr Brent," I said, straightening my spine. I tried to sound firm, but my voice was shaking. "L–l–leave me alone, or I'll tell Felix."

It was lame. I should have been able to tell him what he well knew – that I'd done nothing to be fired for. That *Will* messed up, not me. And that he should do his bloody job.

Of course, I didn't say any of that. Instead, I dodged around him and hurried back to my desk. But I could hear his heavy footsteps behind me. When we were outside his office, he grabbed my wrist and squeezed. I made a small sound of distress, which only seemed to make him grip me harder.

"As if he'll care," he sneered. "Now, are you actually threatening me?" He gave my wrist a firm shake that had me stumbling to the side before he yanked me back up. I looked up and down the corridor frantically, but it was deserted. Tabitha must be in Felix's office with him. "You'll regret this."

"Let go of me," I said, trying to sound strong and annoyed by how shaky my voice came out. But nobody had ever grabbed me in anger and I was terrified.

After a long moment he released me and I skittered back, cradling my wrist.

He rolled his eyes. "Bloody hell, you're so dramatic. I barely touched you."

"S–stay away from me," I stammered. "I don't even know why you're complaining. I've been doing your job with the publicity department."

His eyes flashed with pure fury at that comment as he took a threatening step towards me and I flinched back.

"Watch it, Hop-a-long." His voice was softer now but somehow almost more menacing. "I could finish you at this company and with your precious Felix."

With that he turned away from me and stormed off towards the conference room.

I stood there for a moment, rubbing my wrist and trying to calm my breathing. There would be no two weeks' notice. I wasn't spending one more second working with that psycho.

I grabbed my coat, swiped all my nick-nacks from my desk into my bag, along with all the mountains of stationery I kept scattered about for emergencies, and I booked it out of the building. What I didn't do, unfortunately, was remember to take my notebook from the top drawer.

CHAPTER 21

You have a deal

Lucy

"Jesus, you look awful." Madeline was not known for her tact.

"Thanks, Mads," I said as I took the seat opposite her at the café she'd asked me to meet her in. I loved the place. There were bookshelves everywhere, but also lovely wide alcoves with huge windows – we were in one of them now so that we had the bookshelves behind us and a great view of the street to the side. Madeline poured my tea just how I liked it, and I forced a smile for her. "It's been a rough day, actually."

My throat closed over. Coming here was a mistake. I was still so shaken up by what just happened with Will. I should have gone straight to HR to report him. To be honest, I should have gone to the police. I rubbed my wrist which was still throbbing, and I felt tears sting my eyes again.

"Oh darling," she said in a soft voice, stretching across the table to lay her hand over mine. "What's happened? Has that hunky posh boy broken your heart?"

Madeline knew all about Felix. She'd known about him for a while, even before I'd come to London. I'd made the mistake of telling her who the fae prince was based on once, and she'd been too curious not to over-Google the poor man.

When I moved to London and started working for Felix, Madeline had been annoyed. I did have deadlines after all. But she'd accepted that I needed to be in the real world for a little while to force me out of my shell, and agreed that it would help my writing. Even if my books were based in a world I'd created entirely in my head, they were very character-driven, and I still took inspiration from the people and situations around me. She was also hopeful that it might lead to me being able to tackle public events. But when I got together with Felix, she'd been worried.

"Men like that," she'd warned me, "they're a lot to handle. And you've liked him for such a long time, Luce. Don't get too invested."

But Mads didn't know Felix. She didn't know how he held me, how funny he was, how he made me feel beautiful, how kind he was, how thoughtful. Everyone at the office was drinking iced lattes and fanning themselves all day as Felix still refused to lower the temperature below twenty-five degrees, but all he cared about was whether I was comfortable.

"It's nothing to do with Felix." I took a deep breath and let it out in a shaky exhale. "That guy I work for, Will. He... well he was angry and he grabbed me."

She gasped when I showed her the red marks on my wrist.

"Oh my God, Luce," Madeline said in horror. "Have you called the police?"

"The police?" I frowned at her. "I, er... isn't that going a bit far?"

Madeline's eyebrows went up. "He *assaulted* you, Lucy. No, it is not going too far. At least tell me you've been to HR and reported him there."

I bit my lip, and she growled in frustration. "Right, straight after this you're going back to that shithole and going directly to HR. Then you're going to tell loverboy that his employees are abusive arseholes. Understand me?"

"Okay, okay," I said, putting my hands up in surrender.

"I can come with you if you want," she offered, her voice softer now.

I was tempted to say yes but I shook my head instead. I had to start standing up for myself. "Thanks, hun but I'll manage. Look, let's go over the plans for next month."

She gave me a close look, patted my hand once then pulled back to get some contracts out of her bag. "Right, well, this is the paperwork for the translations. I've renegotiated the Italian deal. They were lowballing us – it was insulting."

My eyes went wide at the figure on the front of the contract from the Italian publisher. "I'm not sure what your idea of *lowballing* is, but if this is my advance then you might want to readjust it."

She smiled. "I told you I renegotiated. This offer is still insulting if you ask me, but I couldn't push them up anymore, and we need to get you into Italy asap."

"Jesus, Mads. You're a proper hard-arse. Where do I sign?"

After we'd gone through the contracts and I'd signed nearly everything, Madeline caught someone's eye over my shoulder and waved, standing up from the table. I frowned in confusion and turned in my chair to follow the direction of her gaze. Harry York was striding across the coffee shop towards us.

"Mr York," Madeline said as he approached. As they shook hands, I was still blinking up at him in shock. "Luce?" Mads prompted, and I jumped out of my chair.

"Miss Mayweather," Harry said in a friendly tone. "It's such an honour to meet you again. I recognised you in the meeting room at Moretti Harding, but it seemed like you weren't that keen on me saying anything. You may not remember but—"

"No, yes, of course I remember," I spluttered out, feeling self-conscious. "I'm so sorry that I ran out of that restaurant. I was a terrible coward that day."

"No, don't apologise," Harry said. "Madeline explained that you found it all a bit overwhelming. I should have started with something less formal. Believe me, I have firsthand experience of what it's like to be shy. You should have met me as a teenager. Please don't be embarrassed. It was very kind of you to send those signed books."

Maddie moved to sit down then and indicated that we should do the same. Harry demurred, saying he'd go and order and could he get us anything.

"What's he doing here?" I whispered to Maddie once he was out of earshot.

"Oh, he contacted me again a few weeks ago after he saw you in that meeting. He wants to see if you'd be open to arranging that book signing now you've breached the boundaries of Little Buckingham. But he was also asking about film rights again. If and when we get a deal on the table, he wants to be a private investor."

"He does?" I felt a blush spread up my cheeks. It was still unbelievable to me that I had such die-hard fans like Harry York. My books were huge epic fantasies. They were all about world-building and complicated storylines woven together, dealing with difficult topics: death, love and loss. There were even some laughs in there. But they weren't set in the real world. There were fairies and elves and lots of supernatural abilities. Of course, I thought my books were good, I just didn't consider them serious enough to catch the attention of the likes of Harry York. "Wow, that's... wow."

"What's wow?" Harry said as he approached our table again, carrying a tray with his americano and my tea with a muffin.

"I was just telling Lucy about your interest in investing in film, and the signing event you'd like her to do."

Harry's face lit up as he sat down. "Oh yeah, I'd love to be the one to reveal LP Mayweather to the world. We'd clear the auditorium for it at the LSE building and provide security for the queue." Security? He thought my queue would need security? "And I'd love to be involved in investing in future film projects, if you decide to go down that road."

"Mr York—" I started.

"Harry, please," he said, and I gave him a smile and a quick nod.

"Harry. Considering how much of an abject coward I was the last time we were supposed to meet, it's very kind of you to think I'd be able to manage a book signing." I cleared my throat and looked down at my tea. "I'm afraid I can be a terrible wussbag about these things. I grew up in a small village and I..." I sighed. "Like you said before, I can get a bit overwhelmed."

"Lucy," Harry said softly and I forced myself to look up at him. "You don't have to be embarrassed. I wasn't lying when I told you how shy I was before – I nearly lost my chance with my wife Verity due to *my* wussbag tendencies. I did lose her for almost twenty years, but that's another story. And I promise not to go overboard, it would just be for a couple of hours. The fee would be generous. Also, afterwards..."

He looked down at his coffee for a moment then back up at me with a new intensity in his expression.

"I run a programme at the LSE. It's a youth project. The area around that part of London has a gang problem, and the schools are rife with bullying. My project provides a safe space for teenagers. We mentor them, provide tutoring if it's needed, try to help them choose their next steps after school and support them through interview processes. They're a great bunch of kids, and well..." He took a deep breath in and out before continuing. "Well, I tend to bang on about your books to the kids, and you've developed a bit of a following. There are some aspiring authors among them who I hoped you might agree to meet with and give them some inspiration? That'd be after the signing, though. So I completely understand if you don't want to give up that much of your time. I don't—"

"I'll do it," I interrupted him, and his shoulders relaxed, his mouth breaking into a wide smile. "No fee." His smile dropped.

"Lucy, believe me, I can afford it." He paused for a moment. "Listen, I was surprised that you had a day job. It's part of the reason I contacted your agent. I want to help you. Give you a bit of a financial boost and maybe a bit of extra promotion."

"Harry," I said through a smile of my own. "My reasons for working at Moretti Harding are complicated. I assure you I don't need a fee for getting free publicity and then helping aspiring authors. If you insist on a fee, then work it out with Maddie. She can take her fifteen percent and I'll ask her to donate the rest directly back into your project."

He was smiling again at that. "Well, great. You have a deal."

Maddie grinned at me. "I knew you'd go for it. See what a great agent I am?"

"The greatest."

"Are you serious about investing... in a film project?" my voice had lowered to a whisper now, as if voicing my biggest dream out loud would make it disappear into smoke.

Harry's eyebrows shot up. "Of course I am."

I looked to the side. "You must really want to see the books on the screen."

He frowned. "Er... yes, I'll admit, just like most LP Mayweather fans, I'm impatient for it to be made into a film. But, Lucy, I may be a super fan, but I'm also a shark. I wouldn't be offering to invest if I didn't think I'd make a shit-ton of money out of it for myself."

I grinned at him. "Really?"

"Really." Harry was looking over at the other side of the coffee shop now and giving a thumbs up. I followed the direction of his gaze and saw his beautiful, dark-haired, very pregnant wife sitting by herself with her eyes glued to Harry and a huge grin on her face. Her gaze flicked to me, and she bit her lip. I gave her a small wave and a smile. She gave me an enthusiastic one back.

"Sorry," Harry said. "Verity's a huge fan as well. She insisted on coming."

"Why's she sitting all the way over there?"

"We didn't want to overwhelm you. She thought it was better that I talked to you about the business stuff first, and then if you were keen, then maybe you wouldn't mind chatting to her as well."

"Oh my God. Get her over here."

Verity York clambered to her feet when I waved to her to come over. She was so lovely and enthusiastic about all things LP Mayweather. Once I'd assured them both that I didn't mind discussing the books at all, that it was fun for me, they really let themselves go. After an hour Madeline had to excuse herself for another appointment but the Yorks were still going strong.

"And the audiobooks are awesome," Verity raved. "You're getting me through the last stages of this endless pregnancy with stupid enforced rest."

"It's not stupid, Verity," Harry growled and Verity rolled her eyes.

"Honestly, your books are keeping me sane," she told me.

"Now, about that map which you've put at the end of book five in the Ransomed Kingdom series," Harry cut in, leaning forward in his chair and using his hands to emphasise his point as he questioned me on the geography of the world I'd created.

To be honest, after a while it felt like the Yorks knew more about my own fantasy world than me. When we finally parted ways, I hugged them both. Verity asked if I'd consider coming over some time, offering reassurances that they would try not to spend the whole time talking about my books.

"I'll ask some normal people," she told me then shook her head in a sharp jerk. "Shit, not that your readers aren't normal people. It's just we're well aware that our fandom is a little... extreme."

I smiled at her. "I love your fandom. I can't tell you how flattered I am. And I really love that I had a hand in getting you together."

They'd told me about their courting phase, when a shared love of epic fantasy books helped their romance along the way. They were *such* a cute couple.

So by the time I left the coffee shop I felt that, after a shitty start, the day had been salvaged. I was in such a good mood, and my confidence had been bolstered so much that I was actually looking forward to going into the office tomorrow and sorting everything out with Felix. Letting HR know about Will. Standing up for myself.

I should have known it wouldn't be that easy.

CHAPTER 22

Broke my trust

Lucy

Felix didn't ring or text me that night. It was the first time we hadn't seen each other in the evening since we got together, and I felt a bit weird about it. But I didn't want to be the clingy girlfriend who couldn't go one night without her man.

We'd only been together for a couple of weeks. I shouldn't be at the stage when I couldn't sleep properly when he wasn't in my bed. That would make me a bit of a desperate case, and the last thing I wanted to do was scare Felix off. He'd had a few stalkery-type situations in the past – I knew that one woman was permanently banned from his building by the doorman after she let herself into his penthouse unannounced when he'd broken up with her. He wouldn't tell me her name, but I got the impression she was a minor celebrity.

Maybe the gloriousness of Felix could turn me into an obsessed weirdo that hung around his building too. The thought was terrifying, but to be honest, I was so in love with him at this stage that I couldn't guarantee my dignity staying intact if he dumped me either.

So the next day when I went into the office, I did it in my smarter stuff – silk shirt and everything. It wasn't the warmest, but I decided that I could sacrifice a bit of warmth to make a good impression for one last time. I strode in there with purpose, leaving my huge puffa at reception so I wouldn't be tempted to sneak it on halfway through the morning, as was my wont. Adrenaline was keeping the blood pumping to my fingers anyway. This was my last day, and I was going to make the most of it.

I started with HR and went directly down there to report Will. Martha, the head of the department, was the one to speak to me after one of her assistants realised what a big deal this was going to be. I could see Martha becoming steadily more and more incensed as I catalogued the ongoing targeted and systematic bullying that I had endured from Will.

When I showed her the bruise on my wrist, her face went red with fury and her voice was thick with restrained anger as she asked if I wanted to report him to the police. I didn't want to go down that road, which disappointed Martha, who was now clearly out for Will's blood.

She told me to go home for the rest of the week, reassuring me that it would all be dealt with officially and that I didn't need to do anything more. I said that I wanted to grab my notebook from my desk and say bye to a few people, but that I'd leave straight after. I knew Will was due to be at a meeting across London all morning, so at least I wouldn't have to run into him.

Unfortunately, when I did make it to my desk, there was a very smug-looking Will sitting behind it. My heart dropped and I felt like I might throw up with fear.

"You're late as per fucking usual," he said with a self-satisfied smile on his stupid face.

"Will," I said in as firm a tone as I could muster. "I've just come to get my things then I'll be leaving. I'm not going to be working for you anymore. Your behaviour has been unacceptable. You should know that I've reported you to HR." There, I said it. I felt unbelievably proud of myself.

Will's face twisted in anger as he pushed up off my desk.

"You little shit," he sneered. "Whingeing about nothing. I've been the best boss to the shittiest employee in the history of shit employees. You should be grateful, not crying wolf to HR."

"I wasn't crying wolf. You—"

"Don't think you can threaten me," he said, taking two long strides towards me. He was in my space so fast I didn't have a chance to retreat further. "I've got some serious shit on you, and now that Felix knows what you've been up to there's no way anyone's going to believe a word that comes out of your mouth."

I frowned at him, my eyes darting to the desk where my notebook was now sitting and then back at his scowling face. I had no idea what he was on about, but I needed my notebook. It had all my outlines in it, and I stupidly hadn't made any copies. I really didn't want to take the chance that Will would destroy it out of spite. He'd clearly been rifling through my stuff. So I took a stupid risk. I darted around him to make a grab for the notebook.

"I've worked too hard to let some cock-tease little shit fuck everything up for me," he said as I rounded him and snatched up the book, holding it to my chest. He lunged at me before I could clear him and grabbed me by the shoulders, giving me a rough shake. "You'll regret making accusations about me. Go back to HR and *take it back*."

I was gripped by real panic, so thick I couldn't think clearly. So instead of screaming like I should have done, I kicked him in the shin in an attempt to get him off me.

"Ow, you bitch!" he spat out, a wild, furious look flashing in his eyes.

Everything from then happened really fast. He threw me back against the wall so hard that I was winded and couldn't scream even if I tried. Pain burst from the side of my head, shoulder and chest. Then he slammed his body against mine, pinning me there. I thought I was going to be sick as his mouth moved to my neck. He licked me over my pulse point before whispering in my ear.

"It doesn't end well for girls like you that get in my way."

Then he let me go and stepped back so suddenly that I had to brace myself to not slide down the wall. I was still wheezing to try to get air into my lungs.

As he slammed the door to his office, there was only one thought in my mind and that was to escape. So I stumbled down the corridor, feeling too shocked to cry even though I could feel my eyes stinging. I made it to Felix's door and lifted my hand to knock on it, but it was yanked open before I could make contact. I let out a huge sigh of relief as I took in Felix in all his glorious, solid handsomeness, holding the door open. But my relief was short-lived.

"Come in, Lucy," he said in a cold tone that caused a shiver to run down my spine. Felix never spoke to me like that. I walked into the office on shaky legs and blinked as I noticed Vicky and Tabitha both standing by Felix's desk facing me. I was still in shock from Will's assault, and my brain was feeling sluggish so I was slow to feel the hostility in the room and notice that Vicky, Tabitha and Felix were all glaring at me.

"Felix," I said in a shaky voice, deciding to ignore the atmosphere and that we weren't alone and get to the point. "Will just—"

"We know all about what's happened with Will," Felix said, cutting me off. I blew out a sigh of relief. Oh, thank God. Somehow, they'd seen what had happened. I wouldn't have to go over it again. Felix would look after me. He'd sort it all out. Everything was going to be fine now. But then, if he knew, why wasn't he coming to me? Why wasn't I in his arms already? My back, shoulder and head were throbbing and I wasn't feeling up to trying to understand what was going on. "He told us *all* about it."

Wait, Will literally *just* assaulted me. He couldn't have confessed already. And to be honest, he didn't seem in a very remorseful mood when he'd thrown me against the wall.

"I don't understand," I said in an unsteady voice.

"How *could you*, Lucy?" Felix snapped, and I blinked in confusion. My head was starting to swim now and I felt shivery with cold and shock. Feeling behind me for the chair, then all but collapsing into it, I winced when pain shot through my shoulder and head.

"W–w–what?"

"How could you betray us like this?"

I did a slow blink, trying to focus on Felix's angry face and make out what he was on about. "I don't know what you mean. Felix, Will just gra—"

"Of course you bloody well know what I mean! I thought there was a weird vibe between you two in that board meeting, but I just put it down to Harry being another sucker who found you attractive. I had no idea that he was paying you off for information."

"Harry York?"

"Don't deny it, Luce," Felix's voice was still tight with fury but also heavy with disappointment. "Will told us everything. He filmed you guys yesterday at that coffee shop."

Felix stepped towards me then, but not to give me the hug that I needed. No, he just loomed over me and shoved his phone in my face. I watched a video of myself, Harry and his wife at the coffee shop. I was sketching a map of the Southern Territory for him in one of my notebooks, and then I ripped out the page and passed it to him. He looked at it reverently for a moment then carefully folded it to put it in his laptop bag. He'd told me he was going to frame it. Why was Felix angry about this? Had he found out I was an author now? I knew he'd be cross when he realised I hadn't corrected him, but it wasn't like I'd ever outright lied.

"Look, I'm sorry I didn't tell you that I—"

"You're *sorry*?" he snapped. "Just a casual sorry? Lucy, you completely broke my trust."

I frowned. "I think that's going a bit far, Felix. I just—"

"You've potentially cost me millions in lost revenue. Cost *us* millions. Hasn't she, Vicky?"

Vicky was looking at me with her head tilted to the side. She no longer had a cold expression on her face. Now, she looked more curious than anything, like she was trying to piece together a puzzle. "Felix, maybe—?"

"Don't make excuses for her," Felix snapped, slashing his hand through the air and making me flinch in my chair.

"I'm not—" Vicky was looking more unsure than I'd ever seen her before now. "I think I need to speak to Lottie, and then—"

"We don't need Lottie here," snapped Felix.

"How on earth could I have cost you millions?" I said, genuine confusion threading through my words. Felix's eyebrows went up in disbelief.

"You've been passing information to Harry York. Information that his clients other than Ollie would be very interested in. It must have been going on for weeks. I wondered why there was another party trying to poach the Hyde Park project. You've been handing him the information straight from the company. Even all the way back when you were at my house party. I just thought it was cute and quirky that you hid away in my library, but that's where the computer was, wasn't it? Those notes you were making on my blotting paper were stolen information from there."

"Why would I give Harry York your company information?"

"For money!" Felix shouted, and I flinched again. "You sold me down the river for *money*. No wonder you can afford a whole flat in Putney. Telling me that bullshit story about low rent. You've been taking a cut from this grubby little deal for weeks and living the high life as a result. I checked with Tabitha. You paid for all those clothes yourself. That's thousands of pounds worth of stuff you were supposed to put on the company credit card. But no, you didn't need to use it, did you? You were already stealing more than enough money for that."

"Felix," my voice had a pathetic pleading quality to it now that made me feel sick to my stomach, but I needed to make him understand. "You've got to listen to me. Will is—"

"Will might be a prick, but he's nothing compared to what a lowlife you are. At least he's looking out for the company."

"No, you don't understand. Felix, he's a total psycho. He—"

"Just get out," Felix snapped.

"I'm not leaving until you hear me out," I tried to make my voice as firm as possible, but it still sounded ridiculously shaky.

Felix didn't bother to respond. He just moved to his desk and pressed the intercom. "Yes, could you come in now, please? Miss Mayweather needs to be escorted to the exit. No stops on the way. We'll send her stuff onto her after we've verified that it doesn't contain any sensitive information."

"Maybe we should listen to her," Tabitha said in a small voice. When I looked over at her, she didn't look hostile anymore. In fact, she looked thoroughly spooked. All the colour had drained from her face and her expression was more worried concern than the cold hatred from before.

"Really, Felix," said Vicky. "I do think we should wait for Lottie."

"I'm not being taken in again!" Felix bellowed as the two security guards that I recognized from downstairs came into the room. Dave and Riley were nice guys. Dave was a single dad and Riley liked to restore old motorbikes. But now here they were, summoned to throw me out of the building. To be fair, they both looked extremely uncomfortable.

"Er, Luce," Dave said, shooting a quick look at a still furious-looking Felix, who just crossed his arms over his broad chest and nodded for them to get on with it.

Riley cleared his throat. "Want to come with us, love?" he asked gently. Too shocked to move, I sat there dumbly for a minute but then flinched when Riley touched my elbow. Oh my God, I was going to be forcibly ejected from the building.

Me, Lucy Mayweather, official goodie-two-shoes and teacher's pet, was practically under arrest.

"Er... don't worry," I said in a small voice. "It's okay, Riley. I can stand up under my own steam." I levered up out of the chair, wincing at the pain in my shoulder again then I thought I'd try one last time. "Felix, if you'd just listen to—"

"I've heard *enough*, Luce," Felix shouted, his face flushed with anger and his hand slicing through the air again. I snapped my mouth shut. Right, well then. I'd had quite enough of arrogant tossers who felt they had the right to be randomly angry with me for one day. I turned and walked away from him. Dave shot forward to open the door for me.

"I'll need to pick up my—"

"You're not picking *anything* up," Felix snapped. "Take her straight outside the building. No stops."

What? I needed my notebook, and my bag was by my desk; it had everything in it. This stupid outfit didn't even have pockets.

"But—"

"*Out!*" The word cracked across the room, and I flinched back as if he'd hit me before spinning around and running out of there.

I slowed to a walk on the way to the lifts. I was in a bit of daze. Dave and Riley shifted awkwardly next to me. When they asked me if I was okay, I didn't really have the strength to answer.

After reaching the ground floor, we walked in silence through the lobby. I was still too numb and shocked to speak. They took my swipe card at the exit, and I just handed it over without any protest.

It was only when I was outside on the pavement, and the freezing wind whipped my hair in front of my face that I realized I hadn't been able to grab my coat from reception. My phone and wallet were still in the building, and my fingers were rapidly turning a ghastly white.

*

"Mikey?" I said through my chattering teeth. Thank God I remembered his number. I'd been so shocked and numb after I was thrown out that I hadn't been able to come up with a plan quickly enough. Then the cold had been so extreme, the shivers so violent that it seemed to cloud my thinking even more.

I'd never been the most practical person anyway – I definitely wouldn't survive in the wild. *My little dreamer* was what Dad used to call me. Well, being a daydreamer is not helpful when you need to think on your feet before your hands freeze off. Seeing as I had no phone, no money, no coat, I didn't really know how I could get home.

After the humiliation of trying to get back in the building to at least get my coat, and being turned away by the doorman who told me it was "more than his job's worth", I started walking in the direction of home. Half an hour of walking later, huddled over with my hands tucked under my arms and my head ducked against the cold wind, I realized that this was not a good plan. In fact, I was in big trouble if I didn't get warm very soon. My fingers had never looked so blue before – it was starting to get scary.

So that's when I swallowed my pride again and ducked into a café that looked friendly from the outside. The staff seemed a little scared of this shivering weirdo who was asking to use their phone – I must have looked a right state.

"I'm in a bit of a pickle." My teeth were chattering so hard that it was difficult to get the words out in a coherent fashion. But once they got a look at my hands, they were quick to set me up on a table next to a radiator, give me a cup of tea and lend me a phone.

"Luce, is that you, love?" Mikey's strong voice made me feel better. Relief washed over me. My big brother would sort this out. "You okay?"

"Er… no, not really. C–c–can you come get me?"

Mikey lived in Little Buckingham, about an hour outside London.

"What's happened?" he said, and the concern in his tone made my throat close over. For the first time that day, I let the tears fall. Unfortunately, that meant getting more words out was even more tricky, but I knew I had to tell him everything.

CHAPTER 23

Unsafe work environment

Felix

"I said leave me alone," I muttered as the door cracked open. In general, this had been working. Everyone was treading on eggshells around me, but if that kept all the bastards away, I was happy. I just wanted to be left to wallow in this misery on my own. So what if Lucy had turned out to be just like that cheating bitch, Lydia? I'd get over it. I refused to acknowledge the small issue of my broken heart. That would make me weak, and I'd learnt long ago that weakness of any kind was not to be tolerated. No, Lucy hadn't broken my heart. I was just pissed off. How had I been gullible enough to let this happen a second time? Another wave of fury washed over me. I was going to focus on that and not the dull ache in my chest or the throbbing behind my eyes.

The most galling thing was the fact I couldn't get Lucy's shocked expression out of my head or how devastated she looked when I asked for her to be removed. I hadn't slept at all last night. Christ, she'd let me down in the worst way, and I still couldn't help worrying if she was okay, which was absolutely ridiculous.

My father's laughter from five years ago rang in my head again after I'd found out what he'd done:

"Well, you've learned a lesson there, haven't you, boy? Trust is for the weak, and love makes you a victim."

I gritted my teeth, but then, just like before, another voice followed my father's:

"It can feel scary to trust people, Felix. But if you won't take the risk, you'll never be truly happy. You have to live life with an open heart."

Henry Mayweather believed in the essential goodness of people. My father would have called him weak too, but I knew Henry had been anything but.

"The police are here."

My head snapped up at that statement. Tabitha was just inside the doorway now, wringing her hands in a most un-Tabitha-like gesture of discomfort.

"What?"

Tabitha bit her lip, and for some reason I felt panic crawl up my throat. Why was she looking so hesitant and worried? Was Lucy okay? I shot out of my seat.

"What's going on?"

Tabitha glanced out of the office and when she looked back at me, I noticed her face was very pale. "They're questioning Will."

I frowned. "Why would they be questioning Will? Shit, I *told* him that I didn't want to report Lucy."

Tabitha shook her head in short jerks, her face, if anything, paler still. "No, no, you don't understand."

"What don't I understand?"

"They're here *for Will.*"

"What?"

"Mr Moretti?" A uniformed officer was at the door to the office now behind Tabitha, who moved aside to let him pass. "Can I have a word?"

"I–I, yes, of course, officer." My mind was racing now. Here *for* Will? What did that even mean? "Tabitha, I'll see you in—"

"It would be helpful if Ms Montgomery stayed, actually," the officer said, and Tabitha sank down into the office chair which Lucy had sat in yesterday, making my stomach drop even further. "I'm Constable Mitchell. Grant."

"Right, er... okay. Grant, what's this about?"

"Mr Brent has been arrested for assault."

I blinked and felt my throat tighten. "What?" I forced out.

"Assault," the helpful Grant repeated. "An incident which happened here yesterday involving a former employee, a..." Grant broke off to check his notepad, and I had to hold back the urge to leap over the desk and shake him, "... a Miss Lucy Mayweather."

"What?" I shouted, adrenaline surging through my body as Grant's words started to sink in. "Where is she?" I strode around the desk, heading to the door. My only thought was to find Lucy and make sure she was okay.

"Mr Moretti," Grant had blocked my exit. "Calm down. I need to get your statement about today's events."

"Where's Lucy?" I said, my voice coming out as a frustrated growl. "Is she okay? Listen, I'll talk to you after I see Lucy for myself."

"Mr Moretti," Tabitha said, getting up from the chair and joining Grant to try to block me. "Please, Felix. Lucy's okay. Just *please* listen to Constable Mitchell before you go off half-cocked." I glanced at her pinched expression and pulled my hands through my hair in an attempt to get a hold of myself.

"Right, okay," I ground out. "What the hell happened?" I looked between Grant and Tabitha. Tabitha looked away and crossed her arms over her chest, her shoulders hunching in on herself. Something was really wrong here.

"I should have said something about Will," she said in a small voice.

"What?" I asked as that dread spread out from my stomach. "What are you talking about, Tabitha?"

"Let's start with establishing the facts," Grant cut in, gesturing for me to walk back away from the door, which I did reluctantly but I did not take my seat again, preferring to stand with my arms crossed, facing Grant. "At approximately ten o'clock yesterday morning, following a meeting with HR, Miss Mayweather attempted to retrieve her belongings from her desk.

"Retrieve her belongings? But Lucy was still working here then," I put in, my eyebrows lowering into a frown.

"She was advised to leave the building for the week after another incident with Mr Brent which occurred the day before," Grant said calmly, and I felt blood rush to my head, leaving my ears ringing. "Your HR manager said that Miss Mayweather had spoken to her about the incident yesterday morning."

"What incident?" I barked out.

"Mr Brent grabbed her wrist, causing significant bruising and was verbally aggressive," Grant said, still looking down at his notebook as he recited the facts.

"What?" I exploded, my fists bunching at my sides. Grant's head shot up at that and he frowned at me. "He did *what*?"

"Felix," Tabitha said. "Let him finish. Take a deep breath. It's not going to help anything if you're not calm."

"It's all documented with your HR department," Grant went on in that annoyingly calm voice. "As I said before, after she reported this initial incident of physical assault, your HR manager thought it best that she give Miss Mayweather the remainder of the week off. However, I believe that there were some of Miss Mayweather's belongings that she needed, including a notebook, so she had to come back to the office to retrieve it, hoping to do this prior to Mr Brent arriving back from a meeting. Unfortunately, he was in the office when she arrived and made another attack on Miss Mayweather. This time, throwing her against a wall. She has bruising to her shoulder, back, head and wrist."

"That – that can't be true," I said in a hoarse voice, feeling my chest tighten in panic. "Will wouldn't do that. Surely there's been a mistake."

"It's all been recorded on the camera facing Miss Mayweather's desk."

"Camera?"

"I had it installed last year," Tabitha said in a small voice, and my heart sank further. "It's a nanny cam. Only starts recording with movement."

"Tabitha, why would you have a camera installed?"

"You've got to understand," she said, her voice now choked with emotion. "I never thought he'd be *dangerous*." Her nose was red now and her eyes had filled with tears. "He was just a sleazy shit, and I'd had enough of it. I thought if I had documented evidence, then it wouldn't be just his word against mine. So, I set up the camera. But then Lucy started and I moved desks to work for you, and I didn't think to…" she broke off with a small sob. "I didn't think to warn her or to check if she was okay. To be honest I forgot about the camera completely. I swear I didn't know he was still doing it."

"Still doing what?"

She threw her hands up as another tear fell. "He was handsy, he'd say things to get a rise out of me, he cornered me a couple of times. All typical alpha bullshit stuff."

"What the fuck, Tabitha? Typical stuff? Jesus Christ, I had no idea Brent was doing this shit. Why didn't you tell me? I would have ripped him apart."

"It was all just low-level bullshit," Tabitha said in a broken voice, and I felt harsh for snapping at her. "But I got a bad vibe from him. A scary vibe. So, I set up the camera. And Felix, I'm sorry, but this office does not invite communication. There's a put up and shut up unspoken rule here. You know there is."

In the back of my mind, I knew Tabitha was right. I'd wanted to create a focused and cut-throat environment. I had thought that was the best way of getting the most out of

163

everyone. Lucy's gentle suggestions about a more *inclusive and open* space floated through my mind, but I shoved all that down. I had to know what had happened.

"I want to see," I said to Grant, whose eyebrows went up.

"Felix," Tabitha said in a warning voice. "I don't think that's such a good idea."

"I want to see what happened in *my* office to *my* girlfriend, right fucking now."

"Your *girlfriend*?" Grant's eyebrows went up as he looked at me. "With all due respect, Mr Moretti, I don't think she's your girlfriend anymore. You had her escorted from the building by security immediately after she'd been assaulted. I mean, I can be a bit of a shit with my missus, but I've never been *that* much of a bastard."

"*After* she was assaulted," I said in a broken voice. "Oh my God." I felt like I'd been winded, and staggered back to lean on my desk. Lucy's face flashed in front of my vision then. She'd been so pale – her freckles standing out starkly against her ashen skin, her hands had been shaking. My gaze shot to the chair that she'd sunk into after she came into my office. I pictured her there, looking so small as I towered over her, her voice shaky and terrified.

"You've got to listen to me. Will is—"

"Will might be a prick, but he's nothing compared to what a low-life you are. At least he's looking out for the company."

My stomach hollowed out, and I thought for a moment I might vomit. I'd defended Brent after he'd assaulted the woman I… oh my God, the woman I love. I loved Lucy. I hadn't even tried to hear her out. I didn't care anymore if Lucy had sold information about the company. Screw the company. Lucy, *my* Lucy, had been hurt, and I hadn't been there for her.

"I want to see that footage," I said to Grant.

"After I've asked you some more—"

"Now!" I barked, and Grant lowered his notebook to pin me with a furious look.

164

"I'm not one of your employees you can bark orders at, Mr Moretti," Grant said in a low, angry tone. "I don't think you understand the situation here. Your employee was *assaulted* on *your* company premises. Twice. You're the one providing an unsafe work environment. I have questions for you, and you're going to answer them to the best of your ability. Then, and only then, will I be sharing footage of the assault. You and your company are not calling the shots here. Am I clear?"

"Crystal," I ground out.

What followed was a tortuous half-hour of questioning about Brent, about Lucy and my relationship with her, as well as Tabitha's previous run-ins with Brent. All the while there was a low ringing in my ears. I needed to see Lucy, needed to check she was okay.

When we were finally done, Vicky came into the room with another officer. Vicky wasn't the most expressive person emotion-wise, but she looked more visibly upset than I'd ever seen her. Lottie was with her this time. I wished Lottie had been here yesterday when I'd thrown Lucy out, but she'd been out at a meeting about her sister and, prick that I was, I wasn't prepared to wait until she came back to confront Lucy, even when Vicky begged me to. Lottie would have known something was wrong. There's no way she would have let this happen. Lottie can sense when someone's lying with almost supernatural precision.

"We made a mistake," Vicky said, as always stating the bloody obvious.

"Did Will do anything to *you*?" I asked.

Vicky shook her head in a series of quick jerks. "No, he's scared of me."

"You, Lottie?"

Lottie shook her head as well, and I could tell that she'd been crying. "I'm always with Vicky, and she's right – that coward is terrified of her. But when I started here, I knew I recognised him. I was a waitress at one of Ollie's bars, and Will was one of

165

a table of blokes who harassed me until Ollie put a stop to it. Will wasn't the ringleader, and he hadn't done anything directly so it didn't seem important. I didn't want to snitch before I'd even started in the role. And yes, he sometimes stood too close and gave me the creeps, but I couldn't exactly complain about him being a mouth breather with a shonky vibe." She lowered her voice to just above a whisper. "And I needed this job."

I closed my eyes slowly. How had I fucked everything up so badly? "Your job would never have been in question, Lottie."

"I'm not good at reading people," Vicky said to the police officer. "I don't pick up on nonverbal cues. I have a..." she closed her eyes for a moment, a frustrated expression crossing her face, "I have a condition. Sometimes I don't see things other people can see. I don't judge social situations in the right way." It was the first time I'd ever heard Vicky fully acknowledge her difficulties and certainly the first time I'd heard her describe it as a condition. She turned to me again. "Felix, I don't think I should be overseeing people. People are not my strong suit. Even with Lottie helping me, I'm not..." she broke off, and I watched her swallow. "This is my fault," she said in a quiet voice.

"We've been over this, hun," Lottie said gently, laying her hand on Vicky's arm. "You don't have to carry all the responsibility."

"Right, we're heading back to the station," Grant said. "We've got all we need for now."

"The footage?" I asked.

"I've got it, Felix," said Vicky, opening up her computer. The police left as Vicky opened the file, and then I watched the woman I love be assaulted right under my nose, right down the corridor from where I was bitching about her over some stupid irrelevant corporate spying. Because, just like my father, I prioritized my business over the people I cared about. Just like my father, I demanded absolute perfection from everyone around me, or else deemed them irrelevant.

When Lucy's head bounced off the wall, I actually did retch and was nearly sick all over the desk. Then I watched as Lucy ran out of shot. Ran to *me*. I jumped to my feet then, pulling my phone out of my pocket as I strode towards the door. My only thought was to find her. To make sure she was okay. To look after her. I was at the lift when I dialled her number but stopped short when I heard a familiar ringtone from back down the corridor. Spinning on my heel, I followed the sound of the ring until I got to Lucy's desk.

"Shit," I muttered as I ended the call and reached for Lucy's bag that was on top of her desk. I looked inside, and my heart sank when I saw her wallet and phone in there. How had she got home?

Then my gaze fell to that bloody notebook, and I felt another flash of doubt. What if...? I picked it up and flicked it open to the first few pages. There were spider diagrams and maps covering every inch of the paper. It reminded me of the notebooks Lucy used to keep as a child, full of her story ideas and the details of the complicated worlds she created. Sprawled across the pages were what looked like character descriptions, story arcs, outlines of some kind of magical kingdoms and fictional family trees – what there wasn't was any classified company information. Nothing that York would find in the least bit interesting.

What the fuck was going on? What even was all this? I was so engrossed in studying Lucy's intricately detailed pages that I didn't hear the approaching footsteps. It wasn't until I'd taken the punch and staggered back, dropping the notebook, that I was aware of my surroundings again.

"What the fuck," I said, my hand not holding Lucy's bag flying to my nose and coming away covered with blood. "Mike?"

CHAPTER 24

"LP Mayweather?"

Felix

"Fuck you!" shouted Mike Mayweather, snatching up Lucy's notebook where it had fallen on the floor and then bearing down on me again. I held up my bloody hand.

"Hey, Mike listen, I don't want to fight you. Is Lucy—?"

"Don't you *ever* say her name to me ever again," he said, grabbing her bag from my hand and then stepping back as he shoved her notebook inside it. "You stay away from my family, you spineless prick."

"Mike, you've got to listen to me," I said, feeling really desperate now. I needed to find out if Lucy was okay, and clearly Mike must know as he'd come to pick up her stuff. His gaze shot from the bag to me and the fury in his eyes almost made me take another step back, but I stood my ground.

Mike and I had fought plenty over the years. We'd grown up practically as brothers, and we'd always been evenly matched. As adults, we were still similar height and build. Mike used physical labour to give him his body whilst I had my own state-of-the-art gym, but the results were the same. We both were a formidable prospect in a fight. I had no intention of fighting him now, though. All I cared about was his sister.

"I had no idea what had happened."

He snorted in disbelief, and I started to panic as he turned to walk away. I strode after him, grabbing his forearm to try to slow him down, but he shook me off. "Please Mike, is she okay? I'm losing my mind here."

He turned to me then, his muscles bunching and a vein throbbing in his forehead. He looked about ready to explode.

"*You're* losing your mind, are you?" he said in a low dangerous voice. I'd never heard him so furious before. I mean he could be a grumpy git, but he rarely went nuclear like this. "You're worried about her now, are you? After you threw her out of your fancy fucking office when she'd just been assaulted?"

"I didn't know she'd been—"

"You didn't let her speak, you bastard!" he shouted. "You and that stuck-up bloody weirdo were too worried about your precious company secrets." I glanced beyond him and saw Vicky, Lottie and Tabitha a few steps away, having emerged from my office. Mike followed the direction of my gaze and gave a derisive snort when he caught sight of them before turning back to me. "I told Mum this was a stupid idea. I told her that Lucy would be eaten alive in this world. That she's better off in Little Buckingham away from sharks like the lot of you."

Vicky cleared her throat. "We had evidence. She met with Harry York. We saw her pass him information. We didn't just—"

Mike started laughing then, cutting Vicky off. "Oh my God, you fucking *idiots*. Are you telling me that you honestly think Lucy would sell information on your shitty company to some finance dickhead? You think she'd do that for money? *Lucy?*"

"It's irrelevant now," I put in. "I don't care what Lucy thought she had to do. I just want to know she's okay. Please Mike—"

"She did not sell anything to anyone," Mike said.

"Mike, I've seen where she lives," I said quietly, not wanting to anger him further but also knowing that we'd been right, at

169

least in this. "The rent for a flat like that is through the roof. There's no way Lucy could afford some—"

Mike started laughing again. "Jesus Christ, you really don't know?"

I frowned at him. "What do you mean?"

"My sister does not need your fucking money."

"What are you talking about?"

"LP Mayweather has her own bloody money."

"LP Mayweather?" I turned the name over in my mind. It was triggering some sort of memory, but I couldn't put my finger on it. Of course, Lucy Prudence Mayweather (Lucy hated the Prudence bit, but Hetty had insisted on naming her after a great aunt) was LP Mayweather, but there was something else – something I wasn't getting. "Mike, I—"

"Work it out for yourself," he said dismissively. "I've got to say that given the man you've become, it's not a big fucking surprise that you've taken very little interest in my sister beyond fucking and firing her. Moretti scum through and through. Blood will out, I suppose. Shame, though, I used to think you were a decent bloke and I never thought you'd turn into your old man."

"Mike," I said in a hollow voice. "I just need to see Lucy. Is she—?"

"You stay away from my family," he said, fury lacing his tone. "Stick with your own kind, you entitled, upper-class prick."

He spun around and stormed off then. When I followed him, he turned, planted one of his large hands in the middle of my chest and gave me a shove. I managed to hold my footing. Mike was forgetting all the times we'd kicked each other's arses as kids. I wasn't the soft London wanker he thought, but I wasn't going to prove that now. I held my hands up, palms forward in surrender.

"Mike, I don't want a fight," I said, trying to keep the panic out of my voice. I needed to see Lucy, and Mike was clearly the route to doing that. Mike snorted.

"I bet you don't." He turned to leave again, and I grabbed his arm.

"Please," I was begging now as he spun around with a furious expression, ready to punch me again. "*Please*, Mike. I just want to see if she's okay. I swear I didn't know anything about what happened. I'm going out of my mind here."

Some of the angry tension left Mike's body. I felt his muscles relax slightly under my grip and he lowered his clenched fist.

"Felix," he said, his voice losing a little of its hard edge. I thought it was a good sign that he was using my first name. "She's not going to talk to you now."

"But—"

"Listen," he said, turning fully towards me as I dropped my hand from his arm. "If the man I knew is still in there, then he'll give her some goddamn space. She can't handle you right now. If you really care about her, you won't bulldoze your way into seeing her just to make yourself feel better. Even you can't be that much of a selfish bastard."

I felt myself deflating. He was right. Rationally, I knew he was right. But the problem was that the memory of that footage was making rationality hard to reach for. I kept replaying the image of Lucy's small frame being thrown against the wall, Brent's body caging her in, and how hard she was shaking after he let her go.

"Just please, please let me know how she is," I said in a broken voice. "I can't—" I broke off to take a deep breath in and out. "I can't stand not knowing. And tell her I'm sorry."

Mike jerked his chin up – it was as much acknowledgement as I was going to get from him, given how angry he was. Then he left, and I knew I had to let him go to her. I felt like shit.

Nobody said anything for a long time. The silence was broken by Vicky, and as usual, she was brutal in her directness.

"LP Mayweather's books are *New York Times* bestsellers, multiple times over," she said, her face fixed on her phone. "Her brother is right. She does not need to sell company information."

171

I moved to Vicky and reached for her phone. She had the Amazon website up. An LP Mayweather book was currently number one in the epic fantasy category. As I looked at the cover, a memory stirred. There was a dagger pointed down in the forefront, with a vast foreign landscape behind. "Number one in epic fantasy, number twenty-two in the store overall. According to the online calculator, and including her backlist, she's doing very well. Of course, she's a hybrid author so some of that money will be going to her publisher. But her self-published works perform just as well. No wonder she was so helpful to Vanessa."

"Vanessa?" I said, distracted as I scrolled through all of Lucy's books. I counted twenty. She had two different series, set in different worlds. "What about Vanessa?"

"Lucy was helping with the advertising campaigns for the new estate."

"She was helping Vanessa? Like *really* helping?" But Lucy was useless at work, wasn't she? Dead weight.

"Yes. She basically took over the social media paid ads. I estimate that she's increased our revenue by twenty percent in the last two months," Vicky said then cocked her head to the side. "You didn't know that? Don't you know anything about her? I thought she was your girlfriend? I thought you grew up together?"

Tabitha snorted. "Men are self-absorbed arseholes." I was still blinking at the phone screen. I didn't really know what to say to that.

I mean, Tabitha was not wrong.

CHAPTER 25

You wrote my story

Lucy

"Earth to Lucy," Emily's voice penetrated my daydream and I came back to myself with a start. "You alive in there, hun?"

I blinked around at the people surrounding me and gave my head a shake to clear it.

"S–sorry," I said in a small voice, pulling my jumper sleeves down over my hands. The sting of the frostnip wasn't as bad this week but it was enough to make me wince as I clenched my fingers together. I was hoping that I'd be able to start typing soon, but so far the pads of my fingers had been too sensitive to even consider it. Seeing as I couldn't hold a pen either the situation was far from ideal. I was already a fair way off my deadline, I couldn't afford any more delays.

"It's okay," Harry said in a soft voice. "Sorry Luce, I was probably droning on a bit. I can understand why you'd zone out."

We were at the LSE building. I'd agreed to meet the teenagers from Harry's project before I left London for good. Mike thought it would be a good opportunity to get me out of the flat, and Emily had driven us up from Little Buckingham so she could come to this meeting with me and then help me pack up. I was moving home.

Chatting with the teenagers had actually been really therapeutic. A few of them brought samples of their work, some of which were brilliant; others actually brought LP Mayweather books with them for me to sign. It was all very relaxed with Harry moderating, and Mikey, Verity and Emily sitting in. I was glad I'd done it but now I just wanted to leave.

I gave Harry an apologetic smile. "No, you're not droning on, I just have a really poor concentration span since..." I trailed off and Emily reached down to give my arm a squeeze, knowing to avoid my sensitive hands.

"We were really sorry to hear what happened at Moretti Harding," Verity said softly.

My eyes flashed to her and she bit her lip.

"I'm sorry, Luce," she said. "News travels fast in our business."

My smile wavered. "Oh, right."

"Lucy really doesn't want to talk about it yet," Emily said after an awkward silence. "I hope you understand. It's all a bit fresh."

It was like primary school all over again. I was free to be the daydreamer, to drift through life with Emily ready by my side to shield me. Just like Mikey used to do; just like *he* used to do.

Thinking about him made my chest ache and started that stupid prickling behind my eyes again. Why couldn't I just forget about the silly sod? It had been nearly a week, and it still hit me in waves. I hated him, like real, real loathing. So why couldn't I stop missing him with a deep ache that almost took my breath away? He'd let me down so badly. I'd totally misjudged him. I thought we had something real. I thought he felt the same.

But, when I looked back on it, I realised that was never the case. It was like the scales had fallen from my eyes now. He was never really mine, was he? He never really *knew* me at all. All those lectures on how to succeed in the real world. His way of succeeding with laser focus, business acumen, boring meetings, and cut-throat stuff. I mean, how could he have ever thought I was interested in that? I even told him that wasn't me. How could he have had so little curiosity to not ask what was? Granted, he was curious *now*. Until I blocked him the number of voicemails and texts I received could attest to that.

Please, talk to me, Luce.

I'm sorry, Lucy. Don't freeze me out.

Baby, please. I'm so sorry. Please let me see you're okay.

Then there were the times he came to the flat. Mikey wouldn't let him in, which was just as well – I was an absolute mess. Mikey had had just about enough of Felix. He told me about how he'd "punched him in his designer-stubbled face" when he'd first seen Felix back at the office. And how the bloody idiot didn't even bother to duck. "It's like he *wanted* to be punched," Mike had said.

Punching people is not my brother's vibe at all, but I'd never seen him as angry as when he picked me up from that café. Me blubbing continuously after I got home and throughout the police interview didn't help either, but he and Mum insisted that this time I had to report the incident to the police. By the time he saw Felix, he was about ready to blow.

The fact that this whole thing would drive a wedge between Felix and the rest of my family made me so achingly sad. Sure, over the last few years Felix had kept his distance. He never came back to Little Buckingham anymore, despite my mum periodically fussing him to visit his mum. Bianca Moretti and Mum were friends now. Mum said that Bianca was lonely and that she missed Felix; that he'd come home more if it wasn't for "that bloody man". (Mum's never been a fan of Felix's dad.) But now Mikey had vowed never to speak to Felix again.

Mum was very quiet on the phone when I told her what had happened. I spared her most of the details, but she got the gist of what went on. She was absolutely furious about Will – fully ready to grab her rolling pin and take the first train to London. I had to explain that "beating him to a pulp" with kitchen equipment might cause problems when we tried to convict him. But she wasn't as angry with Felix as I expected.

"Stupid, stupid boy," she'd muttered. "Never did know what's good for him. That father of his did a real number on him." There was no heat in her tone, just heavy disappointment.

I swallowed and focused back on Harry and his wife.

"Of course, Lucy," Verity said in a shaky voice. "I wouldn't have brought it up it's just..." When I looked up at her I was surprised to see her eyes were wet. "Sorry, stupid pregnancy hormones."

I swallowed as I felt my eyes start to sting as well. When I offered Verity a watery smile she let out a small sob and launched herself at me in a hug, pregnancy bump and all.

"Okay, darling," Harry said gently to his wife. "Let Lucy breathe."

Verity pulled back, wiping tears from under her eyes. "Sorry," she said.

"No don't apologise," I told her. "Hugs are always good."

When Harry's arm went around my shoulders for a quick squeeze, I jumped to hear Felix's voice cracking across the large space.

"York!"

We all turned towards him as he stormed across the atrium. His eyes were fixed on Harry's arm, and a muscle was jumping in his jaw. Harry looked between us for a moment before a sly smirk took over his features.

"Moretti," he said, tightening his arm so he was pulling me into his side. Felix's eyes flashed. "What are you doing in *my* building?"

"Your building?"

I breathed a sigh of relief when Verity broke through the tension, slapping her husband on the chest as his arm went from around me to give his wife a hug and kiss the top of her head.

"*I* designed it, you cheeky sod," she said to her husband and then turned towards Felix. There was a beat of awkward silence with both men staring daggers at each other. "Hello again, Felix."

"Don't even look at my wife," Harry snapped at Felix before he could answer, moving in front of Verity to block her from Felix's view. "And bugger off. I don't want someone who would accuse me of industrial espionage in our building."

"I apologised for that," Felix said through gritted teeth and Harry narrowed his eyes.

"That's all very well, but it's my reputation you threatened. I could sue for defamation of character, you prick. As for what you did to Lucy—"

"Lucy's none of your business," Felix spat out.

"Oh really?" Harry taunted. "She's more my business than yours apparently. Look what happened to her when you made her your business?"

You could cut the testosterone with a knife, which was completely ridiculous, but I wasn't about to make a scene in the middle of—

"Fuck *off*, city wanker," spat out Emily, as she strode over to us, back from her loo break. Emily had never been afraid of a scene. "Who let this dickhead in?"

She walked right up to Felix and gave his shoulder a hard shove. He barely moved, but his gaze did flick down to her.

"Hello, Emily," he said evenly. I was surprised he remembered her. Felix always seemed so above me and my friends back in Little Buckingham.

"You're leaving," she said as she gave him another hard shove, this time with both hands. He still didn't move. It was like his body was made of stone. Probably from his stupid gym in his stupid house. Vain prick. It's not like he needed all those muscles for the boardroom.

Anyway, I didn't care about him and his stupid muscles now. At least that's what I told myself, ignoring the fact that my stomach was flipping and the yearning I had to walk into those muscular arms was so strong I almost couldn't catch my breath.

"I need to talk to Lucy," he said, his gaze going from a now red-faced Emily, who was still putting all her force behind trying to shove Felix out of the building, to me. She carried on shoving and grunting, but his eyes and focus never wavered from my face.

He looked like shit. I mean, don't get me wrong, on a hotness scale of one to smokin' he was still a solid eleven. But his tie was loose, and his shirt was a good few days past needing an iron, and his stubble was no longer designer – it had progressed into a thick, scruffy beard.

My chest felt tight. Was he missing me as much as I missed him? I took a step back, fighting against the urge to go to him and forcing down the acute need to hold him. This wasn't *my* Felix. That Felix had never really existed.

"She's," Emily gave another shove, "not," another shove (harder this time), "going," she was now breathing hard as she gave Felix a continuous push, her feet sliding on the floor unable to get a proper grip, "to speak," another grunt, "to you," a growl, "you fucking prick."

One of her feet did slip then, but Felix grabbed her by both shoulders to steady her, then lifted her gently in the air and put her on her feet to the side while muttering, "Careful, you'll hurt yourself."

Emily was red with rage now. She was not the type of woman able to tolerate being lifted off her feet with very little apparent effort and set to the side. Emily simply wasn't the type of human you set to the side at all. Her face started screwing up and I could see a serious escalation in the offing.

"Em," I said, and everyone's gaze shot to mine. "Stand down."

Emily huffed and crossed her arms, but she didn't go back to physical assault, so I took that as progress. When I was sure that she was no longer in attack mode, I transferred my gaze to Felix. His eyes scanned my face as if he was memorising every inch of it. He took a step towards me, and I took a corresponding one back. His eyes dropped to my feet, and he frowned, but he didn't step closer again. Then he did something so un-Felix, so earnest, it almost shook my resolve. Whilst holding eye contact with me, his blank expression cracked, and naked pain flashed across his features.

"Please," he whispered. Despite the buzz of the room, it was like he'd whispered it directly into my ear. The raw quality of his voice, the absolute desperation had me rocking forward onto my toes. I was so close to just going to him.

He tensed at my movement, his whole body on alert, muscles bunched in tension, practically shaking in an effort to hold himself back. But then I remembered. Felix didn't care about me. He fired me. He hadn't protected me. He didn't like who I was, and he had never really bothered to find out anyway. So I rocked back on my heels, taking another small step back. Felix's eyes flashed before he closed them slowly.

"I don't think she wants to talk to you, Moretti," Harry's voice filled the silence. He was enjoying this. "So, I'll repeat: get out of our goddamn building."

Felix ignored Harry, reaching into his back pocket and pulling out a copy of my book.

"I'll leave once I talk to Lucy," he said, still staring at me.

"Moretti—"

"For fuck's sa—" Emily started, but I cut her off.

"It's fine," I said, just wanting to get this over with. I took a deep breath in and out and walked towards Felix, away from the others. His chest deflated as he let out the breath he must have been holding.

"Lucy... Are you okay?" he asked when I stopped a couple of feet away. Now that I was closer I could really see how terrible he looked. His cheeks were a little more hollow, like he'd lost weight, and there were dark circles under his slightly bloodshot eyes, "I had to see you. I'm so sorry. Lucy, I can't tell you how sorry I am. I should have listened to you. I should never have—"

"How did you know I was here?" I narrowed my eyes at him.

He cleared his throat and darted a look at the interested bystanders, two flags of colour riding high on his cheekbones. "I may have had some security watching your flat."

My eyebrows went up. "What on earth?"

"I'm sorry," he said, that desperate quality still to his voice. "But I was so worried. I can't eat, can't sleep. I just needed to know you were okay. And Will is still out there."

"Felix, that's mad."

"I just can't get it out of my head." He swallowed and his red-rimmed eyes got redder. "Lucy, I saw the video. He hurt you. Your head bounced off the wall like…"

Felix trailed off as he paled so much under his tan I almost felt sorry for him. Almost.

"You can see I'm fine," I snapped, ignoring the throbbing pain in my fingers. To be honest the lasting injuries weren't from Will's assault, they were from being thrown out into the freezing cold and developing frostnip on my fingers.

Felix blinked at me and then looked down at the book clutched in his hand.

"You wrote my story," he said, so low that only I could hear, his words weighted, heavy with emotion. That meant something to him. That I used that story as the basis for my first novel meant a lot to him. I swallowed and then cleared my throat.

"It's not yours," I whispered, stepping closer to snatch the book from him but he held onto it, giving his head a small shake.

"You told it to me first. I'm the *original* LP Mayweather fan. All this lot are a load of Jonny-come-latelys. I knew how talented you were before anyone else. I was the first to believe in you."

I rolled my eyes, still unable to drop my hold on the book, to break the connection. "Some fan. You didn't even know they were published."

"You never told me." There was a hint of accusation and, to my surprise, hurt in his words. "How could you not tell me?"

Anger flashed through me, and I gave the book a tug. He didn't deserve my bloody book. "And when would I have done that, Felix? When did you let me explain? When did you actually ask me what I'd been doing all these years?"

"Lucy, I—"

"No," I snapped, giving the book another tug, but he refused to let go. "You don't get to make excuses. Do you know how much I knew about you before I came up to London? How rabid for information I always was from Mikey? How I scoured those glossy magazines, buying all the ones with you in them with some actress, model or popstar? God, I'm pathetic."

Felix groaned. "No, Lucy. No, please don't say that. You were just a kid when I left. If I'd have known you in the last few years, *really* known you, then I would have devoured every word you'd ever written. I'd have stalked you way worse than you did me."

"Yes, but you *did* know me after I moved here. At least you thought you did."

Felix huffed in frustration. "You never told me. If you'd just told me then—"

"Okay," I conceded. "I should have told you about the books. I never actually lied, and I would have told you if you'd ever asked me once about what I'd been up to." He winced at that, the flashes of colour staining his cheekbones again. "And I know I should have made sure you understood what I was doing working at your company. That wasn't fair. Although when I did try to explain a few times, you cut me off. But I accept that I was essentially lying by omission, and you didn't deserve it. But how could you think me capable of selling secrets to a competitor? How could you even think for a moment that I would sell you out?"

"Luce," he said, that pleading quality back in his voice. "You've got to understand what it looked like. And there's been…

listen, I've been fucked over relentlessly since uni. I should have talked to you about what happened with my ex and about how wary it made me. She really betrayed my trust. I–I can't get into the details but I was completely taken in by her. I'm jaded and cynical, and I... I just jumped to a stupid conclusion."

"I'm sorry you were fucked over," I said, trying to keep my voice steady. "But you've known me forever. That's not me. I thought—" I broke off to take a deep breath and swallowed. "I thought we were..." I closed my eyes so I didn't have to look into his when I said it and lowered my voice to a whisper. "I was falling in love with you."

"Well, I fell in love with you the night I fed you Marmite toast next to my Aga... in fact, no, that's not right. I fell in love with you when I was an angry, hurt thirteen-year-old who was transported to another world by your stories. That's how long you've been it for me. I was just too stupid and fucked up to see it."

I felt my eyes prick again, and this time, the hot tears did form. I let go of the book, my hand going up to my mouth as I stifled a sob and took a couple of steps back.

"Right," snapped Emily as she stepped between us, "that's it, city dickhead. You've made her cry, so your time's up. Get. Out."

"Yeah," put in Harry York as he came up next to Emily to further block Felix from me, assuming a wide stance and crossing his arms over his chest. "Time's up, mate. Why don't you get out before I put you out."

"As if you could," Felix muttered grumpily. "But fine." He put his hands up in surrender. "I'll go. But I'll wait, Luce. Forever if I have to."

I peered around Emily to look at him. He was wearing the same determined expression he used to have as a child when he wanted something. I couldn't remember a single time back then that he didn't succeed, and I didn't want to know what that meant for me.

CHAPTER 26

You both needed a bit of a push

Felix

As I walked up the path to the small, terraced cottage, I felt my chest tighten. I loved it here: the warm kitchen, the laughter, toasted hot cross buns, casual affection – it was the total opposite of my family home. The Mayweathers had a way of making you feel like you were one of them. I never felt like I was just a paying guest or that Hetty was just my nanny. They were family.

I started to feel sick. What does Hetty think of me now? Realising that I'd paused on the path, I shook my head to clear it before I made my feet step forward towards the bright blue door. After I'd knocked, I was bracing to be confronted by a furious Hetty, so when a just mildly grumpy Jimbo, one of the bartenders at The Badger's Sett, opened the door, I was flummoxed.

"Ah, the Moretti boy," Jimbo said, rubbing his hand over his stubble as he looked me up and down. "What you here about, lad? Not still sore about the time I cut your fake ID in half, are you?"

"You always served Mike."

Jimbo's eyebrows went up. "Yeah, well. Back then, Hetty wasn't about to bankrupt my business if I got her boy shitfaced, was she? Nobody wants to piss off the Morettis."

"That's not—" I broke off and took a deep breath in and out. Why was I getting involved in a ridiculous conversation about why I hadn't been served at age fifteen when the rest of the village got away with it? I needed to focus on the task at hand. I was so stressed that I was starting to become as distractable as Lucy, and I didn't have the excuse of being a creative genius to fall back on. "Listen, Jimbo, I'm here to see Hetty."

Was Jimbo Hetty's boyfriend now? That would be... weird. I would have hoped that Hetty had better taste. I mean, it was midday and Jimbo was standing in the doorway wearing his dressing gown and scratching his balls. Charming.

"Hetty?" he asked, his eyebrows up in his hairline. "Hetty's not lived here for over a year, boy."

I blinked. "What? I don't understand."

"That daughter of hers bought her the Moonreach place. Hetty was right chuffed, she were. It was bad enough when Lucy retired her mum. Hetty banged on enough about that to anyone that'd listen in The Badger's. But since Moonreach, she's been fit to burst. She has the bridge club meet at her place now rather than your mum's. Avoids that stick-up-his-arse dad of yours apparently. Can't say I blame her. Never was that keen on your old man."

Moonreach was a beautiful, grade two-listed, large cottage on the outskirts of the village. Hetty would often talk about Moonreach and how she loved it. Old Man Tinsley had lived there. I knew this because Moonreach was the direct neighbour to my parents' house. In fact, it sat between the Buckingham Estate and ours. Not that you could see the house from either my parents' house or Ollie's, as both had a fair acreage.

I blinked again and took a step back. I was beginning to feel very, very stupid. Here I had been feeling bad for Hetty supporting her daydreaming daughter, and all along it was the other way around. I mumbled something to Jimbo as I turned and made my way back to my car.

There was a new gate on Moonreach, much more sturdy than before, with a large sign saying to shut it after yourself. Once I'd driven through it, I realised why. Two hugely fat pigs ambled their way up to my car, snorting like obese asthmatics. They were probably the ugliest creatures I'd ever seen in my life. Behind them, a couple of hens emerged from a bush. One of them was missing half its feathers, and the other was limping. Hetty used to talk about running a small holding. She'd always taken in as many waifs and strays as she could into her tiny cottage. I was guessing that with more space, she'd decided to go nuts.

I smiled for the first time in weeks. My father absolutely hated animals. And there was no way that Hetty would manage to contain this lot in her property; at least, I really, *really* hoped there wasn't.

My smile grew as a llama trotted down the lane towards me. This just got better and better. Old Man Tinsley had only had a couple of dogs, and even they used to drive my dad totally mad.

The llama was staring at me now, its teeth pulling back. I hopped in the car. Not worth being spat at. We had a face-off on the drive for a couple of minutes until the pigs decided to join the llama in blocking my path. One of them lay down in front of my bumper. I decided to cut my losses and drove up into the muddy field to get around them, covering my car in dirt.

I added buying a Land Rover to the list of things to sort out. Once I'd convinced Lucy to forgive me, I was planning on being at Moonreach a fair bit. I would need a vehicle that could handle the mud and didn't scream "poncy city boy" as Mike had dubbed me when he first saw the low-slung Aston Martin that I was currently ruining.

Thankfully, the rest of the driveway was relatively clear – I only had to pause for a moment to let some ducks cross in front of the car.

I took a deep breath when I made it to the front door. They'd painted it the same colour as their old cottage and there were climbing roses up the side. The whole building looked like something out of *Country Life* – thatched roof, thick stone walls, areas of exposed brick and beams.

It was the opposite of my parents' house. My father had done as much as he could to modernise their property, skirting very close to the planning rules and sometimes completely disregarding them. He'd managed to make what had once been a beautiful, old country house into an oversized, glass-fronted monstrosity.

I knocked and waited, my heart in my throat. Hetty opened the door wearing the same apron she'd always worn, some flour on her cheek and in her salt and pepper hair. She was holding a rolling pin, and I braced for impact. But when her shocked expression cleared, her face filled with warmth and she did something completely unexpected. She dropped the rolling pin and pulled me into her for a tight hug. For such a small woman, she was surprisingly strong, pulling me down to her height with ease. I actually felt my throat thicken with emotion. Hetty gave the best hugs.

"Oh, love," she said. "You've gone and got yourself in a right pickle, haven't you?" She pulled back, putting her hands on either side of my face to keep it at her level. "Always were a bit slow on the uptake."

"Er… what?"

She patted my cheek a couple of times. "I sent you my Lucy on a platter. You two were always meant for each other. Your mum and I talked it through and decided that you both needed a bit of a push."

My eyebrows went up. "My *mother*?"

"She wants you happy, love. All those silly women you've been with won't do at all. It was time to put a stop to it. And my Lucy doesn't want anyone but you. Never has." Before I could correct her, Hetty grabbed my arm and started pulling me into the house. As we stepped into the hallway, the barking started. Two massive retrievers came bounding up to us, one of them jumping up on my chest and licking my face, the other wanting to, but too old to manage it.

"That's Samwise. I still leave the naming to Lucy, see," Hetty said. "We've not got very far with training, to be honest. And you know Frodo."

After I'd given the younger dog some fussing, I went down to my knees on the floor to get to Frodo.

"He must be sixteen now?" I said, my voice rough with emotion. "Hey boy," I muttered to him as I rubbed behind his ears the way I knew he liked. "You remember me?" He chuffed, then gave my face a long lick, his tail thumping on the floor. Memories of walks with Frodo and Mike with Lucy trailing behind flooded my mind. I'd always make Mike wait for her, much to his annoyance.

My chest tightened as my memories moved to the old Mayweather dog, Bilbo, and how distraught thirteen-year-old me had sought comfort in his fur after I found out my father took my own dog, Benji to the pound. Mum and I had found Benji at a rescue centre six months earlier, and I'd fallen in love with him despite his scruffy appearance. I was frantic when I came home from boarding school with him missing, and then devastated when I discovered what my father had done. My eyes had been red and puffy from crying on the way to the cottage, but I'd forced them back after arriving.

Unfortunately Mike had been away at scout camp, so it was just Hetty and eight-year-old Lucy there. Hetty had taken one look at me and hustled me into the kitchen where I'd sunk down in front of the Aga and burrowed my face in Bilbo's thick coat. Then little Lucy had come into the kitchen, tilted her head to the side as she stared at me and her dog.

"You're sad," she'd told me.

"A bit, Shakespeare," I'd said in a scratchy voice, sniffing a couple of times but managing not to cry again. Lucy sank down the other side of Bilbo, and her small hand covered mine on his neck.

"Wanna hear a story?" she asked softly.

I nodded, and that's how we stayed. Hetty cooking supper around us and Lucy telling me her story. After an hour, although the aching pain of my dad's cruelty was still there, I at least felt like I could breathe again. How had I forgotten how kind Lucy was? How had I ever thought her capable of betraying me?

"Come on, love," Hetty said softly. I blinked away the memories and looked up at her smiling face before getting to my feet to follow her.

"Is Lucy here?" I asked as we made our way into Hetty's large but somehow still cosy country kitchen, filled with old wood, a Belfast sink, warm tiles, cream Aga. Warm, homely, again the complete opposite of my family home.

"Yes, she's here, but don't worry. She won't have heard you arrive. She's got her special headphones on – can't hear a thing with those things on her ears. Says she needs them to concentrate with Gandalf squawking all day." A cockerel started shrieking right on cue then.

"I'm assuming that's Gandalf?"

"Yes, poor chap's got a nervous condition – squawks all the time. Sad really, all the hens avoid him so, he can't even get himself some. Your mum thinks he's frustrated... sexually."

"What?" I spluttered. Commenting on a cockerel's sexual needs was not an in-character action for my mother. I cleared my throat and rubbed the back of my neck. "*Mum* said that?"

"Oh yes," Hetty said in a breezy tone. "Bianca's *much* less repressed these days."

I didn't want to hear about my mum and her theories about poultry sexual and mental health problems. Thankfully, Hetty was on a mission and she wasn't about to be distracted by Gandalf.

"You really messed up," she said, straight to the point – but then Hetty always was. "What on earth were you thinking?"

I sighed, my shoulders dropping as I sank down into a chair next to the huge, worn kitchen table, running my hand along the smooth wood surface.

"I'm a fucking idiot."

Hetty reached behind her for a blue and white striped pot, opened the lid and held it out to me.

"I only have fifties."

She shook the jar at me and lifted her eyebrows. "Better not say bad words then, young man. You still owe me one pound twenty-five from two decades ago anyway. You always did have a potty mouth." I pulled my wallet out and put a fifty in the jar.

"Well, we'd better sort it out then, hadn't we?" Hetty said as if we were back when I was a kid in the kitchen complaining about a difficult piece of homework instead of sitting here as a full-grown man having broken her daughter's heart. "Nice cup of tea?" A cup of tea was pretty much Hetty's starting point for any crisis, big or small. "Her hands are getting better, so that's one good thing."

"Her hands?" I frowned at Hetty as she put the kettle on. She gave me a cautious look before answering.

"You didn't know about her hands?"

I shook my head, my stomach clenching in dread.

CHAPTER 27

"She was in pain?"

Felix

I had a feeling that I was not going to like whatever had happened to Lucy's hands, my own clenched into fists on the table.

"Oh dear," Hetty said. "Tea first." I waited until a cup of sweet tea was placed in front of me.

"Please Hetty, tell me."

"Take a sip first, love." I complied, not even tasting the tea, but the warmth of it did settle my stomach somewhat. Hetty nodded. "Frostnip."

"Frostnip?" I shook my head. "What do you mean?"

"Well," said Hetty cautiously. "You know she has Raynaud's and cold intolerance, don't you? Doctors never could work out why my Lucy couldn't bear the cold. Had every blood test under the sun – all clear. It's just the way she was made. Should have been born on the Equator, definitely not in England.

"Anyhow, when she left your office, she didn't have her coat, gloves, hat or her bag. And she says she was wearing an outfit you would approve of so she could impress you. Not her normal jumpers and furry boots, but a skirt, heels, thin shirt."

My heart sank as I started to guess where this was going.

"Now, my Lucy, she's a dreamer. Not the most practical soul, but you know that."

190

I nodded, not wanting to hear the rest but knowing I had to.

"Well, she tried to get back into the building to get her stuff, but the chaps on the door wouldn't consider it. Told her they had strict instructions – she was not to re-enter the building under any circumstances. That she was a threat to the company."

I winced, putting the mug of tea down to shove my hands into my hair.

Hetty cleared her throat.

"She didn't know what to do. No phone, no money. And she's shy and doesn't want to impose. She only went into a café to ask for help when she realised she was in trouble, but to be honest, by then it was a bit too late. Her hands were in a really bad way. Frostnip is sort of like a cold burn. Painful for a few weeks but no lasting damage."

"Oh, God no," I groaned, letting my head drop to the table. "I'm an unbelievable bastard." I took another fifty out of my wallet without looking up and slid it to Hetty. "Mike shouldn't have stopped with one punch."

"No, I bloody well shouldn't have." At Mike's angry voice, my head snapped up. He was standing at the back door, rubbing down the dogs. His face was red with anger, his jaw set. "What the fuck is he doing here, Mum?"

Hetty pushed the jar towards him. He dug in his pocket, extracting a pound coin and chucking it in without breaking eye contact with me.

Hetty sighed. "Give the boy a break, Michael. He feels bad enough already. And Lucy's hands *are* much better. She can type now, at least."

My gaze shot to Hetty. "She couldn't type?"

Hetty shrugged. "No. Missed a big deadline as well. It was a bit of a palaver. That's why she's so fussy about using her noise-cancelling thingies and not being bothered by Gandalf. She's on a mission to finish the manuscript."

"She was in pain?" I couldn't help it then; my voice broke over the words, and my throat felt tight. "I caused her pain? I think… I think I'm going to throw up."

With that, I shot up to my feet, only just making it to the small bathroom under the stairs in time to see my breakfast make a dramatic reappearance.

There was silence in the kitchen when I returned after washing my mouth out at the sink and looking at my pale reflection. I sat at the kitchen table again as my hands came up to cover my face. I couldn't look at any of the Mayweathers. How had I sunk so low? How could I have *hurt her*?

"Come on, Felix, love," Hetty's soft voice cut through my self-loathing, her hand had settled on my shoulder, giving it a squeeze. "It'll all be right. You're going to *put* it right. Nothing you couldn't do as a boy was there? Any tree you wanted to climb you were the first up there. Didn't want anything from your dad, so you worked your arse off in the pub with Jimbo to buy a car for yourself, but I know you gave it all to Mikey to help him set up his workshop. And when Lucy was being bullied at school, you went to pick her up and cornered those little shits." Hetty dropped her own pound coin into the jar with her hand that wasn't on my shoulder. "You helped her with her maths. And don't think I don't know that you were the first person to encourage my daughter to become a storyteller. *You* saw that potential."

"Hetty, I didn't even know she'd published her books," I said in an agonised voice. "How could I not have known?"

I looked at Hetty then. Her eyes were fixed on me and slightly narrowed.

"I reckon once you left Little Buckingham you wanted to really *leave*. Too much pain for you here, wasn't there, love?"

I broke eye contact with Hetty to look down at the table. She was right. I had needed to leave this village behind. On some level, I knew I loved Lucy; even as a child, I knew our bond ran deep. And nothing was going to pull me back here, not after what Dad did.

"She'll never forgive me," I whispered, staring down at my tea and feeling the bottom drop out of my world.

Mike huffed. "Ugh, bloody hell. You always were a dramatic little bitch." I glanced at him. He was no longer puffed up with righteous anger; in fact, there was almost a touch of pity in his expression as he sank down into one of the chairs opposite me at the table. "She'll live. It's not like she lost a finger or anything."

I felt the blood drain out of my face. My stomach clenched again.

"Calm down, love," Hetty said. "None of that now. You can't win my daughter back if you're covered in vomit or passed out on the floor."

Vomiting had been a stress response for me as a child, and Hetty was always able to recognise the signs. I took a deep breath to stave off the nausea and took a sip of tea as instructed. Hetty was right – tea really did make everything better.

"Mum?"

I let go of the mug with a clatter at the sound of Lucy's voice. Some tea spilt over the side, but I ignored it. She didn't see me as she made it through the door. That was because, bizarrely, she was pushing a small, fat pony from behind to force it into the kitchen, huffing and puffing with the effort. The small pony's head was in the air, and it was bracing its hooves to try and go back against Lucy's pushing.

"Can we please keep Legolas outside my shed? He keeps butting my arm when I'm trying to write, and he ate one of my maps! This place is a bloody madhouse. You're not meant to have—" She froze, and her mouth snapped shut when she caught sight of me. Straightening up slowly she kept her gaze locked to mine as she reached up to pull her headphones off. "*You're* here."

And I just couldn't help it. I knew I didn't have the right. I knew I had to wait for her to come to me. But there was nothing I could do about it. My legs were pushing up from the chair and taking me over to her before I had really registered

193

the thought to do it. She'd managed to push her way around the pony now and was standing in the kitchen. I stopped right in front of her. Her mouth opened to speak, but she snapped it shut as I gently took both her hands in mine.

Very, very carefully, I turned them over to look at both sides. She winced slightly and my eyes shot to hers.

"They're still a bit sensitive," she said in explanation, and I closed my eyes slowly, feeling the heat building behind them. I hadn't cried in front of anyone since the Benji incident when I was thirteen years old. My father told me that day that crying was for pathetic losers. I vowed then that I would never cry again and that I would hate my father forever. Both promises I'd kept until now.

When I opened my eyes, Lucy sucked in a shocked breath at the tears swimming there.

"I'm so sorry, baby," I said in a ravaged whisper, unable to get anything else past my tight throat.

One of her hands went up to my face. Her thumb swiped the tear that had fallen.

"Felix," she said softly, her voice full of emotion. Then her eyelids swept shut, her hand fell away from my face, the other pulling easily from mine.

I wanted to hold onto her to stop the inevitable retreat but I didn't want to risk hurting her fingers. So I let it slip away as she took a step back. There was total silence in the kitchen now. Mike shifted uncomfortably in his chair – I don't think *he'd* seen me cry since I was six.

"I can't ever take that back," I said, my voice hoarse. "I can't ever take back the fact I hurt you."

Lucy rubbed her hands together and the urge to take them both in mine was so strong I had to shove my own in my pockets.

I sniffed as my eyes started to sting again. Jesus, I couldn't blub again. Heartbroken or no, Mike would never let me live it down.

"Felix, why are you here?" Lucy said in a small voice.

"I told you I wouldn't give up. I–I can't let you go. Please, Lucy, just give me a chance to make it up to you." I paused, swallowing past the lump in my throat. "Please, Shakespeare. I love you."

Lucy looked to the side and bit her lip.

"How could you have forgotten about the stories?" she whispered after a long moment's pause. "I know I didn't push enough to tell you. To make you listen to me when I tried to explain but how could you have forgotten how important the stories were to me? Did you think I just gave them up?"

I took a deep breath in and let it out in a stuttering whoosh. "Of course, I remembered the stories."

Lucy was shaking her head, her hands balled into fists at her sides and I frowned down at them.

"Baby, your hands," I said softly and her eyes flashed but she did relax them slightly – the white knuckles regaining their colour.

"You *didn't* remember. Not until you found out about LP Mayweather," she said. "If you'd remembered, you would have known that I'd never give them up."

"No, that's not—"

"And you're not healthy for me," she interrupted me. I felt the blood drain out of my face. Oh God, I really hoped I wasn't going to throw up again.

"W–what do you mean?"

She sighed. "Felix, I've loved you nearly my whole life. And when you left Little Buckingham you didn't give me a second thought."

"Lucy, I—"

"I'm not saying you should have done," she cut in. "I'm just trying to explain. After you finished uni you rarely came home. You were off to conquer the world. Of course you weren't going to be fussed about a fifteen-year-old girl with hearts in her eyes. But whilst you were off building an empire, I was here writing stories where the heroes all had dark brown eyes, thick hair with a slight curl at the end when it grows out; who were powerful but with hidden soft centres. I wrote about *you*. And if that wasn't enough, I stalked you."

My eyebrows went up at that. I could feel the hope building. "Lucy, I think I would have known if you were stalking me."

She shook her head. "Okay, virtual stalking. I've read every article ever written about you. Every gossip magazine comment and picture. I could probably reel off every one of your ex-girlfriends. I grilled Mikey to the extent he would avoid me after he'd been to London."

"It did get a little weird, mate," Mike conceded, making an eek face that almost made me laugh.

"It got more than a little weird," Lucy muttered. The colour that rose in her cheeks and the discomfort in her expression made my chest feel tight.

"Lucy," I said gently. "Baby, I knew you had a crush on me. You don't have to be embarrassed about that."

Lucy's cheeks were on fire now. I wasn't making this any better. "I came to London for you," she blurted out and I frowned in confusion.

"What do you—?"

"Yes, I needed to leave Little Buckingham. I wanted to stop being such a wussbag and—"

"Don't call yourself that," I snapped, and Lucy rolled her eyes.

"Felix, I could barely leave Little Buckingham without having a panic attack. If that doesn't make me a wussbag, I don't know what does."

"There are different types of bravery," I said firmly. "Putting your stories out into the world – that's real bravery."

"I put my stories out there, but I didn't put *myself* out there. There's a difference."

"Well, you did come to London, didn't you?"

Lucy sighed and crossed her arms over her chest defensively. "I came for you," she whispered, and that hope in my chest swelled so much I almost smiled but she looked too stricken for me to dare. "I mean, that's not what I told myself. I told myself that I needed to stop being a recluse and get out there. That a change would be good for me. That I might as well take a job in your company. But deep down I knew – I just wanted to be with you, which is completely pathetic."

Another lump lodged in my throat as I watched her curl in on herself, hugging her stomach as the colour left her face.

"So, can't you see? That's not healthy, Felix. And it meant that when I did catch your attention, I was too scared to ask for more. I was happy with whatever you could give me." She gave an uncomfortable shrug, darting a quick look at Mike and Hetty before focusing back on me. "I lost myself, Felix. If what happened that day hadn't happened, I would have carried on losing myself in you. Not daring to ask for more. Trying to change to be what you wanted me to be. Accepting that you put work and ambition above me. I'm not suited to your world. I don't fit there. And my obsession with you wasn't healthy for me or you."

I shoved both my hands into my hair as I paced away from Lucy, trying to come up with the right words. Knowing that fucking this up would be very easy if I said the wrong thing. I paced back again and stopped in front of her, closer than before. When I reached for her she flinched back and I had to force my hand to drop back to my side.

"Don't you think I've read every single word you've ever written in the last few weeks? Grilled Mike endlessly, not that the bastard would tell me anything. Lucy, I followed you to the LSE, followed you here. Now, who's stalking who?" I sighed. "Listen, I wish I hadn't stayed away so much after I left uni but my dad…" I trailed off. The last thing I wanted to do was talk about that bastard now. "If I'd seen more of you once you'd grown up, of course I would have fallen for you. Of course I would have done. And we would have had years together. Don't you think I regret that? I regret that bitterly, baby. Especially hearing that you were mine and I didn't even know it. That Davey Turnbull had what was mine because I was too blind and stupid to know what was waiting for me back here."

"Davey Turnbull?" Mike snapped. Lucy's face was on fire now as she rolled her eyes. "How did that prick fly under my radar?"

Lucy narrowed her eyes at him.

"Maybe if you hadn't been such an overprotective caveman I wouldn't have had to sneak around with Davey because you'd scared all the other lads off."

"Please, can we not talk about Davey Turnbull anymore?" I said in a pained voice.

"You brought him up," Lucy said, eyes flashing.

"I'm sorry," I muttered. "I'm not saying this right. Lucy, what I'm trying to get across is that we're meant for each other. I've missed years with you, and I don't want to miss another second."

Lucy looked down at her feet for a moment then she took a step towards me. When she laid her hand over my heart my breath caught in my throat, every muscle in my body tensing.

"I love you, Felix," she said softly, and I started to smile until she shook her head and took a step back and I felt like I'd been punched in the gut. "But you broke my trust." Her voice dropped to a rough whisper. "And I can't go through that again. I won't. I was happy with you, but I never felt secure. My stomach was always in knots wondering when the other shoe would drop. I can't live like that."

"That's my fault," I said, desperation in my tone. "But I can do better. Please, please give me a chance to do better."

She was shaking her head again, and I had an awful sinking feeling in the pit of my stomach. "We're not equals, and I'm not strong enough to handle that type of relationship."

"That's bullshit!" I semi-shouted, and Mike pushed back his chair to stand – clearly not on board with me shouting at his sister, whom I'd already traumatised, and I couldn't say I blamed the guy. I swallowed and forced my tone to soften. "Of course we're equals. No, no that's not right. You're so much better than me. I know I don't deserve you. I know it. But I'm a selfish, arrogant bastard, and I want you anyway."

"It's over, Felix," Lucy told me, her voice now cold. "I'm sorry, but it was over the minute you wouldn't listen to me and threw me away. I can't live like your mother. I can't tolerate a man like your father."

I took a stumbling step back. Lucy's words hammered into me like physical blows. All these years of hating my father, of never wanting to be like him, and here I was – the love of my life could see my worst fear was a reality.

I blinked as I considered the facts. In my quest for more money and power, driven by my desire to outdo my father which I knew he would hate, I'd become a ruthless, workaholic intent on success at any cost. Happy not to make the time to listen to the woman I loved when I was lucky enough to have her. Happy not to care whether the atmosphere in my office was inclusive or fair. Happy to throw away the best thing that ever happened to me.

"Right," I said in a choked voice. "Y–you're right."

"Felix, I—"

"No, no, it's okay. You don't have to say anymore. I–I'll leave."

I ignored Hetty's protests as I stumbled to the front door. I was proud of myself that I managed to clear the borders of Little Buckingham before I stopped in a layby and vomited again into a ditch.

CHAPTER 28

You need to find her again

Felix

I was daydreaming. And when you're supposed to be managing millions of pounds worth of developments, daydreaming is not ideal. But that didn't seem to matter to my wandering mind. It wasn't even the kind of productive daydreaming Lucy often did. It was more along the lines of torturing myself and wishing I could rewind time: never letting Lucy out of my bed, never believing that total weasel, actually asking Lucy about herself, listening to her rather than lecturing her. The list was endless.

It didn't help that, aside from Tabitha, two other associates had also come forward as victims of Will's sexual harassment, which made Tabitha feel even more guilty. Having learned my lesson about not listening, I heard her out and was taught some hard lessons about my management style. Tabitha hadn't felt that the environment in the office was one where she was comfortable disclosing inappropriate behaviour. Terms like *boys' club*, *systemic sexism* and *masculine environment* were used. Great store was put on not whingeing and getting on with the job. Apparently Tabitha believed that unless you made yourself "a robot like Victoria" there wasn't a hope in hell of progressing as a woman.

And even then, even after Tabitha kept her head down and didn't complain about Will, did a good job — she was *still* the one I asked to take Lucy shopping.

"But you're an assistant," I said, bewildered that this was an issue.

"An *executive* assistant who had compiled actual data needed for that meeting you made me miss, which was presented by John instead of me when he hadn't put any of the work in. Would you have asked John to miss the meeting if it had been the other way around?"

Yes, I was definitely learning hard lessons. Everything in the office had to change. An entire culture shift. Less emphasis on being the pushiest, shouting the loudest, more on quiet competence and inclusion.

So, in the end, Lucy was even right about that. It *was* better to be nice, even in business. God knows after the changes the office was brighter and more inviting, meetings were more productive, everyone in the firm was performing better.

It was ironic that I had hated and railed against my dad so much, but when it came down to it I still believed that in order to be successful I had to emulate him. There's no way Dad would tolerate the new soft seating areas with colourful armchairs and sofas, the explosions of personal effects on people's desks now, the baby in a sling at yesterday's meeting, the office dog. But then my dad was a short-sighted arsehole, and if I didn't want to remain one too, I had to change the way I did business.

Vicky approved all the changes. For her, the atmosphere in the office was less a conscious choice and more complete lack of awareness of how the culture and environment in a workplace could affect employee satisfaction and productivity. Nothing ever affected Vicky's productivity. Well, that's what I thought...

"You need to sort my sister out."

I blinked and jerked my head round from staring out of the window daydreaming – because apparently, that's what I did nowadays. Mike was standing in the doorway of my office looking furious with his arms crossed over his broad chest.

"Mike, I—"

"She's miserable and she's stuck in her head, writing all the time. Won't even come out to the pub with Emily. Barely comes out of the office she's set up at Mum's." He stomped over to the chair opposite me and threw himself down in it. "She's gone all weird. It sometimes happens when she's deep in a story. She forgets to eat, won't change her clothes, barely looks up from her computer screen. Her room is covered in maps she's drawn and Post-its with character details or scene ideas on them."

"It sounds like she's gone down the rabbit hole of her next book," I said. "I don't think I can—"

"She's finished the book and has gone straight into another series. No break."

"Mike, I can't tell Lucy what to do. You know that. If anything, I need to respect her wishes *more* after everything that happened."

"She's yours," Mike said simply, and my eyebrows went up.

"Lucy has made it very clear that she is not mine and never will be." I took a deep breath, and my voice was quieter when I spoke again. "And Mike, I'm sorry, but I don't blame her. I don't even think she *should* forgive me. God knows, I can't forgive myself. It's not even just the way I threw her out; it's everything, including me being a dismissive, self-absorbed arsehole, just like…" I trailed off and looked to the side, unable to speak past the lump that had formed in my throat.

"You're *not* your dad," Mike said, leaning forward in his chair and fixing me with his glare. "You never were anything like him. If that's the bullshit you're selling to yourself then you need to start paying attention. Lucy was angry and taken off guard when she implied that. She didn't mean it. I know she didn't. And anyway, it's not like Lucy and Mum are completely blameless in this. You didn't have all the information. They should have told you why Lucy was coming to London, why she wanted to work for you. It was unfair."

I sighed. "Mike, she's asked me to back off. I'm not going to force her to—"

"You know about her hands, right?"

"Yes," I said slowly.

"Well, she can get joint pain with the Raynaud's too. She's not supposed to be leaning over with her back hunched for long periods. And all of that's gone out the window. And, of course, she's not to get cold, and at the moment she's working in the bloody outhouse. There's damp in there. She's in pain, man. Your woman is in pain, and you need to put a stop to it."

"What?" I pushed back from the desk and stood in one sudden movement.

"Back pain and pain in her hands. None of us can convince her to move out of the outhouse, not even that bossy mare Emily." Mike sighed. "My sister doesn't process hurt and loss like most people. She goes into herself. You remember how she was when Dad died?"

Nobody had been able to find Lucy the day after Henry Mayweather died of pancreatic cancer. The whole village had turned out to search. I was home from boarding school for the holidays at the time. I'd known where to look. I'd run over to the cottage and into the back bedroom. There in the depths of the cupboard, behind all the coats and shoes was little eight-year-old Lucy. She was writing in her notebook and she didn't look up when I crawled in after her. It was dark in there, but I could just about make out her face. Tears streaked down each pale cheek slightly as she wrote. It was the absolute silence of the crying that broke my heart the most.

"Hey, Luce," I'd whispered. She didn't look up. "Tell me a story?"

After a few more moments, she blinked and raised her head to look at me. The pain in her eyes caused my chest to squeeze hard.

Then in her croaky little voice, hoarse from crying, she told me her story about a good king who had been cursed by an evil witch to make him fall asleep and not wake up. About how he had a daughter who fought her way to find the antidote that could save him. About how she managed to make her way back and give it to her father before it was too late; and how the kingdom rejoiced when the good king at last woke up again. When she'd finished, her tears had stopped; it was like they'd run themselves dry.

"Daddy won't wake up, will he?" she whispered, and my throat burned as I shook my head. She threw herself into my arms then and I held her in a tight hug, telling her that it would all be okay, something she knew wasn't true.

After a little while, I picked her up and carried her out of the cupboard to Hetty and Mike. I watched as the three of them just fell into each other, collapsing in a group hug with their shared pain. I turned to walk away, but Hetty grabbed my hand and pulled me down with them. I was part of the Mayweather pain, part of their grief, and I felt it acutely.

Henry Mayweather had been more of a father to me than my own.

"Listen, mate, you found her that day, remember?" Mikey asked, his tone uncharacteristically soft. I nodded but couldn't bring myself to speak. "Well, you need to find her again, right? She's not run away this time, but she's gone all the same."

I blinked. What if Mike was right? What if I could find her again? What if she did need me after all? What if I was exactly what she needed? She could daydream to her heart's content. I'd be awake for both of us. I'd make sure all the real-world stuff got sorted.

"Felix, I was just going over the figures for the July reports, and I—" Vicky appeared in the doorway to my office, staring at Mike. She was wearing her pristine white suit, heels, perfect make-up, as always. It was a sharp contrast to Mike's cargo pants, tight thermal and crumbled lumberjack shirt over the top. His beard had a few days growth and his hair was a good couple of weeks past needing a cut. Vicky froze and her mouth dropped open.

"Sorry, love," Mike said, and Vicky blinked at the casual endearment. Nobody really ever had the balls to use endearments with Vicky. "But Felix and I are busy."

Vicky just stood there staring at him. It was bloody awkward, and I wasn't really in the mood to deal with it. Luckily, Lottie came in after Vicky and went straight to her, touching her wrist, which I knew was a signal they'd developed to snap Vicky out of herself when she became hyperfocused on something. It took longer than normal but eventually Vicky noticed Lottie's hand and blinked before coming out of her staring-at-Mike trance.

"Vics," Lottie muttered. "Let's get you back to the office. Leave these guys to alpha it out together."

"I'm sorry about your sister," Vicky blurted out, her weirdly intense focus back on Mike.

"So you bloody well should be," snapped Mike as he glared across at Vicky, who swayed back almost as if she were absorbing a physical blow. "My sister trusted you."

"When it comes to people, I can have poor judgement." She cleared her throat. To my surprise, Vicky actually sounded nervous. I don't think I'd ever heard her nervous before. "I should have listened to Lottie. I should *always* listen to Lottie."

Lottie smiled at Mike and gave him a small wave. "Hi, I'm Lottie, the all-knowing."

"Listen, Mike and I—" I started.

"Can you let Luce know how sorry Vics is?" Lottie said to Mike, completely ignoring me. "We've been trying to contact her, but she's not answering our calls and messages. We miss her. Is she coming back to London?"

"No."

"Yes."

Mike and I spoke at the same time, then he looked at me and raised his eyebrows.

"Yes," I repeated. "Lucy is coming back to London. She's moving in with me and she's staying."

Lottie's eyes went wide. "Oh, right. Well, that's sorted then. Hopefully she's back here for Taco Tuesday. It's Vics's turn and we're making Tabitha come next week."

CHAPTER 29

I accept I've lost that right

Lucy

"Mum, I told you I'm not having any lunch," I muttered, not looking up from the huge spider diagram I was poring over at my desk when I heard the door to the office open.

"You are definitely having lunch."

I spun round in my chair at the sound of Felix's deep voice and blinked up at him. He was frowning down at me, and I immediately felt self-conscious. My hand flew up to my bird's nest of a messy bun on top of my head and felt the multiple pens and pencils embedded in it. I was wearing leggings, a huge jumper of Mikey's which fell to mid-thigh, and I had no fewer than five pairs of socks on my feet.

"What are you doing here?" I said, totally bewildered. Felix was here in Little Buckingham? On a Wednesday? Had the global financial market collapsed? Was I hallucinating? In all the time I'd worked at Moretti Harding I don't think he'd ever taken time off in the week. He shifted on his feet and stuck his hands into his suit pockets (his standard three-piece suit seemed very incongruous with the pokey, cluttered office shed).

"Making sure you eat lunch," he said, as if him popping to Mum's cottage was a regular occurrence. I hadn't seen him in over a month. Now he was walking into the shed like he owned it, closely followed by Legolas (who'd already eaten two of my previous diagrams), put his hand on the radiator and frowned.

"This is way too cold," he said in an irritated voice before pushing away from there to walk to the window and run a finger over the glass, holding it up to show the condensation on the pane of glass. "It's damp in here, Lucy."

"Gah! Legolas! Out!" I shoved the pony away from the desk just before his teeth snapped dangerously close to my newest and most complicated diagram. Legolas snorted at me, and I was, yet again, covered in pony snot. I started pushing him towards the door. It was easier said than done as Legolas was bracing his hooves against me. "Well, help me then," I said to Mr Pristine. "You let Legolas in; you may as well help me eject the little shit."

So Felix Moretti, property development titan, ruthless businessman, most eligible bachelor in London, three-piece-suit-wearing posh boy, helped me push a fat pony's massive furry butt out of my office. When he shut the door on a disgruntled Legolas and turned to me, I took two big steps back, nearly falling over my office chair. Felix reached for me but when his hand met only air, he clenched it into a fist and let it drop to his side. We stared at each other for a moment.

"When was the last time you ate?" he asked.

"Oh my God. Why are you so obsessed with my eating habits? Did Mikey guilt you into coming down here?"

Felix's eyes remained glued to mine, and he crossed his arms over his chest.

"Right," I said, now understanding the situation. Mum and Mikey were worried. For some reason my lunatic brother clearly felt that dragging the man who had broken my heart out to the back end of nowhere to sort me out was appropriate. "You can tell Mikey to jog on. I'm fine. I'm an adult, and I can look after myself."

Felix looked out of the window as his jaw clenched. "You've lost weight," he said. "Lucy, you're not looking after yourself properly. Of course, Mikey's worried."

"I'm fi—"

"And you can't work in here," he went on, cutting me off. "This hut isn't fit for Legolas even. You need a warm, dry environment. Proper insulation. And you shouldn't be crouched over a screen or your desk twenty-four hours a day."

A low, frustrated noise made it out of my mouth that sounded suspiciously like a growl. Bloody hell, when had I ever growled at anyone? But Felix was driving me crazy.

"You're so bossy," I snapped. "I'm not even yours to boss around anymore, and you're still coming here and having a go at me."

Felix looked pained. "Please, love. I—"

"Don't call me love," I said in a low voice, which, to my humiliation, was laced with pain. Just one simple endearment from Felix and I was almost doubled over with the agony of losing him all over again. That was how dangerous this man was to me. That was why I needed to keep my distance, to bury myself in my work and escape reality.

Felix swallowed and looked away for a moment. When he made eye contact again, I could have sworn the pain in his expression was almost equal to mine before he blanked it.

"Okay, Lucy," he said, his voice low and steady, "I accept I've lost that right. I accept I've lost a lot of things when it comes to you. What I won't accept is you not looking after yourself. Now you're coming with me to get lunch, and then you're going to have a break from writing. When you do go back to work it won't be in this *fucking* shed."

My eyebrows went up, and I crossed my arms over my chest. I really must have been a pushover before if he thought I was going to do any of what he just said. Well, spineless Lucy Mayweather had found her backbone. No bossy billionaire was swanning in here and telling me what to do.

"I concentrate better in here," I said, turning away from him to sit back down and start work on the map again. "I can't work in the cottage, it's a madhouse. Out here it's quiet, when people aren't interrupting me." To my surprise, after a brief pause, Felix strode over to me and plucked my hands up off the desk to hold them in both of his. I had to hold back a sigh at the delicious warmth of his large hands enveloping mine. I knew I should jerk them away, but I couldn't quite muster up the self-control to do it. I blinked up at him, overpowered yet again by the sheer beauty of the man. His tight expression from before relaxed now that he was holding my hands.

"At least eat something," he said in a soft voice that made my chest squeeze, but I managed to pull my hands from his with a firm tug.

"Stop fussing over me," I snapped. "I'll eat when I need to eat, and I'm perfectly capable of looking after myself."

Felix sighed, then pushed off from my desk. I did my best to try to ignore him as he felt the damp on the windows again and then tutted when he felt the heat output from the admittedly pathetic mini heater I had plugged in.

"Honestly, it's at least eighteen degrees in here," I told him. "You don't need to worry about it."

"You need it to be at least twenty-four degrees to feel comfortable," he told me, and I gritted my teeth. Trust Felix to lecture me on what temperature *I* was happy in.

"You don't know anything about my temperature regulation."

"I raised the office temperature in a series of degree hikes," he told me. "You stopped shivering at twenty-two degrees, and your hands stopped displaying pigment loss at twenty-three degrees. Twenty-four was when you stopped huddling over to keep warm."

I blinked at him and very nearly smiled. "I didn't realise you were watching that closely." A small kernel of hope started to grow. "You do realise it was madness to make the entire office tropical just to keep one, relatively crap, assistant comfortable?"

He shrugged. "I just wanted you to be warm," he muttered.

"That was really sweet," I said, and hope lit his expression. My chest squeezed, and all I wanted to do was run to him and fall into his arms. But then an unbidden image of Felix's furious face when he berated me before throwing me out of his office popped into my brain. I'd let my guard down with him before and look where that got me.

Plus it was obvious that he was only here because Mike had guilted him into it. My family were worried. I didn't want to worry them, but I really couldn't help it. The compulsion to sink into the other world, the fantasy world I'd created was too strong, and just then that shed was the only place I could do it. The only place I could forget everything and feel fully immersed in the writing. I cleared my throat. "I hope you're not still boiling them alive."

"No," Felix said, looking sheepish, "But I have made some other changes. The office is way more open now. No more old boys' club mentality. More collaboration. Less emphasis on being a dick to get ahead. I even allowed some colour on the walls, personal effects on the desks. We have Cake Monday, Taco Tuesday. You were right – it does make a difference. And you were right about how short-sighted I am. It's not just the sharks that I need to contribute. The best ideas often come from the minnows – they just have to have a forum to speak. It's helped the company immeasurably. I don't know why I've been such a prick for so long. And Will, of course he's been sacked. Tabitha and a few others came forward as well. I'm sure you already know that. He'll have a criminal record."

Yes, the police had told me all of that, not that I'd really taken it in. Much easier to be stuck in my imagination most of the time.

"Tabitha feels really bad. She'd like to apologise to you in person. Vicky too." He let out a brief chuckle. "I think Vicky's taking it the worst. She's not good at being wrong. I gather you're not taking their calls?"

"I'm too busy," I said, looking away from him and back at my map.

"Too busy even to speak to Lottie?" he asked gently. "She's worried about you as well. And she misses you. They all do."

I felt a brief twinge of guilt. I did feel bad about Lottie, but I still wasn't ready to speak to or see anyone from my life in London.

"After I've finished this series. I'll speak to them after."

"But, you'll see them next month, won't you?" Felix asked. When I looked at him in confusion, his head was cocked to the side, his arms crossed again.

"Next month?"

"At the book signing."

My stomach dropped and I gritted my teeth. There were ten missed calls on my phone from my agent. This was an international signing. Epic fantasy and sci-fi authors from all over the world would be there.

"I'm not doing it," I said. There was no way in hell that I was (a) going back to London again (b) being put on display in front of thousands of people, or (c) leaving this shed. The small event at Harry's building was one thing. I'd actually enjoyed talking to the teenagers and I was glad I'd managed to work up the courage to do it before leaving London. But this would be a totally different kettle of fish.

"You have to go up there to negotiate the streaming deal as well," Felix said. I jerked in my chair in surprise as my gaze flew to his.

"What do you know about that? Have you been speaking to Madeline?" I said, annoyance in my tone. First Mikey and now Madeline. Was everyone just going around talking about me behind my back?

"She's worried about you too," Felix said in that gentle tone again.

I rolled my eyes. Maddie was worried about her fifteen percent.

"Lucy, she says your output is insane at the moment. She thinks you need to slow down."

I frowned at this. Okay, so if Maddie was only interested in making money from me then she'd only be happy that my output was crazy high.

"I'm not doing the signing, and I'm not making any deals with any streaming service," I said, turning my back on Felix again. "I just want to stay in my shed and work on my books."

"Okay, love," Felix said softly. I had to blink away tears that suddenly pricked my eyes, so by the time I managed to turn around to tell him to go away he was shutting the door to the shed behind him.

Finally, I thought. He's given up.

CHAPTER 30

I was never the boss of you

Lucy

It was the vibrations that really tipped me off. Oh, and the bloody great hole where the window once was.

"What on earth?" I muttered as I pulled my noise-cancelling headphones down to my neck.

"Hi," a man said from the other side of the hole. He smiled at me like he hadn't just stolen my window. "You alright there?"

"Er, I'm fine," I said slowly. "But I appear to be missing a window."

"Not for long," said another man who popped up next to the first before retrieving a massive new window from the ground. "This'll be installed in a jiffy."

My mouth opened, then closed, then opened again. They were both working away on the windowsill, totally ignoring me.

"I don't need a new window," I said.

"Ah yes, he told us you might say that," said man number one. This information didn't seem to faze him at all.

"Listen, I'm sorry, but my brother's overstepped here," I told them both. "I really don't need—"

"Weren't your brother, love," man number two said. "I know Mike Mayweather. Worked a few jobs with him. Not him that hired us."

My eyebrows went up. "Then who...?"

I trailed off as I put the pieces together, remembering Felix's frown as he wiped some condensation from the window that morning.

"That bossy bastard," I muttered as I pushed up to standing and walked over to the door of the shed, opening it the bare minimum so that Legolas wouldn't be able to make it through and eat my maps. The pony did manage to headbutt me in the groin a couple of times before tossing up his head and trotting up in the direction of the main house kitchen. I followed behind muttering about arrogant, bossy, interfering buggers who need to get over their guilt already and pick on someone else to help excessively.

"Oh good," Mum said brightly when I made it into the kitchen. "Felix said you'd be up soon. I've got your favourite soup in the Aga, love. And I made those bread rolls you like."

"Mum, he's taken my window!" Why was it now acceptable for Felix to stroll around our property stealing the infrastructure? "Whose side are you on?"

"Oh, sweetheart," Mum's overly cheery demeanour cracked then, and when I saw the flash of real worry behind her eyes, I felt ashamed. "There're no sides. There's just me wanting you to be okay."

I sighed. "Mum, I'm fine. You don't need to—"

"You're not fine," she said, her voice cracking. "You've not been fine for weeks."

"You know I get like this, Mum," I tried to explain. "I get absorbed into the story. It's normal."

"You've *never* retreated like this before, Lucy. Well, unless you count after—" Mum broke off to clear her throat, then came over to me and laid her hands on my shoulders to steer me to the table. The dogs ran in from the garden at that point, and between them and my mum it felt like I was being herded into place at the kitchen table. "You've not even been seeing Emily. And you've lost so much weight."

"Mum, I—"

"I'm scared, sweetheart, okay?" Mum said, and I snapped my mouth shut. She sounded scared as well. Really scared. I frowned slightly as I sat in the chair and wrapped my arms around myself. I mean, I guess I *had* lost a bit of weight. As I felt my protruding ribs I grimaced slightly. Okay, more than a bit.

"I haven't felt this scared since after your father died. I can't go back there, Lucy. I felt so helpless. I'm not risking any of that happening again. I know Felix started this all off, but he was wrong. And what's happening now isn't just about that. You're grieving for him just like you grieved for your father, but you can't see that he's right there waiting for you. We should have got you more counselling after your dad died, but we let you get lost in your stories."

"I'm not lost now, Mum," I muttered, but thinking back on the last few weeks I began to doubt myself.

Now that I was confronted by the smell of Mum's soup and fresh bread, I realised just how hungry I was. How had I been ignoring that? I hesitated a moment but then took a chair at the table.

Mum's sigh of relief gave me a pang of guilt as I took the first spoonful of soup. She really was worried. So, I concentrated on eating, at first to keep Mum happy but as the hunger abated, I realised that I could actually think a little more clearly with some food on board. I felt a bit more present. More able to cope. Which was good because the next moment Felix was strolling into the kitchen followed by Rueben, the local electrician.

"Yeah, I know it's a bit nuts, but we *have* to use that shed," Felix said. "It needs a 32-amp supply or I can't fit out the heating system I want to put in there."

Rueben sucked in a breath through his teeth. "You'd be better knocking that old thing down and building from the ground up, man."

"That's not an option," Felix said with a firm shake of his head. He paused in his progress through the kitchen when he saw me sitting at the table. His eyes dropped to my near-empty bowl, then back up to mine, and he smiled. It was filled with relief and affection, and the sight of it made my belly whoosh.

"Listen Rueben," he said, not taking his eyes off me. "If you could just sort the supply, I'd be grateful. Rewire the whole thing. Cost doesn't factor."

Rueben shrugged, gave me a low wave and quick chin jerk before he disappeared out of the front door towards the shed.

"You okay?" Felix asked softly as he walked over towards me at the table. When he drew up next to me, I tilted my head back to look at him. A strand of my hair fell across my cheek and Felix's hand lifted automatically towards it as if to push it back behind my ear. But I flinched away, and his hand dropped down before he took a small step back, his smile dimming slightly. He turned to put a hand on the Aga.

"Back up to temperature then," he said to Mum. Ah, so *that* was why the kitchen was fully tropical. Felix. I should have known.

"Felix, I'm not sure what you're playing at but you're really not responsible for my temperature regulation. And the shed is *fine*."

His eyebrows went up at that blatant lie and I gritted my teeth.

"I'm letting you off, okay," I said, my voice dropping low in the hope that Mum, who was across the kitchen from us, wouldn't be able to hear. "You don't have to feel guilty anymore. And it's not your fault that I've got sucked down a bit of a rabbit hole."

"I'm not doing any of this out of guilt, Lucy," he said, his smile dropping completely now and a frown forming between his brows.

I frowned back at him in confusion. "Then why on earth are you here?"

He looked away from me and his jaw clenched. "We'll get into that later. When you're better."

I shook my head. "I don't have time to get into anything. I'm in the middle of—"

"I know you need your writing now," he said. "I understand that. I'll make sure the shed is watertight, warm and safe. You promise me you'll eat regularly and sleep *in the house* then that's fine. Once I've finished with the shed, you can carry on in your world. For now."

I scoffed. "It sounds like you're *allowing* me to carry on writing. You do realise that you're not the boss of me anymore?"

"I was never the boss of you," he replied softly. "Not really. If anything, it was the other way around. It still is."

I huffed. I didn't understand him at all. Well, he could just jog on with whatever he thought he needed to do. I had no intention of believing him about the guilt thing. There was no other explanation.

And what did he mean by *for now*?

CHAPTER 31

I'll be your assistant

Lucy

"Don't you have to be in London?" I asked for what felt like the hundredth time. Felix had let himself into my shed again, armed with a caramel latte, which he knew I couldn't resist (how he managed to get hold of one in Little Buckingham, I had no idea).

I was now sitting cross-legged on my new ergonomic office chair which had arrived three days ago. My old chair had been removed and replaced within a ten-minute period – I'd actually been sitting on it at the time, but Mikey and Felix had simply lifted me off the chair and onto the new one, totally ignoring my surprised protests.

I was still pretending to be disgruntled – there was no way I was admitting that the new chair was actually super comfortable and way better for my back. It was also the exact colour and make I wanted – as was the wallpaper, newly installed, and the small sofa and throw cushions and the rug on the floor. Someone had clearly been snooping on my Pinterest account.

Felix smiled. "I told you – I'm working remotely. Vicky is more than capable of running the show for the moment, especially with Lottie helping her."

"Have you seen your mum?" I said softly, and his smile dropped. I knew Felix was staying at the pub, and I also knew that would not have gone down well with Bianca Moretti.

"Yeah, a couple of times, when *he's* been in London."

Felix's dad was a real piece of work. I rarely saw him around the village and had never had much contact with him as a child, apart from those few times I heard him shouting at Felix. Once it had been over the only B grade Felix got in his GCSEs. I mean, the boy achieved the highest possible marks in all the other nine subjects, but his arsehole dad stormed over to our little cottage and lost his shit at sixteen-year-old Felix for that one result.

There was a moment when I thought Mr Moretti was actually going to hit Felix, but then Felix had puffed up his chest and stood to his full over six-foot height, muttering, "Try it, old man," under his breath.

My brother had also decided to stand next to Felix and cross his arms over his already substantial chest, and Mr Moretti backed off. It was the first time I'd ever heard my mum swear after she slammed the cottage door in his face. The level of vitriol coming off a father towards his son was so high it stuck with me.

Mum absolutely hated the man.

"Is… she okay?" I asked Felix. Bianca Moretti had always seemed a little fragile to me. She was very glamorous but highly strung. She made a big show of how much she loved Felix, but in my opinion, if she really cared about her son, she would never have allowed him to be exposed to his father's aggression.

He shrugged. "She's fine. Upset that I won't stay at the house, but she knows I'm not ever going to risk breathing the same air as that bastard again, so she'll have to accept it."

I sighed. "Felix, you should just go back to London. I know you hate it here."

Felix frowned. "I hate my father, not Little Buckingham. There's a difference. The office is fine with me working remotely for a bit. And anyway, Legolas would miss me." Legolas was standing next to him with his head on his lap. He was allowed in the office when Felix was in residence – his love for Felix distracted him from eating my work.

Felix blew out a breath and then pulled off his jumper. My mouth went dry at the brief glimpse of his abs and then his glorious, muscled biceps straining his t-shirt. When I managed to drag my eyes back up to his face, he was smirking at me with one eyebrow raised. Even that was sexy. It was completely unfair how attractive the bastard was. His gorgeousness, combined with the steady and relentless campaign to cater to my every need, was slowly chipping away at my resolve.

I would have suspected that the arm and stomach porn he'd displayed was intentional to drive me to distraction, but to be fair to him it was at least twenty-five degrees in the shed.

Felix had not only installed proper electricity and a heating system, but also had the shed clad from the outside to make it completely insulated and watertight. It was slightly ridiculous really. I was too stubborn to move out of the shed, so he'd just reworked everything around me. It would probably have been vastly easier for all involved if there wasn't a small hermit refusing to leave in the mix as they renovated it, but somehow Felix made it work.

And, if I was honest, I did feel better. I was eating now; my ribs weren't protruding in that scary way. The frost nip had completely resolved. I didn't have the back pain anymore. Mum had stopped looking so worried. Mike had stopped his relentless hovering.

If we'd still been together, Felix would have teased me and asked if I was "quite finished checking out the gun show?" But he was more careful around me now, more wary. So, he wiped the smirk off his face and let me blush without commenting.

"Luce," he said gently, and my eyes went back to his, "have you thought anymore about the signing?" I looked away from him and down into my lap.

Yes, I felt guilty, but I just couldn't face all those people. Peopling was hard for me at the best of times but now I just didn't feel safe anymore. After what happened with Will the anxiety had slowly built rather than improve. I mean, Emily had dragged me out to the pub last night, and even that had felt difficult at first. I wouldn't have gone but she basically turned up at the house and kidnapped me.

"I've got a bloody babysitter and I need a pint with my best mate," she'd snapped as she frog-marched me out of the house with Mum waving us off. "You can turtle away on your own time."

Of course, when we got there, as well as Emily's husband Pete, Mike and Felix had appeared. Emily had gradually softened to Felix over the last two weeks. I think she'd become so worried about me that any reinforcements to pull me out of my funk were welcomed. She still called him a "poncy city wanker", but then again she might well have done that anyway, even without what he did to me.

Once we were sitting at one of the tables and I was flanked by Emily and three huge men, my heart rate settled, and I started to feel like I could cope. The Badger's Sett isn't exactly the most ram jam pub, but it was a Saturday and there were a fair few punters.

I'd jumped at a glass falling on the floor and then, to my annoyance, my hand shook as I picked up my glass, so much I had to put it down again. Felix was next to me, and when my hand went back to my lap, he reached subtly under the table and laid his over mine. This was a running theme with Felix. He seemed to know the *exact* moments when I needed contact like this. The feel of his large, warm hand on mine slowed my racing heart and stopped the shakes. It stayed there for the next hour. If the others noticed, they didn't say anything. And at the end of the night, Felix walked me home, still holding my hand, but didn't push it any further.

This new Felix, the one who looked at me like I was the most precious thing on earth, the one with endless patience, the one who just seemed to want to be with me in whatever way he could, support me however I would allow – *this* Felix was very gradually winning my trust, but something was still holding me back.

"I'm not doing the signing," I said. "I've told Madeline, and I just can't go through with it."

"And the meeting with the production company?"

I swallowed and looked down at my lap where I was cradling my coffee. My voice was small when I spoke again. "I just don't think I can…" I trailed off, searching for an explanation that Felix would understand, but that was a feat in itself. How could I explain that I just wanted to hide away from the world and that the potential exposure of my work on screen terrified me? To Felix – the ultimate businessman, only concerned with the bottom line, fearless and alpha and commanding – I would seem pathetic. I *was* pathetic. "I'm not strong enough to cope with that much exposure," I admitted. "I know it's weak, but—"

"That's bullshit," Felix snapped. "You're one of the strongest people I know. It's *not* weak to be naturally shy. It's not weak to be wary after what happened and to want to hide."

He leaned forward then, sitting on the edge of the sofa so that he was only inches away from me in the chair, his beautiful dark eyes focused on me so intently it made me feel like the centre of his whole universe. Having Felix's full, intense attention was a rush like no other.

"But the time for hiding is over now, Luce. You're not going to let this opportunity pass you by. It's *my* fault you were hurt…" his voice broke over the last words and I felt my chest tighten.

"Felix, you're not responsible for what Will did. That's on him."

"I am responsible for not listening to you before it happened and after. I should have seen him for what he was, but I was so wrapped up in my own narrative of how I could be humiliated again, just like I was with my ex."

I sighed. "Felix, you won't even tell me what happened with her. You don't even trust me enough for that."

Two flags of red appeared on his cheekbones and he swallowed, looking away from me for a moment. "Nobody knows what happened apart from your brother."

"Mikey?"

Felix shook his head. "Look, I promise I will tell you. I want to tell you. But it's so sordid. I can't go down that road yet with you. But just know that it clouded my judgment. I let my pride blind me to everything else. And that's not the only time I didn't listen. I should have taken your advice about the office environment. I should have realised what an asset you actually were to the company."

I tilted my head to the side. What had happened to him? My heart clenched at the thought of someone hurting him but I could see he wasn't ready to share anything more at the moment.

"Felix," I said through a small smile, "I was crap at my job."

He huffed. "Listen, I know now that you were helping Vanessa. So, no you weren't crap. Not at the creative side. Not at the advertising side. Yes, organisational skills and business bullshit aren't your bag, but I was so focused on trying to make you into the perfect assistant that I lost sight of who you are. I forgot about all your strengths. And I believed that fucking prick over you."

The absolute agony in Felix's voice was almost painful to hear. I couldn't bear it anymore. So, I put my mug on my desk and leaned forward to lay my hands over his.

"Okay yes, you could have listened. But I wasn't honest with you. I was hurt that you didn't obsess over me like I did over you, that you hadn't asked Mikey anything about me, and so I didn't tell you about the books. I didn't tell you that I was helping the advertising team. You didn't have all the information. That's not your fault. Felix, even without everything that's happened, I'm still a big wimp."

"No, Lucy, that's not—"

"Felix," I said firmly. "I would still be a big girl's blouse about doing the signing and the production company deal. That's just who I am."

"You can't say big girl's blouse," Felix said. "That's sexist. I'm seriously into all the feminism stuff now – Tabitha's sorted me out." Crikey, things really had moved on at the office. "Listen, just try the signing first. The production company can wait." He turned my hands over in his and slid his fingers over my palm. I fought down a shiver at his touch.

"I don't—"

"Think of all those readers, love," he said softly. It was a double-pronged attack – using an endearment and making me feel guilty about my loyal fanbase. "They're dying to see you again."

I looked away from his intense gaze for a moment and felt my cheeks heat again.

"It won't be like at Harry's building. There'll be so many of them at that large of an event," I said in a near-whisper. "I just don't think I can cope with those numbers." Then my voice dropped even lower, and Felix had to lean forward to make out what I was saying. "I'm scared they'll be disappointed. That'll be the real let-down – meeting me."

"You would not be a letdown," Felix said, his voice all growly with anger. The growly quality of his voice combined with the arm porn was making me feel a little lightheaded. My gaze dropped to his mouth, and I leaned towards him just a little more. Only an inch or so separated us now. When I looked up into his eyes his pupils were so dilated that there was only a rim of dark brown left around the edges. One of his hands let go of mine and came up to my jaw, his fingers sliding up from my neck to behind my ear. As my lips parted and my eyes started to close, he pulled back abruptly. I swayed in my seat at the sudden loss of him. He stood from his chair and paced to the door and back again.

"Right," he muttered. "Sorry, sorry. I didn't mean to—" He glanced at me. My cheeks felt like they were on fire now and I could feel a confused frown forming as I looked up at him. He pointed at me. "You need time," he told me. "I promised that I—" He broke off to look out of the window, his jaw clenched so tight that a muscle started ticking there. "Listen, Luce. *I'll* be your assistant at the signing, okay? I'll make sure everything runs smoothly. That you're not overwhelmed."

My eyebrows went up. "*You're* going to assist *me*?" The concept didn't really compute in my brain. Felix as my assistant? Was that even possible? But thinking of the signing, of all those people, imagining myself there with Felix by my side didn't evoke quite the level of panic it had before.

"Well, I mean, if you want me to, I will," he said, then rushed on, "but Luce, it doesn't have to be me. Anyone would come with you – Emily, Vicky, Lottie, Mike, even Bucks would do it. God knows your agent would – that woman scares the crap out of me. I doubt she'd put up with you being made to feel uncomfortable. I know you might not trust me yet. The point is that it's not something you have to do on your own."

I looked at Felix then, at his earnest expression, and something deep inside me that had become twisted, something I didn't even realise had been causing me pain, released.

"I want you there," I said with quiet conviction. "Just you."

CHAPTER 32

The worst assistant

Felix

"Are you warm enough?" I laid both my hands over Lucy's on the table. Whilst they weren't ice-cold, they weren't quite the temperature level I liked them to be. I pulled them into my lap, holding both of them in mine. Lucy glanced down at her hands and then back up at me, a blush sweeping up over her cheeks. Yes, I was getting somewhere with her, but I wasn't going to push things too early. However, I was not above using the chemistry between us and how attracted she was to me to my advantage. "Maybe I should talk to the organiser about whacking the heat up."

"Felix," Lucy said. "It must be over twenty degrees in here. Everyone else will melt if they put the heating up anymore. I'm the only person I can see in a jumper." Lucy was wearing a cashmere jumper dress, thermal leggings and fur-lined boots. I'd become quite the expert in the warmest women's clothing out there.

Once I knew Lucy's sizes, I just started having everything delivered to the cottage. Lucy had been so deep in the writing zone that at first she barely noticed. But since I'd told her I was assisting her, she'd started to emerge from the writing shed more and clocked all the bags and boxes stacking up in her bedroom.

Last week she'd stomped down into the kitchen where I was having a cup of tea with Hetty, a furious expression on her face — well, at least on the part of her face I could see above the pile of coats she was struggling to carry.

"Felix," she snapped before dumping about twenty coats onto my lap. I just about managed to save my tea. When I looked back at Lucy she was standing with her legs braced apart and her hands on her hips. Smiling probably wasn't my best plan, but an angry Lucy was just too adorable, and I was so pleased to be evoking some sort of reaction from her that I didn't care too much if I pissed her off. "Don't you smirk at me." Her eyes narrowed on my face, and I tried to flatten my smile but didn't quite pull it off. "Do you know how many coats I now have in my bedroom?"

I grabbed some of the coats that had fallen to the floor and lifted them all up and onto the chair next to me. "Well, I—"

"This isn't even half of them, Felix!" she snapped. "You're obsessed with buying me clothing."

"Listen, I know you're busy, and I thought that if I did a spot of shopping it would save you time."

"I don't need all this stuff. Nobody needs *twenty-five* coats."

"Er," Hetty put in. "Twenty-four." I glanced at her and then down to Legolas, who was munching on the specialist heated puffa I bought Lucy last week.

"Legolas," I snapped. "That's one of the ones for minus twenty degrees, you bastard."

Legolas gave me a guilty look but continued munching through the lining.

"This is exactly what I mean," Lucy said. "When am I going to ever need to go somewhere that's *minus twenty*?"

"Luce, you need to be maintained at a certain temperature. And that means that—"

"Ugh, I'm not a tropical fish, Felix. You can't just..." she blinked, and her head tilted to the side, the attitude in her stance fading for a moment. "Did you say *you* went shopping?"

I shrugged. "Most of it I ordered online, but for some of it I had to go to specialist outdoor stores and—"

"You bought it? Not Tabitha? B–but you don't have time to go shopping. You've never shopped in your life."

"I didn't really trust it to anyone else."

"Oh." The fight went out of Lucy as she sat down heavily on the chair next to mine. Hetty put a cup of tea in front of her which she took a sip of as she absently stroked one of the thermally insulated cashmere coats lying on the table next to her. "I–I don't... why would you...?"

I dipped my head down so her eyes were level with mine and smiled at her.

"I just want you to be warm, love," I said softly. Her mouth fell open slightly, and her eyes went unfocused.

"Lucy, you say, 'Thank you, Felix, for buying me lots of warm clothes. That was very kind and generous of you'," Hetty told her.

"Right," Lucy muttered. "Uh, thanks." She blinked down at her tea for a moment, then her gaze snapped back to mine and her eyes narrowed again. "No more coats though. I'd need two lifetimes to wear all the ones you've already bought."

I'd shrugged and smiled again when I thought about the delivery that was scheduled for that afternoon.

"I don't care about the other people here," I said, still keeping hold of Lucy's hands. "They can take off a layer if they're hot."

"They'll be down to their underwear if they take off any more layers," Lucy said, the blush still on her cheeks as she looked down at her hands in mine. "And this space is going to fill up with readers soon. It'll be unbearable for people if the heating's any higher."

"Hey, kids," Madeline strutted up to the stand. "So, Lucy, you ready?"

Lucy tugged her hands away from mine and sat up straighter in her chair, her nervous expression returning. Her hand shook slightly as she unnecessarily straightened the bookmarks in front of her.

"Have they sorted out the ticketing system for her?" I asked Madeline, and she rolled her eyes.

"Felix, like I told you already, they don't feel it's needed."

I huffed. "*Those* guys have a ticketing system," I said, pointing to the larger tables at the head of the room. "Why not Lucy?"

"Felix," Lucy said. "I'm not a big enough of a deal for that."

My eyebrows went up. "Luce, you're way up with those guys."

Her eyes went wide as she glanced over to the big names that I knew she was a little awed to even be in the same room as.

"Yes, love, you are," I said softly. "Listen, I'll be back in a sec, okay?"

"Er, okay," Lucy muttered, her gaze still fixed on the other side of the room.

I got up from the table and steered Madeline out of hearing distance.

"I'm not having Luce overwhelmed," I said. "The crowd needs to be controlled properly."

Madeline huffed. "Calm down, Casanova. It'll be fine."

My eyebrows went up. "There are *thousands* of people coming today. What percentage are going to want to see Lucy? How many books are each of them going to bring? Can you see her turning anyone away or refusing to sign anything?"

"Listen, Felix—"

"It'll kill her to disappoint any of her fans," I said. "Trust me, I know her. She'll be devastated. We need more assistants. We need better barriers, and we need a *ticket system*."

Madeline sighed. "You're a pain in the arse, you know that?"

Of course, I was right. I'm always right.

Lucy's table was a bun fight. A massive queue formed within minutes of the doors to the signing opening. She was like a deer in the headlights. Fortunately, due to me throwing my weight around, there were barriers set up to manage the hordes of people and a ticketing system had been hastily added, together with two more queue assistants.

I hate to say it, but when it came to actual assisting, I was... total crap. The tables had well and truly turned. Now *I* was the worst assistant. In fact, one of the signing organisers had to step in to take over the contactless payments and dish out books (that was until we ran out of books).

I was relegated to being the bad guy who told people Lucy was only signing a maximum of two items. *That* I was good at. After all, I'd perfected my arsehole persona for many years.

Lucy was so nervous at first that I was worried she'd shut down. After the first twenty minutes and when Lucy had started stuttering to such a degree that people began to look at her with concern, I told everyone we needed a tea break.

"But, Felix," Lucy hissed as I led her to the empty room next door that was allocated for the authors to have their lunch together later, "we can't just leave. All those people..."

She trailed off and bit her lip, wrapping her arms around her body in a defensive gesture. I needed to get her out of her head. Needed to shock her into life. It might have been too soon, and I still wanted to take things slowly, but I really couldn't see an alternative. That's why I moved into her space, cupped her face with my hands, and kissed her. Her mouth parted as she gasped in shock, allowing me to deepen the kiss as I pulled her stiff body into mine.

I knew the moment that the world fell away for her. She melted into me, her arms uncrossed to slide around my back as I slid one of my hands into her hair and the other around her until I was lifting her up. I placed her on the tabletop behind us and carried on kissing her, stepping between her legs and leaning her back against my arm.

When I finally managed to pull my lips away, I rested my forehead against hers and studied her glazed expression.

"Keep going guys." We both flinched at the voice and turned our heads to see a woman sitting two tables over. She had a cheese sandwich halfway to her mouth and a huge grin on her face.

"Oh my God," whispered Lucy and my arms gave her a squeeze.

"Don't be embarrassed, hun," said the woman, waving her sandwich at us. "This is perfect fodder for my next book. You two ever thought of being cover models?"

"No," we both said together.

"Shame," she muttered, standing from her chair to leave the room. "Anyhoo, continue. Don't mind me."

"She's one of the most famous romance authors on the planet," whispered Lucy, a blush creeping over her cheeks. "Omigod. She spoke to us. She saw us kissing."

I smiled down at Lucy. "I don't think she minded."

Lucy frowned up at me but, I noted, did not do anything to extract herself from my arms. "Why are you kissing me?"

"Well, number one, you're very kissable."

"Felix," she said, swatting my arm which I was also very glad about. I was getting somewhere if Lucy was comfortable enough with me to be swatting my arm.

"And number two, I wanted to break through and get your attention."

Her eyebrows went up. "Get my attention? Aren't there easier ways to do that rather than dragging me off and snogging me in front of famous romance authors who just want to eat a cheese sandwich in peace?"

"No, not really. This was the easiest way."

Lucy snorted.

"Listen, baby," I said, and she swallowed, her expression softening. "I'm sorry. I know I've no right to kiss you, but I just wanted to get you out of your head. All these people, they're here to see you, because of the words you've written. All they want to do is talk about your stories. Just imagine it's me. Think of all the times you've told me about your stories, about the characters. They're on your side. They love the world you've built."

That was the turning point. Lucy came alive after that. There were some maps spread out on her table and she pored over them with the fans (until I did my bad guy routine and moved them along). Madeline even took me aside and asked me if I had "fixed Lucy with my magic dick?". She was nothing if not direct.

I did have a very satisfying moment with Harry the twat when I turned him away and told him to queue like everyone else. I felt a bit bad for his heavily pregnant wife who seemed like a decent human so I had her skip up to the front (there was also the fact I still wanted her to agree to be our architect on the Hyde Park project). But Harry could fuck off.

Unfortunately, that backfired spectacularly when Lucy realised what I'd done and invited the smug fuck to come and have dinner with us after the bloody signing. I tried to dismiss the plan, but Lucy got that look on her face – the one that said she was annoyed that I didn't respect her and her ideas. And seeing as I was deep down the rabbit hole of trying to win her trust I agreed.

Plus there was the fact that I had misjudged Harry. He hadn't been passing any information to his client. Turned out that Will had decided to do that – playing both sides in case he didn't make partner and needed to jump ship to their firm. The CEO of the company was only too happy to rat him out. If I'd have bothered asking around before accusing Lucy I could have found out easily enough and that was on me.

And well, okay, *maybe* Harry's not *that much* of a twatface when you get to know him. And *maybe* having dinner with them wasn't the worst idea in the world. And *maybe* I did learn something from the way Harry does business.

By the end of the day, three things were clear: I should always listen to Lucy; I'm a shit assistant; and I have a magic dick that can snap her out of a fugue. That third fact I planned to use to my advantage, but only when the time was right.

CHAPTER 33

Hurt to hopeful

Felix

"I think they may even have branded Felix the worst assistant they'd ever encountered," Lucy said through a wide smile.

"I told you he'd be rubbish," snapped Emily as she struggled to contain Maisie, her squirming baby, on her lap. "He's always been an arrogant, pig-headed, weasely ba—" She glanced at Hetty who was holding out her swear jar, then down at her own daughter before she rolled her eyes, "—banana-brain."

"Good insult," I said with a smirk.

"Eff off, Moretti," she snapped just as Maisie decided to launch herself forward out of Emily's arms. Luckily, I was close enough to swoop down and catch the baby before her head could hit the wooden table. I scooped her up and secured her on my hip. Maisie, totally unaware of the near-miss she just had, gave me a gummy smile and then patted my face fairly aggressively (like mother like daughter – I'm sure Emily would hit me again if it was socially acceptable).

"Oh well done, Felix," said Hetty as she bustled around me and Maisie to boil the kettle. "You're always such a good boy."

Emily rolled her eyes and made a gagging motion behind Hetty's back whilst Mike let out a grumbly laugh.

"Ugh," Emily groaned. "Now we have to put up with some

sort of hot-guy-baby Levi ad scenario. It's too early in the morning for this, Felix."

I smiled down at Emily as her baby continued to pummel my face. It was the first time she'd called me Felix instead of Moretti since I'd been back in Little Buckingham, which I considered progress. I glanced at Lucy to see her staring up at me with a slightly glazed expression and decided this baby could beat the shit out of me all she wanted if it got that sort of reaction from Lucy. But then the moment was broken by the shrill doorbell ringing, followed by pounding on the front door.

"Felix Moretti!" Mum shouted in between banging. "I know you're in there. You come out here and see your mother!"

"Christ," I muttered as Hetty bustled past me to get the door.

"Now then, Bianca," Hetty said in her firmest tone. "Let's stay calm, shall we."

"Calm my arse!" Mum said. "Jimbo told me he saw Felix two hours ago. It's been like this for weeks. Why am I always the last to know when my son's home? And why do I have to hear it from an inebriated bartender at the post office?" Mum appeared in the doorway then, her normally meticulously styled hair all over the place and her mascara smudged.

"Hi, Mum," I said in a resigned tone. Unfortunately, with Mum, sometimes you just had to ride out the drama. She glanced at me then at Maisie who was still bouncing in my arms, her gummy smile now aimed at my harassed-looking mother.

"Oh my God," Mum breathed, her face paling. "Whose baby is that?"

"Not to worry, Mrs M," Emily put in, getting up from her chair and coming over to take Maisie from me. "This one's mine. You remember me? Emily? My husband Pete fixed your back fence three months ago."

Mum put her hand flat to her chest in a gesture of relief. "Oh yes, thank God for that."

Emily looked up at me, gave me a little eye roll and a small smile, tinged with a bit of sympathy. "Catch you later Lucy, Felix. Thanks for the tea, Hets." She patted me on the arm and mouthed "good luck" and then practically ran out of there. I didn't really blame her – I would have done the same if I could. I sighed.

"Mum, honestly what did you think? That I'd had a secret baby?"

"Well, how would I know?" Mum snapped. "You never tell me anything anymore. I barely see you. You could have had *five* children and left me none the wiser."

I opened my mouth to answer but was interrupted by Legolas trotting into the kitchen straight to Mum. He head-butted her side, and she absently stroked his nose. My eyebrows went up in surprise. Mum was a very anxious person, and she worried a lot about germs. She used to avoid touching Hetty's dogs back in the day. I wouldn't have thought casually stroking a pony was in her repertoire of behaviour.

"Right, come on, Bianca," Hetty said in her firm, let's get on with this tone. "In you come to the kitchen. We can make a cup of tea. Maybe you can convince Legolas to go outside. He does tend to listen to you more than anyone else."

Legolas *the pony* listened to my mum? The most uptight human I knew? I was having trouble processing this. Hetty's no-nonsense tone did seem to snap Mum out of her frozen state though. She moved into the kitchen and to me. I reached for her to give her a hug and kissed both of her cheeks.

"I'm sorry, Mum," I said. "I was going to come and see you. But we only just got back from London."

Mum looked between me and Lucy, her expression going from hurt to hopeful in a heartbeat. "Have you sorted it?" she asked softly. She was talking to me but looking at Lucy.

"Mum," I snapped. "We talked about this, okay? Don't make Lucy uncomfortable."

I'd told Mum the bare facts about what happened with Lucy but warned her not to go overboard. I made sure she was aware

236

that although I was in love with Lucy there was no guarantee that Lucy would forgive me, and the last thing I needed was my mother harassing her. Mum was very pro the idea of Lucy and me as a couple. In her mind I think she saw this as the ideal way of dragging me back to Little Buckingham more often.

What she didn't understand was that, however much I was back in the village, I was not going to be playing happy families with my father.

"You'll sort it," Mum said, then shocked me by moving into Lucy and giving her a kiss and a tight hug. "Hello darling," she muttered into Lucy's hair before letting her go.

"Er… hi, Mrs Moretti," Lucy said softly, darting a confused look at me.

"Oh my goodness. Honestly, Lucy, I've known you since you were a baby. Call me Bianca, please," Mum said as if she was some beloved aunt rather than the previously rather distant ex-employer of Lucy's mum. "Oh!" she clapped her hands together. "This is perfect. You can *both* come over tonight! I'll pop to Waitrose. It can be a proper family get together. Hetty, Mike, you should come too."

"Will Dad be there, Mum?" I asked gently. I was suddenly feeling exhausted.

Mum was getting this manic light in her eyes that didn't bode good things. She was desperate to see more of me. Desperate for me to come home more. Five years ago, when I would agree to family meals with dad, she used to pull out all the stops – cook elaborate meals, buy champagne and make a huge deal out of it. But she got so worked up, wanting everything to be perfect that it was almost unbearable. And my dad was invariably an absolute prick, so we'd start arguing. Cue Mum crying uncontrollably, having full-on panic attacks while I had to try and calm her down – just like I had done my entire childhood. As I hadn't set foot in that house in over five years, I had no doubt that she would be even more full-on than before.

"Yes, of course," she said, feigning ignorance.

"I'm not seeing that man," I said, my tone as firm as I could make it. Mum needed boundaries, and Hetty was right: she needed to calm down.

"He's your father, Felix," she said, her voice taking on that pleading quality that I just couldn't bear to ignore. "Were you...?" she paused and to my horror her eyes filled with tears. "Were you going to leave without seeing me *again*?"

I felt the familiar guilt wash over me and felt myself giving in.

"Mum, I—" I paused and took a deep breath, feeling emotionally drained. After being happily repressed for decades, this heart and soul business was proving to be exhausting. I glanced at the others before leading Mum a little further away. My voice was low, but I was aware that they could probably still hear me. "Don't you remember what happened last time? It took you weeks to calm down. And I—"

The truth was I just didn't want to deal with my father. He wasn't around much when I was a child. When he was he found every chance he could to criticise and berate me. It was more the shouting and putting me down that got to me than the occasional backhander he dealt out. I only ever put up with him for Mum, but after what happened five years ago, I wouldn't tolerate the man for any reason. But the desperation in Mum's eyes was now cracking my resolve.

"Felix, *please*," she said, and I closed my eyes slowly before giving a quick nod. Mum threw her arms around my neck, and I gave her another hug.

"I've got to go!" she said, her tears now dried and her expression full of excitement. "Beef Wellington? That's your favourite darling. And Hetty, Lucy, you'll come?"

"Mum, they don't have to. I can—"

"We'll be there, Mrs Moretti," Lucy said in a firm tone that I barely recognised from across the kitchen.

"Bianca, please," Mum put in.

Lucy nodded and gave her a smile. "Bianca."

"Right!" Mum said. "I'm off to Waitrose. See you all at eight."

As soon as she'd swept out the door I turned to Lucy. "You don't have to come. I have to, but you don't. They're *my* problem."

"I remember," Lucy said softly, and my back straightened. It was so long ago, and she had been so young. I didn't realise how much Lucy picked up on. She always had her head in the clouds, or at least it seemed like she did. She might have been in her own world, but that didn't mean she didn't notice important things. She was one of the most observant people I knew. "And you're *not* going alone."

"Well, that's decided then," Hetty said firmly. "Luca will have to put up with the fur babies as well. I can't leave Frodo on his own, he vomited earlier."

"You're going to take the dogs?" I asked.

Hetty frowned. "Well, of course I am. Oh, I better take Legolas as well."

My eyebrows went up, and I actually cracked a smile. "You're going to take two massive golden retrievers, one of whom has gastroenteritis, and a small pony to my dad's house?"

"It's not just your dad's house, Felix Moretti," Hetty told me. "And your mother loves the animals."

"Since when has mum been spending time with animals?"

"A lot's happened in the last few years, Felix. After I moved here and the animals started breaking through the fences I've been spending more time with your mum. She's good with the animals." She moved to me then and laid a hand on my arm. "They calm her down, love."

I swallowed and then nodded, as my smile faded. "That's good," I said in a rough voice. "Not sure what Dad'll say, though."

"You leave that dad of yours to me," Hetty said, and before we could respond to that ominous statement, she bustled off to the back door and shouted for Mikey.

"I guess we're all going then," I said as I shot an uncertain glance at Lucy. "Luce, you know that Dad can be…" I trailed off, and it was her turn to squeeze my arm.

"We can handle your dad."

CHAPTER 34

Ancient history

Lucy

We couldn't handle Luca Moretti.

I doubted that Satan himself could handle Luca Moretti. He was an unbelievable prick. If life was fair, Luca would be as ugly and awful as his personality, but unfortunately that was not the case. No, he was basically an older version of Felix: tall and powerful despite his advancing years, his salt and pepper hair perfectly styled. He was in a suit and his lip actually curled when he took in us Mayweathers: Mikey and I were both wearing jeans and thick jumpers, Mikey still had his work boots on, and my trusty Uggs were warming my feet.

I suppose I should have changed, but when I asked Felix how fancy his mum would expect us to be and if I should wear a dress, he'd frowned, saying it was too bloody cold for that and that I looked perfect as I was. That was a stretch seeing as I was wearing thermals and a ridiculously thick jumper. But judging by the way he subtly tried to crowd me towards the Aga in the kitchen at every opportunity, I think my thermoregulation trumped all other fashion considerations in his mind.

There were still times when he glanced at my hands with a worried expression. The red marks had faded now, but it was like he had to keep checking. That tortured look would come back into his eyes, his jaw would clench and he'd grind his teeth.

Yesterday, when I reminded him that I was absolutely fine, he lost his shit, ranting on about the danger of prolonged cold exposure to people with Raynaud's, spouting all sorts of facts I'd never heard of. He'd clearly been researching and working himself up into a right tizzy.

"Felix, enough!" I'd snapped, and I think my commanding tone shocked him into silence. "Enough now." His hands were clenched into fists at his sides. I stepped to him and covered them with mine. He immediately relaxed his fists and took my hands in his, his expression softening. "You've got to stop worrying. There wasn't any permanent damage and—"

"But there *could* have been, love," he said, back to that tortured tone of voice. "There could have been all sorts. I read an article that said—"

"Enough of the articles, you nutter!" Honestly, he needed to calm down. "My hands are fine. *I'm* fine. But you won't be if you carry on obsessing on what could have happened."

He'd promised to calm down about it, but it seemed that didn't extend to allowing me to wear anything less than Arctic clothing to walk half a mile to his mum's house.

Mum was in one of her boiler suits with a wax jacket over it that she was yet to take off. Even Felix was relatively casual, looking edible in jeans that sat so perfectly on him it actually made me feel a little lightheaded. After a string of awkward greetings, Luca turned to Felix.

"Couldn't have put a shirt on for your mother?" he asked. The guy hadn't spoken to his son in five years, and this was the first thing he said?

The one bit of satisfaction I had was when the dogs jumped up on him, and Samwise licked his smug face. The expression of pure disgust was something I wished I'd caught on camera (it was just as well that I'd made an executive decision to keep Legolas in the hallway). But that was the only highlight so far.

Bianca made being on edge into an art form. She was so obviously thrilled to have her son home that she was vibrating with nervous energy. Bianca didn't care what we were wearing or that she was in a full evening gown; she just cared that we were there. And she greeted us as though she hadn't seen us in years rather than just a couple of hours ago, hugging us all in turn, even a surprised Mikey. Luca seemed to want to ignore the fact we were even there. Instead, he took every opportunity to get digs in with his son.

"I hear you lost the Framlingham Estate," he boomed out at Felix. (Luca did a lot of booming, and the drawing room, as they called it, was so big that it echoed off the walls, stopping all other conversation.)

Felix narrowed his eyes as he considered his father. He was clearly furious but holding back, no doubt for his mum's benefit. His knuckles were white where he was gripping his beer bottle (the fact he and Mikey had asked for beers and proceeded to drink them straight out of the bottle had also drawn a sneer from Luca for some fucked up, posh person reason, no doubt) and he had that small 'v' in between his brows, which I knew was a sign he was under stress. I tried to tell myself that worrying about Felix's stress levels wasn't my job anymore, but all I could think about were the times I stroked his head to calm him and make that v disappear in the past.

"Let's not talk business, Dad," Felix said in a low, controlled voice, and Luca boomed out a laugh.

"Yes, no business now boys," Bianca said in a high-pitched, nervous tone. "I'll be back in a jiffy. Just need to check the beef."

"Right, yes I thought you wouldn't want to talk about losing out in front of your new little girlfriend."

"Her name is Lucy, Dad. She's standing right here."

"I'm not his girlfriend," I put in but then wished I hadn't when I saw a cruel smile spread across Luca's face.

"Oh really? That *is* interesting. Your mother told me different, Felix. Dump him, did you?" He took a step towards me with that creepy smile on his face, and I instinctively moved back towards Felix.

"Yes, Dad, she dumped me."

Luca snorted. "Not the first and won't be the last."

Felix turned to him and took a deep breath in, letting it out slowly. His knuckles were white where he was gripping his beer.

"Well, yes. I suppose you're right. But Dad, not quite sure I could have anticipated the last one. Why would I suspect that my own father would bribe my girlfriend to pass details of a land deal I'd been working on for two years to a competitor?"

I gasped. Mum started coughing on her gin and tonic. The room went silent. Is that what happened five years ago with Felix's ex? Bloody hell, what kind of monster was this man?

"I did you a favour there, boy," Luca said, absolutely no remorse in his voice. "You certainly do pick them, don't you? What about that other one? The famous one?"

"You know her name Dad," Felix said through his teeth.

"She dumped you as well, didn't she? Went off with that actor fellow." He snorted.

Felix opened his mouth to reply but just when he was about to speak, Bianca swept back into the room, her smile faltering at the palpable tension in the air.

"I'm sorry, Mum," Felix said, his voice thick with anger as he put his bottle of beer down on the side. "Fun as this has been I can't stay any longer and put up with this." Bianca's face set with determination as she looked between her husband and her son.

"Oh no, please, darling," she said. "Luca, we talked about this." There was a real bite in her voice that I'd never heard before and she was staring daggers at her husband, who just shrugged a shoulder.

"Calm down, both of you," he said. "You always were too sensitive, Felix."

"Please stay, darling," Bianca said in a pleading tone. Felix hesitated then gave a tight nod and picked his beer up again. Bianca gave him a shaky smile. "Right, well come through in five minutes. Liddy and I are just finishing setting the table." Liddy had been the Morettis' cook for many years.

Once Bianca had swept out of the room again, Mum took a step towards Luca, putting her own drink down before she spoke.

"I've looked after a lot of children in my time," Mum said, and all eyes turned to her in surprise at her slightly random statement.

Luca smirked. "Ah, do go on, Hetty. I'm sure this will be a fascinating anecdote."

Mum returned his smile, totally unperturbed by his condescending tone.

"Well, what I was going to say was that I've looked after many, many children, and your son was certainly *not* an oversensitive child. In fact, he was one of the most resilient and determined children I'd ever come across."

"We'll have to agree to disagree there," Luca said. "But as he's *my* son I think I'm a bit more qualified to comment as I know him significantly better than the hired help."

Hetty's eyebrows went up. "Oh right. So how does Felix like his tea?"

"What the hell has tea got to do with anything?"

"Hmm, favourite food, then? Or what was his best-loved toy as a child? What was his first fight over? What is his worst childhood memory?"

"Is this some sort of bullshit test?" Luca scoffed, his face going bright red with anger.

Mum held up her fingers one by one as she listed off the answers. "Milk, one sugar. My chicken pie. Mr Cristos – a furry monkey he took everywhere until you caught him with it on a rare family trip out. I think it was actually a business lunch where you and your colleagues were all supposed to bring family. You said Mr Cristos was a "bloody embarrassment" and chucked him in the bin before leaving the house. Luckily I was prepared to fish him out again, wash him and then replace him in Felix's bed before he got home. But the poor child spent the entire day thinking his most precious possession was gone forever. And you screamed at him for over an hour when you got home from the lunch because he'd cried. He was *five*."

"I–I–I…" Luca spluttered. "He couldn't drag that mangled old thing all over the place. It was embarrassing."

"Luca," Mum said in a low voice. Luca flinched at her use of his first name. I'd never heard Mum call him anything but Mr Moretti. "He. Was. *Five*."

"This is all ancient history. Who cares what—?"

"I have *not* finished," Mum said and to my surprise, Luca's mouth snapped shut. She held up a fourth finger. "Felix's first fight was with one of his posh boarding school chums who called my son a 'token townie' and my daughter a 'weird little freak'. Your *sensitive* son broke that boy's nose. We had to have a long chat about anger management and not solving things with your fists or flying into a rage at the drop of a hat. It's something Felix had to unlearn. Something *someone* had been modelling at home for him from the start."

"I don't know what you're implying but—"

"His worst childhood memory." Mum held up a fifth finger and then paused. Bianca, who had been in the kitchen, was now standing in the doorway, her eyes glassy with unshed tears. Felix glanced at his mum, then moved to Mum and laid his hand on her arm.

"Hetty, that's enough now," he said softly, then lowered his voice even further. "Mum can't…" he trailed off. Mum looked at Bianca and then gave Felix a sharp nod of agreement.

"Well, maybe we can bloody well eat if we've finished going over ancient history," said Luca.

"Right, yes! Let's go through," Bianca said in a falsely bright tone.

The tension hanging in the air was almost unbearable. I wasn't sure how Felix survived it as a child. I'd never felt so angry in my life. The white-hot rage building inside me towards Felix's father was actually a little scary. Containing it was becoming more and more of a challenge. Felix must have noticed because on the way through to the dining room he leaned into me.

"Are you okay?" he whispered. Yes, that's right, this man who'd just been put down and attacked by his father for the last half hour was asking me if *I* was okay. I took his hand in mine, gripping it firmly.

"I'm fine," I replied in a low, tight voice. "But your dad is a total dickhead."

He smiled down at me, flashing his white teeth against that tanned skin. "I've noticed." His smile dropped as we finally made it to the dining room door. "Best to not rise to it, though. For Mum."

Of course, he'd want to protect his mother. I'd never really appreciated how fragile Bianca was until now or how much of a strain that must put on Felix. I gave him a stiff nod, resolving to tamp down the rage and not give in to the strong desire to punch Luca in his smug, condescending face.

Unfortunately, I didn't realise how much worse Luca could get. I didn't brace nearly enough. The next hit, whispered slyly to Felix on the way into dinner, but in a stage-whisper meant for everyone to hear, was directed at me. That I could handle.

"Would've thought you'd manage to keep hold of the help's kid, boy," Luca said through a smirk. "But then, even batting well below your weight, you still can't hold their interest, can you?"

Felix, who'd kept his cool throughout all the character assassination directed at him, was clearly at the end of his tolerance for his dad's bullshit when it came to me. He spun around in a sudden movement, so fast it was all a blur for a moment and the next thing I knew he had his dad pinned against the wall under a fancy painting. He did it as silently as possible, and they were hidden from the entrance to the dining room where his mum was waiting to serve dinner.

"Listen, you piece of shit," he hissed, keeping his voice low enough that his mum couldn't hear, gripping his father by the top of his shirt and then giving him a shake. "Don't ever turn your venomous bullshit on Lucy. Don't look at her. Don't talk *to* her or *about* her. If I catch you *breathing* wrong in her direction, I'll do what I should have done years ago and kick your arse from here to The Badger's Sett."

He released him in another sudden movement that had Luca stumbling forward, gasping for breath.

"How dare you," he spluttered, his voice hoarse. "How dare you attack me in my own home."

"Not a great feeling, is it *Dad*?" Felix said in a tight voice. "Being attacked in your own home. Welcome to my world."

"You can't do this. Your mother won't—"

"I *can* do this, and if you don't want Mum to hear the full story about what happened with Lily, then I'd shut your mouth. It wasn't just secrets she was selling to you, was it?"

"I don't know what you're talking about," Luca said, straightening up and shifting on his feet.

Felix's eyebrows went up, and Mikey cleared his throat. "Mr Moretti," Mikey said in a low but conversational tone. "You fucked her on the reg behind Felix's back. Don't you remember I found you fucking her when I delivered your kitchen table five years ago? Bianca was away."

"You can't prove anything."

Mikey shrugged. "Er... not strictly true. I took pictures on my phone."

Luca's face paled then, a hint of panic creeping into his expression. "You wouldn't tell Bianca," he said, the confidence in his tone wavering. "It would break her."

"She's already broken, Dad," Felix said, the anger had drained out of his voice, and he just sounded tired now. "You broke her a long time ago. But for the moment, we can hate each other in private rather than upsetting Mum."

"I don't hate you," Luca said, and Felix sighed.

"Dad, let's not get into this now."

"But, I don't. I did you a *favour* with that woman."

"What's going on out here?" The sound of Bianca's voice made everyone freeze in the corridor. Legolas chose that moment to trot past us all, weaving around us and conveniently stepping on Luca's foot.

"That was a horse," Luca said as he watched Legolas's backside disappear into the corridor in the direction of the drawing room. "There's a goddamn horse in my house."

"Don't be ridiculous, Luca," Hetty said in a brisk tone. "Horses in the house? Honestly, whatever next."

Luca's mouth opened and closed a couple of times like a goldfish before he glanced at his son and snapped it shut.

CHAPTER 35

"Get. Out."

Lucy

Dinner was tortuous. The atmosphere was thick with tension. Luca continued to have little digs at Felix and Bianca.

"Ha, one thing my wife excels at is overcooking the bloody beef. So, Felix, still working under a female boss?"

"She's my partner, Dad. As you well know."

"Hmm, took you long enough to build up your portfolio though, didn't it?"

Bianca got more and more on edge, dropping serving spoons and apologising way too much over the state of the meal. Felix sank more and more into himself, his eyes gradually becoming dull and resigned – just like he used to look as a child after a run-in with his father. Mikey and Mum managed to steer the conversation away from Luca, talking about things he clearly wasn't a part of. By all accounts, Mum had managed to drag Bianca out from under his control a lot more since moving to Moonreach. But the way they were ignoring him seemed to further enrage Luca, who just became more poisonous. But it wasn't until he went *there* that *I* lost my shit.

"Well, at least your dogs are a proper breed, I suppose," Luca said to Hetty. "Not like that awful thing you and your mother brought home, Felix."

Everyone at the table froze.

"Don't, Dad," Felix said in a low voice.

"What?" Luca said, all innocence. "I did you a favour there too, didn't I? You and your mum getting all soppy and wanting to give that fucked-up mongrel a home. It was embarrassing."

The silence was thick and awful. Bianca's eyes had filled with tears. I remembered Benji, Felix's dog. They'd been inseparable the year before Felix went off to boarding school. He'd loved that dog. Then there was that horrible day when Felix came to the cottage with red-rimmed eyes. The day I told him a story with his face buried in Bilbo's fur.

Mum told me Benji had gone off to live on a farm. It had been a year after Dad had died, which we'd all taken badly, Felix grieving as much as us. So the loss of Benji was particularly acute.

I never questioned what had happened, but there was a sick dread forming in my stomach and a vague ringing in my ears as I listened to Luca. Suddenly, the rage overtook the shyness and, for the first time in my life, I didn't care if I was the centre of attention as I pushed back from the table in one violent movement and stood up.

"Lucy?" Mum asked.

Everyone's gaze was fixed on me now, but I only had eyes for Luca.

"What did you do?" I managed to get out past my throat, which was now thick with fury. My voice didn't sound like my own – it was low and biting.

"What are you talking about, young lady?" Luca said, feigning innocence again.

"What did you do with that dog?"

"That dog was a fucking embarrassment. I did us all a favour."

I looked at Mum. "*That's* his worst childhood memory, isn't it?" I asked, and Mum gave a short nod. I turned back to Luca, my hands bunching into fists at my side.

"Get. Out." I said, my voice shaking with fury.

"What?" Luca's eyebrows went up.

"You heard me, get out."

"You can't tell me to get out of my own home."

"You are a sadistic, narcissistic, disgusting excuse for a human being. You don't deserve to be here. How on earth you produced a man like your son is beyond me."

"Some lower-class employee's brat isn't going to tell me to leave my own home. Who the *hell* do you think you are?"

"I don't work for you anymore, Luca," Mum put in. "I haven't for a long time, remember?"

He waved his hand in a dismissive gesture, clearly to him once an employee, always an employee.

"Your son is successful, clever, shrewd and a brilliant businessman," I said. "But more than that he's kind, funny, loving, good fun, charismatic. He's the kind of man people gravitate towards. You're the kind of man they avoid. There's more power in his way of being than yours. He's more influential than you, more successful and you can't *stand* it."

"Can't keep a woman, though, can he?" Luca sneered.

"That is because *you*," I pointed a finger at Luca then, "have fucked him up. *You.* That's why he did what he did to lose me. *You* made that happen."

"And I wouldn't be so sure about your ability to keep a woman either, Luca," Bianca put in. When I looked over at her, she was standing herself, glaring at her husband. "I told you what would happen if you didn't behave tonight. I wanted to wait until after the Mayweathers had left, but Lucy has put it *so* much better than I would have. Get. Out."

"Bianca, darling," Luca said in a placating tone, standing from his chair and holding his hands up. "There's been some misunderstanding, but it's nothing we can't sort out as a family."

"You took that dog to the pound," Bianca said, her voice shaking with barely contained anger.

"Oh my God," Luca groaned. "That was *years* ago. Why are you all banging on about it now?"

"You broke his *heart*," she said, her eyes filling with tears. One escaped and she swiped it from her cheek in an angry gesture. "Just like you broke mine. You made me lesser. You made it so I would tolerate my beautiful boy being shouted at over and over again. Being shoved out of the way. Being put down. B–b–being hit. I watched him become a shadow of himself. I knew the only time he was happy was at that tiny little cottage with Hetty, so I threw myself more and more into my charity work to justify him spending more time there. I agreed to go to all those stupid business dinners and to host those unbearable parties so that my son wouldn't be exposed to *you*."

"This is all total bullshit," Luca blustered. "I gave you a good life, Bee. You and Felix both."

Bianca shook her head. "You wouldn't know a good life if it smacked you in the face. For you, it's all show and appearances. No love, no warmth. Nothing that matters. So now you can indeed get out."

"Where the hell do you want me to go?"

"How about you stay with your secretary in her little flat that you pay for?"

Luca blinked once and the colour drained out of his face.

"Or with any of the other women that you sleep with? I'm sure one of them will have a spare room for you. But if you think that now your business is failing, you'll have access to *my* money, you can think again. Don't even think about trying. The trust is ironclad. I think my parents always knew you would do this." Bianca, coming from a very rich family, was the one with the real money in that marriage.

"I'm not going anywhere."

"Wrong," Mikey said, standing from his chair and sauntering over to Luca. "You'll be leaving, mate."

He took hold of Luca's arm and lifted him to his feet. Luca tried to shake him off, but he was no match for my brother.

"Felix," he said, looking at his son for support which just showed how deluded the man was. Felix stood, went over to the other side of Luca and together with Mikey pulled him away from the table.

"Fine, fine," Luca spat. "I'll go. You don't need to strong-arm me like bouncers."

Mikey and Felix let him go and he straightened his suit jacket, pulling the cuffs of his sleeves down in sharp, angry movements. He attempted to leave with as much dignity as possible, but Legolas chose that moment to trot into the dining room straight up to him and head butt him in the groin. That pony was a pain in the arse, but in that moment all was forgiven as far as I was concerned. It was perfectly timed and made Luca's exit that much more satisfying. Luca stormed off as fast as he could, given the severe pain he was now in thanks to Legolas. Not much later we all heard the front door slam and tyres screech on the drive.

"Well, that's done," said Bianca, breaking the tense silence. Then, surprising us all, she turned on the spot back to her chair at the head of the table and took her seat. She whistled, and Legolas came trotting in, followed by both dogs. She gave Legolas an apple that she'd plucked from the fruit basket and chucked the dogs a huge piece of beef Wellington each.

CHAPTER 36

Pretty-boy business types

Lucy

"Woah, this is nuts," I muttered under my breath, all of my nerves superseded by shock. The office was completely unrecognisable. Something nudged my leg, and I looked down to see a small, scraggly terrier at my feet, his tail wagging as he stared up at me. He looked just like Benji.

"Lucy!" I tore my eyes away from the *actual animal* in Felix's office to focus on Tabitha. She was smiling, which was a little disconcerting. I managed a small one of my own as she bounced, yes *bounced* up to me (also disconcerting – Tabitha was not a bouncy human). "You're here."

"Well, yes I—" I was cut off as the wind was knocked out of me by Tabitha's hug. What the hell was going on?

"It's so good to see you again," she said, swaying me from side to side. It took a moment for my shock to fade and return the hug. When she finally pulled back, she kept both her hands on my shoulders to keep me near her as she searched my face. "You look fabulous." A blush crept over my cheeks at the unexpected praise, and I bit my lip. "Does Felix know you're here?"

"No, I…" I felt my blush deepen as I started to realise how mad my plan was. "I wanted to surprise him."

The last thing Felix would want in a workday would be a surprise visit from me. When I worked here his pace was relentless – back-to-back meetings with not even a lunch break. The man was a workaholic.

I shuddered at the memory of his anger at being interrupted during his negotiations with the Framlingham Estate when I'd brought him a birthday cake. How could I have forgotten about that? I'd been stupid thinking I should surprise him. Work Felix didn't like surprises. I'd let myself be lulled into a false sense of security recently by Little Buckingham Felix, but I'd forgotten that this version – the one that ruled the office with an iron fist – was not kind, sweet, funny and hot (well, okay maybe he was still hot – it was impossible for him not to be, but that's where the similarities ended).

"Oh dear," I whispered. "I think maybe this was a mistake."

I tried to take a step back from Tabitha but her grip on my shoulders tightened and she frowned down at me.

"Hey, no way are you shooting off again," she said, removing both her hands from my shoulders and looping her arm through mine so she could steer me further into the office space. Since when did Tabitha and I walk around arm-in-arm? "He's in a meeting at the moment, but I'll show you around the place whilst you're waiting. You won't recognise it."

The dog at our feet barked once and Tabitha laughed. My eyebrows went up. I could count on one hand the number of times I'd heard this woman laugh. Her arm dropped from mine as she bent down to stroke the dog, who immediately flopped onto his back so she could scratch his tummy. After sufficient tummy scratches, Tabitha further shocked me by reaching down and scooping up the scraggly ball of fluff in her arms. To be clear, this was not a non-shedding dog, not by a long stretch – her previously pristine suit jacket was now covered in cream fur. The dog licked her jaw and she giggled.

"Lucy, meet Pippin," Tabitha said, and I automatically lifted my hand to give Pippin scratches under his cute little face. A small smile tugged at my lips at the name. "He's our new office dog."

"Office dog?" I said, my eyebrows going up in surprise.

Tabitha frowned at me. "Yes, it was your idea, wasn't it?"

My mouth fell open but the ability to speak deserted me as I remembered my advice from months ago. I looked away from Pippin and Tabitha, my eyes darting around the office: plants everywhere, desks strewn with personal effects, walls painted warm colours, a beautiful, fancy coffee machine taking pride of place in the central area, flanked by brightly coloured, comfortable looking sofas and funky armchairs. Tabitha let Pippin down and he trotted off to a large, fluffy dog bed next to the sofas.

"Where are the walls?" I muttered, focusing on the far side of the office. Instead of the walls and the heavy oak doors into the partners' offices, there was floor-to-ceiling glass. Light streamed in through into the communal space, which was no longer bleak, dark and grey.

"Oh, they were the first thing to go when Felix started making the changes," Tabitha said, linking arms with me and drawing me further into the office. "After what happened to you..." I stiffened and her words cut off. "Oh Lucy, I'm sorry, hun. I didn't mean to just blurt that out. I–I..." she paused. When I looked at her, I was shocked to see unshed tears in her eyes. "I'm so sorry about what happened." she was speaking in a very-un-Tabitha-like broken whisper now which didn't sound right at all.

"Hey," I said, trying to make my voice firm, "It wasn't your fault and I'm okay, I promise."

"I should have reported him," she said, still with that broken voice. "If I'd have known that he was going to do it to you and the others I would have done, but I just... I *need* this job and I didn't think anyone would believe me."

"It's on him, Tabitha," I said. "His behaviour is on him." I reached across and gave her hand a squeeze. "Listen, I'm sorry he targeted you as well. I didn't know about that either. I know now that Will and the unfair office environment were why you were…" I hesitated, not quite knowing how to phrase the next.

"A raving bitch?" Tabitha put in for me with a smile which I managed to return. Thankfully that broken quality in her voice had receded, as had her tears.

I cleared my throat and glanced away. "Er, I wouldn't say that… I just—"

"Hey, it's okay," she said. "I've been reliably informed that I was a bitch. I'm cool with it."

"Yup, total b-word." We both turned to see Lottie and Vicky approach. Lottie had a big smile on her face and Vicky's expression was set to her normal piercing gaze.

"Thanks, Lots," Tabitha returned on an eye roll.

"You can always rely on me to bring the honesty," Lottie said. "Hello, stranger," she said to me as she pulled me in for a hug. Hugging was clearly the new office protocol. "We missed you." Lottie pulled back and scanned me from head to foot. "You look hot."

I blushed again. "Felix has an obsession with buying me jumper dresses." Lottie's smile grew huge.

"I bet he does."

"You're back," Vicky said simply. No hug from her, but that wasn't a huge surprise. Office protocol or not, a hug would be a step too far for Vicky.

"Er, yes," I said hesitantly. "I just popped in to say hi."

"I was incorrect and acted on poor information when I last saw you," Vicky continued. Now that I was really looking at her, I could see the subtle signs of stress on her face. Her jaw was tight, her face looked pale. "It was wrong. Very wrong. You have my sincere and deep apology. Had I known you'd be coming in today I would have prepared it in writing."

I shook my head. "Vicky, it's fine. You don't have to—"

"It is *not* fine," she snapped, shocking me with the uncharacteristic display of emotion. "You were hurt." She shut her eyes for a moment. When she opened them, there was real pain there. "I was wrong, and I'm never wrong."

"Vicky, I—"

"I'm never wrong except for the one time that it mattered, when it was about someone being hurt, not just about making more money. *That* time I was wrong."

"Okay, but Vicky it's over now. And we all make mistakes."

"Not me. Not until now."

"Come on, Vics," Lottie said in a gentle voice. "We talked about this. You need to give yourself a break, right? Maybe now you've seen Lucy for yourself you can let this go."

Guilt swamped me for staying away for so long and not answering messages from everyone. Vicky had clearly been imagining the worst.

"I'm sorry I didn't come sooner, Vicky," I said. "But honestly, I'm fine. I've been writing and it sort of sucked me down a rabbit hole so I could forget about everything else. But I should have let you know I was okay."

Vicky's eyes went wide. "You have no responsibility to let me know anything. *I'm* the one with the responsibility."

"Vics, you can't be—" Lottie started but Vicky cut her off.

"I was in a position of responsibility. I was the boss. I should have seen what was going on. I should have insisted on taking things further when I saw Will with you at the party." She lowered her voice. "I have difficulty reading people. It's a problem."

Lottie sighed. "You're better than you think you are, Vics."

"Only because I have you to help me," Vicky returned. "And you *tried* to tell me about him, but I did not listen to you. Unforgivable. Now, if you'll excuse me, I need to prepare the numbers for the meeting this afternoon. Numbers I understand." She turned on her heel and strode away from us, her back poker straight and her shoulders stiff.

Lottie sighed again. "She's taken this hard. I expect that by the time you leave, she'll have a five-page apology printed out for you."

"Oh dear, poor Vicky. It wasn't her fault."

"Vicky's hard on herself and she's not used to making mistakes."

"She's lost weight," I said, and Lottie nodded.

"Vics finds emotions tricky. When she's upset she can't really express it properly so it sort of manifests physically. Not eating is one of the ways I can tell she's upset. She struggles with some of the textures and…" Lottie broke off and bit her lip. "Sorry, I really shouldn't say too much. It's not really mine to share, and trust is really important with Vics."

"Is she still having trouble sleeping?" Tabitha asked and Lottie nodded.

"I'm not sure what to do to snap her out of it, to be honest. She's never really been this bad before. It might help now that she's seen you're okay."

"I hope so," I said, watching Vicky behind the glass in her office. She was typing at a furious pace, a look of fierce concentration on her face.

"Maybe your brother should pay us a visit again."

"Mikey?" My eyes went wide as I looked at Lottie who was grinning. "Mikey was here?"

"Oh yeah," Tabitha put in. "Your hot brother stormed in here and gave us all what for. It was quite spectacular."

I groaned. "Oh no, he's such an over-protective numpty."

"I don't think anyone could ever describe that man as a numpty," Lottie said through a smile. "And he made *quite* the impression on Vicky."

"He did?"

"I've caught her looking at his website a few times. That photo of him next to his tools and that massive table he custom-made? Vicky stared at that for half an hour straight last week. I thought she'd had a stroke."

"Vicky fancies my brother?" I had to swallow back laughter. Vicky and Mikey were total opposites. The last man I could see Vicky with would be my rough-and-ready, flannel-wearing, unshaven, bitter-drinking, scruffy brother. I'd never even seen Vicky wear a pair of jeans.

Lottie shrugged. "Weird I know. But since she found out about what happened to you, the only time she's seemed at peace was when she was looking at that photo of your brother. I've never seen her behave like this. You wouldn't believe the number of blokes that try to get in her pants, and she brushes them off like flies. But then they're all pretty-boy business types, maybe she needs a *real man* like Mike. No offence, Luce – I know you kind of like pretty-boy business types." Lottie winked at me, and I gave her a shy smile.

"Enough about blokes," Tabitha said, linking arms with Lottie and me and dragging us both further into the office. "Let's show you round, Lucy. Look, the conference room wall has gone now as well. Felix wants a more open environment. No more silos and not sharing ideas. And it's working. Way more communication, everyone pulling together. Profits are actually up. It's crazy."

We came around the corner and that's when I saw him. He was sitting in the middle of the conference table, holding court. Everyone's focus was on him and what he had to say. But when he glanced up from his laptop and opened his mouth to speak again his eyes locked with mine and he stopped mid-sentence. Surprise crossed his expression before that wide glamorous smile lit up his face. Everyone was still watching Felix. Some frowned in confusion at his silence. Others turned to see what he was looking at.

I froze like a rabbit in the headlights as he rose from his seat.

CHAPTER 37

No to going slow

Felix

She was here.

For the last two weeks since that dinner at my parents, I thought I'd better give Lucy a bit of space, but it had been hellish. After apologising to the Mayweathers for the shitshow that was that evening, I'd left for London. What Lucy did for me, standing up to my father for me like that... I was totally overwhelmed by it, to be honest. And I realised that I still had to work on myself before I could deserve her properly. I had to become a better man for her. I couldn't just continue to bulldoze her into forgiving me and being with me, or I was just as selfish and controlling as my father.

But if being around her and showing restraint was difficult, actually being completely apart from her was worse. At least when I was with her I could have some sort of Lucy fix without going cold turkey. Kissing her at the signing to snap her out of her funk had backfired on me spectacularly. I was craving her before the kiss, but feeling her in my arms again, having her soft body melt into mine and having her taste in my mouth made everything ten times worse.

I barely slept at night and when I did I dreamt of her. I was an addict. So, when I saw her through the glass, right here in my space, my next move was automatic. Screw this meeting, screw these investors. Lucy was here. She was here and she was looking at me with that hope in her eyes again. Looking at me like she used to.

"Felix?" Paul, the head of a multinational investment company we were negotiating with, said. "You alright, mate?"

There was some confused muttering around the table as I rose to my feet, my eyes locked with Lucy's still. I'm not sure if I even managed to mutter an apology as I strode away from the table and out of the room.

"Oh shit," I heard Tabitha mutter as I walked directly to them. "Felix, you pillock. Can you please go back in there and finalise the deal before you snog your girlfriend? We're just showing her round the... oh bloody hell, never mind."

I hadn't even spared her or Lottie a glance as I made my way straight to Lucy. To be honest, I wasn't aware of much else at that moment. I just went to her as if on automatic pilot. All I knew is that I had to taste her again. I had to have her in my arms again. So, I didn't even pause as one hand went to her jaw, the other arm wrapped around her back to lift her off her feet and I kissed her.

"Felix!" Tabitha snapped and I heard Lottie giggle. I lowered Lucy back to her feet and reluctantly broke the kiss to smile down at her.

"Hi," I said through my smile. She blinked up at me in shock then the corners of her mouth turned up.

"Hi," she whispered.

"Right, well, shall I actually save the bloody deal or what?" Tabitha said, but I'm afraid I was still beyond registering her.

"I missed you," I said to Lucy. Tabitha huffed and I heard her stalk off to the conference room muttering about *lovestruck weirdos*.

"I missed you too," Lucy said back.

"Er, Felix," Lottie said, her voice shaking with amusement. "You know how you got rid of all the walls and put glass in instead? Well, pretty much everyone in the office is watching you right now."

I managed to pull my gaze from Lucy's and glanced around to confirm Lottie was right – everyone was indeed watching us. Some were pretending not to, but most were fairly blatant about it. Employees no longer worrying about pissing me off because I wasn't a growly bastard anymore had its drawbacks. I shrugged, but then when I looked down at Lucy, I realised she was not quite as at peace with our public display as me. Her face was bright red, and her smile was faltering. I couldn't have that.

"Right, come with me." I grabbed her hand and led her away from Lottie and the rest of the office.

"Have fun kids," Lottie called after us as I headed for the lift.

"What are you doing?" Lucy said as the lift doors closed after us. I looked down at her and smiled, still so ridiculously happy that she'd come here. That she was in London. That she came to find me. "You can't just walk out of that meeting. Felix, you've worked on that deal for months. It means everything to you."

I frowned and squeezed her hand which was still in mine. "It doesn't mean everything to me. Not even close." I turned to her and reached for her other hand, pulling her closer and fixing her gaze with mine. I took a deep breath. It was time to lay it out for her. Time I was honest. "Lucy, I don't know if you've worked it out by now, but *you* mean everything to me. I think you always have."

Her mouth fell open and her eyes went wide as she searched my face.

I squeezed both her hands to reassure her. "It's okay if you don't feel the same way. I know I haven't earned that yet. I'm not pushing for anything more than you're willing to give. We can take things slow, and I—"

"No," Lucy said, cutting me off and my heart sank. Right, I was a strong negotiator. I'd fucked up, yes, but I could claw this back.

"Lucy, baby please just give me another chance. We don't have to—"

Lucy was shaking her head back and forth, a frown on her face, her freckled nose wrinkling. "No, I mean… no to going slow." I blinked at her, lost for words and it was her turn to squeeze my hands. "That's why I came here, Felix. You're driving me crazy with this *wait until you're ready* malarky. I'm ready, goddamit! I can't concentrate anymore. I think about you all the time. I can't sleep and when I do I dream about…" she trailed off and her eyes went to the side, a blush staining her cheeks. When she spoke again it was in a whisper. "I *need* you."

From then on my body took over. There was a roaring in my ears as a wave of white-hot desire swept through me. On instinct, I released Lucy's hand to punch the lift emergency stop button. We came to an abrupt halt. Lucy's eyes shot back to mine.

"What are you—? Ompf!"

I'd reached down, lifted her up to balance her on the rail next to the lift control panel so that her face was level with mine and her legs were wrapped around my hips, then pulled her skirt up around the top of her thighs. My hand that wasn't supporting her against the wall came up to the side of her face to tilt her head back, and my mouth slammed down on hers. Her lips had parted in shock, so it was easy for me to deepen the kiss. After a moment, her soft moan into my mouth threw off the last of my control. One of her hands went into my hair, the other under my suit jacket to pull at my shirt and get to the skin of my back. I rocked against her as my mouth moved down her neck.

"You're so beautiful," I muttered against her skin, my voice hoarse with need. "I missed your taste, missed the feel of your skin." I pushed her dress off her shoulder and then cupped her breast with my free hand over her bra. "This has to go," I said as I kissed down from her collarbone to her chest, pulling down the cup of her bra so that my mouth could close over her nipple.

Lucy had been making needy little suppressed sounds until then but when I pulled her nipple into my mouth, she started moving against me as she cried out.

"Felix, please."

The desperation in her voice and the way she was grinding into me made me forget where we were. Forget that I was taking things slow with Lucy and building her trust.

Christ, I forgot my own name.

The roaring in my ears intensified as my hand went to the soft skin of her thigh, sliding up and taking her skirt with it until I was at the edge of the lace of her underwear. She gasped as I slid in the waistband and down. My finger slipped into her heat as my thumb pressed on her core. She rode my hand with jerky movements before reaching around and tackling my fly. I let out a deep groan as she freed me, and as her small hand encircled me I felt a rush so intense it almost felt like I might pass out. Her other hand came up to my jaw and she pulled my face down to hers.

"Please," she repeated, her voice so saturated with need and near desperation that any control I had been exerting was a thing of the past. I stepped back just far enough to grasp her underwear and yank it down her legs, letting it fall to the floor as I lifted her a little higher, pushing into her hard and fast. I closed my mouth over hers to swallow her scream. Her hand was clutching at my hair now, the other digging her nails into my back as she jerked with each thrust. My head shifted back slightly so I could look at her. Her eyes were rolled back in her head, her hair had fallen out of its ponytail to frame her face. Her incredible breasts were bouncing as I powered into her. "You. Are. So. Fucking. Beautiful," I ground out in between strokes. Her eyes came to mine, only a thin rim of blue around the dilated pupils.

"I love you," she gasped then tensed as if realising what she'd just revealed. I couldn't have that, so I moved my hand between us and pressed where she needed as I continued to thrust, angling to what I knew would hit the perfect spot. She moaned again, losing herself as she flew over the edge. As she spasmed around me, my movements went out of control, and sparks went off behind my eyes as I followed her in the most intense orgasm of my life.

Lucy was limp in my arms, staring up at me with a dazed, sated expression before she blinked a couple of times and came back to herself, stiffening when the realisation of where we were, what we'd just done, and what she'd just admitted to me swept over her.

"Oh my God," she whispered as I lowered her to her feet.

"Is everything okay up there?" a voice came over the tannoy and Lucy's eyes went wide. I cleared my throat and pressed the intercom to reply.

"We're fine. I think the emergency system triggered itself. I've nearly sorted it."

"I can override the—"

Lucy squeaked, and I quickly cut him off to reply. "No need."

"But—"

"Leave it," I snapped.

"Yes sir," came the reply and I thought I could hear a suppressed snort of laughter in the background.

"Oh my God," Lucy repeated.

I'd now managed to rearrange myself back into my trousers and tuck my shirt back in. My tie and jacket were still in place so, apart from maybe my hair being tousled where Lucy had been grabbing onto it, I was pretty much back together.

I turned back to Lucy, who was still very much not back together and felt a huge wave of protectiveness crash over me. She was still blinking at the intercom in horror. Her dress was hanging off her shoulder, her hair was all over the place, half her skirt was still rucked up near her waist, she was only wearing one shoe and her cardigan was lying next to us on the floor. Then she shivered and I flew into action.

"It's all fine," I said in a low, reassuring voice as I gently lifted her bra strap back onto her shoulder, pulling the cup over her breast, then settling the dress back where it should be and smoothing her skirt back down.

"They know what we were doing," she said in a horrified whisper.

I tried and failed to hold back my smile.

"Felix," she snapped as I bent down to pick up her cardigan. "This isn't funny!"

I put her cardigan on her, then buttoned up the front, picked up her shoe, lifted her foot so she had to balance holding onto my shoulder and slipped her shoe back on. Then I stood in front of her, my hands going to her hair to finger comb it back from her face.

Despite my efforts, Lucy looked exactly like she'd had a good seeing to in a lift, something I did not want my security team to witness. I pulled her into me, enclosing her in my arms and kissed her forehead.

"No, they don't," I lied, and her eyebrows went up.

"Yes, yes they do!"

"Well," I shrugged. "I own the building, and I pay their salaries, so if I want to shag my gorgeous girlfriend in the lift, they can suck it up and jog on."

"Ugh, you are impossible."

I grinned down at her and went to the control panel, punching in the code for the car park so we could avoid the staff seeing her. The lift started moving and I pulled Lucy into my side, kissing the top of her head and feeling more content than I had in months.

"Where are we going?"

"I'm taking you home."

"Felix, you've got to go back up there. What about the meeting?"

"Baby, if you think I'm going back into a bloody business meeting after that you've totally lost it."

"B–b–but—"

"I'm taking you home." We were next to my car now. Lucy looked from it to me in surprise as if she couldn't quite work out how she got there. Then she shivered again, and I frowned.

"Felix, you can't—"

I pulled open the passenger side door and pushed Lucy forward by putting pressure on the small of her back.

"Get in the car. Now." I used that commanding tone and watched her eyes glaze slightly.

"You're so bossy," she muttered as she slid into the car but there was no heat behind it. Lucy liked a little bit of bossy in her life. I smiled as I slammed the door after her.

On the drive back to my house Lucy was quiet. I could feel her tension build even as I took her hand in mine and held it on my lap, driving with one hand to keep it there as if she might slip away from me at any moment.

But after what she'd just revealed to me, after everything, Lucy Mayweather was not slipping away. Not ever again.

CHAPTER 38

I know it's a bit much

Lucy

"Wow," I said as Felix led me into the hall, and I drew to a halt. "This is… this is *different*."

"Different good?" Felix asked, turning to me, his hand still holding mine.

From the moment I'd seen Felix today he'd been touching me. It was as if he was reassuring himself that I was real and that I was here with him. That, and the way he was looking at me, was at least some reassurance after I told the bastard I loved him. He responded by giving me the most glorious orgasm of my life which was great, don't get me wrong, but what it *wasn't* was him saying he still loves me too.

Maybe he didn't still feel that way anymore? Maybe that's why he backed off?

I looked up at him and his expectant expression and studied it for a moment. There was a subtle tension around his eyes. My answer to the transformation of his house was important to him. I wasn't sure why. I mean, the man could decorate however he wanted. Maybe he mixed it up on the reg? But this was quite the change – gone was the grey and white, gone were the clean lines. Instead, the walls were painted a warm ochre, almost orange colour, there were plants in colourful pots, an old-fashioned hat stand was next to the front door. The sideboard was the same gorgeous, polished oak as the floors.

"It's beautiful," I breathed, and his shoulders relaxed slightly. "But I wouldn't have said it was your taste."

"Tastes change," he said dismissively, pulling me on through the hallway.

"Felix," I said as we came to a stop in the kitchen. I gave my hand a tug and he frowned as I pulled it from his. "Listen, just because I said... I mean, I know I said something in the heat of the moment. I don't want you to feel that you have to..." I huffed and pulled my hands through my already messy hair. When I spoke again my voice was only just above a whisper. "Look, can we just forget about it?"

"No," Felix was facing me with his arms crossed over his chest. "No, I don't think we can." I felt a spark of panic.

"Listen, it's okay if you don't feel that way now." My voice rose as I tried to convince him. "You just have to forget about it, and we can pretend that I never—"

He uncrossed his arms and came for me with a determined expression on his face. Grabbing my hand, he pulled me along back out of the kitchen and into the corridor. When we got to his study, he hesitated with his other hand on the doorknob.

"Okay, I wasn't going to show you this yet because you might think I'm a little crazy. It's a bit... full on."

"Full on? What do you—?" I gasped as he opened the door and pulled me inside. "This... what did you do?"

I blinked at the walls. Felix's boring panelling had been replaced by floor-to-ceiling shelves. Two entire walls worth, full of books. I dropped Felix's hand and glided forward to the nearest wall. My hand trailed over the spines of the books. The shelf I was touching was all epic fantasy, including every Tolkien ever written. My eyes scanned along the entire wall – complete with a small sliding ladder for the higher shelves – and fell on the far side of the room.

"Oh, Felix," I breathed.

All the special edition book covers for my books were framed in between the shelves. But the most spectacular element was the huge map of Minora on the remaining wall, and how it linked to the other two kingdoms in my books. I moved over to it automatically, my eyes sweeping from the rich green of the forests to the bleaker desert landscapes bordered by mountain ranges. It was so detailed. And it filled the *entire wall*.

Felix's large, heavy desk had had a makeover and was now positioned so that it had a view of the garden out of the vast picture window, the seat of which was piled with cushions of all colours. A new sofa was opposite the desk – big, squashy and a warm burnt orange colour. I felt my eyes sting.

"I know it's a bit much," Felix muttered, sounding uncharacteristically unsure of himself. He shoved his hands in his pockets and shifted slightly on his feet. "And a bit stalkery. I mean, I knew most of your favourite authors of course, but I might have had your mum snoop into your Kindle too. I guess I just felt like I needed to *do* something. Somehow if I built you your perfect room, if I made this house somewhere you'd want to be, then maybe, maybe you'd want to be here. With me."

My eyes were still stinging, and my throat felt tight as I looked at him. His shoulders were tense as he cleared his throat and avoided my gaze to look out of the window. I couldn't get my words past the lump in my throat, so I decided to act instead. When I burst forward Felix's startled gaze shot back to me. His hands were only just out of his pockets in time to catch me as I jumped into his arms, my legs encircling his hips. I took his gorgeous face in both my hands and covered his cheeks, forehead, nose and finally mouth with kisses. He let out a shaky relieved laugh as I continued my attack.

"You like it then?"

I leaned back slightly to look at him, returning his smile with one of my own, even as a tear fell down my cheek. "Of course I like it, Felix. I *love* it."

"I love you, you know," he said.

"I do know," I said through my smile as another tear fell.

"I know I've said it before, but I'm sorry I let you down. I promise, I *swear* it'll never happen again. And you can daydream, go down a writing rabbit hole, disappear into your books; I'll be here waiting. I'll be here sorting the real world for you. I mean, all those times I lectured you about changing, and it was me that needed to bloody well buck my ideas up. I just—"

I cut him off with a kiss then rested my forehead against his. "I couldn't stay in my weird little dreamy comfort zone forever. Okay, maybe I don't need to be a fully corporate animal like you, but I *do* need to be able to handle some public-facing stuff if I want the books out there."

"But—"

"And I wasn't happy, Felix. You pushed me, yes. Were you right all the time? No. But that doesn't mean that some change wasn't good for me too."

He rolled his eyes. "What am I going to do with you?"

"Well, you can keep me."

His eyes lit and his smile widened. "You'll stay with me here?"

"Felix, you've built me a blooming library, had a map of a fictional world I made up painted on an actual wall, given me multiple orgasms, supported me in my career, tolerated my mother, let a small horse molest you endlessly and eat your belongings for me." I softened my tone as I went on. "You made sure I was warm, you stopped me from disappearing into my world. Of course, I'll stay with you."

His eyes clouded for a moment. "I didn't always make sure you were warm. I haven't always supported you."

"You've supported me since I was five years old. Nobody, not even Dad, listened to my stories like you did. I loved you then, and I love you now."

"And you'll stay?" he said as if wanting to clarify the situation, wanting to get some sort of verbal agreement I wouldn't back out of. "Here?"

"Well, yes. But we have to go back to Little Buckingham on the reg. The mothers would lose their shit if we stayed away. We can stay in my shed. It's practically a three-bed house now, thanks to you and your crazy ways."

"I guess I can spend more time in Little Buckingham, especially now Dad's out of the picture."

"Plus, Legolas misses you."

He shuddered. "I'll spend time back home, but you have to train that fucking pony."

"Sure."

"You're not going to train him, are you?"

I bit my lip. "No."

He buried his face in my neck and burst out laughing. I wrapped my arms around him and squeezed him with my thighs.

"Did you decorate your bedroom?" I asked, smiling at the hundreds of books on the wall opposite.

"Of course."

I cleared my throat. "Maybe we should…"

"Uh, uh," he said, striding over to the sofa and lowering me down. Once we were there and I was wrapped in his arms, he kissed the top of my head. "Tell me a story."

I snuggled into his side and let out a frustrated huff. "I'd rather see your bedroom," I grumped, and he chuckled.

"Humour me, Shakespeare," he said softly.

I sighed but the emotion in his voice made me relent. So, I started to tell him the story of the next book I was publishing. This was about a grumpy but damaged king of a savage world who ruled with an iron fist, killing anyone standing in his way; and the half-fairy daughter of the local witch who makes him see that there might be another way to govern.

The king just happened to have dark brown eyes and a dimple on his right cheek.

Ten minutes in Felix relented and carried me to his bedroom.

"Mummy, can you tell us a story?"

Lucy

"Lucy?"

I blinked as I felt a warm hand on the back of my neck, swimming up from my daydream and turning towards the sound of my husband's voice. There he was, towering over where I'd been sitting in the window seat, hugging my knees and staring out over London.

Felix had added this arrangement into his office shortly after I moved back in with him. He knew daydreaming was essential for me and he said if I could do it anywhere I might as well do it in his office so he could see me anytime he wanted. I wasn't about to object. I had a steady stream of caramel lattes, Marmite toast and anything else I might want here after all.

One of the other reasons was that when I was into a story, I sometimes forgot to eat. Felix was not so keen on that scenario. So the window seat it was. There were comfortable cushions, and a desk that suspended over me should I want to write. I had an office laptop and Kindle given the amount of times I'd forget my own. Sometimes Felix would be out at meetings. Sometimes he worked alongside me. Sometimes he'd kiss the side of my head or snuggle in behind me as I worked. Sometimes he'd lower all the blinds to the rest of the office...

Yes, it worked for me in a big way.

"Oh sorry, were you there long?" I smiled up at him as I reached for his waist, pulling him into me. He chuckled as he lowered himself next to me on the seat, wrapped his arms around me and leaned back so I could snuggle into him.

"Only the standard amount of time. Don't worry, you ignoring me is good for my ego."

"I don't mean to ignore you," I objected, twisting around to look at him. "I just go a bit..."

"Doolally."

"Yes, doolally."

"It's okay, Shakespeare. I know your brain is thinking up the next universe for you to write in. Just so long as you continue to visit us mortals in this universe, I'm happy."

He kissed my temple and gave me a squeeze. "You warm enough?"

Felix had ditched his suit jacket and tie. His sleeves were rolled up giving me plenty of muscular arm porn to admire. It may have been winter, but you wouldn't have known it sitting in here. Felix had put in a separate heater for his office after people started standing in the fridge to try to cool down when he'd overheated the whole floor. Everyone was happier that way, and I'd assured Felix that I wasn't going to die of hypothermia if I had to do the occasional walk to the bog or to see Vicky, Lottie and Tabitha at a reasonable twenty degrees.

"They're here," he said in a cautious voice, and I stiffened.

"W—what? Oh crikey, I completely lost track of time. We'd better—"

I went to stand up, but Felix's arms tightened around me to keep me in place.

"Felix," I said, panicked now. "We shouldn't keep them waiting."

"They're here for you, Shakespeare," he said in a soft voice. "You're going to see if you want to work with them. Not the other way around."

"B–b–but it's a real production company," I squeaked. "Maddie'll kill me if I don't—"

"Maddie works for you. Just like I work for you."

I huffed out a laugh. "You don't work for me, you daft article."

"I'll have you know that I'm the... what was it now? 'The worst, most unrelentingly crap assistant in the history of publishing'."

Ooh, Maddie had been *really* angry with Felix after the last signing. To be fair to her, he had been a bit growly and overprotective and he may have told a producer to bugger off when he tried to corner me about a deal after the signing had finished. But by that stage I'd been on my feet for eight hours, my wrist was hurting and I had a headache from all the peopling. Steven Spielberg himself could have approached me and Felix would still have told him to jog on.

"I thought you were excellent," I said. "And you've got a cute butt which counts for a lot in an assistant."

"Is that right?" he muttered, his hand coming up to tilt my face towards his so his lips could brush mine. "I think that might constitute sexual harassment, Mrs Moretti," he muttered against my mouth, and I smiled.

"Maybe my assistant could do with a little harassment. Maybe then my caramel lattes wouldn't be so few and far between."

"You had a latte half an hour ago, you little minx. I'll show you harassment."

With that he slid his hand up my jawline and covered my mouth with his. Just as I was getting lost in the kiss, I heard a sharp tap on the glass.

"Shit, Felix we forgot the blinds," I squeaked, and he huffed out a frustrated sigh. I jumped when the sharp tapping started again and turned to see a furious Maddie standing outside the glass window to the office flanked by an amused Lottie and a curious Vicky.

"I guess we better get up," he said reluctantly as Maddie wrenched the door open.

"Honestly, Felix," Maddie snapped, steam practically coming out of her ears. "You guys canoodle 24-7. Do you have to when an entire production team are boiling their arses off in the next room?

With no rush at all Felix lifted me up and moved us both to standing, taking my hand and then strolling to where Maddie was standing in the doorway. I groaned.

"Felix, please tell me that you're not boiling those telly executives alive in there, you maniac?"

He shrugged, completely unrepentant. "I've no idea how long this meeting could go on for. I wanted you comfortable."

"You're impossible," I said as we started towards the conference room.

"They're on our turf, so I... Luce? You okay?"

I'd come to a sudden stop in the corridor. I could see the executives through the glass. There were five of them. Five. Why did it require five of them to speak to little old me?

"Lucy?"

"I don't think..." I whispered, shaking my head and taking a step back. "I mean, I just write silly stories about fairies and stuff. I can't understand why anyone would..."

Felix moved to stand in front of me so that his large body was blocking my view of the conference room. He put both his hands on my shoulders to anchor me in place.

"Lucy, look at me," he said, his voice firm.

I blinked and looked up at his handsome, determined face.

"Now you listen to me, Shakespeare," he said. "Your stories take people to other worlds. They give people joy. They're about good and evil, love and sacrifice. They are not silly. Understand me?"

I bit my lip. "Er... I guess—"

"*They* need *you*. Not the other way around. Now we're going in there to kick some streaming service arse and get you the deal you deserve with the control over it you want."

"I just—"

"Think how proud your dad would have been, Shakespeare," he said softly. I closed my eyes and Dad's voice echoed in my brain.

"Storytellers change the world, love," he'd said. "There's nothing as powerful as a good story told well."

"Okay," I told Felix, new determination in my tone as I squared my shoulders. "I'm ready."

Felix smiled at me and then gave me a brief, hard kiss before we both headed into the meeting. When I looked up it was to see all the eyes in the conference room fixed on us through the glass. Maddie rolled hers. But I didn't care. I was the keeper of stories and if I wanted to kiss my husband before a meeting then I would.

"Good afternoon, ladies and gentlemen," Felix said as we walked into the room. "This is Lucy Moretti, pen name LP Mayweather, and I will be assisting her today."

*

Four years later...

Felix

"Get. Off. Legolas. Now!" Bea stamped her foot as she glared at her twin brother. One of her bunches was higher than the other, she had her hands on her hips with her short, chubby legs braced wide as her dark brown eyes flashed with fury.

Legolas had found his calling as an entertainer for our three-year-olds. He would happily trot around the village and the estate with either one of the twins on his back. But both Henry and Bea very much considered Legolas theirs, and there was a little too much of me in both of them for either one to concede defeat.

"Imma ride to Gramma's!" shouted Henry, giggling hysterically as Legolas trotted off in the direction of my mother's house.

Lucy and I had built what my mother and Hetty both agreed was a "modern monstrosity" in between Moonreach and my mum's estate. For the last five years we'd lived between here and London but, given how good the village school was and how much the kids loved it here, we were likely to be based much more in Little Buckingham going forward.

"Henry Moretti!" I shouted as Legolas started picking up speed. "You come back here!" Legolas, ever willing to piss me off, broke into a canter just at the point I decided to pick up Bea and give chase. The old bastard barely managed a trot usually, but he had it in for me after years of preventing him from eating Lucy's maps. "Jesus Christ," I said as I saw the gate was open.

"Cheese and rice," Henry shouted gleefully – now thoroughly enjoying being a passenger on the all-out run across the countryside we were having to do.

I was going to kill that pony.

We followed them over the field and through the gate. I knew where the furry menace was headed now as The Badger's Sett pub garden came into view. Henry squealed as Legolas jumped the small fence separating our land from the pub's.

Unfortunately it took a little longer for me to negotiate the fence with Bea in my arms, so by the time we made it into the garden, Legolas had already knocked over a couple of tables and snatched an apple right out of Emily's youngest daughter's hands.

Emily snorted. "Good luck, Moretti."

"What the bloody hell kind of show are you running there?" shouted Jimbo as we ran into the back door after Legolas. There was a trail of destruction in here too.

"Free Sunday lunches for everyone," I cried over my shoulder and a cheer went up amongst the patrons despite the carnage we'd left behind.

"And drinks, you tight git," Mikey called after me, and I gave him a one-finger salute as we emerged onto the street.

"Daddy!" Bea admonished. "You mustn't finger swear."

"I was waving at your uncle."

"That was not a nice wave. I knows all about finger swears. Theo Harding does them all the time."

Well, Theo Harding was a little shit just like his dad, who I would be having a word with once I'd found that bloody pony. I was really panicking now. Little Buckingham didn't get a lot of traffic, but it only took one car to—

"Missing something?" My head snapped around and I breathed a sigh of relief. Standing there in front of the village shop was my very beautiful and very pregnant wife holding onto the reins of a not-looking-in-any-way-sorry Legolas with one hand, and the hand of our overexcited son in the other.

Bea wriggled in my arms to get down and then ran over to them. "Daddy said 'cheese and rice' *and* he finger swore at Uncle Mikey."

I scowled at the little snitch, but she stuck her tongue out at me and hid behind her mother's legs. Lucy sighed.

"I was gone for twenty minutes, Felix," she said.

I threw up my hands. "They're totally unmanageable."

"We are not unmanny-at-all," Bea said, her hands going to her hips in indignation. "*Mummy's* never lost one of us."

"That's because your mother is perfect," I said as I stalked over to them, plucked Henry off the ground to tuck him under one arm then reached down to tuck Bea under the other before tickling them both. Then, with the kids still under my arms I leaned forward and kissed Lucy.

"Ew, gross," complained Henry as they both wriggled out of my grip.

"Daddy, you do some things good," put in Bea, clearly concerned that she might have hurt my feelings.

"Oh really? What's that then?"

"You give really good cuddles. You can throw us in the air super high. You let us climb trees way higher than Mummy. And you... can cook really good pancakes."

"Well, thank you for that performance review."

Lucy smiled up at me as she burrowed under my arm and kissed my neck. "Your dad does have his strong points."

Lucy had been worried that the daydreaming side of her would make parenting difficult. It took a lot of reassurance when she first fell pregnant for her to believe that she wouldn't just one day forget the twins existed as she dreamt up another story. I worked mostly from home for the first three months after they were born, and then she'd often come into the office with the twins. But it turned out that, when it came to the kids, inattention was not a problem. Lucy was in fact way more of a helicopter parent than me, hence my allowing Henry off the lead rope and the ensuing chase across Little Buckingham.

"Mama, I'm tired," Henry said in a small voice, and we looked down at him to see him swaying on the spot. Henry was a full-power kid, but when his battery ran out, he just sort of deflated. I scooped him up, and he nuzzled into my neck.

"Sorry, Daddy," he said around a yawn.

"I'm riding Legolas home," Bea declared, using the opening of her brother's exhaustion to her full advantage. So that's how we walked through the village – Bea riding Legolas, one of my arms around Lucy and the other holding up a muddy, nearly asleep Henry.

When we arrived back at the house, Bea was just as exhausted. I listened to Lucy tuck them into their beds for a nap and waited outside the door for what I knew they'd ask. Almost in unison the question came:

"Mummy, can you tell us a story?"

Jacob is different

Lucy

"It's the daydreaming again, I'm afraid."

Ugh. I was beginning to really dislike Jacob's new teacher.

"Honestly, I'll ask everyone to get changed for games, and ten minutes later Jacob's still staring off into the middle distance. He's completely away with the fairies."

"Okay," Felix said slowly. "Apart from the daydreaming, how is Jacob actually doing?"

Mrs Huckleberry huffed. "It holds the class up, you see. He's just totally a flibbertigibbet."

I blinked at her and pressed my lips together to stop the laughter I could feel building.

"And don't even get me started on break times. Yesterday the bell rang to call all the children in and, again, *no* Jacob. We found him lying on his back in the middle field, staring up at the clouds."

"I'm sorry," Felix said, sounding anything but, "did I hear you right? You're telling me you lost my son on the school grounds?"

"We did not lose Jacob," Mrs Huckleberry snapped, very unwisely in my opinion. "He lost himself in his own world, just like he does ninety per cent of the time."

"I thought I'd made it clear two weeks ago that I would not be happy if there were any further signs of a lack of supervision at break times." Felix's voice was low and deadly now. Mrs Huckleberry's face paled as she belatedly realised how angry my husband was.

Two weeks ago, Jacob had been pushed over and kicked by some of the other boys. And the person to pull them off him had not been a teacher; it had instead been a little girl. Not just any little girl, mind. Even at seven years old, Margot Harding was a force to be reckoned with. Now, Margot was not a daydreamer – not by a long shot. She was a laser-focused, ruthless little dynamo. But she loved Jacob. Always had. And by the time she'd been pulled off those three boys, one of them had a broken nose, another's eye was almost swollen shut and the other was limping. Neither Margot nor Jacob had a scratch on them, which was not the case with the boys. Despite the fact they were all a year older than her and nearly twice her size, she'd brought the lot down.

That had been a fun meeting with the headteacher, Mrs Clayton. After she'd started off about how the school didn't condone violence and that Margot would need to be disciplined, Ollie had lost his mind. He was not happy about the fact it had been his tiny daughter versus three older and much larger boys.

"B–b–but she doesn't have a scratch on her!" protested Mrs Clayton. "Did you *see* the other boys?"

"She'd better not have a scratch on her," Ollie had said in a dark voice, causing Mrs Clayton to swallow nervously.

Then the reason for Margot's violence came out and Felix went nuclear. I don't think the meeting went quite the way Mrs Clayton expected. It started as a disciplinary meeting for Margot and Jacob, but concluded with her apologising profusely and reassuring us that the bullying would be tackled. That clearly wasn't the case.

"W—w—well there was supervision, but Jacob also has to take some personal responsibility for his actions. I need him to start bucking his ideas up a bit."

"His ideas are *why* he daydreams," I put in. "His mind is just full of them, and it can overwhelm him sometimes."

I could tell that Mrs Huckleberry was suppressing an eye roll at that, and I gritted my teeth.

"Ideas do not get shoes on and get things done in a timely fashion, I'm afraid," she said in a prim voice.

"Ideas are how we fix the world's problems. Every innovation started with an idea. Every story that changes lives starts with ideas. They're more important than you can even comprehend."

"I do not think that Jacob is coming up with solutions to global warming instead of putting his shoes on."

"How do you know?" snapped Felix. "Listen, Jacob is who he is, and we wouldn't change him for the world."

"Now the twins were a different story. Always so on the ball. No daydreaming. Exemplary students. I tell Jacob all the time to try and live up to his siblings because—"

"You do what?" Two streaks of colour had appeared high on Felix's cheekbones, and his hands had balled into fists. "Are you telling me you regularly compared my youngest son to his older siblings? What the hell kind of show are you running here?"

I laid my hand on Felix's arm and gave him a warning squeeze. Having been on the receiving end of the "why can't you just be more like your brother" for my entire childhood I knew exactly how awful it was.

"Jacob is different from his siblings," I told Mrs Huckleberry, something she already knew, and then went on to tell her some other things she also needed to know. "He's different, full stop. But different doesn't have to be bad. We need all the daydreamers we can get in this society, and shaming children out of it is not the way to go."

I stood up then and Felix followed my lead. "I'll see you in the meeting with the headmistress," I told her, and she frowned in confusion.

"There isn't a meeting scheduled with the headmistress," she said. I leaned over her desk slightly, fixing her with a steady stare.

"Oh, there will be," I said, the threat in my voice unmistakable.

As we left her classroom, Felix took my hand in his and gave it a squeeze. My throat was tight but I needed to hold it together as we were about to get to our boy.

Jacob gave us a big grin as he ran out of the school gates to us.

"Hey, Mum, Dad! I think I've come up with a way to reduce the emission of fossil fuels from domestic log burners! See, it's all a question of filters and—"

"Hug first," I said through my thick throat. He tilted his head as he looked into my eyes which were watery.

"You okay, Mum?" he whispered, and I gave a firm nod.

"Better than okay, love."

He launched himself into my arms and then into his father's, keeping on about the filters for the log burners. So much for Mrs Huckleberry saying that Jacob's ideas weren't how to fix global warming. That was one of the differences between Jacob and me. Jacob tended to daydream about how things worked and how problems were solved; I daydreamed stories, but for both of us we needed to go "doolally" regularly for the ideas to come. It was as essential as breathing to us. I looked down at his shoelaces and sighed. Undone again.

"That sounds fab, darling," I said as I cupped his cheek. "But you need to stop sometimes to do the real-world stuff, okay?" He glanced down at his feet and the tips of his ears went pink.

"Right, Mum," he said, kneeling down to lace them up quickly.

"I don't know about that," said Felix as he smiled down at his son. "The real world is pretty boring. You be you, Jake."

Jacob grinned up at his father. If there was one person in the world who accepted and appreciated my daydreaming boy for exactly who he was, it was my husband.

Just like he had with me.

The End

Read on for Tabitha's story.
Exclusive paperback content.

Apology accepted

Alex

"Who's dealing with the negotiations then if Moretti's swanned off to the country? I want to get this sorted today."

"I think his assistant Tabitha is abreast of all the relevant details," said Luke, my business partner. "Felix said she can answer all our queries just as well as him."

"Great," I snapped, holding back an eye roll and trying to ignore the completely illogical zing of anticipation I felt at hearing her name. The woman absolutely hated me, and I wasn't exactly her biggest fan either. "Can't we deal with someone else?" I said, my voice laced with irritation.

"Have you got a problem with Tabitha?" Luke asked me, his eyebrows going up in surprise. "She's pretty goddamn competent if you ask me. We'll probably get further with her than a lovestruck Moretti anyway. Apparently he abandoned a meeting about one of the biggest land deals in London last week to chase after his girlfriend."

I shrugged. "I'd just rather deal with someone else. She winds me up."

"Careful, Alex." I flinched at the sound of Tabitha's voice, way too close. Shit, how much had she heard? "Your misogyny is showing."

She didn't break stride as she swept past both of us, high heels clicking across the tiled floor and, bizarrely, a scruffy little dog following in her wake. God, she was beautiful. Her suit hugged her curves as she sashayed through the office. She only spared me and Luke a brief dismissive glance, but it was long enough for me to get a good look at those gorgeous green eyes, which tilted up at the side just slightly. She looked defiant and completely in control, but I could see the tight set of her mouth giving her away.

I'd upset her.

Again.

"Fuck," I muttered under my breath.

Luke sighed. "Fuck is right. We do actually want to do business with these people, mate. You might want to rein in the dickhead for a day."

My shoulders slumped.

There hadn't always been this animosity between me and Tabitha. In fact, it had been the total opposite when I first met her at a drinks party at Felix Moretti's house. She'd been standing across from me in the same group when Ian Mowat had started banging on about his haulage company, and I caught her stifling a yawn. Ian was one of my friends, but he could be a boring bastard about his lorries. I'd quirked an eyebrow at her, and she'd snorted into her drink. Then, when I tilted my head to the side in invitation, she took my lead and we both left the group, making our own cosy group of two and staying that way for the rest of the night.

I didn't tell her who I was, deciding to feed her the normal bullshit line about how I worked in finance. She didn't need to know about my tech company which was one of the fastest growing start-ups in the industry, recently valued at £2.4 billion – this kind of information I tended to keep to myself until I was sure I could trust a person. Tabitha was effortlessly sexy, witty and fun, and by the end of the night, I'd decided that she was going to be mine.

Fucking Felix ruined everything though with his shitty timing, coming up to us both, slapping me on the back and calling me by my real name before I'd had the chance to explain anything to Tabitha. I had to suffer through painful small talk with him whilst Tabby was struck dumb in shock, until finally Felix was called away.

"Alex Costas?" she breathed at me once we were alone again. Her face drained of all colour as she spoke. "I-I thought you were called Xander?"

"I can explain. I just—"

She shook her head, taking a few steps back. "Mr Costas, I had no idea who you were. If I'd had any clue as to your identity I would never have complained about my work environment, especially with you in negotiations with Moretti Harding. I realise you must think me totally unprofessional but—"

"Tabby, please," I'd begged, taking her hand in mine. "I would never say a word. It doesn't matter—"

"Doesn't matter?" She snatched her hand back, her eyebrows going up as her voice rose.

I shrugged. "So I know that the atmosphere at Moretti Harding isn't great and the coffee is shitty. It's not like you gave away any corporate secrets."

She was looking really pale now. "D-did you do it deliberately?" she whispered.

I frowned. "What do you mean?"

"Lie about who you were. Did you do it to test me? Get information out of me before you sign the contracts?"

"No, of course not." I was losing patience now. "Tabitha, you're a low-level employee. I'm hardly going to target you for some light corporate espionage." She took a step back and her eyes shuttered. "Shit, listen I'm sorry. That came out wrong. I—"

"Low-level employee," she repeated slowly as she crossed her arms over her chest. "So why *did* you lie then?"

I grabbed the back of my neck, shifting on my feet in discomfort. "Listen, I rarely tell women my real identity. I have to be careful."

She tilted her head to the side and her eyes flashed. "Ah, it's only *women* you lie to."

I sighed. "You're getting the wrong end of the stick. I have to be careful. I—"

"You don't think *I* have to be careful?" she snapped. "You have no idea how careful I am normally. I can't believe I let my guard down. It's easy for you — billionaire, tech giant, man... for *me* things are a little more complicated. You may think I'm just a *low-level employee*, but my career matters to me. And risking my professional reputation on a man who's given me a fake name, no doubt so he can fuck me with impunity, is not going to help my struggle against the misogyny and disrespect I already battle on a daily basis."

She took another step back and then stalked away.

I beat a retreat that night but, unfortunately, in the weeks that followed I'd made my feelings embarrassingly clear. I sent her flowers, chocolates, even jewellery. All items were returned straight back to me, unopened.

Eventually our paths did cross again. This time at the Moretti Harding offices. I knew she was an assistant to the guy I was discussing the development with, but what I didn't know was just how far she was willing to go in her quest to *assist* him. When Luke and I rounded the corner to Will's office we caught him and Tabitha in the reception area, right in each other's personal space, so close it looked like he was about to snog her right on her desk. Tabitha sprang away from Will with a guilty expression and a red face as soon as she saw us approach. Will just straightened his tie and led us into his office with a smug look.

"Bit of advice boys," he said once we'd shut the door of his office with Tabitha still outside at her desk. "Get yourself hot as fuck assistants that are willing to shag for a leg up in the company. That one's an ambitious little minx. Keeps you dangling for months, then *bam*, by the time she's let you in there you're willing to give her whatever pay rise she wants."

We hadn't done business with Will that day. Mainly because I'd told him he was an arsehole and then left his office in short order. I did stop at Tabitha's desk on my way out though after telling Luke to go on to the lifts without me.

"I thought I'd offended you at that party, and that you were too principled to go out with me given that I was negotiating with your company," I said to Tabitha in a low voice. She froze behind the desk and looked up at me like a deer in the headlights. "You really had me going with your little game. Keep me on the hook until I'm totally desperate for you, just like you did with Will. Jesus Christ! What's the appeal of that prick?"

Her face paled and for a terrible moment I actually thought she might throw up, but she swallowed before her green eyes flashed and she blinked up at me.

"Get *the fuck* out of here," she said, her voice low and shaky with fury.

I rolled my eyes. "Don't pretend you're all affronted after you've been caught in the act, darling."

"How dare you call me 'darling'."

"God, this moral high ground thing is really wearing a little thin when you're actually willing to screw that joker to get ahead. I mean, who's next? Felix? Harry York?"

"I can assure you, Mr Costas." She kept her gaze steady on me and for some reason my chest tightened. "I will never let a man in the corporate world get anywhere near me, *ever* again. *Never*. Now, get out of my office right fucking now."

I frowned. Before she looked away from me, I could have sworn I saw a sheen of wet across the green of her eyes.

"Tabby, I—"

"Are you deaf? Get the fuck *out*."

"Is there a problem here?" I turned to see Felix with his arms crossed over his chest at the other end of the corridor. I looked back at Tabitha for a moment, but her gaze was fixed on her computer screen, tapping away at the keys and looking totally unruffled by the last five minutes. I huffed and stormed over to Felix, informed him the deal was off but offered no further explanation. His employees were his problem.

Well, now I *had* to deal with the very Moretti Harding employee I most wanted to avoid. This was not going to help with my unwanted dreams of her at night when I couldn't get control of my subconscious. That incident had been over a year ago, but I was still plagued by the woman.

I turned to Luke with a sigh of resignation. "I'll try and rein it in, but she fucking hates me."

"Well, she's been bloody good about my apology," Luke muttered. "And I was way more in the wrong than you. At least you called the fucker an arsehole."

"What did you have to apologise for?"

He blinked at me. "You know, for Will Brent."

"Why are you apologising to Tabitha about Will Brent?"

"Holy shit, you really don't know? Everyone's been talking about the shit that went down here for weeks."

"I avoid the subject of Moretti Harding like the plague," I told him. "I'm only here today because we literally cannot move the development forward without them."

Luke sighed. "Will Brent is a creepy arsehole."

"This is not news."

"Yes, but apparently that particular creepy arsehole was sexually harassing a lot of the female staff here. Especially Tabitha. What we walked in on that day was part of it. She actually set up cameras to gather evidence, and then handed it all over to the police when Will assaulted Felix's girlfriend, the stupid bastard."

"What the fuck are you talking about?" I'd stopped dead in the middle of the corridor, feeling the colour drain out of my face. Luke frowned at me.

"Er... well, I kind of assumed you knew. I mean, you grabbed the guy and called him an arsehole, and after nuking the deal you waited behind to talk to Tabitha. When I found out about the harassment, I presumed that you'd noticed what I didn't and that you were probably checking in with her that she was okay?"

"Holy shit," I muttered. I reached up and gripped the back of my neck as a feeling of total helplessness and nausea washed over me. I had never felt like more of a terrible human being than in that moment.

"Alex? What's wrong?"

"I am the biggest prick on the planet, that's what's wrong."

Luke shrugged, grinning over at me. "Tell me something I don't know."

"Ugh, shut up, you smug twat. We'd better get into the conference room. Then I need to have a private word with Tabitha."

"What the hell for? I'm the one that needed to apologise."

"Trust me, I've got a fuck ton more to apologise about than you."

Tabitha

I clenched my hands in my lap to stop them from shaking. Bloody Felix, buggering off to Little Buckingham and leaving me to deal with these bastards. I mean, okay, he might have come back if I'd explained why I hated Alex Costas, but up until recently Felix hadn't been the most approachable boss, and I still wasn't comfortable showing him any sign of weakness.

I took a deep breath in through my nose and let it out through my mouth. Competent professionalism was the mantra of my entire career, and it wasn't going to be shaken by some jumped-up tech bro with delusions of grandeur. The double doors opened, and there he was, all gorgeous, dark-eyed, broad-shouldered, six-foot-three of him

"Hi, Tabitha," Alex said softly as he took the chair opposite me. He smiled a tentative smile which just confused me. I frowned at him briefly, then looked over at Luke Morris who gave me a low wave and a grin. Now Luke, I could tolerate. He'd apologised to me at least, not that he had anything to be sorry about. And I would never hold a grudge against someone with that level of golden retriever energy, all blonde hair and sunny smiles, unlike his business partner, whose icy demeanour was legendary.

"Mr Morris, Mr Costas," I said, giving them a brief nod. "Now if we could—"

"Alex," Alex interrupted.

I lifted an eyebrow and fixed him with what I hoped was a glacial stare, but the heat I could feel building in my cheeks likely ruined the effect. "I'm sorry? What are you—?"

"Not Mr Costas. Call me Alex."

"Oh? I was under the impression your first name was Xander. My mistake." I sniffed and looked back down at the plans in front of me. "Mr Costas, if you open to page three, you will see a comprehensive financial plan with all the costs of the project laid out. I can address any queries you might have now, or you can email me them after the meeting."

I heard him sigh but I didn't look up. That man did not deserve my eye contact. After establishing that we were doing this on my terms, the meeting progressed without incident. They had a few questions, but there were no more ridiculous insistences for me to use Alex's first name and no more softly spoken interruptions, which I told myself I was glad about.

When it was clear there was nothing further to discuss, I snapped my folder shut and pushed up from my chair. "You'll be following up directly with Felix," I told them both with fake bravado. I had no idea if Felix would want that, but I did know that I couldn't cope with any more of this ridiculous tension. Alex narrowed his eyes at me.

"What if we want to work with *you*?"

I shrugged. "Take that up with Mr Moretti," I said as I swept past them.

I thought I'd escaped when I saw them both stride off towards the lifts. My shoulders slumped in relief as I collapsed back in my office chair, scooping up Pippin to sit in my lap so I could stroke his soft fur.

"Since when do you have an office dog?"

I startled in my chair and Pippin broke off from licking my neck to look up at the large man looming over us. Alex was very good at that – looming.

"I-I thought you left," I managed to get out around my tight throat. It had been a long day. Covering for Felix whilst he was away sorting things out with Lucy was proving difficult. I'd spent way too much time over the last week stroking the egos of clients whose noses were out of joint not to be interacting directly with the boss. I was so over corporate bullshit, and Alex being here just topped it all off.

"I'm a total dickhead," he said out of the blue and I blinked up at him.

"Okay," I said slowly. "You're not going to get any argument from me on that score. Not sure why you see the need to announce it to my office though."

He shoved his hand into his hair in a gesture of frustration. I wasn't sure whether it was with me or with himself.

"I misinterpreted what I saw that day. It's no excuse, but I was already coming from a place of frustration that you wouldn't even give me a chance, and I… well, I jumped to conclusions like the dickhead that I am. I should never have spoken to you that way."

I looked away from him out of the floor-to-ceiling window that Felix had installed last week and, to my annoyance, I felt my eyes start to sting.

"Apology accepted," I whispered, not trusting myself to speak any louder. "You can go with a clear conscience."

To my absolute shock Alex did not take the out that I'd given him and just leave. No, instead he rounded my desk, fell into a crouch in front of me and laid his hands over mine on Pippin's fur. Pippin, the traitor, seemed delighted by this development and proceeded to lick Alex's hand. Alex smiled and gave the dog some head scratches before his gaze came back to mine.

"I will never have a clear conscience about that day," he said with real feeling. "I will never forgive myself for not dragging him away from you and marching him into Felix's office."

I shrugged. "I mean, you did call him an arsehole."

"Too bloody late and for the wrong bloody reason."

I shrugged again and to my horror a tear escaped, but before it could run down my cheek Alex had reached up to wipe it away. "You weren't the only one to assume that..." I trailed off then cleared my throat. "Sexism is rife in business. You're not the first man to make me feel small."

Alex groaned. "I would never want to make you feel small, Tabby."

That use of my nickname made my chest feel tight and I could feel my eyes start to sting again. Bloody hell. I was a professional woman and this was the middle of my office for Christ's sake. I needed to get a hold of the situation.

"Listen, Alex," I said, sniffing back my tears, straightening my shoulders and pulling my hands from under his. Then in order to preserve my sanity, I pushed back so that my chair, complete with me and Pippin in it, rolled a few feet away from him. "I don't know what you're playing at now, but as far as I'm concerned, you're one of the baddies in my story. I pigeonholed you over a year ago, along with Slimy Will, and it's there you'll stay."

His jaw clenched, and his eyes flashed as he straightened from his crouch and smoothed down his tie. He stared down at me for a long moment before taking a step towards me, to which I responded to by scooting further back. Raw frustration crossed his expression before he masked it.

"Now, I've got a massive amount of work to get done," I said, "so if you would kindly bugger off, that would be appreciated."

Annoyingly, it was like I could feel his hands on mine for the rest of the day, and at night, when my subconscious had free rein, the feeling got even stronger. All my dreams were full of Alex and me engaged in a very different kind of conference room meeting. One where he swept all the documents off the long table so that he could lay me down on there and kiss me.

So I woke up the next day even more tired than before, and I blamed him for that too.

Alex

You're one of the baddies in my story.

This was how much of a twat I'd been. Shoved into the same bloody category as Will the rapey arsehole. Well, I wasn't prepared to be the baddie in Tabby's story. I was going to be the goddamned hero if it killed me. And it might well kill me by the looks of things.

I swore as I stumbled over another pile of rubble. What the fuck was she doing at the building site? When Felix told me this was where I could find her, I told him he was a total wanker. Not great for our working relationship, but still, he should not have allowed Tabby all the way out to this part of London on her own in order to check out the location.

Granted, this neighbourhood had been identified as a potential candidate for significant gentrification (that was why I was keen to invest in this development in the first place), but that would not be happening any time soon, and currently it was not an area that young attractive women should be going to alone.

"Not *allow* her?" an incredulous Felix had spluttered at me. "You try not allowing Tabby anything. The woman would have my balls. She does what the fuck she wants and I trust her judgement."

Bloody wetwipe. Tabby was his employee for God's sake.

Finally, she came into view. I would have smiled at her outfit if I wasn't so bloody infuriated. She was in a tight-fitting suit and four-inch heels, with absolutely no concession to the uneven ground and totally unbothered to be surrounded by men twice her size, all wearing heavy work gear.

Well-aware that I had to tread carefully here, I hung back and observed how she dealt with the situation. Max, one of the lead architects on the project, was scowling down at her. This was no surprise; scowling was Max's standard expression. I'd seen grown men cower under that scowl, but Tabby appeared to be totally unbothered. By the end of their discussion he even seemed to give her a nod of respect, which was certainly unusual for Max. Unlike his business partner Verity, Max was not good with "the clueless bloody suits", as I'd heard him refer to property developers and investors.

She was smiling when she finally waved goodbye to them and handed the foreman her hard hat, but when she turned to leave and her eyes met mine, her smile dropped.

"What are you doing here?" she hissed as she gracefully picked her way over the building debris with surprising ease.

"Maybe I wanted to see the progress on site myself," I said, taking her elbow to steady her when she was level with me, then gritting my teeth when she shook me off.

"Whatever," she muttered. "Probably checking up on me to make sure I don't fuck things up. Next you'll try to mansplain the building trade to me and—"

"Mansplain the building trade? I know nothing about the building trade."

We were back on the more even ground of the pavement now and Tabby picked up the pace. I had no idea how she motored along so fast in those stilts she had strapped to her feet.

"Then why are you here?" she snapped in frustration. My car pulled up next to us then and I darted in front of her to

302

bring her to a stop. Her gaze went from me to my car and then narrowed.

I held my hands up in surrender. "I just don't want you walking around here on your own. It's not safe."

Tabby exaggeratedly looked up and down the empty road we were on and raised an eyebrow at me. I held back a frustrated growl.

"You know this is a dodgy area, Tabby. How were you planning on getting home?"

She rolled her eyes. "Same way I got here, dickhead. On the tube like a normal person who doesn't have private cars following them around London."

I did growl then. "Felix is such a self-absorbed twat."

"What are you on about now?"

"Felix, letting you take the tube. He should have—"

"Letting me?" Her voice rose in indignation. "Nobody *lets* me do anything. I'm perfectly capable of—"

"I know you're perfectly capable, baby," I said softly. She froze as she looked up at me, and I suppressed a smile as I watched her pupils dilate whilst the pink in her cheeks deepened. Maybe it was a bit soon for endearments since she still seemed to despise me, but I knew the effect I had on women, and I was willing to use all the weapons I had at my disposal to win Tabby over. "But please, *please* let me take you home. I'm literally begging you. No strings attached, I promise."

She sighed and gave my car a brief, longing glance. Given how exhausted she looked, I was hoping a lift home in a comfortable, well-heated vehicle would appeal enough for her to be willing to put up with me.

"Fine," she muttered, and I smiled. "But I'm not your baby."

I pressed my lips together to keep in the smart-arse remark I wanted to come back with, and held the car door open for her. When she sank into the rich leather, resting her head back and letting out a small sigh, it took all my self-control not to reach for her then and there.

303

After a brief introduction to my driver, I turned to her and studied her face.

"You work too hard," I told her.

She huffed. "Word of advice, big guy. You don't want to imply to a woman that she looks tired. It tends to piss us off."

"Shit. I didn't mean you look tired. You look beautiful. You always look beautiful. I just mean that… well, I know Felix is dumping his work on you, and I don't think it's fair. You looked done in when you were sitting with your dog after that meeting."

"I was done in because of how bloody stressful that meeting was."

"I'm sorry, Tabby." My voice was rough as my chest tightened with guilt.

Her eyes flicked to me, and I hoped it wasn't just wishful thinking, but I thought her expression may have softened. This close I could smell her light perfume and see the tiny freckles under her make-up. Her hair was falling out of its severe style, her suit was creased and had a light covering of construction dust over it, and I'd never seen her look more beautiful.

"And I know I've said it before, but I really am so *so* sorry about everything that happened last year as well." My eyes flicked to my driver then back to her. "Listen do you mind if I put up the privacy screen?"

She blinked at me. "You have a privacy screen? Like a billionaire in a bad romance novel?"

My lips twitched and I nodded.

She shrugged. "Go for it."

"I really am sorry," I repeated as the thick, tinted, sound-proof glass screen went up between us and the driver. "I'd do anything to go back and change the way I behaved."

She rolled her eyes. "You don't have to expend all this effort out of guilt, you know. And you don't have to keep feeding the whole office every day either. It's getting a bit ridiculous."

"I didn't want to single you out, and I wanted to respect your professional reputation, but I know how hard you're working and I want you to eat lunch."

Again there was that softening of her expression. I was getting somewhere.

"I do like sushi," she muttered.

"I know," I said through a smile. We'd talked about our favourite foods that night at the party before she found out who I was. We'd talked about everything.

"You're forgiven, okay? You can go off with a clear conscience."

"You think I'm doing this out of guilt?"

She turned to me and I couldn't help leaning into her.

"I feel bad about what happened, but that's not why I'm out here." I reached up to her face, giving her time to pull away, but she stayed where she was. She shivered when my fingers traced her delicate jawline. "I'm way too much of a self-interested prick to go that far with an apology."

"Really?" she breathed. My mouth was a hair's breadth from hers now. My whole body tensed in anticipation.

"I can't stop thinking about you, Tabby," I said in a tortured whisper. Her eyes slid closed, and I could see that this was my opening. I could kiss her now and she'd let me. But would that help me win her over? If I touched my mouth to hers, if I crossed that line, I wouldn't be able to stop. She didn't need to be coerced by another pushy arsehole. So instead, I swore and pulled away.

"Shit, I'm sorry," I said, throwing myself over to my side of the car. "I'm being totally inappropriate." My voice was full of all the self-loathing I was now feeling. "You're right. I'm as bad as—"

"Don't say it!" she snapped, and I froze in shock as she lurched across the space between us, silencing me by putting her fingers over my mouth. "I was wrong. You're not like him."

She moved her hand to my jaw and leaned into me, her soft breasts pressing against my chest.

"Maybe *I'm* taking advantage of *you*," she muttered, her lips grazing mine. Her scent was all around me now, and I could see the flecks of blue in the green of her eyes. My heart felt like it was beating outside of my chest. I didn't think I'd ever been as turned on in my life. Then she moved again, straddling my lap to kiss me.

The feel of her lips on mine was enough to snap me out of my frozen state. One of my hands buried into her soft hair whilst the other clamped around her hip, pulling her closer as I deepened the kiss, sliding my tongue inside her mouth when she moaned.

The kiss was hard and desperate, full of months of contained need on both sides until I stilled underneath her when I realised we'd arrived at her block of flats.

"Bloody hell," she breathed, her cheeks flaming as she moved to get off my lap, clearly embarrassed now. But I was not ready to be without her softness against me. Not by a long way. So my hand at her hip tightened as the other went up to her jaw to tilt her head back and meet my gaze.

"I'm going to be the hero of your story, understand me?" I said firmly.

She raised an eyebrow, and when she smiled at me I felt like I'd won a huge victory.

"I really got to you with that baddie stuff, huh?" Her tone was teasing, but I gave her a solemn nod.

"I'm in love with you, Tabby, so yes, hearing that killed me."

Her eyes went wide. "You love me?"

"Completely, totally and pathetically. Why do you think I pushed so hard to work with Moretti Harding again? I found love at a boring business party I'd been dreading, and then I fucked it all up. But if you'll give me a chance, I'll spend the rest of my life making it up to you."

"The rest of your life?" she breathed, searching my face and then melting into me. "It's mad and completely out of character for me," she said after a long pause. "But I love you too. So if you want to be the hero of my story then I guess I can be the heroine of yours."

If you enjoyed reading *Daydreamer,*
you will love *Gold Digger* –
the next book in the *Daydreamer series.*
Read on for an excerpt now.

CHAPTER ONE

Arse over tit

Lottie

Posh people were weird. They lived in huge houses with too many bedrooms and way too many toilets. I mean, the toilets in this house outnumbered the people five to one. It was ridiculous. But I wasn't complaining. Let them be weird if it meant I earned a decent wage. Because posh people might have liked a vast array of bogs to choose from, but they sure as fudge nuggets didn't like cleaning them.

That's where I came in.

Only on that particular day I had a small problem with my posh-bog-cleaning gig, in the form of a skinny, eight-year-old girl who had a tummy ache and didn't want to go to school. Just before we turned the corner into the square of posh people's houses, I squeezed her hand gently and then squatted down in front of her. My heart clenched when I saw a tear track down her cheek. She was all bundled up in her puffa coat but with her pyjamas underneath and clutching Keith, her very-much-in-need-of-a-wash soft toy pony.

"Right, lovebug," I said, carefully wiping the tear away and then settling my hands on her small shoulders. "Remember the plan? It's going to be like when we play hide and seek. Only you'll be hiding for a *really* long time. Still got some of that book left to read?"

Hayley nodded at me, her big, brown eyes huge and serious in her small, freckled face. I sighed, and my heart clenched again. Hayley had been through enough. If she had a tummy ache then she deserved to have a day at home with me, snuggled up on the sofa drinking Lucozade in the warm, not trudging through freezing London and having to hide in a scary, huge, posh-person house whilst I cleaned toilets. But I knew that Hayley's stomach ache had more to do with how much she hated school than anything, and I was not about to risk this job.

These particular aristocrats paid well above the odds, and I simply could not afford to be labelled as unreliable. Even if I *could* afford to drop today's hours, which I could *not,* the risk of losing the job altogether was too great. We were edging towards desperate, and there was no safety net, not for Hayley and me; there never had been.

"I've put loads of snacks in your bag. All your favourites plus a bottle of Lucozade, but if you feel like you're going to throw up, it might be better to wait to eat at home."

Please, please, God, don't let her throw up in that house. I'd been there when the interior decorator came last week. The woman had recommended a four-thousand-pound chaise lounge. If a weird, extra-long chair for *one person* cost four grand, then an eight-year-old vomit disaster could take me years to pay off.

"How's your tummy feeling?"

Hayley scrunched her freckled nose as her hand came up to make a so-so gesture.

I sighed again.

"Use your words, lovebug," I gently reminded her. Her eyes dropped from mine as she looked to the pavement, toeing a piece of gravel with her fluffy boot. I hated having to nag her, but I worried that if I didn't make her speak, at least to me, her vocal cords would atrophy from disuse.

"It's okay," she said eventually, her voice so small that it was almost drowned out by the city noises around us, despite the fact that we were on a quieter London street (posh people live on quiet, leafy streets in London – the bus noises, exhaust fumes, screeching tyres and shouting were for us lesser mortals). "I won't throw up. I promise."

I felt my nose start to sting and pulled her into me for a tight hug, smushing Keith the Pony between us. Blinking rapidly, I forced the tears back. I tried to never cry in front of Hayley if I could help it. She needed to believe I was strong, reliable. She'd been let down enough already by adults who couldn't cope. I would not have her believe I would let her down too.

Once I was sure that my tear ducts were back under control, I pulled back to stand up. Taking Hayley's hand in mine again, I squared my shoulders and turned into Buckingham Square.

Nestled in the heart of Kensington, Buckingham Square was beautiful. The large, ornate buildings surrounded a small central private garden in the centre. You had to be a resident of the square to use that gated piece of land. It was nothing like the common around the corner from our block of flats – rather more in the way of well-maintained roses and mature trees, and fewer used needles, burnt-out patches of grass, beer cans and homeless people. I'd yet to pluck up the courage to ask for the key so that I could maybe eat my lunch in there, restricting myself to only longing glimpses over the fence. It was like a little oasis of nature right smack in the middle of London. Even looking in from the outside fed my soul.

Hayley froze outside the imposing Buckingham House, and I glanced down to see her eyes wide and her mouth open.

"It's huge," she whispered, her unprompted words a testament to her shock. "I thought you said they weren't the royal family?"

"No, lovebug," I said, tugging her along towards the side staff entrance. The longer we were out here, the more chance

313

there was of us getting caught. "Remember, that's *Buckingham Palace*? Buckingham House is different."

What I didn't say was that the residents of Buckingham House weren't *that* far down the line of succession. The duke was about thirty-fifth the last time I Googled him. I shivered at the thought of the duke. My obsession with him was way out of hand. But I challenge any red-blooded female to work for someone like that and not indulge in some light internet stalking. The man was almost inhumanely attractive – powerful, a multi-billionaire if Wikipedia is to be believed, practically fucking royal and, to top it all off, he had a dry sense of humour that rivalled even my own, which was of the desert variety. Not that he would ever share his humour with me. He barely even ever looked at me. I was staff and, therefore, practically invisible to god-like beings such as the Duke of Buckingham.

But there were a couple of times when I did feel seen. Last week I'd been emptying the bin in the corner of the kitchen as the duke and his creepy brother-in-law, Blake, came in. I was ignored, as usual, as they discussed the meetings they had on that afternoon, but then Blake said:

"I'm sorry, old boy," his posh accent booming through the space, "but it simply won't fit. You can try to squeeze it in, but it'll be unbelievably painful for everyone involved."

I tried, I really did, but it was too tempting. So, before I managed to rein myself in, I muttered, "That's what she said," under my breath.

The problem was, although I used to swear like a sailor, I'd managed to train myself out of it after Hayley came to live with me, but leaving a perfect *That's What She Said* joke hanging was just too much for me to manage.

I bit my lip, hoping neither of them had heard (staff were, after all, supposed to stay as invisible as possible – much like the house elves in *Harry Potter*). I tried to make a quick exit, but when I turned around and flicked a glance in the duke's direction, he was closer than I thought he'd been, and his blue gaze was pinning me to the spot. Blake clearly hadn't heard, thank God, and was blabbering on about some other nonsense, totally unaware that his brother-in-law was staring at me or that I even existed. But the duke wouldn't stop staring, and I couldn't seem to move.

Eventually, one of his dark eyebrows winged up, the corner of his sexy mouth quirked on one side, and I swear I almost passed out with a lust head-rush right there in the kitchen, holding a bag of rubbish which smelt like last night's curry.

Then, just like that, the moment was over. He looked back to Blake, and I sucked in some much-needed oxygen, having held my breath throughout the entire unspoken exchange. As I scurried out of the kitchen, I felt my face heat with embarrassment. Why did I have to draw attention to myself? I mean, if I was going to draw the duke's attention, I'd rather it hadn't been whilst I was wearing leggings and my cleaning t-shirt, which proclaimed my love for Take That and had a tear in the collar, with my hair piled on top of my head like I was some ridiculous pineapple, and holding a smelly bag of rubbish.

And anyway, getting your employer's attention when you were in a service role was never good. The last cleaning job I had proved this when the husband, who I'd thought a pretty nice guy up until then, started invading my personal space. For a while, I thought I was being paranoid or overly sensitive, right up until the day he grabbed my arse.

That's where friendly banter with employers had got me, and was one of the reasons I now kept my head down, even if the thought of the duke grabbing my arse – or any other part of me – made me lightheaded. The man was a walking wet dream. I should know as *my* dreams were full of him.

That was another result of my late-night internet stalking, falling asleep to dreams of him calling me into that dark-wood, oldy-worldy, big man office of his, grabbing the scarf I wore in my hair off my head, sealing his mouth over mine and bending me over his thousand-year-old priceless antique desk.

315

Ah, the consequences of an over-active imagination and the frustration of a non-existent sex life.

There was no room for smoldering blue-eyed, tall men with muscular frames, wearing immaculate suits and designer beards in my life. I needed to concentrate on survival.

Anyway, The Stepladder Incident a few weeks ago had taught me that the duke, rather than finding me irresistible like my last employer, in fact had a full-blown allergy to touching me. Which, whilst mind-blowingly embarrassing, was fine. At least, that's what I told myself.

The only interaction I allowed myself with him now was through our daily game of chess. Not that we sat down together to play. It's just the chess set was always out in the snug, and whenever I cleaned the room it was in, I made my move. There was always a countermove the next day. So far, I was winning three games to one.

Hayley and I scurried in through the kitchen. Luckily, the catering staff weren't here this early. Either posh people made their own breakfast, or they were happy to subsist on strong coffee from their fancy coffee maker until noon – I suspected the latter.

I hurried down the massive corridor to the double doors of the drawing room. No sitting room for these peeps – no, it was all *drawing rooms* and *snugs*. There were multiples of both; depressingly, the smallest snug had more square footage than our entire flat. Slipping inside, I towed Hayley along to the spiral staircase in the corner of the large, high-ceilinged room. There were various armchairs and uncomfortable-looking brocade sofas facing each other in the centre of the huge space, a large fireplace on one side and tall windows with views over the gardens on the other.

"Up here," I whispered to Hayley, motioning for her to climb up first – it was steep, and I was known for my clumsiness. If she fell, I'd rather she landed on me; and if I fell, I'd rather not take her down with me.

The mezzanine had rows of bookshelves, and a billiards table sitting in the middle. Since the bookshelves were largely filled with encyclopedias, which, thanks to the internet had been surplus to requirement for years, and I didn't think anyone had played bar billiards since the 1800s, Hayley was likely to remain undiscovered up here.

She tucked herself into a corner with the cushions I'd swiped on the way up, and snuggled into Keith whilst I helped her out of her coat and laid it over her like a blanket.

"We made it," I whispered, trying to sound excited rather than the acute relief I was actually feeling. "That was fun, right? Secret mission complete."

I wanted Hayley to think this was all a bit of a game and not to worry too much. The problem was she was an observant little thing – just like me. We could both read people and atmospheres with almost supernatural accuracy. The social worker called it hypervigilance. Apparently it was common in people with our background. Hayley would have picked up on the tense line of my shoulders, the worry in my eyes. My bright, fake smile wouldn't be fooling her.

My hand pressed to the centre of my chest before I pressed it to the centre of Hayley's. It was our non-verbal *I love you*. Hayley was smiling a small smile by the time I was done, which was the most I could ask for. Big bright smiles, giggles and such were not part of Hayley's make-up anymore, but I was determined to change that. So I kissed her forehead and straightened up from kneeling to start back down the spiral staircase.

Unfortunately, I'd only managed to get halfway down when a rich, deep voice sounded from the corridor, getting closer. When the double doors opened and those blue eyes locked with mine, I did what I do best – I tripped, and fell arse over tit down the steps.

To read the rest of Lottie's story,
find *Gold Digger* available now
at a bookstore near you.

ACKNOWLEDGEMENTS

I'll start by saying a massive thank you to my readers. I never dreamt that people would take the time to read the stories I have thought up in my freaky brain, and I am honoured beyond words. I am also eternally grateful to the reviewers who have taken a chance on me – your feedback has made all the difference to the books and is the reason I've been able to make writing not just a passion but a career.

Special mention for Susie's Book Badgers - you are wonderful humans, and your support means the world.

My fantastic alpha readers – Small Suse, Aurelia, Carly, Jane, Ruth, Jess, Katie and Andy – your feedback was essential and much appreciated.

Thank you to my agent, Lorella Belli, for your support and encouragement.

To Jo Edwards my brilliant editor and dear friend – thank you, thank you and I'm so sorry about all the semicolons!

Thank you to the wonderful team at Keeperton for believing in the Daydreamer series and bringing the books to a wider audience.

Last but not least thanks to my very own romantic hero. I love you and the boys to the moon and back.

Susie Tate is a #1 Amazon bestselling author of addictive, feel-good contemporary romance. She can be counted on to deliver uplifting but also heart-wrenching stories that make her readers laugh and cry in equal measure. Her charismatic but flawed heroes have to work hard to earn their heroine's forgiveness but always manage to redeem themselves in the end.

The real and raw themes that underpin Susie's books are often inspired by her experiences working as a doctor in the NHS for the last twenty years. Susie worked in a range of hospital specialities before becoming a GP, during which time she looked after a women's refuge for victims of domestic violence as well as being child safeguarding lead for her practice. Susie's medical career gives her a unique insight and understanding of the social, psychological and physical issues some of her characters face, lending authenticity to her writing.

Susie lives in beautiful Dorset with her wonderful husband, three gorgeous boys and even more wonderful dog. Her very own romantic hero and husband, Andy, suffers from Motor Neurone Disease (aka ALS). Susie's career as an author has allowed her to spend more crucial time with Andy and their boys after this devastating diagnosis. Susie and Andy work to raise awareness about MND/ALS and support charities like the MNDA and My Name5 Doddie, who are searching for a cure and supporting sufferers.

 Arndell

Connect with Arndell
Love this book? Discover your next romance book obsession and stay up to date with the latest releases, exclusive content, and behind-the-scenes news!

Explore More Books
Visit our homepage: keeperton.com/arndell

Follow Us on Social Media
Instagram: @arndellbooks
Facebook: Arndell
TikTok: @arndellbooks

Stay in the Loop
Join our newsletter: keeperton.com/subscribe

Join the Conversation
Use **#Arndell** or **#ArndellBooks** to share your thoughts and connect with fellow romance readers!

Thank you for being part of our book-loving community. We can't wait to share more unforgettable stories with you!